DEATH IN KASHMIR

ALSO BY M. M. KAYE

FICTION

The Far Pavilions
Shadow of the Moon
Trade Wind
Death in Kenya
Death in Zanzibar
Death in Cyprus
Death in the Andamans
Death in Kashmir
The Ordinary Princess (for children)

AUTOBIOGRAPHY

The Sun in the Morning
Golden Afternoon
Enchanted Evening

DEATH
IN
KASHMIR

A MYSTERY

M. M. Kaye

St. Martin's Minotaur
NEW YORK

Map of Kashmir drawn by Reginald Piggot

www.minotaurbooks.com

ISBN 0-312-26310-4

First St. Martin's Minotaur Edition: December 2000

D 10 9 8 7 6 5 4 3 2 1

For GOFF
and the delectable valley
With all my love

CONTENTS

Author's Note	xi
Pronunciation Guide	xiii
Part I GULMARG	1
Part II PESHAWAR	67
Part III SRINAGAR	87
Postscript	237

'Who has not heard of the
vale of Cashmere . . . ?'
Thomas Moore, *Lalia-Rookh*

AUTHOR'S NOTE

When I first began to write murder mysteries—'whodunits'—I would try
to write at least two thousand words every day: Sundays excepted. If I
managed to exceed that, I would credit the extra number to a day on
which I knew that some unavoidable official duty or social engagement
would prevent me writing at all. It was my way of keeping track of the
length of each chapter and controlling the overall length of the book, and
at the end of each day I would make a note against the date of the number
of words I had written and considered worth keeping. Which is why I have
on record the exact day and date on which I first met my future husband,
Goff Hamilton, then a Lieutenant in that famous Frontier Force Regiment,
the Corps of Guides.

It was on a Monday morning and the date was 2 June 1941, and I
happened at that time to be living in Srinagar, the capital city of Kashmir,
which is one of the loveliest countries in the world. Goff, who was up on
short leave, fishing, had called in to give me a letter that he had promised a
mutual friend to deliver by hand. I presume I wrote something that day,
since I was actually at work on my daily quota when he arrived. But there
is no entry against that date—or against a long string of dates that followed.

The manuscript stopped there, halfway through a chapter. Because
what with getting married, having two children, working for the WVS and
also for a propaganda magazine, and living in a state of perpetual panic for
fear that Goff would not get back alive from Burma, there was no time to
spare for writing novels. It was not until the war was over and the British
had quit India, the Raj become no more than a memory and Goff and I
and the children were in Scotland, living in an army quarter in Glasgow
and finding it difficult to make ends meet, that I remembered that I could
write, and decided that it was high time I gave the family budget a helping
hand.

I therefore dug out that dog-eared and dilapidated student's pad in which I had begun a book that I had tentatively entitled *There's a Moon Tonight*, and read the two and a half chapters I had written during that long-ago springtime in Kashmir.

It didn't read too badly, so I updated it to the last months of the Raj instead of the first year of the war, and when I had finished it, posted it in some trepidation to a well-known firm of literary agents in London, who fortunately for me, liked it. I was summoned to London, where I was handed over to one of their staff, a Mr Scott, who was considered the most suitable person to deal with my work on the grounds that he himself 'knew a bit about India'. He turned out to be the Paul Scott who had already written three books with an Indian setting, and would one day write *The Raj Quartet* and *Staying On*, and as he became a great friend of mine, my luck was clearly in that day. I hope that it stays in, so that readers will enjoy this story of a world that is gone and of a country that remains beautiful beyond words, despite mankind's compulsive and indefatigable efforts to destroy what is beautiful!

I would also like to mention here that having recently seen the TV versions of Paul's 'Jewel in the Crown' and my own 'Far Pavilions', and been constantly irritated by hearing almost every Indian word mispronounced (some even in several different ways!), I have decided to let any readers who may be interested learn, by way of a guide which follows, the pronunciation that my characters would have used in *their* day. In some cases no syllable is accented, in others the syllable on which the accent falls will be in italic type, and the rest in roman. The spelling will be strictly phonetic because too many words were not pronounced as they were spelt, e.g. *marg* (meadow), though spelt with an 'a', was pronounced *murg!* And so on . . . Thus leading to considerable confusion!

PRONUNCIATION GUIDE

The right-hand column shows how each word should be pronounced: the stress is on the italicized syllable(s).

Apharwat	Apper-waat
Banihal	Bunny-harl
Baramulla	Bara-*mooler*
Bulaki	Bull-*ar*-ki
bunnia	bun-nia
chaprassi	ch'*prassi*
chenar	ch'*nar*
Chota Nagim	*Choter* N'geem
chowkidar	*chowk*-e-dar
Dāl	Darl
feringhi	fer-*ung*-ghi
ghat	gaut
Gulmarg	Gul-*murg* (Gul rhymes with pull)
Hari Parbat	Hurry *Purr*-but
Hazratbal	*Huz*-raatbaal
Jhelum	*Gee*-lum
khansamah	khan-*sah*-ma
khidmatgar	kit-ma-gar
Khilanmarg	Killan-murg
maidan	*my*-darn
mānji	*maan*-jee
marg	murg
memsahib	*mem*-sarb
Nagim Bagh	N'geem Barg
Nedou	*Nee*-doo

pashmina	*push*-mina
Peshawar	P'shower
Rawalpindi	R'l'*pindi*
sahib	sarb
shikara	shic-*karra*
Srinagar	Sr'in-*nugger*
Tanmarg	Tun-*murg*
Takht-i-Suliman	Tucked-e-*Sul*-eman
tonga	*tong*-ah

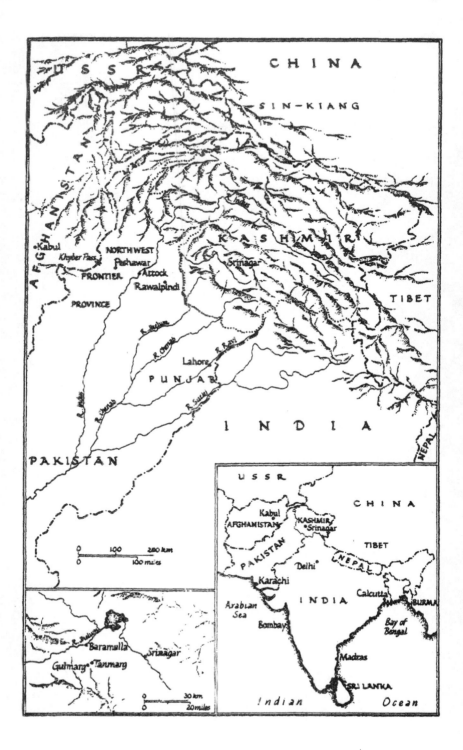

Part I

GULMARG

'The white peaks ward the passes, as of yore,
The wind sweeps o'er the wastes of Khorasan;
But thou and I go thitherward no more.'
                    Laurence Hope, *'Yasin Khan'*

1

Afterwards, Sarah could never be quite sure whether it was the moonlight or that soft, furtive sound that had awakened her. The room that except for the dim and comforting flicker of a dying fire had been dark when she fell asleep, was now full of a cold, gleaming light. And suddenly she was awake . . . and listening.

It was scarcely more than a breath of sound, coming from somewhere outside the rough pinewood walls that divided that isolated wing of the rambling hotel into separate suites. A faint, irregular rasping, made audible only by the intense, frozen silence of the moonlit night.

A rat, thought Sarah, relaxing with a small sigh of relief. It was absurd that so small a thing should have jerked her out of sleep and into such tense and total wakefulness. Her nerves must be getting out of hand. Or perhaps the height had something to do with it? The hotel stood over eight thousand feet above sea-level, and Mrs Matthews had said——

Mrs Matthews! Sarah's wandering thoughts checked with a sickening jar as though she had walked into a stone wall in the dark.

How was it that awakening in that cold night she had been able, even for a few minutes, to forget about Mrs Matthews?

Less than a week ago, in the first days of January, Sarah Parrish and some thirty-odd skiing enthusiasts from all parts of India had arrived up in Gulmarg, that cluster of log cabins that lies in a green cup among the mountains of the Pir Panjal, more than three thousand feet above the fabled 'Vale of Kashmir'. They had come to attend what was, for most of them, their last meeting of the Ski Club of India. For this was 1947, and the date for India's independence—the end of the Raj and the departure of the British—had been set for the following year.

Beautiful mountain-locked Kashmir was one of India's many semi-independent princely states which, by treaty, were in effect 'protectorates' of the Government of India, ruled over by hereditary Maharajahs, Nawabs, Rajas or Ranas who were 'advised' by a British Resident. And though access to this particular State was not easy, since it is walled in on every side by high mountains, it has been regarded for centuries as an ideal hot-weather retreat from the burning plains—the Great Moguls, in their day, making the journey on elephants, horses or in palanquins.

The British had followed where the Moguls led, and made it one of their favourite playgrounds. But because the State would not permit them to buy or own land in Kashmir, they had taken to spending their holidays there in houseboats on its lovely lakes, in tents among the pines and deo-dars, or in rented log cabins in Gulmarg, which is little more than a grassy bowl among the mountains that overlook the main valley. A bowl that some homesick Briton (presumably a Scotsman?) converted into a series of admirable golf-courses, and which during the winter and early spring is blanketed deep in snow.

Every year, during this latter period, the Ski Club of India would hold one or more of its meetings in Gulmarg. And on these occasions the ram-bling, snow-bound, summer hotel would be opened to accommodate mem-bers and their friends. This year had been no exception, and anyone and everyone who could possibly manage to get there had done so. The weather had been perfect and the party a gay one: until, with shocking suddenness, tragedy had struck.

Mrs Matthews—grey haired, sociable, delightful—had been picked up dead from among the snow-covered boulders near the foot of the Blue Run.

She had not been missed until late afternoon on the previous day, as dusk was falling and the skiers converging on the welcoming lights of the hotel—straggling up from the nursery slopes, or down from the snowfields of Khilanmarg that lie high above Gulmarg where the pine forests end. Even then it had been supposed that she was in her room.

She was there now. They had brought her back to it and laid her on the bed, and Sarah wondered, with a little prickling of the scalp, if the compar-ative warmth of the narrow, pinboard room had been sufficient to thaw the dreadful stiffness from those frozen, contorted limbs.

A terrified coolie, bringing firewood to the hotel, had stumbled upon that sprawling figure in the dusk, and Sarah had seen her carried in: a grotesque jumble of widespread arms and legs that could not be bent or decently straightened.

Sarah had liked Mrs Matthews—everyone liked Mrs Matthews—and the unexpected sight of that rigid corpse had filled her with such shudder-ing nausea that, unable to face the prospect of food, she had retired early and supperless to bed and had taken a long time to fall asleep. Now all at once she was wide awake; and with little prospect of dropping off again while her room remained bright with moonlight, and that faint rasping sound frayed at her nerves.

Strange that there should be rats up here in winter, with the snow lying deep for so many months and the huts shuttered and deserted. Hadn't she once read somewhere that they could not stand extreme cold? Perhaps Kashmiri rats were different . . . Sarah tossed and turned restlessly, and wondered irritably what had possessed her to draw back the curtains? At the time, it had seemed pleasant to lie and look out at the snow and the night sky, but she should have realized that sooner or later the moon would shine into the verandah and reach the window of her room.

Earlier in the evening, because the atmosphere of her small bedroom had seemed close and stuffy after the crisp night air outside, she had half opened her bathroom window and left wide the communicating door between the two rooms. But the logs that had blazed in the fireplace a few hours ago were now only a handful of grey ash, and the room was very cold.

The prospect of getting out of bed in order to draw the curtains and close the bathroom window was not a pleasant one and Sarah shivered at the thought. Yet now, in addition to feeling cold, she was also beginning to feel hungry and regret foregoing her supper, and there was a tin of biscuits on the bathroom shelf. She could fetch a handful and close the window and the bedroom curtains at the same time. Reaching out a reluctant hand for the fur coat that was doing duty as an extra blanket, she huddled it about her shoulders and slid out of bed. Her soft, sheep-skin slippers were ice-cold to her shrinking toes, but they made no sound as she crossed the room and went through the open doorway into the bathroom.

The small, wooden-walled suites in this wing of the hotel were all alike, each consisting of a bed-sitting room, plus a narrow, primitive bathroom, the back door of which opened onto two or three shallow wooden steps that led down to a path used only by those hotel servants whose duty it was to clean the bathrooms or to carry up hot water for the small tin bathtubs.

Sarah did not bother to switch on the light, for the open window allowed the cold glimmer of moonlight on snow to fill the small bathroom with a pale glow that was more than enough to see by. But she had taken no more than two steps when she stopped short, listening to that barely audible sound that she had supposed to be the gnawing of a rat. It was clearer now—and it could not possibly be a rat, because rats did not gnaw metal. Sarah stood quite still, holding her breath and straining to hear. There it was again! So soft a sound that had it not been for her opened door and window she would never have heard it. The stealthy rasp of a file on metal.

This time it was followed by the faint rattle of a window-frame; though there was no breath of wind. And suddenly she realized what it meant. Someone outside was trying, with infinite caution, to file through the fastening of a window. Not her own, for that stood open. Whose, then?

The room to her left was unoccupied, and since the one immediately beyond it belonged to Major McKay of the Indian Medical Service, who held strong views on the value of fresh air and boasted of sleeping with every window wide in all weathers, it could not be either of those. The room on her right was occupied by a Miss Rushton, a girl in her midtwenties, while in the one beyond it, between Miss Rushton's room and one occupied by a Colonel Gidney, lay the body of Mrs Matthews.

Sarah shivered at the thought of that locked room and its silent occupant, and clenching her teeth to stop them chattering, moved cautiously forward until, standing flat against the wall, she could peer out obliquely from her half-opened window. A wide bar of shadow lay across the slope and the path below, but beyond it the snow sparkled brilliantly in the moonlight, thinning the shadows with reflected light so that she could see quite clearly the rickety wooden steps that led up to Janet Rushton's bathroom door.

There was someone standing just beyond those steps: a shapeless figure whose hands, showing dark against the weather-bleached woodwork, were busy at the level of Miss Rushton's window. There was also a metal object lying on the window-sill—she could see it gleam in the reflected moonlight. A jemmy, perhaps? or some improvised crowbar?

Sarah's immediate reaction was one of pure rage. Mrs Matthews not twelve hours dead, and already some ghoulish coolie from the village, or a dishonest hotel servant, was breaking in to steal the dead woman's belongings! Because of course it must be that, and the would-be thief had merely mistaken the window, since Janet Rushton, the girl in the next room, wore no jewellery and appeared to have brought little more than a change of skiing clothes and slacks with her; which made it highly unlikely that anyone bent on random theft would take the trouble to file through the catch of her window. Particularly when she, Sarah—an obviously more profitable victim!—had obligingly left hers wide open!

She decided to shout and bang upon the window, confident that this would be more than enough to scare any thief away. But even as she opened her mouth to carry out this laudable intention, the figure turned its head and her shout died unuttered: for it had no face . . .

For a moment it seemed to Sarah that her heart stopped beating. Then in the next second she realized that she was looking at someone who was wearing a mask: a hood of some drab material that completely covered the wearer's head and neck, and had holes cut in it for eyes. In almost the same instant she realized that the object lying upon the window-sill, so near to those purposeful hands, was a gun. And all at once she was afraid. Afraid as she had never been before in her short twenty-two years of life.

This was no ordinary thief. No pilfering Kashmiri would wear a mask or carry firearms. Besides, of what use were such precautions against a dead woman? Then it *must* be Miss Rushton's room that was his objective——

Sarah backed away from the window inch by inch and regained her bedroom. Her breath was coming short as though she had been running, and it seemed to her as though the thudding of her heart must be as audible as drumbeats in the silence. Janet Rushton . . . she must warn Janet . . . Her cold fingers fumbled with the handle of the verandah door and managed to turn it. I mustn't run, she thought: I must go quietly. I mustn't make a noise . . . She forced herself to ease open the door slowly so that it made no sound.

The narrow wooden verandah that ran the length of the wing was bright with moonlight, and outside it a sea of snow glistened like polished silver, blotched by the dark bulk of the main hotel buildings. In front the ground fell steeply away until it reached the more or less level ground of the golf-course and the *maidan*,* beyond which it swept upward again to meet the inky shadows of the deodar forests and the cold brilliance of the night sky.

It had snowed for half an hour or so earlier in the night. Snow lay thick upon the verandah rails, and a powdering of blown crystals covered the wooden floorboards with a thin, brittle carpet that crunched crisply under Sarah's slippers. The small sound seemed terrifyingly loud in the frozen quiet of that silent, sleeping world: 'Loud enough to wake the dead' . . . the phrase slipped unbidden into her mind, and the picture it conjured up did nothing to lessen her tension.

She reached Janet Rushton's door and turned the handle; only to find that the door was locked. But either Miss Rushton was already awake or she was an exceptionally light sleeper, for Sarah heard a swift rustle from inside the room as though someone had sat up suddenly in bed. She tapped softly, urgently, upon the rough wooden panel of the door, and still there was no reply; but as though disturbed by the sound, an overhanging mass of snow at the edge of the roof detached itself and fell with a sighing *flump* into the snowdrift below the verandah rails, setting her heart racing again.

* An open space in or near a town, a parade-ground.

And in a fresh access of panic she grasped the door handle and rattled it urgently.

There was a swift movement from inside the room, and after a moment a voice breathed: *'Who is it?'*

'It's me—Sarah Parrish!' whispered Sarah in ungrammatical frenzy: 'Open the door. Quick! *Oh hurry!'*

She heard a bolt withdrawn and the click of a key turned in the lock, and the door opened a few inches; a narrow slit of blackness in the moon-flooded verandah. Janet Rushton's voice, curiously taut and breathless, said: 'What is it? What do you want?'

'Hush!' begged Sarah urgently. 'Don't make a noise! There's someone trying to get in through your bathroom window. You've got to get out of there, quickly. He may be in by now! I saw him—it . . .'

Janet Rushton still did not speak and Sarah, exasperation suddenly mingling with her panic, thrust with all her strength against the close-held door and stepped over the threshold.

A hand gripped her arm and jerked her forward into darkness, and she heard the door close behind her and the rasp of a bolt shot home. *'Don't move!'* whispered a voice beside her—a voice she would never have recognized as belonging to the gay and gregarious Miss Rushton—and the next instant something cold and hard was pressed against the side of her neck. Something that there could be no mistaking. A small, ice-cold ring of metal.

Sarah stood quite still, rigid with shock, while in the darkness a hand went over her body with a swift and frightening efficiency. There was a short gasp, as if of relief; then: 'Now tell me what you want,' said the harsh whisper.

Sarah touched her dry lips with her tongue: 'I've told you. There's someone trying to get in by your bathroom window. For heaven's sake stop playing the fool and let's get out of here!'

The cold rim of metal did not move, but in the moment of silence that followed there came a faint and unidentifiable sound from somewhere outside the building, and suddenly the cold pressure was withdrawn. There was a swift movement in the darkness beside her, and Sarah was alone. She heard a door open and the sound of someone stumbling against a chair in the dark bathroom, and turning, groped her way to the electric light switch and pressed it down.

The harsh yellow light of a single shaded bulb revealed a counterpart of the bare wooden walls and shabby, utilitarian furniture of her own room. It shone down upon the narrow tumbled bed and struck sparks from the edges of a pair of skates that lay upon the floor, lit up the slim lines of the skis that leant against the cupboard, and glinted wickedly along the short polished barrel of the weapon in Janet Rushton's hand . . .

Sarah's eyes, narrowed against the sudden light, lifted slowly from the small, ugly weapon to the face of the girl who stood in the bathroom doorway, watching her.

Janet Rushton was an attractive girl of the healthy, outdoor variety, whose chief claim to good looks lay in fresh colouring and abundant curly blond hair, rather than in any regularity of feature. But there was no vestige of prettiness in the face that stared back at Sarah above the gleaming barrel of the little automatic. The blue eyes were hard and unwavering in a face so white and haggard with fear and desperation as to be almost unrecognizable.

She came forward into the room, drawing the door shut behind her with her free hand without turning her gaze from Sarah's, and said softly: 'There *was* someone there: the window-catch has been filed through and there are marks in the snow. But whoever it was must have heard us and gone. What happened? Who was it?'

'How on earth should I know?' demanded Sarah heatedly. She had been more shaken than she would have thought possible, and her receding panic was rapidly being replaced by wrath: 'I went into my bathroom to get some biscuits, and I heard a noise outside. I'd already heard it, and I thought at first it was a rat; but it was someone trying to open your window, and . . .'

'*Who was it?*' interrupted Miss Rushton in a harsh whisper.

'I've just told you! I haven't any idea!'

'Was it a man or a woman?'

'Why, a—' Sarah checked, brows wrinkled, and after a moment's thought said slowly: 'A man, I suppose. I don't really know.'

'You don't *know?* But that's absurd! It's almost as bright as day outside.'

'Yes, I know. But you see he—it—was in the shadows and close against the wall. Anyway it never occurred to me that it could be a woman. I thought it was some coolie or a hotel thief, who meant to burgle Mrs Matthews' room and had mistaken the window.'

'*Why should you think that?*' The question was sharp with suspicion.

'What else should I think?' snapped Sarah, exasperated. 'No one is likely to raise much fuss if half Mrs Matthews' possessions are stolen, because the chances are that no one will be able to say what's missing. You can't tell me that any ordinary sneak-thief is going to take the trouble to break in at your window when mine is already open. Of *course* I thought it was Mrs Matthews' room he was after! I was just going to shout and scare him off, when . . . when . . .' Sarah shivered so violently that her teeth chattered.

'When what? Why didn't you?'

'He—it—turned its head, and it hadn't got a face.' Sarah shivered again. 'I mean, it was wearing a sort of tightly fitting hood with holes for its eyes, and it had a gun. I–I knew then that–that it couldn't be some ordinary little thief, and I was scared out of my wits. All I could think of was to get you out of your room before that creature got in. And,' concluded Sarah stormily, exasperation and wrath overcoming her once more, 'all I got for my pains was a gun jabbed into me!'

Janet Rushton gave a sharp sigh and dropped the gun into the pocket of the windbreaker coat she wore over her pyjamas. She said uncertainly: 'I–I'm most awfully sorry. It was terribly stupid of me. I'm afraid I lost my head. But I . . . you startled me. I'm always nervous in this country—especially in a hotel. It makes me feel safer having a gun, and I——'

'Oh, rubbish!' interrupted Sarah tersely. 'You aren't the nervous kind; I've seen you ski! There's something very peculiar about all this, and I don't like it. What's going on?'

A slow flush rose in Miss Rushton's white face, and faded again, leaving it if possible paler than before, and all at once Sarah was smitten with compunction: the girl looked so exhausted and desperate. Her anger ebbed away and she smiled unexpectedly into the drawn face: 'I'm sorry. I didn't mean to be cross and scratchy, and I don't want to do any of this "fools rushing in where angels fear to tread" stuff, but it's beginning to look to me as though you're in some kind of a jam. Are you? Because if you'd like any help, here I am. I've got quite a good shoulder for crying on, and a bottle of aspirin and a tin of salts in the next room. Just state your preference. We aim to please.'

She was relieved to see an answering smile replace the look of tension upon Miss Rushton's face. 'That's nice of you—considering the hysterical reception I gave you,' conceded Janet in a more normal voice. 'Thank you for coming in as you did. I can't apologize enough for treating you like that, but you see I've–I've been rather worried lately. Oh, it's only a purely personal matter—but . . . Well, I suppose I've been letting it get on my nerves a bit. I was half asleep when I got out of bed, and I didn't realize who you were when you came bursting into my room in the dark. It was a bit unnerving, you know. I . . . I don't know what you must think of me."

Her voice seemed suddenly to fail her, and she took a few jerky steps to the nearest chair, and sitting down abruptly, as though her legs could no longer support her, helped herself to a cigarette from a box on the table beside her and looked vaguely about her for a light.

Sarah handed her the box of matches that stood on the chimney-piece, and said lightly: 'You lie very badly, you know. Still, if that's your story, you stick to it. I'm going to make up the fire and wait here while you smoke that cigarette, and after that, if you're feeling any better, I'll get back to my own room.'

She turned to the task of stacking pine chips and fir cones from the wood-box onto the still faintly glowing embers in the fireplace, and blew them into a blaze while Miss Rushton lit the cigarette with uncertain fingers and smoked it in silence.

Sarah added some dry aromatic deodar logs to the fire and sat back on her heels: 'There. That'll blaze up beautifully in a minute or two. It's a pity we haven't got a kettle. I'd like to go all girlish and make a pot of tea.'

Janet made no comment. She had been watching Sarah make up the fire: studying her intently. Now she stubbed out the end of her cigarette in the ashtray on the table, and getting to her feet, walked over to the fireplace and stood leaning against the chimney-piece, staring down at the bright leaping flames. Presently she said abruptly: 'Why did you think I was lying?'

Sarah leaned back against the side of an armchair and looked up at her with a disarming smile. 'I didn't think. I knew.'

'What do you mean?'

'Do you really want to know?'

'Yes, of course.'

'Well, I'm not exactly an idiot, and as you've already pointed out, it's almost as bright as day outside—and you took a good long look at me through the crack of that door! Half asleep, my foot! You knew exactly who you were shoving that gun into, and—well, I'm curious. That's all.'

The pale face above her flushed painfully in the glancing firelight, and Sarah said contritely: 'That was rude of me. I'm sorry. You don't have to tell me anything if you don't want to, and if you're feeling better now I'll go back to bed. At least this business should give everyone a laugh at breakfast!'

She stood up and held out her hand: 'Good-night.'

Janet Rushton looked from the outstretched hand to Sarah's face, and turning away to pull up the small chintz-covered armchair, she sat down again and said haltingly: 'Don't go just yet . . . please! I–I'd be very grateful if you'd stay a little longer and just . . . just talk to me until I feel a bit less fraught. You don't know what a relief it would be to sit back and listen to someone else, instead of sitting here by myself and–and thinking about . . . Besides, after that thief scare, I couldn't feel less like sleeping. So if you could stay for a bit . . . ?'

'Of course,' agreed Sarah cheerfully, resuming her seat on the floor and clasping her arms about her knees. 'What would you like me to talk about?'

'Yourself, I think.' Janet's voice, which had been noticeably quiet, returned to its normal pitch, and Sarah automatically raised her own to match it.

'Story of my life? *"Me,"* by me. Mankind's favourite topic! All right. I'm afraid it's not wildly enthralling, but such as it is, you shall have it. Let's see . . . Well, to begin with, like most of us I'm a mixture of England–Ireland–Scotland and Wales, which nowadays adds up to "British" to save time. But I was born in Cairo of all places, because Dad was in the Foreign Service and he and Mother happened to be posted there at the time. I even have a vague recollection of being carried round the Pyramids, sitting in front of Mother on the back of a camel. I suppose I was about three then, and . . . But perhaps you've been to Egypt?'

'Not yet. It's one of the places I've always meant to visit one day—ever since I heard about Tutankhamen's tomb when I was in primary school.'

'I mean to go back there too, one day. To see all the things I missed. I remember a lot more about Rome, because I was older when Dad was posted there, and I still haven't forgotten all my Italian—or any of the other languages I picked up at the various schools that "Foreign Service children" go to. It was a marvellous life for a child. I can't think of a better one and I only wish . . . Oh well, I don't suppose that any of the places I remember will ever again be quite the same as they were before the war. Just as Vienna was never the same after the First World War! *"Babylon the great is fallen, is fallen . . ."* ' Sarah sighed and dropped her chin on to her clasped hands.

'You were lucky,' observed Janet. 'My father was in the Indian Army, so like most "children of the Raj", I and my brothers got shipped back home at a very early age, to be "educated". A lot earlier for Tony and John and Jamie than for me. After that we only saw our parents about once every two years until our school days were over and we came back here again. Didn't you ever go to a boarding-school in England?'

'Yes. But not until I was fourteen. That was because . . . Well, my parents were due to go to America, and they were taking me with them, like they always did. But it–it was the year the war broke out. We'd been on holiday in England that summer, and we sailed on the *Athenia* at the beginning of September.'

'The *Athenia?* But wasn't she———?' Janet stopped abruptly and Sarah nodded.

'Yes. She was torpedoed the day after war was declared, and . . . and my parents went down with her. There weren't enough lifeboats, you see.'

A log burst into flame and the fire blazed up and crackled merrily.

Janet said: 'I'm sorry,' and Sarah gave a sharp little sigh.

'So am I. It seemed such a . . . such a pointless waste. They were both so . . . Oh well, that's how I finished my school days in a boarding-school in Hampshire; because Dad had managed to pitch me into a lifeboat with a lot of other children, and we all got back safe and seasick to England, where I was scooped in by my grandparents and eventually sent to Gran's old school. It got bombed twice while I was there, and the first time we moved into two wings of someone's Stately Home, and when that went too, into a clutch of Nissen huts that were a lot warmer. Then, as soon as I struck seventeen, I left and joined the W R A Fs. I was demobbed last year, and as I wanted to see our Vanishing Empire before it vanished for keeps, I jumped at the chance when my Aunt Alice suggested that I come out and spend a few months with them in Peshawar.'

'What made you come up to Gulmarg?'

'Why, skiing of course! What else? We always went skiing during winter and spring holidays before the war, and I was given my first pair of skis before I was five. So when the Creed's told me about this meeting, and offered to give me a lift in their car, up and back, I couldn't resist it. I was afraid I might have forgotten how to ski, but thank goodness it seems to be one of those things that you don't forget—like riding a bicycle.'

'Who are your aunt and uncle?' asked Janet.

'The Addingtons. Aunt Alice is mother's eldest sister, and Uncle Jack's commanding the Peshawar Brigade at the moment. You've probably met them.'

'Yes,' said Janet slowly, 'they were up here last year. I wondered why your name rang a faint bell—it was your uncle, of course. I sat next to him at a dinner party last year and he mentioned you. It seems you had a good war record.'

'No more than anyone else in the Women's Services,' said Sarah with a laugh: 'That's just Uncle Jack blowing the family trumpet. He didn't do too badly himself, what with a bar to his D S O after Alamein, and another in Burma. I only got the usual service medal.'

'Plus a commission in record time,' observed Janet thoughtfully.

Sarah blushed vividly. 'Well . . . yes. And, as that more or less concludes our broadcast from Radio Parrish, I'd better be going. That is, if you're feeling a bit less fraught?'

'I think I am,' conceded Janet, 'but if you're prepared to stay a little longer I'd like to tell you something. I don't suppose I should, but in the circumstances it seems preferable to letting you go on being curious—and possibly "giving everyone a laugh" with the story of this business tonight. Besides, God knows I need help—you were right about that.'

Sarah gave her a puzzled look, and abandoning her intention of leaving, settled back to wait with a curious mixture of expectancy and apprehension. But Janet seemed in no hurry to begin. Instead, she turned her head and looked searchingly about her as though to make sure that there was no third person in the small room, and Sarah's gaze, following hers, lingered upon the door that led into the darkened bathroom, across which lay the long shadows of the tall, polished skis. The heavy curtains over the windows hung still and smooth in the firelight, and the painted parchment lampshade cast a circular shadow upon the wooden ceiling. The silence in the small room was all at once oppressive, and Sarah had the sudden and disturbing fancy that the cold silent night and the frozen snowdrifts had crept closer about the outer walls to listen.

The flames whispered and flickered in the silence and a drop of moisture fell down the chimney and hissed upon the glowing logs.

Miss Rushton rose stiffly and crossing to the bathroom door opened it to reach in and switch on the light. Closing it again, she stood for a moment looking at it thoughtfully, and Sarah, watching her, remembered that her own bathroom door could only be fastened with a drop-latch fitted with a flimsy catch from the bedroom side, although the opposite side was fitted with a bolt. Janet Rushton dropped the latch into place and came back to her chair: 'I'm going to tell you this,' she said softly, 'because—well, partly because I've got to tell you something and I'm too dog-tired to think up a lie that would hold water. And partly because in case anything happens to me I should like someone to know.'

She stopped as though that explained everything, and Sarah said sharply: 'What do you mean? What could happen to you?'

'I might die—like Cousin Hilda.'

'Cousin Hilda? . . . Oh, you mean Mrs Matthews? I'd forgotten she was a relation of yours; no wonder you're feeling upset. It was a ghastly thing to happen. But there's no need to be morbid about it. After all, it was an accident that could only happen once in a blue moon.'

'It wasn't an accident,' said Janet Rushton quietly and quite definitely.

'What on earth do you mean?'

'I mean that Mrs Matthews was murdered.'

The night and the silence and the brooding snowdrifts seemed to take a soft step closer and breathe about the isolated wing of the dark hotel, and the little flames that rustled about the deodar logs whispered . . . *murdered . . . murdered . . . murdered.*

'That's ridiculous!' exclaimed Sarah indignantly. 'Major McKay's a doctor, and he said it was an accident. He said that she must have slipped on that rotten snow and hit her head on those rocks as she fell.'

Yet, unaccountably, she did not believe her own words. There had been something about Janet Rushton's incredible, unemotional statement that carried conviction in the face of all sane judgement and reasoning.

'I know what they said. But they're wrong. I know she was murdered. You see, we had been afraid of this for some time.'

'*We?*'

'Mrs Matthews and I.'

'But—but . . Oh, I know she was your cousin, but *really,* Janet!'

'As a matter of fact, she wasn't related to me at all. That was only camouflage.'

Sarah came to her feet in one swift movement. 'I think,' she said evenly, 'that you must be over . . . a bit over-imaginative.'

Janet Rushton smiled a little wryly. 'Why didn't you say "over-dramatizing yourself"?' she asked. 'It was what you were going to say, wasn't it? No: I'm not over-dramatizing myself. I only wish to God I were!' Her voice broke on the last word and the fingers of her clasped hands twisted convulsively together. 'I'm sorry: I thought you wanted to help. But I can quite see how far-fetched and Horror-Comic all this must sound to you. If it's any comfort to you, it sounds pretty crazy to me, so I don't know why on earth I should have expected you to believe it. I ought to have had more sense.'

'But I do—I mean, I can't . . . Oh, *hell!*' sighed Sarah despairingly, subsiding once more onto the hearthrug. 'I'm the one who ought to be saying, "I'm sorry," not you. And I really am sorry. I suppose I thought for a moment that you must be making fun of me just to see how much I'd swallow, and I reacted by doing a Queen Victoria: the *"We are not amused"* line. Can I change that instead to "Go on, convince me"? Please, Janet. I mean it.'

Janet's attempt at a smile was not entirely successful, but the nod that accompanied it satisfied Sarah, who smiled back at her warmly. But that brief check had evidently served to reawaken the older girl's sense of caution, for she stayed silent for an appreciable interval; sitting very still and apparently listening, though as far as Sarah could hear there was no sound from outside the room, and only the flutter and purr of flames and the occasional crackle of a burning log from inside it. Nevertheless, Miss Rushton continued to listen, and presently she rose to her feet, and crossing over to the outer door, switched off the light, and drawing back the bolt with her left hand (the right one, Sarah noted, was hidden in the pocket that held the little automatic) eased open the door.

The flood of moonlight that lay along the verandah had narrowed as the moon moved up the sky, but the long, snow-powdered arcade with its fringe of glittering icicles hanging from the roof-edge above was silent and deserted, and the only marks upon it were the prints of Sarah's footsteps.

Janet stood in the doorway for a moment or two, looking about her and listening to that silence. Then, stepping back, she closed and bolted the door, switched on the light again, and having checked the window fastenings and made sure that the curtains were closely drawn, looked across at Sarah and said very softly: 'You won't mind if I turn on the radio, will you? Cousin Hilda and I used to use it whenever we wanted to talk in a place where we could be overheard, so I know all the available stations backwards, and one of them puts on a discussion group around this time of night—or at least, that's what it sounds like. I've no idea where it comes from or what language they're talking, but voices make a better cover than music. So if you don't mind . . .'

She stooped to remove a small battery radio set from a chest of drawers that stood against the wooden wall between the door and the window, and placing it on top, adjusted the knobs and switched it on, releasing an excitable babble of voices that would have done credit to a family of Neapolitan fisherfolk enjoying a domestic row.

The volume, however, while not sufficient to disturb the slumbers of any fellow-guests further down the verandah, was more than enough to prevent anyone outside the room from separating the lowered voices of Miss Rushton and her visitor from the medley of masculine and feminine chit-chat and the incessant whine and crackle of static.

'I see what you mean!' commented Sarah, automatically keeping her voice below the level of the invisible disputers: 'Well, go on with what you were telling me. I'm all ears.'

Janet returned to her chair, and leaning forward, elbows on knees, to warm her hands at the fire, said carefully, as though choosing her words: 'You must have heard of the Secret Service, though I imagine it never occurred to you that very ordinary people like Cousin Hilda—Mrs Matthews—and myself could belong to it. No!' as Sarah made a startled movement and seemed about to speak, 'let me finish. People like us—like me—are only small fry. Our job is just to collect information: odds and ends of rumour and talk and gossip that can seem meaningless by themselves, but when added to other scraps collected by other people can—may—mean a

great deal. Well, some months ago the department we work for picked up a
. . .'

She paused, apparently searching for a word that would not commit her
too far, and finally selected an ambiguous one: 'A trail——'

2

Sitting by the fire with her sensible, schoolgirlish hands spread out to the blaze, and speaking in a carefully controlled voice that was pitched to reach no further than Sarah's ears, Janet Rushton told how she had been sent to Kashmir to contact and take her orders from a Mrs Matthews, who, since it might cause comment if an unmarried girl were to live alone, would pose as a relative so that the small houseboat on the Dal Lake near Srinagar, that had already been taken in Janet's name, could be moored next to Mrs Matthews' much larger one. How between them they had found out what they had been sent to find out: only to discover with horror that it was no more than the tip of a submerged and deadly iceberg whose presence no one had even suspected . . .

The situation was not one that they were equipped to deal with, and the enormity of the lurking menace had made it necessary for them to pass on the details of their discoveries to someone in higher authority. Yet their orders specifically forbade them to make any move to leave the State without the permission of their department. Since none of their various Kashmiri contacts operated at a sufficiently high level to be entrusted with such potentially lethal and unstable dynamite, Mrs Matthews had sent off the equivalent of a 'Mayday' call for help—though she was well aware that it would not be easy for anyone of their own nationality, or any non-Kashmiri for that matter, to arrive in Srinagar and get in touch with them without being noticed and talked about: for the simple reason that by then the year was drawing to a close.

The hordes of summer visitors had all left long ago, and the fact that she and Janet had been able to remain without exciting remark was because both had a talent for sketching in water colours, and November happens to be among the loveliest of months in the valley, as it is then that the snowline moves downward to meet the forests, the chenar trees put on every shade of red from vermilion to crimson, and willows, poplars and chestnuts blaze yellow and gold.

As painters, this annual transformation-scene had provided them with an impeccable reason for staying on when all the other visitors had left. Just as it had previously given them an admirable excuse not only to drive, ride, walk or be paddled in a shikara* to any spot they cared to see, but to fall into casual conversation with innumerable strangers who would pause to watch the artists at work, linger to ask questions and offer advice, and finally squat down beside them to talk. An end that had, according to Janet, played no small part in their selection for this particular assignment.

It was during this period, when the last of the leaves were falling, that Mrs Matthews had sent off that 'Mayday' call and sat back to wait for the help that she assured the anxious Janet would not be long in arriving. But four days later the *Civil and Military Gazette,* one of India's best known daily newspapers, had carried a small paragraph reporting the accidental death of a Major Brett who had apparently fallen from his carriage on the Frontier Express, *en route* to Rawalpindi: 'Foul play was not suspected, and the police were satisfied that the unfortunate man had at some time during the night, and while still half asleep, opened the side door of the carriage by mistake for the bathroom door . . .'

The accident was clearly not considered important enough to rate the front page, and had been tucked away on an inner one among a rag-bag of assorted news. But according to Janet, Mrs Matthews had read and re-read it, looking uncharacteristically shocked and upset.

'I'd never seen her look like that before,' said Janet. 'She was always so calm and good-tempered . . . even at the worst times. I asked her if he'd been a friend of hers, and she said no, she'd only met him once: he'd been in the room while she was being given her orders. But she couldn't help wondering if he had been on his way to meet us, because she didn't believe the accident story. He wasn't the kind to make that sort of silly mistake.'

'But surely, if the police——?' began Sarah breathlessly.

'If one of–of our people dies in an accident, we let it go at that. Officially, anyway. That may sound callous, but it's a lot safer all round than asking a flock of questions that can only lead to embarrassing answers. Cousin Hil—Mrs Matthews—said we mustn't worry, because if he *had* been the one, and on his way here, someone else would be sent instead. But–but I worried. I couldn't help thinking that if it wasn't an accident, and he'd been killed to stop him coming here, then–then the people who did it might know about us. And that if anything were to happen to us, no one would ever know what–what we knew.'

When the last leaves had fallen and cat-ice began to form on the lakes, the two of them had abandoned their houseboats and moved into Nedou's

* A flat-bottomed, canopied punt.

Hotel in Srinagar, to wait with ever-increasing anxiety for an answer to that urgent call for help. Knowing only too well that with every day that passed it would become more and more dangerous for anyone to answer it, because at that season of the year no casual visitor in their right mind cares to undertake the long, cold and frequently hazardous journey along the winding mountain roads that lead to the valley. Unless they have a very good reason for doing so. One that leaps to the eye or is easily explained! Though even then such rare wildfowl are apt to be conspicuous.

One such reason accounted for Mrs Matthews and her young cousin being able to take up residence, and without causing so much as a raised eyebrow, in the almost empty hotel where, apart from the suites occupied by a few elderly permanent residents living on their pensions, only a handful of rooms were kept open for the use of occasional visitors: the fact that both women were skiing enthusiasts.

Like the watercolour sketching, this had been a point that had not been overlooked by their employers; and Gulmarg, the little summer resort that had become one of the favourite playgrounds of the Raj and the chief meeting-place of the Ski Club of India, lay within easy reach of Srinagar—a car drive of twenty-four miles to the village of Tanmarg on the insteps of the mountains, followed by a four-mile ride on the back of a sure-footed hill pony up the steep and stony bridlepath that zig-zags upward through the forest, bringing the visitor to the shallow bowl of Gulmarg which lies in the lap of the tall ridge of Apharwat.

Both women had brought their skis with them, and everyone in the hotel was soon aware that they had skied in Europe before the war, and on several occasions since then at meetings of the Ski Club in Gulmarg, whenever there had been sufficient members to make it worthwhile opening the snow-bound hotel for ten days or so. 'You don't find people coming up here to ski on their own,' explained Janet, 'because it isn't worth opening it for just two or three people. And skiing on the level ground in the valley isn't much sport.'

Two days after they had moved into the hotel in Srinagar, and while they were becoming seriously worried over the lack of response to their 'Mayday' signal, a violent snowstorm had swept in from the north; blocking the passes, closing the Banihal route and both the Murree and Abbottabad roads into the valley, and ensuring that no plane could cross the mountains to land on Srinagar's still somewhat makeshift airfield. Telephone, telegraph and power lines fell before the onslaught of wind and snow, blacking out all Kashmir and isolating it from the outside world for more than a week. And even when it was over, the sky remained dark and threatening, with stormclouds hiding the high peaks, the airfield blanketed in drifts ten to twenty feet deep, the city snow-bound and avalanche threatening the toiling gangs of coolies who fought to clear the winding road through the mountains beyond Baramulla. The Banihal route could not even be attempted and was to remain closed for several weeks.

The first bus to struggle through brought sacks of mail, and Janet and Mrs Matthews had skied over to the post office on the Bund to collect their letters. They had also volunteered to fetch the rest of the hotel mail, and it was only after they had distributed this that they had time to open their own, most of which consisted of Christmas cards. The rest was of no interest except to the recipient, but one envelope—posted unsealed in the manner of printed circulars—contained a ten-page Christmas catalogue issued by a well-known store in Rawalpindi.

Mrs Matthews, to whom this had been addressed, glanced through it and left it open on the writing-table in her room for the remainder of the day, where the room bearer and any hotel servant whose duties brought him there—not to mention the odd resident who dropped in for a drink and a chat—had ample opportunity to see it, and to leaf through it if they wished. But later that night, when the majority of guests were safely in bed and the curtains were close drawn, she had removed from her small paperback library of favourite books that accompanied her everywhere, Stella Gibbons' *Cold Comfort Farm;* and with its help decoded the message that the Christmas catalogue contained——

'She told me about it next morning while we were skiing on the Takht,' said Janet. 'The man who had fallen from the Frontier Express *had* been on his way up to see us. But it didn't necessarily mean that the opposition had connected him with us, so we were not to worry. Someone else would be arriving as soon as possible and would identify himself in the usual manner. Cousin Hilda said he'd be arriving that day, because if the mail bus had got through it meant that the Murree-Baramulla road was passable, and that judging from the date on the envelope, the catalogue had been posted in Rawalpindi just over a week ago. He must obviously have been snowed up in some Dâk bungalow on the road.'

She stopped and fell silent for a space; staring bleakly into the leaping flames, until at last Sarah said in an uncertain whisper: 'Didn't he come?'

Janet dragged her thoughts back from whatever unpleasant paths they had been wandering along, and said 'Yes. He came. His name was Ajit Dulab and he was one of the best game shots in the country. And one of the best polo players, too. He was supposed to be up here to see if he could bag a snow-leopard—they get driven down to the lower hills by bad weather. The State put him up in one of the Maharajah's Guest Houses, and a senior official gave a cocktail party for him to which we were all asked. To cut a long story short, he managed to arrange a meeting with Cousin Hilda—she was going to give him a skiing lesson—and she told him everything. And the next day he said the weather was too bad for shooting, so he bought a couple of snow-leopard skins at a shop on the Bund, and left.'

'Then what are you worrying about?' asked Sarah. 'It's his headache now, not yours!'

'He never got back,' said Janet in a hoarse whisper.

'You mean . . . you mean he was *murdered?*' gasped Sarah.

'I don't know! I suppose it could have been an accident. Just–just bad luck. That road can be very dangerous; cars and buses and lorries are always going over the edge. There are so many places where the mountain-side drops straight down below it for several hundred feet into the gorge where the river runs—and no one gets out of that alive. Apparently his car was swept over by an avalanche.'

Sarah released her breath in an audible sigh of relief and said: 'Then it *must* have been an accident!'

'Perhaps. But avalanches can be started by people, and someone could have been waiting . . . it could have been done on purpose. If only we could have been sure that it was an accident we'd have felt . . . well, better, I suppose. But we weren't sure. We didn't even know, afterwards, if someone else had been sent up here or not. Perhaps someone was, and didn't make it either . . . like–like the other two.'

'Do you mean you had to sit here and wait and do nothing?' demanded Sarah, astounded. 'Haven't you got a radio transmitter, or a receiving set, or anything like that? I should have thought——'

'Small, portable transmitters,' interrupted Janet shortly, 'not only don't work well among mountains, but transmissions can be picked up by people they're not intended for. And worse still, traced! It would have taken no time at all for word to get around that someone was transmitting in code from the valley, and then the hunt would have been up—and the game with it!'

'Oh. Yes, I see. But surely you could have telephoned?' said Sarah—intrigued by this glimpse of the mechanics of spying, but puzzled by the slowness and elaboration. 'The lines must have been mended by then. Or why not just send off a telegram?'

'In *India?*' said Janet scornfully. 'Just how long have you been out here?'

'Only a month and a bit,' admitted Sarah. 'Why?'

'Well for your information, there is no such thing as a secure telephone in all India—let alone in Kashmir! The Viceroy and the C-in-C and the

Director of Central Intelligence, and one or two other bigwigs, probably have a scrambler apiece; but no one else would be able to get their hands on one. Certainly not in a Native State! The lines go through endless telephone exchanges and can be tapped almost anywhere by a child of two. As for telegrams, they get passed from hand to hand and everyone reads them—see *Kim!*'

'But if they were in code?'

'Codes,' retorted Janet impatiently, 'are the worst give-aways of all, because except for very brief ones that sound like sense—and boring sense at that!—a message in code instantly focuses attention and curiosity, and plenty of suspicion, on both the sender and the receiver. In our business no one writes down anything. Unless . . .' she hesitated, and for a brief interval her gaze seemed to leave Sarah and turn inward again to some disturbing mental picture that her words had conjured up; and when she finished the sentence it was in a completely different tone, and almost inaudible: '. . . unless we *have* to—if there's time.'

Another icy little prickle ran down Sarah's spine, and goaded by it, she said with a trace of tartness: 'But the message Mrs Matthews got in Srinagar must have been in code. The Christmas catalogue.'

'Yes, that's true. But since it came through the post, it got held up for a good many days by the storm—like that man who came up to see us. And no one could have read anything different into it, or even realized that there was anything else to read, except the person it was addressed to. Because only that person would have the key. A different key each time! It's almost the only code in the world that's impossible to crack, because nothing's written down, and you go by numbers—and the words are in another book. But unfortunately it doesn't work except for fairly short messages, because it isn't just *any* numbers. And what we had to say needed a lot of words and explanation.'

'It all sounds appallingly complicated to me,' observed Sarah disapprovingly.

'So is learning to walk a tightrope over Niagara, I imagine! Or finding one's way across the Gobi Desert. And this is worse than either. In the end we got another message, in much the same way as the other one. It told us to move up to Gulmarg for the Ski Club Meeting, and that the agent who would contact us here would be a skier. And also how we could meet him without anyone knowing.'

It had sounded a pretty good idea, said Janet. Skiing in Gulmarg, in her opinion, being an infinitely better reason for coming to Kashmir in winter than trying to bag a snow-leopard. But the brief message had concluded with a single, dreaded word that in their tabloid dictionary stood for

'Watch out—you have obviously been spotted!' It had shaken Janet badly, for despite the suspicions that had been raised by the deaths of those two agents, she had persuaded herself that the second was almost certainly due to a genuine accident, and that if the first was not, there was no need to suppose that the killers had any suspicion as to who the victim was travelling to meet. But now one small word had destroyed all that . . .

'I was so sure we were safe,' whispered Janet. 'I didn't believe that anyone could possibly suspect a middle-aged, gossipy widow who liked to paint and knit and go to coffee parties and whist drives, or a girl who played golf and tennis and went out sketching, and danced and picnicked with subalterns up on leave. But I suppose we must have made a slip somewhere . . . Or else someone has turned traitor: that–that does happen . . .'

Her voice broke and died out, and she swallowed convulsively as though her mouth had suddenly become dry. Once again her hunted gaze travelled swiftly and furtively about the little room—to the crackling radio, the closed, blank doors and the windows where the faded curtains hung still and undisturbed. And when she spoke again it was still in a whisper.

'After that message came, I was afraid . . . terribly afraid. Mrs Matthews wasn't. She was wonderful. But she took extra care. She carried a gun everywhere, and she made me carry one. She saw to it that our doors and windows were locked and barred at night, and that we didn't eat or drink out of any dish or jug that someone else hadn't helped themselves from first. I'd have given anything, then, to leave. But we had to wait for the one who was to meet us here. We *had* to. But he still hasn't come, and now Cousin Hilda is dead; and I'm afraid . . . *I'm afraid!*'

Sarah reached out a steadying hand and said with an attempt at calm good sense that she was far from feeling: 'Now you know you don't mean that. That's just hysteria.'

Janet Rushton jerked back in her chair and said angrily: 'You don't believe me! You think I'm either mad or imaginative, don't you? *Don't you?*'

'Actually,' said Sarah slowly, 'I don't. Though heaven alone knows why I don't! But I do think you are exaggerating the situation a little. Major McKay is an Army Doctor and both he and Dr Leonard say that Mrs Matthews' death was an accident. So for all you know it *may* have been just that. An unlucky accident.'

Janet Rushton's laugh was not a pleasant sound as she brushed Sarah's hand off her knee: 'Listen, my poor innocent, I may be frightened, but I'm not a fool. My nerve may have cracked a bit, but my brain hasn't—yet! I've already told you that Mrs Matthews carried a gun. Well it wasn't on her when she was found, and there could only be one reason for removing it. The murder had to look like an accident, and if there had been a loaded automatic on her it would have raised doubts in even the woolliest of minds; not to mention giving rise to a lot of awkward questions. People, even middle-aged widows, do not usually carry loaded weapons unless they are afraid of something.'

Sarah said: 'Couldn't it have dropped out into the snow when she fell? Or perhaps the coolie who found her may have stolen it?'

'She wore it in a little holster under her arm—like I do in the daytime—and someone must have searched her body to find it. No coolie would have touched a corpse found under these circumstances, because he would have been too afraid of being accused of having something to do with her death. And even supposing a coolie *had* tried to rob the body, do you suppose for one moment that he would have gone to the trouble of removing the holster as well? It would have been easy enough to slip out the gun, but it can't have been so easy to remove the holster and the sling. It must either have been cut away or her ski-coat taken off and replaced, which could only have been done while her body was still warm, because afterwards she —it——'

'I know,' said Sarah hastily, 'I saw them bring her in. But how do you know the gun wasn't there when they found her? Major McKay may have taken charge of it.'

'Because,' Janet's voice was once more barely audible, and she shivered uncontrollably, 'I found her at about four o'clock. Before the coolie did.'

'*You!*'

'Yes. I–I was worried. I hadn't seen her since dinner-time the night before, because when I went to her room after breakfast she'd already left and the room servant said she'd gone off with the Khilanmarg party. So it wasn't until you and Reggie Craddock and the Coply twins came back early from Khilan, and said you hadn't seen her, that I began to get really worried. I went out to look for her myself. I don't know why I went straight to the gully . . . except that Reggie had warned us that the snow there was dangerous, and I was afraid that——' Janet left the sentence open, and then finished abruptly: 'Anyway, I found her.'

'But—' whispered Sarah breathlessly, 'but that must have been long before the coolie found her! Why didn't you fetch somebody?'

'What was the use? She was dead. She had been dead for hours. Even I could see that. Besides, I couldn't afford to have my name brought into it, so I came back to the hotel by a different route and said nothing—it had begun to snow again by then, so I knew that my tracks would be covered.'

Sarah said sharply: 'What are you going to do now? Why don't you go to the police?'

'The *police?*' said Janet scornfully. 'Of course I can't go to the police! What would I tell them? Give away the results of months of work and planning, and ruin everything at the eleventh hour? Or say I "just had a feeling" that it wasn't an accident—and be told that I'm a hysterical female for my pains? No. There isn't anything I can do but wait.'

'*Wait?*' repeated Sarah incredulously. 'Wait for what, for heaven's sake?'

'I've told you. We have to meet someone here. I can't go until he comes. Mrs Matthews is dead, but I know all that she knew. And I have to pass it on to the right person. After that, like you said, it's somebody else's pigeon and not ours—mine—any longer.'

Sarah wanted to say 'suppose he doesn't come?' but stopped herself in time: it seemed an unnecessarily cruel remark in the face of the girl's desperate fear. She said instead:

'Why don't you take a chance and write it down for once—the important part—and risk posting it? Yes, I *know* you said that agents in your department don't put anything in writing because letters can go astray or be stolen and cyphers can be decoded. But it also seems,' she finished crisply, 'that agents can be killed!'

'Yes,' said Janet Rushton slowly. 'Agents can be killed. That was why I didn't believe you when you came to my door tonight. I thought it was a trap. That you had come to kill me.'

'You *what!*'

'Why not? If anyone had told you a few hours ago that I was a Secret Service agent, would you have believed them?'

'Well . . .'

'Of course you wouldn't! Because I don't look like your idea of a Secret Service agent.'

'Yes, I suppose so. I see. No wonder you pulled a gun on me! I thought you must have gone mad; or else I had.'

'I know,' said Janet wearily. 'I realized that if you weren't one of—*them* —then I would have done something that was going to be appallingly difficult to explain away. But I had to do it, because the other risk was so much greater.'

'How do you mean? What other risk?'

'If you had been one of them and I had hesitated for fear you might not be, I should have had no second chance. It was better to risk letting myself in for a lot of awkward questions and complicated lying than to risk that. You see, it's not just my own life that's at stake. It's far more important than that. Now that Mrs Matthews is dead I'm the only person who knows what she knew. I was never any more than a sort of second string to her. She gave me all my orders. But now I'm on my own and I've got to keep alive. I've got to! I can't let her down. I can't let it all be lost.'

The tired, passionate voice cracked queerly on the last word and after a moment Sarah said curiously: 'What made you decide that I was on the level?'

Janet Rushton smiled wanly. 'Oh, partly intuition I suppose, but mostly simple arithmetic.'

'I don't understand.'

'Don't you? It's very easy. You hadn't any weapon on you and you had told me the truth—there *had* been someone at the window: someone who must have been there quite a while, for they had made a very neat job of filing through that catch. Well, if you weren't on the level you wouldn't have warned me.'

'Oh I don't know,' said Sarah with a smile. 'I might have planted him there as a sort of decoy duck.'

'Yes. I thought of that too. You learn to think of most things in this job. But that didn't add up either. If you had planted someone at that window you could only have done it to provide an alibi: an excuse for getting in or for getting me out, supposing I had refused to open the door to you. Your reasoning could have been that before letting you in I might run to the bathroom window and check up on whether you were speaking the truth, and then, convinced of your *bona fides* by a sight of the decoy duck, I would of course have opened the door.'

'Then what makes you think—' began Sarah.

'I didn't go to the window first,' interrupted Janet. 'I made certain instead that you had no weapon on you; and by the time I got to the window, whoever had been there had heard us and gone. It did occur to me then that possibly it was a plot: not to kill me, but to gain my confidence. But if it had been that, then it was an entirely pointless gilding of the lily for your decoy to take on a long, cold and exceedingly tricky job on my window merely to provide an alibi, when the briefest demonstration would have served the same purpose equally well.'

'I see,' said Sarah slowly; and shivered. 'You seem to have it all worked out. And—just for the record of course—I am on the level, you know.'

'I know,' said Janet, with an odd inflexion in her voice. She raised her tired, hunted eyes from a contemplation of the glowing logs in the small brick fireplace and gave Sarah a long and curiously calculating look.

The logs fell together with a little crash and a sudden spurt of flame, and Sarah stood up slowly and said: 'What is it you want me to do?'

Something taut and watchful in Janet Rushton's face relaxed, and she said: 'You're certainly not stupid.'

'Not particularly. You wouldn't have told me all this merely in order to stop me chattering at the breakfast table. If that was all you were after, you'd have fallen back on the complicated lying. You were weighing it up all the time I was telling you the story of my life, weren't you? I'm quite sure you could have thought up a convincing explanation for me, but you decided to tell the truth instead. There had to be a reason for that.'

'There is. The reason is that I'm–I'm desperate. I'm in a corner, and so I'll have to take a chance.'

'And you're taking it on me. Is that it?'

'Yes. You appear to have a reasonable amount of intelligence, and you couldn't have done well in the W R A F, or been such a good skier, without a fair amount of physical courage. And I need help. Will you help me?'

Sarah held out her hand. 'Shake,' she said gravely; and smiled.

The other girl's fingers, cold and tense, closed tightly over hers for a brief moment. 'Thank you,' said Janet with real gratitude, and getting up from her chair she crossed to the writing-table, pulled open a drawer, and taking out an envelope and a fountain pen returned with them to Sarah.

'If my luck's in,' she said, 'you may not have to do anything. In fact, I hope to God you won't! But just–just in case, I'd like to have your address on this, and to know that if you should ever get it you'll do something about it. I'm not sure what, but I shall have to leave that to you, and I've a feeling that you won't let me down.'

'I'll try not to,' replied Sarah soberly. 'But why *my* name? Surely——'

'I daren't put anyone else's. *I daren't!* Because it could give that person away. But you're different. You're not one of us and you don't know anything. You are only someone I met skiing, so it's just possible that this will get to you without trouble if–if anything should happen to me.'

'Nothing's going to happen to you,' said Sarah firmly. She took the proffered envelope, noting as she did so that it was sealed, and though not empty, did not contain very much——certainly not more than one or at the most two sheets of thin writing-paper. And accepting the pen, she scribbled her name and address on the envelope and returned it.

Janet stood weighing it thoughtfully in her hand, and when she spoke again it was so softly that Sarah could barely catch the words and had the impression that she was talking to herself:

'The next problem is going to be getting this safely locked up when no one else is around, which isn't going to be easy if I'm being watched. Unless . . . Yes, that would do. I can take it down with me tomorrow——' She gave a small, brisk nod, as though in confirmation of some plan, and thrust the sealed envelope into her pocket. 'And now,' said Janet in her normal voice, 'I think you'd better get back to your own room.'

'Are you quite sure you'll be all right?' asked Sarah uneasily. 'After all, that window's open now, and a child could deal with the door-latch. I'll stay if you like. Suppose he—it—whoever it was—comes back?'

'Don't worry,' said Janet. 'No one is in the least likely to have a second try tonight. The lights are enough to advertise the fact that I'm awake and ready, and I shall leave the bathroom light on and wedge a chair under that door handle.'

'Well, if you're certain it's OK,' said Sarah doubtfully. 'Anyway, promise me that if you hear any unexplained noises you'll bang on the wall and yell.'

'I promise,' said Janet with a pale smile.

She crossed to the door, and drawing back the bolt opened it cautiously and glanced rapidly up and down the deserted verandah before turning back to Sarah. 'It was nice of you to come,' she said awkwardly. 'I—I can't tell you how grateful I am.'

'Nonsense,' said Sarah lightly. 'I was meant to come. Predestination or whatever it's called. Fate, I suppose: "There's a divinity that shapes our ends, rough-hew them as we may," and all that. Good-night, dear.'

The door closed softly behind her, and once more she heard the click of the key turning in the lock and the muffled rasp of the bolts as they were pressed home. A few seconds later the radio was switched off and the night was quiet again.

Sarah stood for a moment looking about her, her back to the door. After the comparative warmth of the firelit room the verandah was an icy cavern of pale shadow that stretched emptily away past closed, secretive doors and shuttered windows. The white, glistening waste of snow lay piled all about the rough wooden walls and hung thick and heavy upon the low roofs, blotting out the sharp angles of the buildings and drawing soft, curved lines against the frosty sky.

Far away across the *marg** a tree cracked sharply with the sound of a distant pistol shot, as its sap froze inside the rough bark. The thin sound, a pinprick in the silence, echoed faintly round the bowl of the sleeping *marg*, and Sarah, who had moved towards her own door, checked sharply. But it was not that faint sound which had stopped her.

The moon had risen higher into the night sky and half the verandah now lay in shadow. Only a narrow bar of cold white light remained at its edge,

* A meadow. In this case all the open grassy spaces of the three golf-courses were known collectively as the *marg* and the polo-ground as the *maidan*.

fretted with the sharp pattern thrown by the verandah railings. But in the reflected light from the wastes of snow beyond the railings, Sarah could see quite clearly on the film of white snowflakes that lay upon the verandah floor the prints of her own fur-lined slippers.

But there was now another set of footprints upon that pale and fragile carpet. The footprints of someone who had walked on tiptoe down the deserted verandah and paused outside Janet Rushton's door . . .

3

The sight of those footmarks was more shocking to Sarah than anything that Janet had told her, and as she stared down at them she felt as though she had been abruptly and violently propelled out of a make-believe world into one of chilling reality. For though it would not be true to say that she had disbelieved Janet, she had consciously allowed for a certain amount of exaggeration due to the effects of sorrow, fear and shock. Now, suddenly, it had become real to her. Because the proof was here before her eyes.

Her first instinctive reaction was to warn Janet. But even as her hand went out to knock once again on that door, she checked and turned back to look down again at those betraying prints. Whoever had made them had clearly not stayed listening very long; which meant that they had not been able to hear anything and been forced to retreat, disappointed. And since Janet had suspected that there might be an attempt to eavesdrop, and had guarded against it—and had also, in Sarah's opinion, endured enough for one night!—there seemed little point in bursting in on her a second time merely to tell her that she had been right.

There was, of course, something far more useful that she herself could do: follow that line of prints and find out where they led to! But even from here she could see that they had entered the verandah by way of the three stone steps at the far end, and left again the same way. And since the possibility that whoever made them might be lurking somewhere among the black shadows cast by the end of the hotel wing, waiting to see if anyone would do just that, was too daunting to be faced, Sarah fled back to her own room, and once safely inside it locked and bolted herself in.

After all the alarums and excursions of the past hour she had not expected to be able to fall asleep again. But here the experience gained during the war years, when she had learned to make use of every opportunity to snatch what sleep she could between air-raids or the departure and return of home-based bombers and fighters, stood her in good stead.

Her eyes had already closed and she was almost asleep, when it occurred to her that the second set of footprints, like her own, had been made by a woman . . .

It was at breakfast next morning that Reggie Craddock, the Secretary of the Ski Club, made his announcement.

He referred briefly to the tragic death of Mrs Matthews, and to his own previous warning that the Blue Run was unsafe for skiing. The snow, said Reggie Craddock, was rotten in places, and due to the thawing of a stream, most of the track was ice and very dangerous. No one, under any circumstances, was to ski in or near the run for the remaining four days of the Spring Meeting, and anyone found doing so would be automatically suspended from membership of the Club. He added the bald information that Mrs Matthews' body was being taken down to Srinagar that day for burial, and sat down with evident relief as a babble of low-toned conversation broke out around the tables.

Sarah glanced across the dining-room to where Janet Rushton's blond head gleamed in the brilliant morning sunlight that streamed through the snow-fringed window-panes. Janet's face showed no visible traces of her last night's panic, and Sarah, noting that she was wearing a dark tweed coat and skirt in place of her usual ski-suit, presumed that she would be accompanying her supposed cousin's coffin down to Srinagar and attending the funeral there. At the moment she was talking to Hugo Creed—a large and jovial character, built on generous lines, who was temporarily on the non-skiing list owing to an unfortunate altercation with a tree on Red Run.

Janet had been commiserating with him and Major Creed had evidently said something that amused her, for her laughter came clearly across the room, and hearing it, Sarah was tempted to wonder if the happenings of the previous night had not been a particularly vivid nightmare, or the product of a feverish imagination? But though she might possibly have been able to discount Janet's story, she could not forget those clear, betraying prints on the snow-powdered floor of the verandah.

Later that morning, on her way to the post office to send off a letter to her Aunt Alice, she had stopped to look behind her more than once, haunted by an uncomfortable feeling that she was being followed. But except for a few distant figures stumbling upon the nursery slopes below the hotel, the shimmering sweep of the snow-blanketed *marg* was empty and glittering in the clear sunlight that was thawing the snow to a soft slush under her skis, and there were fewer skiers than usual, since several of the older members had accompanied Janet down to Srinagar, from where they would return after a post-funeral luncheon at Nedou's Hotel.

She was on her way back from the post office when she saw the Creeds, who were watching a beginners' class on the nursery slopes, and went over to join them. She had known them in Peshawar and been driven up to Kashmir in their car, and despite a considerable disparity in their ages, Mrs Creed (Antonia by baptism, but 'Fudge' to her many friends) had become a particular friend of hers.

'Hello, Hugo,' hailed Sarah, coming to anchor beside them: 'Why isn't Fudge pushing you around in a bath chair? I thought you were supposed to be on a bed of sickness?'

'Not quite, my child,' said Hugo comfortably, closing his eyes against the sun-glare. 'No bones broken, or anything like that. A mere matter of bruisery. I'm as stiff as an old boot, and Fudge has been rubbing me with pints of embrocation, with the result that I smell like a sewer. You can wind me from five hundred yards, but I am becoming hourly more supple.'

He brushed away some melting snow from the bench he was seated upon, clearing a space for Sarah: 'Come and sit down. I know of few more invigorating pastimes than watching one's fellow-man earnestly endeavouring to remain upright while sliding down a snow slope of one-in-one with six feet of planking strapped to his boots. Take that one, for instance: observe the exaggerated caution of his advance. Now he's off— that's the stuff!—now he's gaining speed—his skis are crossing—now he's dropped a stick——Wait for it! . . . *Magnificent!* The purler of a lifetime. I have no doubt that Messrs Metro-Goldwyn-Mayer would have paid him thousands to record it for a custard-pie comedy, and we get it all free. *Bravo, sir! Bravo, indeed!*'

'*Do* shut up, Hugo!' begged Fudge. 'Don't laugh at him Sarah! It only encourages him. That's Major McKay. Reggie says he'll never make a skier, but he will try; he spends hours on the nursery slopes. He's looking simply furious, poor dear, and spitting out snow.'

'And doubtless a few teeth as well,' said Hugo, interested. 'Did I ever look like that when I was learning to ski, Fudge?'

'Worse,' said Fudge, 'far worse. Like Henry VIII doing the splits.'

'I resent the comparison,' said Hugh with dignity. 'Anyway, you have got your numbers wrong. Henry certainly, but not eight. Five, I think. Or whichever one Laurence Olivier recently introduced to the public. Many people commented at the time upon his close resemblance to myself. "Larry old boy", they said, "or is it Hugo?" Quite embarrassing it became. Cease giggling, Sarah. It does not become you.'

'I'm sorry,' said Sarah laughing, 'but I've often wondered who you reminded me of, and of course it's Henry VIII.'

'There!' said Fudge triumphantly, 'What did I say? Thank you, Sarah.'

'It's a plot,' sighed Hugo. 'But I forgive you, Sarah. You're so pretty.

When I have sent this harridan of mine to the block, may I hope that you will step into the vacancy thus created? No security of tenure, of course.'

'I'll think it over,' promised Sarah. 'Are you two coming on the Khilan party tomorrow?'

'I'm coming,' said Fudge. 'Hugo won't be able to make it, worse luck, but I am deserting him for the night. I wouldn't miss my last chance of a night at the ski-hut for anything.'

'There's wifely devotion for you,' observed Hugo sadly. 'Does she forego her selfish pleasures to stay and anoint my creaking joints with yet more embrocation? Not on your life! She leaves me cold and rushes off to ski with snakes-in-the-grass like old Reggie. Hello, Reggie. Rounded up your numbers for the hut tomorrow?'

'Yes,' said Reggie Craddock, panting up the slope below them, his skis slithering and skidding on the slushing surface. 'Hell take this sun! The bally place is a bog. If this thaw keeps up, goodbye to our last four days skiing.'

'Never mind,' comforted Hugo. 'You can all have a jolly time tobogganing on the slopes with the hotel tea-trays. Nice, clean, boyish fun. Who's for the hut tomorrow?'

The ski-hut stood on the snow slopes of Khilanmarg, which is the long plateau, high above the bowl of Gulmarg, where the tree-line ends and the forests run out at the foot of Apharwat, the long bare ridge of mountain, seamed with gullies, that rises above it for another fourteen thousand feet. Khilanmarg, the Meadow of Goats, is well named, for in summer it provides a grazing ground for flocks of goats and sheep who crop the grassy levels and scramble about on the rocks and the steep slopes of the mountainside above. But in winter the snow turns it into perfect skiing ground, and it was a practice of the Ski Club members to go up in parties to Khilanmarg and sleep the night in the ski-hut, which gave them more skiing time on the following day, since it eliminated the long pull up through the forest paths from Gulmarg, fifteen hundred feet below.

Reggie said: 'Quite a goodish crowd staying the night, and some only coming up for the day. Fourteen of us for the hut I reckon. Let's see, there's Sarah here, and Fudge of course, and the Coply twins. And Mir Khan and Ian Kelly, and those two birds from Calcutta—what are their names? Thingummy and Something.'

'Thinley and Somerville,' prompted Fudge.

'Yes, that's it. And myself of course, and Meril Forbes and the Curtis girl, and Helen and Johnnie Warrender. That's the lot I think.'

'Oh, dear! Is Helen really coming?'

'So she says. Why?'

'Nothing, only——'

'*Miaow!*' interjected Hugo.

'I wasn't going to say anything!' protested Fudge indignantly.

'I'm sure you weren't. I know how dearly you love Helen.'

'Now who's being catty? *Miaow* yourself! But I won't pretend she doesn't madden me. She's like–like——'

'Quite,' said Hugo. 'Biscuit crumbs in the bed. You need say no more.'

Sarah, who had been checking names on her fingers, said suddenly: 'But that makes thirteen, not fourteen. You'll have to rake in someone else, Reggie. You can't take up a party of thirteen. It would be unlucky.'

'It was fourteen when I made out the lists,' said Reggie, 'I must have forgotten someone.'

'Me,' said Hugo sadly.

'Of course. *Damn!*'

'Don't apologize,' said Hugo with a gracious wave of his hand.

'I wasn't. I was just wondering who to rake in to take your place.'

'It can't be done. There's only one of me: the country carries no spares. I am what *Fifi et Cie* would doubtless label an "Exclusive Model".'

'I wish you wouldn't chatter so much,' said Reggie irritably. 'I can't think straight while you babble. Do you suppose we could get Tomlin to take your place?'

'He's sprained his wrist.'

'Curse, so he has. What about Stevenson?'

'He's umpiring the beginners' race tomorrow.'

'Oh well, I expect we shall raise someone. Anyway, I'm not superstitious myself, and if Fudge and Sarah will refrain from commenting on the fact, I don't suppose anyone else will think of counting heads. Sarah can keep her fingers crossed and drape charms round her neck if it really worries her.'

'Sound common sense,' approved Hugo. ' "*A Solomon come to judgement!*" If you can bring yourself to believe that certain things are unlucky, you must also be able to believe that certain other things are lucky. So if you see my dear wife plodding up to Khilan tomorrow, Reggie, festooned with horseshoes, bristling with white heather, and clutching a four-leaved clover in one hand and an outsize log of wood in the other, you will know that she is merely taking suitable precautions against disaster.'

'There's the lunch gong,' said Reggie. 'I think I'll push off. Good Lord —look at McKay! Golly what a toss! It's a wonder they don't break their necks, isn't it? Has he been doing that sort of thing all morning?'

'Without ceasing,' replied Hugo. 'It's very nearly perpetual motion. Still, it provides the bystanders with a lot of good, clean fun, and if his rugged bulldog spirit forbids him to chuck the whole idea and take up ballroom dancing instead, he will undoubtedly succeed in breaking his neck in the near future, ruining a perfectly good pair of skis in process. Then we can all have a jolly laugh and you can put the nursery slopes out of bounds.'

'Considering Mrs Matthews is being buried today, I don't think that's a particularly funny remark,' observed Reggie Craddock frostily.

'Oh God!' said Hugo. ' *"We are not amused!"* Sorry, sorry, sorry. Lead me lunchwards, Fudge, before I put my foot in it further. Coming, Sarah?'

The rest of the day passed without incident, and watching Janet Rushton at supper that evening Sarah decided that she was either a remarkably good actress, or had allowed the shock of finding Mrs Matthews' body to exaggerate her fears.

That night there were no unusual sounds from the other side of the thin wooden wall of her bedroom; but Sarah found herself unable to sleep, for the deathly silence of the previous night was broken now by a soft chorus of drips from the thawing snow on the roof falling with a stealthy, monotonous patter into the piled snowdrifts below the verandah rail, pitting them with small, dark, ice-fringed holes. There was a breeze too: a faint uneasy breath of wind that sighed and whispered along the dark verandahs and under the snow-laden eaves, and combed through the black deodar forests behind the hotel with a sound like far-off surf.

An hour or two after midnight it died away and frost drew a silent finger along the rooftops; checking the thaw and re-hanging fantastic fringes of icicles from every gutter and ledge. Silence flowed back across the *marg,* and Sarah slept at last. To be awakened by a discreet tap upon the door and the arrival of her morning tea.

Bulaki, her down-country bearer, reported that it had snowed in the early hours of the morning and that the hotel's Kashmiri servants said that bad weather was coming. He looked cold and unhappy, and his dark face appeared blue and pinched and as woeful as a monkey's. He inquired between chattering teeth if it was still the Miss-sahib's intention to spend the next night in the Khilanmarg ski-hut, and on receiving a confirmatory answer observed darkly that no good would come of it.

The ski-hut, said Bulaki, was damp and insecure. It was also a place of evil omen, for had not the first ski-hut been buried by an avalanche—and with no less than three young sahibs within it at the time? He himself had spoken with a man who had helped to dig out the bodies of those same sahibs, and . . . At which point Sarah had cut him short with some haste, and having repeated her intention to spend the night in the Khilanmarg hut, requested him to pack what she would need for the expedition while she was at breakfast.

Twenty minutes later she stepped out into the snow-powdered verandah and descended the hill to the dining-room, which was situated in a large block some distance below the wing in which she slept. The hotel buildings lay scattered over the top and sides of a steep little hill that rises out of the centre of the shallow bowl in the mountains that is Gulmarg—the 'Meadow of Roses'. A bowl that in summer is one vast, green golf-course, walled about by forests of pine and deodar and chestnut, and dotted and encircled by innumerable little log huts that bear a strong resemblance to those of a mining camp in any Cowboy film.

Despite Bulaki's warnings of bad weather it was a glorious morning. The sun had not yet reached into the bowl of Gulmarg, but it lit up the mountain tops that rose above it and glittered upon Sunrise Peak in a dazzle of light. Breakfast was a hurried meal, and immediately after it some twenty or so members of the Ski Club packed their rucksacks with sandwiches and Thermos flasks, and strapping on their skis set off on the long climb through the pine forests up to the open snowfields of Khilanmarg.

The day had been all too short, and with the lengthening shadow of evening a chill had crept over the snowfields, and those of the party who were returning to the hotel drained the last drops of tea from their Thermos flasks, ate the last crumbs of cake, and buckled on their skis for the homeward run. One by one their small figures, dark against the rosy-tinted snow and dwarfed by the lowering bulk of Apharwat whose steep sides rise up from the gentle slopes of Khilanmarg, swooped away across the sparkling levels to vanish among the shadows of the pine woods.

Sarah, who had been skiing in Christmas Gully with Ian Kelly and the Coply twins, paused on the ridge of the Gully to watch the nightly miracle of the sunset. 'Isn't it wonderful!' she said on a breath of rapture.

A girl's voice spoke from behind her: 'Yes, it is pretty good, isn't it? Like a transformation scene in a pantomime—not quite real.'

Sarah turned sharply to find Janet Rushton leaning upon her ski-sticks at the rim of the Gully and looking down to where a spangle of lights pinpricked the distant cup of purple shadows that was Gulmarg.

'Hello!' said Sarah, surprised. 'I didn't know you were staying up here for the night. I suppose you've taken Hugo's place? The fourteenth man.'

'Yes. I couldn't resist it. I didn't mean to stay, but Reggie brought pressure to bear. Said the party might develop the jitters if they discovered they were thirteen. Load of old rubbish really; and anyway, his efforts have been wasted.'

'But you're staying?'

'Yes; I said I would. Besides—well anyway it's too late now. The others have gone and it would only cause comment if I insisted on rushing after them on my own.'

'Why? What's happened?'

'Nothing much, except that Evadne Curtis has developed tummy trouble or cold feet or something, and I've just heard that she decided to go back to the hotel after all, and those two, Thinley and Whatsisname, have gone down with her. She comes from their part of the world and it appears that both of them are rivals for her hand. So naturally neither of them was going to let her go with the other. All very understandable, but it means we're now only eleven and I needn't have said I'd fill in for Hugo, after all. Oh well——!'

Sarah was conscious of a sudden wave of relief. She had watched the small dark figures of the homeward-bound skiers vanish among the pine woods with a feeling of heavy foreboding that she had not wished to analyse, but which she now realized had its roots in the fear that somewhere down in that rapidly darkening hollow far below, death lay in wait for Janet; death tiptoeing along the black, snow-powdered verandahs of the old hotel, or lurking among the shadows at the foot of Blue Run. But now Janet would not be there. She was here, and safe; far above the shadows of the black, watching trees and the secretive wooden walls of the old hotel. Here in a clean, fresh, frosty world. Safe . . .

Sarah laughed aloud in sheer relief. 'Come on,' she said, 'race you to the hut.'

She was a good skier; but Janet was an excellent one, and drawing ahead effortlessly she arrived with a swish of flung snow at the hut a full sixty seconds ahead of Sarah, who found her leaning against the far corner of it and dusting the snow off her suit. Her gaze was on the dim hollow far below them and her face in the waning light was once again strained and anxious.

She said abruptly and in an undertone: 'I shouldn't have stayed up here. It's too great a risk. I've been a fool. I should have gone back with the others.'

'*Risk?*' repeated Sarah sharply. 'What do you mean? What risk is there in staying up here?'

'It's not that,' said Janet. 'It's . . . oh well, perhaps it doesn't matter.' She turned to glance up at the steep slope of the mountainside that rose behind the small hut, and at the clear star-pricked sky above it, and added with apparent inconsequence: 'Anyway, there's a moon tonight.'

A tangle of dark figures shot past them in a flurry of snow to collapse in a confused heap before the hut door. 'Get your skis out of my hair, Alec!' demanded Ian Kelly. 'Where are the others, Sarah?'

'Some of them have arrived and some of them are just arriving,' said Sarah. 'Hello Reggie. Where have you been?'

Reggie Craddock and his two companions, a tall slim Indian with a face that would have graced a Greek coin, and Meril Forbes, a thin sandy-haired girl with pale eyes and a multitude of freckles, came round the side of the hut and joined the group by the door.

'Up to the top of Gujar Gully,' said Reggie, unstrapping his skis. 'By the way, you all know each other, don't you? Miss Forbes, and Mir—I can't remember all your names, Mir.'

The tall Indian laughed. 'One is sufficient. But we have all met before.'

'Speaking for myself, very painfully,' said Ian Kelly. 'I cannoned into Mir coming down Red Run two years ago and I'm still black and blue. Where did you learn to ski, Mir? Up here?'

'No, in Austria, and then in Italy. I had not skied up here before this year. It is good snow.'

'Best in the world!' asserted that loyal Secretary of the Ski Club, Reggie Craddock. 'By the way, I'm thinking of doing a run to the Frozen Lakes tomorrow morning. Five-thirty start. Anyone coming with me? What about you, Janet?'

'No thanks. Too much of a slog. I feel like idling for a change.'

'I will go,' said Mir Khan, 'and so will Ian. It will do him good. He is putting on weight. Two years ago he was a gazelle—a fawn!'

'Ah youth! youth!' sighed Mr Kelly. 'I was young then—at least nineteen. All right, I'll martyr myself. Coming with us, Sarah?'

'I'll think about it,' said Sarah. 'Come on, Janet, let's see if anyone's got the lamps lit and the stove going. I'm frozen.'

The door closed behind them and within minutes the last gleam of daylight faded from off the mountain tops. Stars glittered frostily in the cold sky, and far away, beyond the towering peak of Nanga Parbat, a flicker of lightning licked along the ranges. But overhead the sky was clear and cloudless, and paling to the first pallid glow of the rising moon.

The interior of the ski-hut was partitioned into three sections: a living-room with a men's dormitory leading off from it to the left and a women's dormitory to the right. A double tier of bunks ran round three sides of each dormitory wall; fourteen bunks to each room, with an additional three bunks in the living-room in case of need. But the days when the ski-hut could be filled to capacity had gone, and Reggie Craddock had been both surprised and pleased at being able to muster the handful who now replaced the thirty-one of earlier years.

Fudge Creed, who was engaged in drying socks at the iron stove that stood in the middle of the women's half, welcomed Sarah and Janet with enthusiasm, and dropping her voice to a feverish whisper said: 'My dears! Thank heavens you've come: another ten minutes and I should have sunk through the floor. I never realized before how lowly are my antecedents, and how few, if any, of the right people I know. I don't believe there is a single peer whom I can call by his first name—let alone his nickname!'

Janet burst out laughing and looked at once younger and less anxious. 'Helen, I suppose! Where is she?'

'Having her skis waxed next door.'

'I thought I heard female voices from the men's side as we came through. All most reprehensible!'

'*Ssh!*' warned Sarah. 'Here comes your little chum.' But it was not Helen Warrender who pushed open the door and entered, but Meril Forbes: a colourless young woman in every meaning of the word, who despite an over-abundance of freckles might have been quite pretty had it not been for the hunted expression she habitually wore. Meril had the misfortune to be an orphan and to possess, as her sole relative and guardian, an elderly and autocratic aunt who lived more or less permanently in Kashmir. If she had ever possessed any character or will of her own, it had long ago been submerged in the strong waters of her aunt's personality, for Lady Candera was one of those domineering old ladies who employ outspokenness to the point of rudeness as a form of social power politics, and are feared and deferred to in consequence.

'Hello, Meril,' said Janet, sitting down on the floor before the stove, and tugging off her boots. 'Glad to see you were able to come up for the meeting after all. I thought I heard something of your not being able to make it. What happened? Aunt Ena suffer a change of heart?'

Meril's face flushed faintly under its powdering of freckles. 'Something like that,' she admitted. 'First she said she wouldn't hear of it, and then suddenly she told me I could go.'

'If I were you, I'd take a chopper to the old pest,' advised Janet candidly. 'No jury would convict. You've got a sweet, kind nature, Meril; that's your trouble. What you need is to get roaring drunk and recite the Declaration of Independence to your aged aunt.'

Meril Forbes smiled wanly. 'She's been very good to me on the whole, you know. I mean, if it hadn't been for her, I should have had nobody. She's done a lot for me.'

'Oh well,' said Janet, getting up, 'as long as you feel like that about it. What do you suppose there is for supper? I've had nothing but some sandwiches since breakfast.'

'I can tell you,' said Fudge, with some satisfaction: 'Mutton broth and stew. Both good—I made 'em. Lots of coffee—me again. And lemon cheese-cakes sent up by the hotel. What do you suppose I've been doing while you three were frivolling around the snow-slopes with your boy-friends? Cooking the supper—that's wot!'

'Bless you. I had visions of having to do it myself. Let's go and knock the stuffing out of it without delay.'

The remainder of the party were already gathered about the stove in the living-room, sipping cautiously at a weird concoction of hot rum, lemon, and various other mysterious ingredients procured and manufactured by Johnnie Warrender.

'Ah—*les* girls!' exclaimed Johnnie, waving a steaming glass. 'Come and try a snort of this, darlings. Just the thing to keep out the cold. A "Hell's Belle"—that's what they're called. Jolly good name, too, hell's bells!' He laughed uproariously. It was evident that Johnnie was already 'well on the way'—a not unusual condition for him. Sarah accepted a glass and retired with it to the farther end of the room where she sat sipping it gingerly and observing her fellow-guests with interest; in particular, Johnnie's wife, Helen, who was talking to Mir Khan and Reggie Craddock.

The other women in the party were wearing slacks and woollen pull-overs, as were the men. But Helen Warrender, alone of the party, had brought a more exotic change of clothes for the occasion: a smartly draped wool dress, low-necked and short-sleeved, in a vivid shade of emerald green. Her silk-clad legs ended in green shoes with rhinestone buckles, and there were a pair of large rhinestone clips at the neck of her dress, and matching ones on her ears.

This was another woman who, like Meril, could have been pretty, per-haps even beautiful, if her face had not been marred by its expression: in her case one of chronic boredom and discontent that no amount of cleverly applied make-up could conceal. A lavish use of lipstick failed to disguise the bitterness of the sullen mouth or the downward droop of its corners, while the glittering, scarlet nail-polish that she favoured only seemed to emphasize the restlessness of the hands that fidgeted ceaselessly with an endless chain of cigarettes, lit one from the other and thrown away half smoked.

All in all, decided Sarah, Mrs Warrender struck a strident and incongru-ous note on the rough-and-ready surroundings of the ski-hut. A note as artificial and out of place as the rhinestone ornaments that twinkled and flashed in the smoky light from the kerosene lamps.

The room was very hot, and the waves of heat from the crude iron stove, allied to the thick haze of cigarette smoke, the babble of voices and the fumes of Johnnie's 'Hell's Belle', combined to make Sarah very sleepy, and as soon as possible after the meal, although it was still barely past nine o'clock she retired, yawning, to her bunk.

The others were not long in following her example, for they had risen early and it had been a long and healthily tiring day. Moreover, the best skiing tomorrow would be before breakfast while the snow was still crisp and dry from the night frost. By ten o'clock the last oil lamp had been extinguished and the ski-hut was dark and quiet.

It must have been an hour before midnight when Sarah awoke, for the moon was well clear of the heights above Khilanmarg, and its cold clear light, intensified by the glittering wastes of snow, lent a queer luminous quality to the darkness in the little ski-hut.

She lay still for a minute or two, gazing out at the shadowy, unfamiliar outlines of the narrow room with its dimly seen tier of bunks, and listening to the muffled and rhythmical rumble of snores proceeding from the other side of the partition, where Mr Reginald Craddock was presumably sleeping on his back. A wandering breath of wind from Apharwat soughed under the snow-hung eaves and whispered its way across the empty white levels, and down in the pine forest a branch cracked sharply, breaking under the weight of snow.

A moment later that distant sound was repeated from somewhere inside the hut. And of a sudden the darkness thinned, and Sarah found herself looking at the clear outlines of the little iron stove which less than an instant before had been a dark blur. A second later she realized why this was so: someone had opened the hut door.

For a moment or two she lay still, listening. But beyond that sudden creak of a hinge there was no further sound, and she sat up cautiously and peered out over the edge of her bunk.

There was only one entrance to the ski-hut, and that was by the door that led into the living-room. But the inner door between the women's side and the living-room was open; and so also was the outer door of the hut, for the living-room was bright with moonlight and by its reflected glow Sarah could just see the faintly snoring bundle in the next bunk that was Meril Forbes.

The bunk beyond it was Janet's, but it was empty, and the reflected light from the open doorway of the room beyond showed the tumbled blankets and glinted faintly on the sides of the little stove. And suddenly, horribly, Sarah remembered again that line of footprints on the empty verandah, and the way the light had glinted along the barrel of the little automatic in Janet Rushton's hand . . .

The next moment she was out of bed and thrusting her feet into her ski-boots. Pulling her heavy coat off the bunk, she dragged it about her shoulders, and was at the door and across the living-room, and looking out into the night. Something moved against the wall of the ski-hut, and as a shadow blotted the gleaming brightness of the snow she said, *'Janet!'* in a gasp of relief.

The shadow checked, and Janet's voice said in a sharp whisper: 'Sarah! What on earth are you doing out here? Get back at once before you catch pneumonia!'

'I heard the door creak when you went out,' explained Sarah between chattering teeth. 'It woke me up, and when I looked out of my bunk and saw you weren't there I was afraid something had happened.'

She wriggled her arms into the sleeves of her coat, and buttoning it up about her stepped out into the snow, and as an after-thought, turned and very quietly closed the door: there was no necessity to wake others in the hut. The hinge creaked faintly again, and the latch fell into place with a soft click.

Janet Rushton was leaning against the wall of the hut, strapping on her skis. She was fully clothed and wore a neat dark skiing cap tied over her yellow curls, and a thick woollen muffler about her throat. She sang softly, just under her breath, as she tugged at the stiff straps and buckles: an old tune that Sarah had heard the dance bands play on the radio and at dances in wartime England—how long ago?

'The moonlight and the moon,
And every gay and lovely tune that's played for you,
Were made for you.
The Summer and the Spring,
And that golden wedding ring,
Were only made for you,'

sang Miss Rushton.

She fastened the last strap, and straightening up, pulled on a pair of fur-lined skiing-gloves and picked up her ski-sticks. In the clear moonlight Sarah could see that her eyes were sparkling and she looked young and gay again, and as if a heavy load had been lifted from her shoulders.

'What are you up to?' demanded Sarah. 'What's happened, Janet? Where are you going?' Her whisper was sharp in the stillness.

'Hush! You'll wake the others. Come over here.' The snow crunched crisply under their feet as they moved out into the moonlight and away from the shadows of the ski-hut.

Janet said: 'He's come, Sarah. He's come at last. Now everything will be all right and tomorrow I can go away from these horrible mountains and be free again. Look over there!'

She caught Sarah's arm and pointed with one gloved hand to where, far below them, the moonlight filled the bowl of Gulmarg with milky light.

'What?' whispered Sarah. 'I can't see anything.'

'There, among the trees, to the left of the Gap.'

On the far side of Gulmarg, from among the furry blanket of the distant treetops that showed iron-grey in the moonlight, a single speck of light glowed like a minute red star in a stormy sky. A pin-point of warmth in the immensity of the cold, moonlit world that lay spread out before them.

'I can see a speck of light, if that's what you mean,' whispered Sarah. 'A red light.'

'Yes, that's it. We've been waiting for that light for days. Ever since we came up here one or other of us would watch for it every night, and I'd begun to think it would *never* come. That's partly why I decided to stay the night up here—to tempt my luck. I knew that if it did I could see it from here just as well as from my room at the hotel. Perhaps better.'

Sarah said: 'But what are you going to do? You can't go down there now.'

'Of course I can. I'm a good skier. Better than almost anyone here. I can get there in under half an hour.'

'Don't be absurd!' They had been speaking in whispers, but Sarah's voice rose perilously: 'You'd never find your way through that forest by night.'

'*Ssh!* You'll wake somebody. I'm not going that way: I'm going down Slalom Hill and the Blue Run. Reggie Craddock did it in ten minutes and I can do it in eight. After that I'll cut straight across the *marg*. Say another twenty minutes at most.'

'Janet, you're mad. You can't do it! And you can't go by Blue Run. You heard what Reggie said about it—and–and——'

Janet laughed softly, her breath a white mist on the still air. 'It's all right, Sarah. Don't look so horrified. I'll keep to the edge of the run, and I know the route like the back of my hand. Don't worry, there won't be a murderer waiting for me down there at this time of night, and I'll be back long before morning. If I'm not—if I'm delayed, I'll go straight back to the hotel instead and pretend I got up early for the run down. Tell the others that, will you, if I'm not back in time?'

Sarah said: 'I can't let you go like this. Something—anything—might happen! Look, if you'll wait just a minute while I get my skis and put on a few clothes, I'll come with you.'

'No. You're a grand girl Sarah, but you're not a good enough skier.

You'd probably break your neck on that run, and that would hold me up.'
She smiled at Sarah's anxious face. 'I'm all right. Really I am. Look.'

She thrust her hand into a pocket of her ski-suit and drew out the little
automatic. For a moment the moonlight winked and sparkled on the cold
metal, and then she slipped it back again and fastened the pocket with a
small steel zipper.

'Do you mean to say you've been carrying that thing around in your
pocket all day?' demanded Sarah, illogically shocked.

'Not in my pocket: in its holster, here——' Janet patted her left armpit.
'But I realized at the last minute that no one was going to notice a lump on
my ski-suit at this time of night, so I took it out and put it in my pocket
instead; easier to get at it there. Not that I shall need it tonight. Or ever, I
hope. But I have to carry the whole works with me, because I daren't risk
leaving it behind, for fear that some helpful tidy-upper like Meril comes
across it and starts asking a whole floorful of agitated questions.'

Sarah said abruptly: 'Janet, what do you get out of this?'

Janet paused, and her face in the moonlight was suddenly sober and
thoughtful. After a moment she said slowly: 'None of the things that most
people work for. No great material rewards or public success. Excitement
perhaps; but most of all, fear. Fear that makes you sick and cold and
brainless and spineless.'

'Then why——?'

'My father,' said Janet, 'was a famous soldier. And my grandfather and
my great-grandfather. All my family have always been soldiers. But my
eldest brother was killed on the Frontier in '36, and John died in Italy, and
Jamie in a Japanese prison camp. I am the only one that's left, and this is
my way of fighting. One has to do what one can. It isn't enough just to be
patriotic.'

Sarah thought suddenly of another Englishwoman, long dead, who had
faced a German firing-squad, and whose immortal words Janet Rushton
had unconsciously paraphrased: *Patriotism is not enough.*

She held out a hand. 'Good luck, Janet.'

'Thank you. You've been a brick, Sarah, and I'm terribly grateful. I wish
I could show you how much I appreciate it.'

Sarah smiled at her; a companionable smile. 'For a sensible girl,' she
said, 'you certainly talk an awful lot of rubbish. Take care of yourself.'

'I will,' promised Janet. 'Don't worry.'

She leant forward and swiftly, unexpectedly, kissed Sarah's cold cheek.
The next moment, with a strong thrust of her ski-sticks and crisp swish of
snow, she was gone—a dim, flying figure in the cold moonlight, dwindling

away over the long falling levels of the snowfields to merge into the darkness of the forest. A shadow without substance.

Sarah turned away with a little shiver and made her way back to the hut: suddenly aware of the intense cold which had numbed her hands and feet and turned her cheeks to ice. Janet was right, she thought, shivering. I shall catch pneumonia—and serve me right!

The moonlight slanting over the deep, smooth snow on the ski-hut roof turned it to white satin, below which the log walls showed inky black with shadow. And the night was so quiet that Sarah could hear, like a whisper in an empty room, the far, faint mutter of thunder from behind the distant mountains of the Nanga Parbat range on the opposite side of the valley. But she had not taken more than two steps towards the hut when she heard another sound; one that was to remain with her and haunt her dreams for many a long night to come. The creak of a door hinge . . .

Sarah checked, staring. Frozen into immobility by the sight of the door that she had so recently closed. Someone must have eased it open while she talked with Janet in the snow, and was now closing it again—slowly and with extreme care—and presently she heard the faint click as the latch returned softly to its place. But it was a long time before she dared move, and standing in the icy moonlight she recalled, with a cold prickling of the scalp that had nothing to do with the night air, Janet's carelessly confident words of a few moments ago, when she had spoken of the Blue Run: *'There won't be a murderer waiting down there for me at this time of night.'*

Perhaps not. Perhaps because a murderer had been waiting here all the time. Close beside her under the snow-shrouded roof of the little dark ski-hut on Khilanmarg.

4

It was not until Reggie Craddock's alarm-clock announced with a deafening jangle that it was 5 a.m., and sounds of movements on the other side of the partition betokened the reluctant arising of Messrs Craddock, Kelly and Khan (the remainder of the party being impervious to the joys of pre-dawn skiing), that Sarah at last fell into an uneasy sleep.

She had lain awake for hours, huddled shivering among the blankets in her narrow bunk. Listening to the monotonous rumble of snores that proceeded from the other side of the wall, and the snuffling breathing of Meril Forbes. And seeing again and again the stealthy closing of that door.

Someone had been standing there, watching and listening. And if it had merely been somebody roused from sleep, as she herself had been, surely they would have called out? In that bright moonlight it would have been impossible not to see Janet and herself, or fail to recognize them; and anyone who thought they heard voices and decided to investigate, would have hailed them. Besides . . . Sarah shivered again as she remembered that closing door: it had been eased shut so slowly, so very gently . . .

There were eleven people in the hut, including herself and Janet. But she could not eliminate any of them, because by the time she had plucked up the courage to move again and re-enter the hut, whoever had closed the door had had ample time to slip quietly back into their own bunk.

Sarah went over in her mind all she knew of the party gathered in the ski-hut.

There was Reggie Craddock, the Secretary of the Club: a stocky little man in the late thirties, who possessed a handful of cotton mills and a consuming passion for winter sports. He had served during the war with an Indian regiment and had only recently been demobbed, and having been born and spent the best part of his life in India, he was well known from one end to the other of that gregarious country. It seemed unlikely, on the face of it, that Mr Craddock of Craddock and Company, lately a member of the Bombay Grenadiers, would be employed in subversive activities or mixed up in murder.

Then there was Ian Kelly. Of Ian she knew a little more since he was a young man who liked to talk about himself, especially to pretty girls—in which connection it may be pointed out that Miss Sarah Parrish was a very pretty girl. But nothing he had told her had led her to believe that he could be in any way mixed up in espionage. In the first place, he had been dancing attendance on her throughout the day of Mrs Matthews' murder, and so could not conceivably have performed that deed himself. He had also, in the last year of the war, won an M C and been three times mentioned in dispatches. That in itself seemed to preclude the possibility of his being employed as a foreign agent.

Johnnie Warrender . . . There was very little she knew about Johnnie Warrender, beyond the fact that he possessed an irritating wife and apparently played—or had played—polo. She must ask Fudge about him. He seemed a pleasant enough person; wiry and restless, verging on the forties, and with an open-handed and hail-fellow-well-met disposition. His failing appeared to be drink, for hardly an evening passed without Johnnie getting what he himself described as 'creditably illuminated', while his bar bill at the end of each month must have reached four figures in the local currency.

Mir Khan. Another unknown quantity. She had been introduced to Mir Khan by Ian Kelly during her first day in Gulmarg, but she had never had much speech with him. He was a friend of Reggie Craddock's, and Reggie appeared to have an enormous admiration for him. Though how much of this was due to the fact that Mir could out-ski Reggie any day of the week, and was reputed to be one of the finest shots in India, she did not know, since she was aware that her countrymen's attitude towards proficiency at games and sports was apt to cloud their judgement, and that provided a man could smite a ball farther, or with more accuracy, than his fellows, and could be counted upon to hit a sufficient amount of birds on the wing, they automatically voted him a 'good chap' and pronounced him to be an 'excellent feller' and 'one of the best'.

Mir possessed these abilities to a marked degree; in addition to much charm of manner and a string of strange prefixes to his name that marked his affiliation to a princely house. He had been shooting snow-leopard beyond Gilgit, and had stopped off at Gulmarg for the Ski Club Meeting on his way south. But there was no reason to suppose, because he was popular and charming and friendly, that he was not also anti-British.

After all, thought Sarah, tossing in the darkness, it *is* his country and we *are* the 'White Raj'—the conquerors, even though we're on the verge of quitting! *Was* it Mir Khan who had stood watching in the darkness from the hut door? Where had he been on the day that Mrs Matthews died? As far as she could remember, with Reggie Craddock and a party on the slopes beyond Khilan. All the same she put a mental query against Mir Khan . . .

That left only the Coply twins. Cheerful, charming, overflowing with good spirits, they had arrived in India at the tender age of eighteen, only a few months before the fall of an atom bomb on Hiroshima had ended the Second World War. To their disgust they had seen no active service, and this was to be their last leave in India before they left to join their regiment in Palestine.

Sarah would have dismissed them as possible suspects if it had not been for two things; both of which, under the present circumstances, she found a little disturbing. There was Russian blood in them, and they had been out skiing alone on the day of Mrs Matthews' death. Their father, now a General in the Indian Army, had married a White Russian, and the twins themselves were bilingual. Sarah had met Nadia Coply in Peshawar, and had written her down, with the cruelty of youth, as being fat and affected.

It was Nadia, a strong-minded woman, who was responsible for christening the twins Boris and Alexis, but time and a British public school had substituted Bonzo and Alec, and Bonzo and Alec they remained. Certainly Nadia, if her own stories could be trusted, had been a member of the old Russian nobility, for she was fond of relating with a wealth of dramatic detail how as a small child—'and *so* beautiful'—she had sat upon the knee of the Tsar and been fed with bon-bons from a jewelled box. A woman with her antecedents would be hardly likely to have anything but enmity for the Communists. Still—there was Russian blood in the twins and they had been out alone together for most of the fatal Thursday.

Sarah turned restlessly in the darkness. If only it were possible to know exactly when Mrs Matthews had died. But no one would ever be sure of that. The intense cold could play tricks with bodies, and even the doctors would not give an opinion on it. They had said that they thought she must have died roughly four or five hours before her body was brought back to the hotel, which had been at 7 o'clock. But Janet had found her about four, and her body had been stiff already, because Janet had said——Sarah's thoughts shuddered away from the remembrance of that frozen, contorted corpse.

The Coply twins *could* not be responsible. They were so young. And yet —and yet? Sarah remembered photographs she had seen of German prisoners shortly after the fall of France. Batches of fair-haired boys in their teens and twenties, who only a short time before had been machine-gunning women and children in the streets of small market towns, and dropping high explosives upon roads packed with helpless civilian refugees. No.

Youth by itself was no alibi in these days. Youth could be hard and ruthless and intolerant, and without pity for old age and weakness.

What of the women?—for it had been a woman who had made those footsteps, though Sarah was convinced that the faceless creature who had sawn through the latch of Janet's window was a man. Fudge could be written off at once. Meril wouldn't have the guts, and allergic as she was to Helen Warrender, Sarah could not believe that that determinedly elegant and feline woman, with her constant references to the 'Right People', would involve herself with anything so socially damning as murder.

Reggie Craddock, Ian Kelly, Johnnie Warrender, Mir Khan, the Coply twins, Fudge, Meril Forbes and Helen. One of those people. Sarah's aching brain reviewed them all, over and over again in an endless procession, until the muffled whirring of Reggie's alarm clock broke the evil spell of the night, and she fell asleep at last: to dream of Janet, helpless and panic-stricken, pursued down endless dark verandahs by faceless figures.

She awoke tired and unrefreshed to the smell of burning bacon fat and the welcome sound of a boiling kettle, to find that the rest of the party were already out taking advantage of the early morning snow, with the exception of Meril Forbes, who was preparing breakfast with a vast amount of energy and ineptitude. There was no sign of Janet.

'Mrs Creed said to let you sleep,' said Meril, flapping helplessly at the reeking smoke that filled the living-room from the neglected frying-pan. 'She did try and wake you once, but you seemed so fast asleep that she said we'd better leave you. They're skiing in the Gully; all except Reggie. And Mir, I suppose.'

'Who's they?' asked Sarah, wrinkling her nose at the fumes.

'Oh, all the rest of them,' said Meril vaguely.

In the face of Janet's parting request Sarah did not like to inquire after her, but since Meril had not mentioned her the chances were that she really had got back in time, and without her absence being noticed. She was probably out skiing with the others.

Sarah dressed, shivering in the cold hut, and went outside.

The sun was still hidden behind the rim of Apharwat, but its reflected glow made a glory of the snowfields. The sky was a pale wash of turquoise against which the mountain peaks cut violet patterns, and from somewhere among the pine woods below the *marg* a thin line of smoke from a wood-cutter's fire rose unwavering into the still, morning air. But despite the clear radiance of the dawn there was something curiously threatening and oppressive about the breathless chill of the morning; a vibration of unease. And Sarah, looking away across the distant valley, saw that the great rampart of the Nanga Parbat range was hidden by a pall of dark, grey-brown cloud that spanned the horizon from east to west and tinged the sky above it with a foreboding yellow stain. As she watched, lightning flickered in the belly of the cloud and she could hear, faintly, from across the cold mountain ranges, the mutter of a far-distant storm.

Meril Forbes' voice, harried and anxious, exclaiming: 'Oh *bother!* I've burnt the bacon again!' recalled Sarah to a sense of duty, and she offered herself as assistant cook and was gratefully accepted. There was nothing much to be done about the bacon, so she turned instead to the task of preparing large quantities of coffee and toast. But the thought of Janet worried her, and presently, deciding on the indirect approach, she said carelessly: 'Who's looking after Bonzo and Alec? I imagine Reggie didn't take them with him?'

'Not much!' said Meril, clattering cups and saucers at the far end of the room. 'They're as much use on skis as a couple of porpoises. Worse! No, they've gone off to Christmas Gully with the others, to practise breaking their necks. They went off about an hour ago, and if they're not back soon I think we might start breakfast without them, don't you? The others won't be back for hours if they've gone to the Frozen Lakes.'

There was a crisp swish of snow outside and a cheerful voice announced: 'Home is the skier, home from ski, and the hungry home from the hill! Sarah, my beautiful, you are a lazy little grub and a disgrace to your nation. Why didn't you come with us instead of hogging it in your bunk?'

'I am allergic to early rising,' said Sarah firmly. 'What are you doing around here, Ian? We didn't expect you back for hours. Where have you left the others?'

'To their own devices. We decided to go our separate ways. I expect old Reggie's still messing about somewhere at the back of Apharwat, and Mir went off to Mary's Shoulder: said he wanted to practise jump-turns or something. I thought I'd had about enough, after mucking about for a couple of hours admiring the sunrise, so I decided to come back and admire you and the bacon instead.'

'Oh dear!—I'm afraid the bacon's burnt,' said Meril guiltily. 'But you can have a boiled egg.' She went to the door and peered out. 'Here are the others coming now. Where's Janet, Ian? Has she gone to the Lakes with Reggie, or did she go with Mir?'

'Neither,' said Ian. 'She didn't come with us. You forgot we were torn from our snug bunks at the ghastly hour of five ack emma. She'll have gone with the others.'

Meril looked puzzled. 'But she didn't. I mean, she'd gone already when they went, and we thought she must have decided to go with you.'

'Well she didn't,' said Ian firmly, 'and if I may be permitted to bring the conversation back to food, if you think one egg is enough for me, Meril dear, you have committed an error of judgement. I require at least six.'

Meril said anxiously: 'But then if Janet didn't go with you——'

Sarah interrupted hurriedly: 'She must have gone off early on her own, I think. She said something last night about fetching up at the hotel for breakfast; probably wanted to see the beginners' race this morning.'

The arrival of the Coply twins, smothered in the snow of frequent falls, together with Fudge and the Warrenders, put a stop to the conversation; and half an hour later, as they were washing up the breakfast things, Reggie Craddock put in an appearance, having abandoned his proposed trip to the Frozen Lakes owing to doubts as to the weather. There was no sign of Mir Khan, who was apparently still engrossed in the practice of jump-turns on the snow ridge known as Mary's Shoulder.

Reggie ate a hurried breakfast and looked at his watch. 'It's fairly early yet,' he announced, 'so I suggest we slide down and head off the people who are coming up here for the day. I don't like the look of those clouds at all. There's a nasty storm coming up, and I've a feeling it'll be here a lot sooner than we think. I'm not for having a packet of people caught up here by bad weather. What do you say, Johnnie?'

Johnnie Warrender lounged to the door and looked out above Gulmarg to the far side of the valley, where the sky was darkening above the cloud bank that concealed the Nanga Parbat range. The sun still shone serenely, but the curious, dirty yellow stain above the black bar of cloud was spreading rapidly over the cool blue of the sky, and there was an uneasy mutter in the air.

'Perhaps you're right,' conceded Johnnie, who was looking tired and cross in the morning sunlight. There were dark pouches under his eyes and he had cut himself shaving. 'Personally I shouldn't say it'll be here for hours yet—if at all. It may go down the valley and miss us altogether. However, it certainly looks as though something sticky was brewing over there, so I suppose we'd better play safe.'

They had rolled up their bedding and the various items that would be carried down by coolies, packed their rucksacks and strapped on their skis, when Reggie Craddock asked: 'Where's Janet?'

'Gone down ahead,' said Ian Kelly. 'What about Mir?'

'Oh, Mir's quite capable of looking after himself. I couldn't spot him anywhere when I came back, so he's probably gone down too. But in case he hasn't I'll leave a note on the door to tell him we've gone on ahead.' Reggie scribbled a few words on a page of his pocket diary, ripped it out, wrote Mir's name across the front in block capitals, and tucked it under the latch where he could not miss seeing it. 'Come on, we'd better get going if we want to stop the rest of them coming up. We'll go down by Red Run. You two'—he addressed the Coply twins—'had better stick to the path. I won't have you risking your necks on the top half of the run. We'll give you a quarter of an hour's start. Shove off.'

The twins broke into injured protests, but Reggie was adamant. Fudge volunteered to accompany them to see that they got down without mishap, and after a moment's hesitation Helen Warrender decided to go with them too. She was not a particularly good skier, and disliked fast running except on open snow.

Fifteen minutes after their departure Reggie Craddock gave a hitch to his rucksack and set off down the slope with Sarah, Ian, Johnnie Warrender and Meril behind him. They fanned out on the crest of Slalom Hill and each took their own line, swooping down over the crisp shimmering surface like a flight of swallows; dipping, swaying, turning in a swish of flung crystals, and leaving behind them clear curving tracks on the sparkling snow. The icy air, whipping past them, sang a shrill crooning song in their ears as they swung round the Brooklands curve and shot over Hill 60, and presently they were among the tall tree trunks; swerving and swinging down the track under the dark snow-laden boughs of pine and deodar.

It is not far short of the first houses that Red Run is crossed by Blue; the junction of the two runs bearing the appellation 'Dirty Corner' for reasons not unconnected with the frequent and simultaneous arrival at this point of both Blue and Red runners moving at speed and arriving from opposite directions.

Sarah shot down the curving track, jump-turned with expert precision, and emerged into the straight stretch above the junction of the two runs a bare yard ahead of Ian Kelly—only to check violently, in a flurry of snow.

She saw Ian, swerving wildly to avoid her, shoot past and cannon off a tree trunk to fall with a whirl of skis, sticks, snow and startled swearwords into a piled drift, and heard Reggie shout behind her as he came to an indignant standstill a yard or so to her left, the others stemming behind him on the slope. But she did not move. Her eyes, fixed and dilated, were on the two figures immediately ahead of her. The Coply twins, who were standing at the junction of the two runs.

Alec was bending down, dragging frenziedly at the straps of his skis, while Bonzo, his hands cupped about his mouth, alternately shouted something unintelligible up the slope, and pointed down it.

'*What the hell—!*' said Reggie Craddock violently. He thrust strongly with his ski-sticks and shot away down the track; the others following behind him, except for Sarah, who stayed where she was, held in the grip of a sudden, sickening premonition of disaster. It was only when she heard

Ian swearing in the undergrowth and saw Reggie and the others reach the twins that she forced herself to follow them.

Alec had rid himself of his second ski by the time she reached them, and was running down the Blue Run slipping and stumbling on the treacherous surface, while Meril was saying in a high, cracked voice that sounded as if it came from a gramophone: 'But they took Mrs Matthews away—I know they took her away! She can't still be here. They took her away!'

Sarah took one look at the sprawled figure that lay at the foot of the icy slope below them, a dark smudge against the whiteness, and took the slope at a run. She heard Reggie's warning shout and Meril's scream, and then Alec had caught her, and they had fallen together among the snow-covered boulders beside that other figure that lay so still.

It was Janet of course. Sarah had known that it would be. Perhaps she had known it, subconsciously, from the moment when she had awakened in the ski-hut, heavy-eyed and sick with apprehension, to find that Janet had not returned. The Coply twins, gesticulating in the snow, had only supplied the dreadful confirmation of what she already feared to be true.

Sarah reached out and touched her. Janet lay on her side in the snow in a curiously confiding attitude, almost as though she were asleep. Her knees were bent, and her arms lay stretched at her side, her hands still gripping her ski-sticks. There was a little scarlet stain on the snow under her head, and her blue eyes were open. There was no trace of either surprise or horror on her dead face, but rather a faint, definite impression of scorn: as though she had expected death and derided it.

Sarah became aware of Reggie Craddock swearing violently under his breath, of Meril's hysterical sobbing, and of Fudge's arms about her, pulling her away.

'Come away, Sarah. Don't look dear. We can't do anything; she's dead.'

Sarah jerked herself free and stood up. She had seen all she wanted to see in those first few minutes, and verified it when she had reached out to lay her hand on a pocket of Janet's snow-powdered ski-suit.

The narrow metal zip-fastener was closed, but the gun had gone. And it was not until after they had carried the slim, stiff figure up the hill to the hotel, and laid it in an empty room in an unoccupied wing, out of consideration for Miss Parrish's nerves, that Sarah learned—by way of Dr Leonard's wife, Frances, who has assisted her husband to remove the dead girl's clothing, so that he and Major McKay could conduct a thorough examination to eliminate any possibility of foul play—that nothing unusual had been found. Which could only mean that the holster and its sling had also been taken, since its discovery would certainly have aroused a good deal of curiosity and speculation.

5

'Where are you going, Sarah?' Ian's voice sounded as cheerful as ever.

'Out,' said Sarah briefly. She pulled on her skiing gloves, and picking up her ski-sticks, stepped out of the over-heated atmosphere of the hotel lounge into the chill of the darkening afternoon.

'Then I'll come with you and keep an eye on you.'

'No thank you, Ian,' said Sarah, allowing him to adjust and buckle on her skis. 'I'm only going across the *marg*, and I'd rather go by myself if you don't mind.' She drew the loops of her ski-sticks over her wrists as Ian fastened the last strap and stood up, dusting the snow off his knees.

'Don't be silly, Sarah. I know this business has been a bit of a jolt for you, but there's no reason why you shouldn't behave in a rational manner. There's a hell of a storm coming up, and it isn't going to help the situation if you get yourself lost in it. At least let me come with you if you feel you must go mooching about the *marg*.'

Sarah said: 'But I don't want you, Ian. And don't worry, I won't get lost. See you at tea-time—and thanks for your help.'

She slid swiftly away down the snow-covered path, gaining momentum as it dipped sharply downwards, and vanished round a curve of the hill, leaving Ian Kelly to mutter evil words and return moodily to the hotel and the subdued groups of skiers discussing the latest tragedy in the lounge.

At the bottom of the hill Sarah swung to the right, and skirting it, made for the end of the Red Run and turned up into the forest.

The sky was by now completely overcast and, although it was barely two o'clock, the day had darkened to a twilight dimness. Little gusts of wind were blowing across the open *marg*, but under the snow-ladened boughs of the forest trees the air was cold and still, as Sarah picked her way carefully between the tree trunks and presently reached the junction of the two runs where the twins had stopped that morning. Brushing the snow from a tree stump she unfastened her skis and sat down facing the slope of Blue Run, and propping her chin on her hand, thought deeply.

Of one thing only she was completely sure. Janet, like Mrs Matthews, had been murdered. Not for one moment did she believe the doctor's diagnosis of accidental death due to a fall at speed and the striking of her head against a rock. She was certain that the blow that had killed Janet had been deliberately inflicted, for to prove it, as in the case of Mrs Matthews, there was the missing gun.

The question was *how?* Sarah went back once more over that conversation with Janet in the moonlight outside the Khilanmarg hut, and once again she seemed to hear Janet's low confident laugh as she said: 'It's all right Sarah. Don't look so horrified. I'll keep to the edge of the run, and I know the route like the back of my hand. Don't worry. There won't be a murderer waiting down there for me at this time of night.'

The edge of the run . . .

Sarah stood up, and carrying her skis, walked up the side of the Blue Run, keeping among the trees. Presently she crossd to the other side, and less than a minute later came upon what she was looking for: the track of a single skier on the extreme right-hand side of the run, among the tree trunks.

Turning she followed the track downhill, and at the junction of the runs stopped to fasten on her skis before picking up the trail again. It ran down the hill following the line of Blue Run, passed without pause the small scarlet blotch that marked the spot where Janet's body had lain, and continued for a couple of hundred yards until the trees thinned at the edge of the *marg;* at which point it turned right and was lost among a maze of crossing and recrossing tracks made by a beginners' class.

Pausing again, Sarah leant against a snow-powdered tree trunk and stared out across the sullen levels of the *marg* with unseeing eyes——So Janet had not been killed on the way down from Khilan after all. She had kept to one side of that treacherous, frozen run and had gone on across the open levels of the *marg,* to keep her appointment somewhere among the dark pine trees where that red spark of light had shown like a small, evil star on the previous night. That meant that she must have been killed on her way back to Khilan, her mission completed. But there was something wrong there too . . .

Sarah turned and glanced back at the lowering ridge of Apharwat, coldly white against the slate-grey sky, and realized as she did so that although Janet might have come down from the ski-hut by the Blue Run, she would never have returned by that route, since the quickest way down would have proved the hardest way back. She would have come by the forest path. So why had her body been found on the Blue Run?

A theory was forming itself slowly in Sarah's mind, and she leaned her head against the rough bark of the tree, and shutting her eyes, tried to visualize Gulmarg as she had seen it last night from the snowfields of Khilan, following the direction of Janet's hand pointing down at that far small speck of light.

'About level with the Gap,' said Sarah, speaking aloud. 'And not more than a quarter of a mile this side of it.'

She opened her eyes and turned to look in the direction of the hotel, and from there, frowning, to the lowering sky overhead. Then, with a sudden squaring of her small jaw, she set off resolutely towards the Gap.

Fifteen minutes later she was among trees again at the far side of the *marg*, and she had found what she was looking for. Halfway across, a single track had detached itself from the multitudinous tracks of the beginners' slopes and struck off alone towards a point to the right-hand side of the Gap. It was not in a direction ordinarily frequented by members of the Club, and Sarah was fairly certain that she was following the track that Janet's skis had made on the previous night.

The track herringboned up the slope below the road that runs round the edge of the golf-course, and on reaching it, followed the road for several hundred yards, before turning off up a side path between the trees: and following it, Sarah found herself standing before a rickety wooden gateway beyond which, half hidden by tree trunks and snow-laden branches, stood a low, log-built bungalow of the usual Gulmarg pattern.

The log-built 'huts', as all houses here are called, are only occupied during the summer months. When autumn comes and the chestnut trees add their splashes of bright gold to the pine forests and the snows begin to creep down from the mountain tops, the population retreats to the house-boats and hotels of Srinagar in the valley below, and the huts remain shuttered and empty until the following May. This one was no exception—apart from the fact that there were tracks on the short path leading to the front door and that the top bar of the gate had been swept clean of snow.

At least three people had entered and left the bungalow within the last twenty-four hours. Probably more, for the track Sarah had followed was crossed by others, coming from the direction of the Gap, and there were two more leaving the gate, so close upon each other that they might almost have been a single track. Yet despite this, the house appeared completely deserted.

The roof was hidden under a thick covering of snow, and a fringe of icicles hung from the eaves. The door was closed and there were rough board shutters nailed over all but one of the windows. But the blank, rime-fringed panes of that single unshuttered window looked out, free of the encroaching trees, towards the hotel, and above it to the heights of Apharwat and the long snow slopes of Khilanmarg . . .

It was from this window then, thought Sarah with sudden conviction, that the light that had lured Janet to her death had shone last night. And drawing a deep breath, she pushed open the unlatched gate and walked up the path towards the house.

Her ski slipped and slithered where the tracks of those earlier visitors had hardened the snow to ice, and a sudden thin gust of wind, herald of the coming storm, blew across the *marg* and soughed among the deodars; sloughing off snow from over-weighted branches and whispering about the crude pine walls of the empty house.

Sarah tried the front door cautiously, and finding that it was not locked, took her courage in both hands and pushed it open. The hinges creaking protestingly, and suddenly, daunted by the darkness and the silence inside, she would have turned and run back down the trodden path and out into the open *marg* but for the thought of Janet setting off alone in the moonlight for that last long ski-run through the lonely woods . . . 'Sarah!' apostrophized Miss Parrish, in an angry undertone, 'you are a lousy little coward—and anyway, it can't be worse than the V-bombs!'

Unfastening her skis and leaving them beside the path, she set her teeth and stepped over the threshold of the silent house.

The air inside was stale and very cold, and the house smelt damp and musty. But there was a faint scent of cigarette smoke in the small dark hall, and another fainter smell that was barely more than the ghost of an odour: a sickly smell; sweetish, cloying and wholly unfamiliar.

Sarah wrinkled her nose and stooped to pick up a half-smoked cigarette. She touched it gingerly, almost as if she thought it might still be hot, and then dropped it back on the floor with a little grimace of disgust. The door had partially closed and now she saw that a chair stood behind it. It was an ordinary verandah chair with a wooden back and arms and a sagging cane seat, and someone had been sitting in it comparatively recently for beside it lay a couple of cigarette-stubs and a film of scattered grey ash.

There was something on the arm of the chair that made Sarah's heart leap like a trout on a line: a small, triangular splash of blood that showed wet and vivid against the unvarnished wood. But when she removed a ski-glove and put out a shrinking finger to touch it, it was not blood at all, but only a fragment of thin shiny red rubber, such as might have been torn from a child's balloon, which had caught in a crack of the wood.

The bathos of the discovery, coming on top of that terrified leap of the heart, sent her off into a sudden and uncontrollable gale of giggles that contained more than a touch of hysteria. Oh, for heaven's sake! thought

Sarah, mopping her eyes with the glove, I *must* stop seeing horrors at every turn. This isn't getting me anywhere!

She controlled herself with a considerable effort, and looked about her. To the left of the hall in which she stood were three doors which when tried, proved to be either locked or bolted on the other side, while to the right a narrow passage led to another doorway, presumably a sitting-room. The passage was dark and smelt of rats, pinewood and cheap varnish, and there were marks on the uncarpeted floorboards: smears of damp and traces of discoloured snow. Sarah advanced along it cautiously, and trying the door at the end found that it was unfastened and opened easily.

When the track she had followed across the *marg* had turned up to the gate among the pine trees, she had not doubted that it was to this house that Janet had come last night. But if she had needed proof, it was here ——This, then, was the room with the unshuttered window.

The trees that huddled close about the small house had left this one window clear, so that it commanded an uninterrupted view, in a direct line ahead, of the *marg*, the hotel, the rising wall of forest behind it and, higher still, the distant expanse of Khilanmarg.

There was very little furniture in the room—any upholstered item such as sofas and armchairs having presumably been stored in one of the locked rooms. But there was a small round table drawn up before that single unshuttered window, and on it, among a litter of spent matches, cigarette-ends and grey ash, stood an old but obviously serviceable Petromax lamp. The glass of the lamp was red, and the room was a degree warmer than the rest of the cold house. And once again Sarah was aware of an odd smell that mingled with the scent of stale cigarette smoke. But this time it was a different smell, and vaguely familiar. She stood still, sniffing the close, stuffy air——*Cordite!* Someone had fired a gun in that little room. Had it been Janet?

A sudden, shuddering horror of the cold, shuttered house and the locked rooms that lay at the far end of the narrow passage overcame Sarah, and turning swiftly, she closed the door behind her, shooting home the bolt with trembling fingers and shutting herself in with the scanty wooden furniture and that betraying lamp.

A low growl of thunder shuddered through the cold air and echoed among the mountains; and once again a sharp gust of wind licked across the *marg* to moan among the pine trees, rattling the window-panes and whining through a knot-hole in the pinewood wall——

No. Not a knot-hole. A bullet hole.

Sarah pulled herself together and walked quickly across the room to verify it. But she had seen too many bullet holes on too many targets to be mistaken, and she turned back to the table. The floor was a pool of shadow in the waning light, but there was a half-empty box of matches beside the lamp, and she stretched out a hand for them and lit one with unsteady fingers. A little flame flared up and sputtered weakly at the end of the match as she held it towards the floor, and a moment later it flickered out. But not before she had seen the ugly, sprawling stain that disfigured the rough planking of the dusty uncarpeted floor.

There was no mistaking what had caused it. Someone had died in this little cold room—and within the last twenty-four hours, for the blood in the cracks between the floorboards was still faintly sticky. It could not have been Janet, because Janet had been killed by a blow on the temple, and there had been very little loss of blood, while whoever had made the stain upon the floorboards had lost a very great deal of it—more than a man might lose, and live. Besides, it was out of the question that any murderer would have risked carrying a dead body a mile or so round the *marg* to dump it on the worst stretch of the Blue Run.

Quite suddenly Sarah remembered the ski-tracks she had seen leading away from the gate; the two tracks that had not been parallel, but so close upon each other's heels that they almost seemed a single track. And in a swift flash of intuition she saw the ugly explanation of those tracks, and did not doubt that were she to follow them they would lead round the roadway that skirted the *marg*, and, deviously, through snow-blanketed undergrowth and small side paths to the edge of the Blue Run. Or that they had been made by Janet and her murderer—Janet walking ahead, driven like a sheep to the slaughter-house, with a gun at her back, to stand at last in the bright moonlight at the foot of the icy slope on the Blue Run awaiting the savage blow that killed her, with that scornful half-smile that death had not been able to wipe from her face.

Sarah straightened up with a little sigh and leant against the table, steadying herself with her hands on the dusty surface. She looked round the room slowly and intently, and down at the ash and the cigarette-stubs on the table, and the single blood-soaked stub that lay on the stained patch of floor. There had been at least two men, then: one who had lit the lamp and waited here for Janet, and rolled and smoked his own cigarettes; and the other who had waited in the hall, sitting on the chair behind the door and smoking a popular and widely advertised brand . . .

Sarah slipped the box of matches into her pocket and forced herself to unbolt the door and return down the dark passage to the hall, and once there she struck another match and held it above her head. But beyond the scattered cigarette ash, the burnt-out stubs and the small triangular fragment of rubber on the chair behind the door, she could see nothing that might give a clue to the identity of the person who had sat there waiting in the dark. Even that strange, elusive suggestion of an odour, that had tainted the close air when she first entered the house, had gone—dissipated by the cold current of air from the open door.

The match spluttered out, scorching her fingers, and she dropped it on the floor and lit another and another, and stood for a long time staring intently about the small shadowy hall as though she could force the silent bolted doors, the dark walls and the blank, shuttered window-panes to tell her what they had seen.

Yet there was, decided Sarah, little they could have told her beyond what they and the ski-tracked snow outside had already shown her; and checking the sum total of that mute evidence she made her own deductions.

The man who had lit the lamp and set it in the window must have waited a long time in the cold sitting-room at the end of the passage, for there were close on a dozen cigarette-ends scattered upon the table top and lying on the dusty floor. Because Janet had been late——

Owing to an unexpected twist of fate that had prevented Hugo Creed joining the party on the previous day, she had, at the eleventh hour, taken his place. With the result that when the signal lamp was lit she was not, as expected, in her room at the hotel, but in the ski-hut on Khilanmarg, and expert skier though she was, that long run down in the moonlight must have taken her over half an hour, so that someone else had got there before her. Someone who carried a gun and must have killed not only Janet, but the agent she was hurrying to meet: the man who had lit the lamp and waited for her in the small cold room at the end of the passage, and who had died on the dusty floor among the scattered cigarette ash.

Yet why hadn't Janet, hurrying silently over the snowy *marg*, heard the reverberation of that shot and been warned in time? The night had been so still. So deadly still that even enclosed within the walls of a room, the sound must have echoed across the *marg*. How was it possible that Janet had not heard it? Or had it been fired after she had entered the dark house? The chair behind the door and the two cigarette-stubs seemed to disprove that theory, for one of the latter had been smoked as far down as possible, while the other had not been lit long before being abandoned, and it had not been pressed out but thrown, barely half-smoked, onto the floor. Both spoke clearly of someone who had waited, sitting at ease in the darkness behind the doorway, and who had not had so very long to wait . . .

It was then that Sarah remembered one of the few sounds that had broken across the silence of the icy night. The sharp cracking of a forest tree as sap froze under the bark or an over-burdened bough broke under its weight of snow, and which had sounded like pistol shots. The crack of a distant automatic would have passed for a more familiar sound, and there would have been nothing to warn Janet that she was walking into a trap. Janet, who had said: *'Tomorrow I can go away . . . and be free again!'*

She must have come up the short, snow-covered path confidently, and never known, until she pushed open the door into the dark hall, that freedom of a different sort was waiting for her that night. And perhaps when the spring sunshine had melted the snow from the forest, some wandering woodcutter might stumble across the rotting corpse of the man who had lit that lamp and waited for her, and whose blood had soaked into the floor of the cold, shuttered house among the pine trees. Though even that was unlikely, for there were too many lonely ravines and tangled gullies in the forests, where a body might lie undiscovered until the jackals and the prowling leopards had scattered its bones.

Another warning growl of thunder reverberated among the mountains, and the rising wind slammed the open shutter of the room at the end of the passage, sending Sarah's heart into her mouth. But close upon the heels of that sound there came another and far more frightening one—the soft creak of a floorboard, twice repeated, from one of the three rooms that lay behind those locked doors. It broke Sarah's nerve, and in a frenzy of panic she dropped the matchbox and ran headlong from the house.

Lightning quivered across the *marg* as she snatched up her skis and ski-sticks and fled down the snow-covered path and through the gate that now swung crazily in the wind. But though the instinct of self-preservation urged her to run and keep on running, once out of sight of the house common sense reasserted itself, forcing her to stop and fasten on her skis— it being obvious that whoever had been lurking on the far side of one of those locked doors could not have been wearing skis, and once she had strapped on her own she could easily outdistance anyone on foot.

Her fingers were so clumsy from cold and panic that it took her the best part of three minutes to fasten the stiff straps. But she managed it at last, and picking up her ski-sticks from where she had dropped them in the untrodden snow, she turned off the road to cross the *marg*.

The first snow had begun to fall as she left the house, but now all at once, with the wind behind them, the whirling white flakes were driving down so thickly that she could not see more than a yard ahead of her. Sarah hesitated briefly, and then changed direction, intending to do a traverse on the slope which would bring her out towards the main road that ran from the Gap to the Club. The road leading up to the hotel branched off this halfway, and though it would take longer, there was less chance of losing herself in the storm. But she had barely gathered speed when a dark form loomed up through the driving snow immediately ahead of her.

She swerved wildly, but too late, and cannoning into something solid, would have fallen but for a hand that gripped her arm and held her upright on the slope. Panic struck her afresh, and she tried to wrench herself away; but the grip on her arm might have been steel, and a man's voice said harshly: 'Who are you? What the devil are you doing here?'

Sarah opened her mouth but found she could make no sound. Her throat seemed contracted with terror, and the wind drove the thick snowflakes into her eyes and blinded her, turning her face to a solid mask of snow.

'What's the matter? Lost your voice?'

Her captor put out a hand in a heavy ski-glove and brushed the snow roughly from her face, peering down at her from the whirling dimness. She had a fleeting impression, blurred by the driving snow, of height, and a pair of eyes, flint-grey and very angry, before her own eyes were once more blinded by snowflakes.

The voice, which she could not recognize, muttered something under its breath, and for a moment the grip on her arm was relaxed. In that instant, with a strength born of fear, Sarah wrenched her arm free, thrust strongly with her ski-sticks and was away.

The slope was in her favour, and since the unknown man was facing the opposite way, it would take him a second or two to turn in his tracks. The storm was in her favour too. She thought she heard a shout behind her, and swinging sharply to her left, vanished into a seemingly solid wall of whiteness.

Twenty minutes later, blinded with snowflakes and buffeted by wind, breathless, shaken, and having lost her way at least half a dozen times, Sarah reached the hotel.

She was only just in time, for the snow that had blotted out the *marg* as she struggled across it was but a fraction of the storm to come. All that night it raged over Gulmarg in a screaming blizzard of whirling snow and shrieking wind. Snow and wind that wiped out for ever the tell-tale tracks across the *marg* and along the deserted forest road. And two months later, when the *marg* was green again and summer visitors came riding up the steep winding track that led up from Tanmarg at the foot of the hill, the *chowkidar*, the Indian caretaker of one of the huts among the pine woods, spring-cleaning the hut for the arrival of its tenants, found a dusty, red-glassed Petromax lamp in one of the rooms, and quietly annexed it. There was also a curious stain on the grimy floor, but when the carpet was laid it could not be seen.

The storm had raged for two days and nights: turning from snow to hail, and from hail to driving, blinding rain that washed away the thick snow-caps from the huddled roofs and brought the avalanches thundering down the steep slopes of Apharwat.

On the third day they buried Janet in the sodden little cemetery that the rain had temporarily thawed to a point where the ground was no longer frozen solid. And that done they went down the hill to Tanmarg and the waiting cars, through the slush and the dingy patches of discoloured snow, while a sad wind moaned through the forests behind them.

'Goodbye, Sarah. Pleasant journey. Write to me sometimes. Thal is a boring spot. Not that we shall be there much longer I gather.'

'Goodbye, Ian. Of course I will. Goodbye, Meril. See you again some-time, I hope.'

'Oh, sure to. You'll be up in Srinagar for the summer anyway, won't you?'

'No. I'm going to spend the summer with some friends in Ceylon.'

Reggie Craddock came up blowing on his fingers and looking ill and cold: 'Goodbye, Fudge. You and Hugo are giving Sarah a lift down, aren't you? One of the damned buses hasn't arrived, so I suppose I shall have to hang about for hours just to be sure everyone gets off safely. I'm sorry this show ended the way it did. Ghastly business. I suppose I should have set a guard on that run, or roped it off or something. Pity women hate doing what they're told. Damnable affair. Oh well, hope we shall see you again this summer. I shall be in Srinagar again if I can get any leave. Odd to think it may be the very last time any of us will ever get the chance. Can't really believe it, somehow. You and Hugo coming up, I suppose?'

'Yes—for a fond farewell and all that. I don't suppose there'll be many people up. See you then; and don't worry too much about—about Janet and Mrs Matthews, Reggie. You couldn't have prevented it.'

Reggie nodded moodily and turned away as Major McKay pushed through the crowd of chattering coolies.

The Major too looked tired and harassed, and it occurred to Sarah that unpleasant as the two tragedies upon the Blue Run had been for the members of the Ski Club, the main weight of unpleasantness must have fallen upon him. He was limping slightly, and his normally ruddy countenance appeared pallid and depressed under the patches of sticking-plaster, souvenirs of his dogged struggles upon the nursery slopes, that adorned it. He shook hands punctiliously with Fudge and Sarah, and having wished them a good run to Peshawar, turned to Meril Forbes: 'You're for Srinagar, aren't you Meril? What are you doing for transport?'

'Oh, I'm all right, thank you,' said Meril. 'Aunt Ena has sent the car for me. It's only your bus for Rawalpindi that hasn't arrived yet.'

'Well it isn't going to be any use to me when it does arrive,' said the Major morosely: 'I've just heard that I have to go to Srinagar again. I thought we had dealt with all the formalities connected with this unfortunate business, but it seems—well, the point is, do you think you could give me a lift in your aunt's car?'

'Of course I can. How horrid for you, though.'

'I'm afraid your skiing holiday hasn't been too pleasant, George,' said Fudge sympathetically.

'I cannot imagine that it has been pleasant for any one of us,' said Major McKay austerely. 'Personally——'

A fanfare of blasts upon an electric horn interrupted him, and Fudge said hurriedly: 'That's Hugo. He wants to get to 'Pindi in time for tea. I must fly. Goodbye, George. Goodbye, Meril dear. Come on, Sarah.'

They left Meril and Major McKay and the remaining skiers standing in the cold wind among the trodden snow-banks and the crowds of jostling coolies. And a few moments later Hugo's big, luggage-laden Chevrolet rolled out of Tanmarg on the start of its two-hundred-and-forty-mile journey down the long, winding, mountainous Kashmir road towards the sun and dust and roses of Peshawar.

Part II

PESHAWAR

'There needs no ghost, my lord, come from the grave,
To tell us this.'　　　William Shakespeare, *Hamlet*

6

'That,' said Sarah reflectively, her eyes following the white-clad figure on the racing polo pony, 'is by far the most attractive man in Peshawar.'

Sarah, Hugo and Fudge Creed were seated in deck-chairs at the edge of the polo ground, watching a knock-up game between two scratch sides.

'I thank you,' said Hugo graciously, tipping his hat a shade further over his nose to keep the sun-glare from his eyes: 'You were referring to me, of course.'

'Oh, I don't count you——'

'In that case, I withdraw my gratitude.'

'Don't interrupt, Hugo! I was going to say, I don't count you because you are a sober married man and therefore technically out of play. If you weren't married to Fudge of course, I dare say I could go for you in a big way.'

'Kindly avoid the use of imported slang, my child,' begged Hugo. 'Besides, the expression you have just made use of never fails to put me in mind of a determined dowager at a free tea making a feline pounce upon the last austerity bun. And to return to the subject of your original remark, which I now take, in lieu of myself, to refer to Charles Mallory, if you are thinking of working up a romantic interest in him you can save yourself a lot of trouble by following Mr Punch's celebrated advice to those about to get married: *"Don't!"* '

Sarah laughed. 'I'm not. But why not?'

Hugo tilted the brim of his hat with one finger and peered sideways at her. 'Can I be sure of that?'

'I'm afraid so. I've tried out my fresh young charms on him for weeks now, without the slightest result. In fact I think he is the only man who has ever snubbed me firmly and with intention, and I don't mind telling you that it's a salutary experience.'

'*Hmm,*' said Hugo sceptically. 'It also, apparently, has its attractions—judging from the vast sale of novels by women writers, devoted exclusively to square-jawed heroes of the "pick 'em blond and knock 'em down" variety.'

'I,' said Sarah serenely, 'am neither blond nor susceptible to brutality.'

'No. You are red-headed and green-eyed and snub-nosed, and I frequently wonder why the local wallflowers don't gang up on you and scratch your eyes out, instead of eating out of your hand.'

'Charm,' said Sarah complacently. 'Charm and personality, coupled with a sweet disposition. Things you wouldn't know anything about. Stop snuffling at my ankles, Lager!' She bent down and scooped up a small black and tan dachsund puppy who was skirmishing round her chair. 'Tell me more about my Secret Passion, Hugo. Why would I be wasting time and trouble on him?'

'On Bonnie Prince Charlie? Because he's immune, my child. Inoculated, vaccinated and everything. There isn't a woman for miles around who hasn't tried out her technique on him, only to retire with it badly bent and in drastic need of repair. He prefers sport of the outdoor kind to games of the indoor variety.'

'He also, if you want to know,' put in Fudge, who had been idly listening to the conversation from a deck-chair on the other side of Sarah, 'speaks five languages and half a dozen dialects, and is what Reggie Craddock would call "a chap's chap". Finally, alas, he has a revoltingly glamorous girl at home who answers—judging from the outsize photographs that adorn his rooms—to the name of Cynthia, and who wears a gigantic solitaire on the correct finger, presumably donated by the said Charles.'

'Yes,' said Sarah with the ghost of a smile. 'So I noticed.'

'Oh you did, did you? How and when—if it's not too personal a question?'

'Jerry Dugan and I called in on him on our way to the Club the other day. Jerry wanted to borrow a stirrup-leather or something. She is lovely, isn't she?'

'Well up in the Helen of Troy class, I should say. Very depressing.'

'What did I tell you?' said Hugo. 'The chap is a mere waste of anybody's valuable time.'

'Well, maybe you're right. Hello, here's Aunt Alice coming to ask me why I'm not wearing a topee—or whatever those dreadful pith mushrooms are called—and whose side is winning. And I don't know the answer to either.'

A plump, grey-haired lady in a flowered silk dress was bearing down upon them from the direction of the row of cars parked at the edge of the polo ground.

'Sarah dear! No topee! You'll only get sunstroke. Now which side is

winning? No thank you Hugo, I'll sit here. Why isn't the Maharajah playing? Rajgore. I mean?—I see Captain Mallory is riding one of his ponies.'

'There's been a bit of a flap in the State. Some enterprising burglar has
made off with the Rajgore emeralds,' explained Hugo. Adding with a re-
gretful sigh: 'I wish it had been me! I think I shall set up as a sort of Raffles
when I get the sack from the Army. All these Princes and Potentates
simply dripping diamonds are an open invitation to crime.'

'So *that's* why Captain Mallory is playing his ponies! Sarah dear, how
many times have I told you that it's dangerous for you to be out without a
topee before four o'clock?'

'But it's after five, darling,' Sarah pointed out, 'and you know I haven't
got a topee, and too much vanity to wear one if I had. And anyway, I don't
believe anyone has worn one out here for the last ten years. You haven't
got one yourself.'

'Oh, but we're used to it dear. The sun I mean. But coming from Hampshire——'

'Auntie darling, I do wish I could get it out of your head that the whole
of Hampshire is a cold and draughty spot full of damp and fogs.'

'Not fogs dear. Blizzards. I remember once when your mother and I
spent Christmas with our grandparents at Winchester it never stopped
snowing and blowing. I had to wear a woollen vest over my combinations.
Which team did you say was winning, dear?'

'I don't know darling. The one Johnnie Warrender is captaining, I suppose. I've been gossiping with Fudge and not really paying very much
attention to the game. Anyway, it's only a sort of knock-up, isn't it? Here's
Uncle. Uncle Henry, did your lot win?'

'Naturally said General Addington, collapsing into a deck-chair and
fanning himself with his hat: 'I was umpiring, and saw to it. As a matter of
fact,' he added thoughtfully, 'they came very near to losing, in spite of
Johnnie's best efforts. That young protégé of the Governor's is hot stuff.'

'So Sarah thinks,' interrupted Fudge maliciously. 'Don't you, Sarah?'

'Does she, indeed? There used to be a song in my young days,' mused
the General, 'that said something about

> "I've seen the hook being baited,
> I've been inoculated;
> They can't catch me!"

Don't waste your time, Sarah.'

'Hugo has just been giving me much the same advice. A bit more of this,
and I shall get really intrigued.'

'That reminds me,' broke in Mrs Addington brightly, 'I *knew* I'd forgotten something. I've asked that nice Mallory man to dinner tonight. The Charity Dance at the Club, you know. Another man is always so useful. And, as I told him, I had no idea until I wrote out the table plan just after tea, that I'd asked thirteen people, or of course I'd have asked someone else. Some people are so odd about sitting down thirteen.'

Sarah felt a sudden uncomfortable shiver up her spine: where had she heard a conversation like this before? Of course! . . . Hugo had fallen out of the party to Khilanmarg and left it thirteen, which was why Janet had decided to come. She gave a little hunch to her shoulders as though to shrug off the uncomfortable memory and said: 'Aunt Alice, you didn't really tell him that did you?'

'What, dear?'

'Tell him that you were only asking him because you'd discovered at the last minute that you had a party of thirteen?'

'But there aren't thirteen now, dear. He will make the fourteenth, so it's quite all right. Not that I'm in the *least* superstitious myself—except about black cats of course. I once very nearly ran over one on my bicycle and only half an hour later I heard that April the Fifth had won the Derby— just as I said he would.'

'How much did you have on him?' asked Hugo, interested.

'Oh, I didn't have any money on him. I never bet. But it does go to show that there is something after all in those old superstitions, doesn't it?'

Sarah abandoned the unequal struggle and relapsed into a helpless fit of giggles, while Fudge, returning to the previous topic, said: 'I wonder he didn't refuse, or invent an excuse or something. It's not like Charles to let himself be bounced into going to Club dances.'

'Oh, I don't expect he'll come to the *dance*, dear. I told him that as long as he came to the dinner that was all that was necessary. I'm sure no one will mind *dancing* thirteen. Not that they could, of course. And I can't think what you're giggling about, Sarah dear. He didn't at all mind my being frank with him, whatever you may think. He's a very nice-mannered young man, and I can't imagine why Mrs Crawley and Mrs Gidney, or Kidney, or whatever her name is, and Joan Forsyth and that Roberton woman are so catty about him.'

'Suffering from a sprain in the technique, I expect,' offered Fudge. 'Are they catty about him?'

'Well, dear, you must admit it's a little *odd*. I mean after all the war *was* on still—when he arrived here, that is. And then when his regiment went off to Palestine or the Pyramids, or one of those places where they were always capturing hundreds of Italians—though what on earth they wanted them for I cannot imagine—what did we do with them when we had them? Just *think* how much food they must have eaten! And no spaghetti or anything. Still, I believe they provided one or two quite good dance bands in places like Muree, or was it Mussorie?'

Sarah said: 'Aunt Alice, what *are* you talking about?'

'Captain Mallory of course, dear. You aren't paying attention. A lot of people have been inclined to criticize him severely. For being a sort of A D C I mean—while we were still at war. They feel that he should have been fighting like the rest of them; his regiment I mean—not Mrs Kidney and the Roberton woman, though goodness knows they fight enough. But I must say, we did think it a little *odd* of the Governor to insist on a regular officer when there were so many tobacco people about who were so much cleverer at running things, and danced *quite* as well. But then of course so many people are silly about a man who doesn't do any fighting in a war. So stupid of them, because it's so much more sensible *not* to, don't you think? If we all just *didn't*, I mean, well where would people like Hitler have been?'

'In Buckingham Palace and the White House I imagine,' grunted her husband.

'Don't be silly, dear. How could he have been in two places at once? But as I was saying, Sarah dear, he was always being some sort of an A D C somewhere while the war was on—Captain Mallory I mean, not Hitler—and when it was over he still stayed on here, and now they're sending his regiment off to Palestine, or some place where they still seem to like fighting, and of course everyone thought he'd go, as it couldn't be *too* dangerous now—I mean not like D-Day, and Burma—but it seems he'd rather stay here instead.'

'I think,' said General Addington, rising from his deck-chair and addressing Sarah, 'that your aunt has said quite enough for one evening. Let us remove her before worse befalls. Come along, Alice, it's past six already and your fourteen guests will be arriving in under two hours.'

'Only eleven guests, dear. The other three are Sarah and you and I. Goodbye, Antonia. Goodbye, Hugo. You two really must come and see us some time. Drop in for drinks some evening won't you? . . . Oh, you're coming to dinner tonight? How nice.'

'*Alice!*'

'Coming, Henry dear. Come along, Sarah. You mustn't keep your uncle waiting.'

The procession departed down the dusty length of the polo ground to where the General's car waited by the roadside.

7

There was a pile of mail addressed to Miss Parrish on the hall table of the big white bungalow on the Mall: letters that had arrived by the afternoon's post and had been put aside to await her return. Sarah pounced upon them hungrily—aware of a sudden pang of homesickness at the sight of the English stamps on the bulging envelopes—and retired to her room to indulge in an orgy of news and gossip from home.

She was still reading half an hour later when her aunt tapped on the door to announce that she had forgotten to write out the place cards for the dinner table, and would Sarah please try and get down early and do this for her?

Sarah started guiltily, and hastily skimming through the last two sheets of the letter in her hand, bundled them all into her dressing-table drawer. There was still one envelope unopened which she had left to the last because it bore an Indian stamp and looked as though it might be a bill or a circular since the address was typewritten. But there being no time to read it now, she slipped it into her evening-bag before scrambling hurriedly out of her linen frock and into a bath.

It was perhaps half an hour later that she left her room and crossed the hall in a cloud of grey tulle powdered with rhinestones, her red head burnished to a sophisticated smoothness and her green eyes shining like peridots between curling lashes whose natural darkness was a perpetual thorn in the flesh to several of her red-headed but sandy-lashed acquaintances.

There was someone waiting in the unlighted drawing-room. A too early guest, lurking abashed in the shadows, thought Sarah; wondering why the servant who had shown them in had not turned up the lights. The last of the daylight still lingered in the garden, but the drawing-room was almost dark, and she pressed down the switches as she entered and advanced with a smile to apologize for the omission. But her eyes—or was it her senses?—had evidently played tricks with her, for there was no one there.

The big, high-ceilinged room was empty, and Sarah looked around it with a puzzled frown, for the impression of someone waiting there had been so vivid that for a moment or two she found it difficult to believe that she had been mistaken. Probably a shadow thrown by the headlights of a passing car from the road beyond the garden wall, she thought. Drawing up her shoulders in a little shiver, she went out onto the wide verandah where dinner had been laid that night because the approach of the hot weather had made even the big rooms of the old bungalow seem too warm and stuffy.

The sky behind the feathery boughs of the pepper trees at the far end of the garden was turning from lemon yellow to a soft shade of green, and the air was sweet with the scent of roses and jasmine and fragrant with the smell of water on dry, sun-baked ground. But looking out over the fast darkening garden, Sarah was conscious of a disturbing and inexplicable sense of unease; though mentally reviewing the events of the past day she could find nothing to account for this sudden feeling of foreboding that possessed her.

A faint sound behind her made her turn swiftly, expectantly. But it was only a small beady-eyed lizard that had rustled across the matting, and not . . . not . . . what? What *had* she expected to see? A girl in a blue skiing suit? Yes—that was it! She realized, with a cold shiver of incredulous horror, that she had turned expecting to see Janet!

From the moment that Sarah had arrived back in Peshawar, over two months ago, everything that had occurred during the closing days of the Ski Club Meeting had seemed to fade into unreality. It was as though it had all been a nightmare from which she had awakened to find herself in a safe and familiar room. And since she had no intention of leaving that room, she had thrown herself with an almost feverish gaiety into what social life there was left in the Station, and thrusting the memory of Janet into the background of her mind had done her best to forget the snowfields of Khilanmarg, the Blue Run, and a line of footprints on a deserted verandah. She had very nearly succeeded in doing so—to the extent, at least, of persuading herself that her imagination, and Janet's, had run away with them, and that the ice of the Blue Run had been the sole cause of those two tragedies.

Of the house among the pine trees she would not let herself think at all, for fear that it might break down her escapist line of reasoning. But now, suddenly, she was remembering Janet again . . . Was it because of this party tonight—the party that would have been thirteen?—and because if she herself had not told Reggie Craddock that he ought to get a fourteenth member for the party at the ski hut, Janet would never have stayed? But that, thought Sarah defensively, would have made no real difference to Janet's fate, since she would still have seen that red spark of light from the hotel and gone out to keep her rendezvous with——

'Sarah!'

Mrs Addington made an abrupt appearance at the far end of the verandah, wearing a gaily coloured kimono over a pair of pink lock-knit bloomers of almost Edwardian aspect, and with her hair tightly screwed into innumerable metal curlers.

'What is it, Auntie? Good heavens! Do you know that it's almost five past eight and you asked your guests for 8.15? Or have you forgotten there's a dinner party?'

'Of course I haven't, dear. I never forget anything. In fact I've just remembered something. The Creeds are coming tonight. Antonia told me so this evening.'

'I know they are,' said Sarah patiently. 'You asked them at least six weeks ago.'

'Yes, yes, dear. Don't interrupt me. I only wanted to say that I'd quite forgotten them when I was writing out the table plan. So of course I hadn't really got thirteen people after all—there were fifteen.'

'Oh darling, you are hopeless! And you black-jacked the unfortunate Charles Mallory into coming to your party entirely under false pretences. I'm ashamed of you!'

'Well that was what I wanted to ask you about, dear. Do you think we can ring him up and tell him we don't need him after all? It's the savoury, dear: Angels-on-Horseback. So *humiliating* if there are not enough to go round. He didn't seem particularly anxious to come, so I'm sure he'd be only too delighted to get out of it.'

'I don't doubt it,' said Sarah dryly. 'But he's not going to get the chance! No, darling: I refuse flatly to let you trump your already ace-high reputation for tact. You and I can either pretend to a loathing for Angels-on-Horseback, or cut the whole course off the menu. Take your choice.'

'Yes, perhaps that will be best. And now I come to think of it, dear, I don't believe it was Angels-on-Horseback after all. I changed it to cheese straws, and the Khansamah* always makes hundreds of those: last time we had them at the tennis tea next day. The ones that were over, I mean. Mrs Kidney said it was *such* an original idea. Good heavens! Is that a quarter past eight? You really shouldn't keep me here talking, dear. I shall *never* be ready in time!'

* A cook.

She disappeared with the speed of a diving duck as the little gilt clock in the drawing-room struck the quarter.

Sarah's wide net skirt whispered along the matting of the verandah as she passed round the long table with its load of silver and cut glass and bowls of Maréchal Niel roses, assisting portly Mohammed Bux, the *khidmatgar*,† to rearrange the table for the addition of two extra places.

She held her aunt's table plan in one hand and a small pile of name cards in the other, but it might have been noted, had anyone been there to look over her shoulder, that she did not distribute the cards entirely in accordance with the original plan. The revised arrangement, apart from the inclusion of the Creeds, contained one alteration; for when, half an hour later, the guests were seated, Major Gilbert Ripon, who should have sat at Sarah's right hand, had been relegated to the far end of the table, while Captain Mallory occupied that place.

'Not that it was worth the trouble,' confessed Sarah later, leaning over Fudge's shoulder to peer at herself in the looking-glass of the cloakroom at the Peshawar Club, 'because he talked almost exclusively to that hearty Patterson girl, and on the only occasion that we managed to start a conversation, Archie Lovat kept chipping in until in the end they forgot all about me and discussed the last day's hunting across my prostrate form for about ten minutes. After which, of course—*did* you hear her Fudge?—Aunt Alice suddenly noticed the alteration in her dinner plan, and being Aunt Alice, naturally commented upon it at the top of her voice: curse the darling old mothball! And Charles Mallory sort of lifted one eyebrow and looked slightly surprised—damn him—and Gilbert Ripon glared and that revolting Patterson girl giggled. All in all Fudge darling, one of the more frosty of my failures.'

'Not so frosty, really,' commented Fudge consolingly, powdering her nose with care: 'After all, he *has* come on to the dance, hasn't he?—despite all those outspoken comments by your well-meaning but muddle-headed aunt. And that, let me tell you, is no mean concession on his part. He isn't often seen around at dances. Oh well—good luck darling, but don't say I didn't warn you!'

'And if you warn me just once more,' retorted Sarah, 'I shall begin to suspect your motives; so stop fussing about with your face and let's go off and dance.'

Being a popular girl, the queue of would-be partners was a long one, and it was almost halfway through the evening before Charles Mallory was able to dance with his hostess's niece. He proved to be a surprisingly good

† A butler.

dancer, which for some reason she had not expected him to be, and Sarah clapped enthusiastically for an encore.

The band, which had been playing a gay and rather noisy quickstep, obliged with a waltz, and when the verse ended its leader crooned the refrain in an adenoidal whisper: . . .

> 'The moonlight and the moon,
> And every gay and lovely tune that's played for you,
> Were made for you.
> The Summer and the Spring,
> And that golden wedding ring,
> Were only made for you . . .'

Sarah's silver-shod feet stumbled and checked and Charles Mallory felt her go rigid in his arms, and glancing down at her saw that her face had suddenly lost every vestige of colour.

'Shall we sit out the rest of this one?' he suggested. 'I'm not very good at waltzes.'

Sarah said: 'Please,' in a small, breathless voice, and Charles led her out of the hot, crowded ballroom into the cool night air of the Club garden, and once there propelled her firmly across the lawn and put her into a wicker chair.

He stood looking down at her for a moment with a slight frown between his eyes: she certainly did look oddly shaken, and he said curtly: 'Wait here and I'll get you a drink.'

He left her sitting in the starlight, and returned a few minutes later carrying a frosted glass in each hand. Sarah thanked him, still in a small voice, and drank in silence while Charles pulled up a second chair, and sitting down, watched her over the rim of his glass without appearing to do so; his own face in shadow.

In the ballroom behind them the band, evidently pleased with their choice of an encore, embarked on a repetition of the song, and Sarah shivered so uncontrollably that her teeth chattered against the edge of her glass.

For the past few weeks life had been so gay that she had thought herself free of the nightmare of Gulmarg. But for some reason it seemed to have returned that evening to haunt her, and though she had tried to push it away it had followed her. Now it was here too—born of a trite, haunting melody—and suddenly she was back once more in the eerie moonlight outside the snow-shrouded hut on Khilanmarg, and Janet was fastening on her skis for her last run and humming that soft, catchy tune . . .

'The Winter and the Fall, and the sweetest words of all, were simply made for you,' crooned the leader of the band.

Sarah said: 'Why *must* they go on and on playing that thing!' There was a sharp edge of hysteria to her voice, and Charles Mallory leaned forward and removed the glass from between her unsteady fingers. 'You'll spill that, and spoil your dress,' he said in a matter-of-fact voice. 'It isn't much of a tune, is it? But they'll stop in a minute.'

He offered Sarah a cigarette, and when she refused it, lit one himself and embarked casually on a surprising story about an impoverished dance-band leader in a Budapest café, who had been born a Prince of an Imperial House: talking to give her time to recover herself and to take her mind off the music that drifted through the opened windows of the ballroom behind them.

Presently the band stopped and as the dancers came streaming out into the cooler air of the lantern-lit garden Sarah said: 'I'm sorry. It was stupid of me to behave like that. I don't know what's got into me tonight. But that tune reminded me of something unpleasant, and . . .'

'What are you two gossiping about?' cut in Helen Warrender brightly. 'I'm sure it must be something terribly interesting. Can we listen?'

Charles stood up and she plumped herself firmly into his vacated chair, ordered her partner to fetch her a brandy and soda, and turning her back upon Sarah said: 'Isn't it hot, Charles! I'm simply sticking to my frock. That's the worst of taffeta; even though one pays an absolute fortune for a model, it behaves like flypaper in the heat. Thank goodness we shall be leaving for Kashmir the week after next. I really couldn't stand this heat much longer. We're staying with the Douglases at Murree, on the way. I expect you know him, don't you? He's Lord Seeber's son. *Such* a darling. Do fetch another chair, Charles. And one for Tim.'

Charles collected two more chairs and a small green-painted table as Helen's partner returned across the lawn bearing drinks.

'Thank you, Tim. Oh damn! They've put ice in it! Why can't they keep the sodas cold instead of drowning them with ice cubes? Never mind—it's not really your fault. Give me a cigarette will you, Tim?'

The obedient Tim obliged and took the vacant chair, and Helen hitched her chair round to face Captain Mallory: 'Tell me, Charles, what did you think of the polo this afternoon? As a whole, I mean? Do you think we shall ever be able to raise enough people to play at all regularly? Of course if Johnnie had really been playing up to his handicap this afternoon, we'd have beaten you by much more. But then it's not really worth trying against these scratch teams.'

Charles said solemnly: 'Thank you, Helen.'

'What for? Oh! but I didn't mean *you*, Charles. I've seen you play at Delhi and Meerut, and I think it's so sporting of you to play with this ragtag and bobtail. But I suppose we should be grateful even to them. After all, they do give us some practice games. Oh really, Tim! You know I never smoke gaspers! Thank you, Charles. As I was saying——'

Sarah yawned, and opening her evening-bag pulled out a slim enamelled vanity-case, and with it something that fell on to the grass at her feet. It was the uninteresting looking envelope that she had not had time to open with the rest of her mail, and had pushed into her bag to read later. Picking it up she glanced at her companions, but as Mrs Warrender's taffeta-draped back obscured Charles Mallory and determinedly excluded her from the conversation, and the unsatisfactory Tim had removed himself and his rejected gaspers into the night, she shrugged her shoulders and opened the envelope; holding it so that it caught the light of the lanterns that hung in the trees behind them.

There was a second envelope inside the first one, together with a covering note from a firm of lawyers in Rawalpindi, dated two days previously, which—when translated out of the complicated jargon so beloved of the legal profession into plain English—informed Miss Parrish that the enclosed letter had been included in a packet placed for safe keeping in the office safe of the Manager of Nedou's Hotel in Srinagar, Kashmir, in January, by the late Miss Janet Elizabeth Rushton. The Manager had handed this packet 'upon her demise' to her bank, to be forwarded to her lawyers who had retained the contents until her will had been proved and probate obtained. Which fully explained the long delay, since lawyers and solicitors, like the mills of God, grind slowly . . .

Sarah turned her attention to the sealed envelope which bore her name and address in her own handwriting, and which Janet must have given, unobserved, to Mr Croal, the Manager of Nedou's Hotel, on the day that she had gone down to Srinagar to attend the funeral of Mrs Matthews. And holding it once again in her hand it was as though a cold breath from the snows and the shadows of black pine forests crept across the crowded lawn.

This, then, was the cause of the queer feeling of uneasiness and foreboding that had awaited her on her return to the big house among the pepper trees: the reason why the wraith of Janet had seemed to stand so close behind her that evening.

Sarah could see her with an uncomfortable vividness, standing in the small firelit room and weighing this same letter in her hand. She had said something about 'taking it down with her' . . . To Srinagar of course, where she and Mrs Matthews had taken rooms at Nedou's Hotel for the winter, and where Mrs Matthews had been buried because the snow lay too deep and the ground was too hard up in Gulmarg . . .

The wax of the seal broke under Sarah's cold fingers and fell upon the soft filmy layers of her skirt like small splashes of blood, and she brushed them away with a shiver of horror and drew out the two sheets of paper that the envelope contained: 'I left a record,' wrote Janet in a firm school-girl hand and without preamble or explanation, 'on the houseboat *Waterwitch* owned by Abdul Gaffoor, in Srinagar. Go there as soon as possible and look for it if anything happens to me. I paid in advance for the boat up to the end of June this year, and arranged that if I did not occupy it myself, any friend of mine who held the enclosed receipt could do so in my stead.' Then, in a wavering scribble, as though her nerve and her hand had suddenly failed her: 'I know I ought not to have done this, but I felt I had to. I can't say anything more. I can't. But it's there.'

The letter was unsigned and there was no clue as to the person or persons for whom Janet had originally intended it. In all likelihood it had only been written after Mrs Matthews' death. Probably an hour or two before Sarah herself had run to Janet's door in the moonlight, to warn her of that faceless figure in the snow.

The second piece of paper was a receipt for the rent, paid in advance up to the end of June 1947, for the houseboat, *Waterwitch;* and written on the back of it, signed by the houseboat's agents, were the terms of lease.

Sarah re-read the short note with its brief, incredible instructions and final agonized cry three times before the words had any meaning for her. It was impossible, fantastic, that she, Sarah Parrish, should be sitting in the Indian starlight, in the ancient city of Peshawar, holding in her hand a clue to international mysteries involving, perhaps, the lives and destinies of countless people. A few lines written by a murdered girl . . .

She read it once again, slowly and deliberately, as though she could drag from the paper the hidden thing that lay behind the bald words; the knowledge that had been Janet's when she wrote it, and which, but for this scrap of paper, would have died with her. And yet it told so little. Who had she meant it for when she wrote it? What had she meant to do with it? Why had she written it at all?

To that last question, at least, there appeared to be an obvious answer: because she had been afraid of death. Not so much on her own account, as for the knowledge she possessed. She had been terrified that the knowledge might be lost, and for that reason had been driven to take a desperate risk. Two risks! The chance of written information falling into the wrong hands, and the possibly greater one that her sudden decision to trust Sarah Parrish could prove to be a disastrous mistake . . .

Mrs Warrender, who had produced a large vanity-case adorned with a regimental crest, and had been powdering her nose as she discussed the old days at Ranelagh and Hurlingham, snapped the case shut and turned to Sarah: 'You'll be going up to Kashmir for the summer I suppose, Sarah? We're going up the week after next. Not that it's any fun now. But I suppose this is the last season we shall ever have, what with the handover set for next year, so . . . Oh hello—is that the notice about the races?'

She leant forward and calmly twitched the sheet of paper from between Sarah's fingers.

Sarah did not stop to think. She reached out and struck the letter out of Mrs Warrender's hand, and with the same movement managed to knock her scarcely touched glass off the table, splashing its contents over the scarlet folds of Mrs Warrender's taffeta dress and filling her lap with fragments of half-melted ice. Mrs Warrender screamed and sprang to her feet, and Sarah, standing up, placed a small silver shoe on the forgotten sheet of paper, swished her billowing skirts over both and apologized in a flurry of carefully simulated concern and embarrassment.

Mrs Warrender glared at her like an angry cat and said, in the same breath, that it didn't matter at all and that the frock was ruined; and allowed Charles Mallory to mop off the surplus with his handkerchief.

Sarah said: 'I can't think how it happened. I must have knocked against the table. Perhaps if you went straight home and put the dress into water it won't stain?'

'Nonsense! It's quite impossible to wash taffeta. I shall have to send it to the cleaners. Thank you, Charles. That's enough. It'll dry in a minute or two. No, of course not! I wouldn't dream of taking it off. Look, it's drying already. Tim can—Tim! Where *has* that damn' boy got to? Really, one's junior officers these days are worse than useless! There's the band starting again. Come and dance this one with me, Charles. I was supposed to be dancing it with Johnnie, but you know what husbands are like. Anyway, he's sure to be tight by now and he always cuts my dances.'

Charles said: 'I'm sorry Helen, but I'm afraid I've got this dance with Miss Parrish.' His voice was pleasant but very definite, and he did not look at Sarah. He looked instead at Mrs Warrender, meeting her eyes with a bland gaze.

Helen Warrender, as Fudge had pointed out, was a stupid woman. But there was that in Charles's lazy gaze which even a stupid woman could read, and she flushed a dark and unbecoming red, looked from him to Sarah and back again, and spoke in a voice that was suddenly strident.

"I'm *so* sorry! I didn't realize I'd broken up a tête-à-tête. In that case I'll go and hunt up Johnnie.' She turned to Sarah and said with a metallic laugh: 'Don't take him too seriously, will you? In case you didn't know it, he's *heavily* engaged. Aren't you, Charles darling?'

Charles's expression did not alter, but he drew back a chair as though clearing a path for her, and with a toss of her head she swept away across the lawn, her taffeta skirts hissing angrily over the dry grass.

Sarah stooped down and picked up the sheet of paper, surprised to find that her hands were shaking and her knees trembling with reaction from rage. She sat down abruptly, and reaching for her unfinished drink, drank it thirstily, and putting down the empty glass looked up at Charles.

'Thank you,' she said with the ghost of a smile. 'That was very good of you. Could you—would you add to your kindness by lending me your lighter for a moment? No, I don't want a cigarette thank you.'

Charles handed over a small silver cigarette lighter and Sarah snapped back the catch and held Janet's letter to the flame. The thin paper, having fortunately escaped being splashed with Helen's brandy and soda, caught alight easily and flared up, burning quickly until at last there were only three words left visible in the bottom corner—*'But it's there!'*. Sarah watched them fade with tears prickling behind her lashes, and thought: Oh! poor Janet! and dropping the blackened fragments onto the lawn she ground them into the parched grass with her heel.

'And now,' said Charles, 'perhaps you'll tell me why you flung that brandy and soda over Helen Warrender? Not, of course, that she hadn't been asking for some such demonstration. Still you must admit it was a little drastic.'

Sarah flushed. 'I didn't—I mean—it was really a sort of accident.'

Charles raised a sceptical eyebrow: 'Yes?'

'You mean "oh yeah?",' corrected Sarah crossly.

Charles's voice held a hint of laughter. 'My mistake; I thought you'd done it on purpose.'

'All right, then. I did do it on purpose and she had asked for it. So what?'

'Nothing. I was merely interested. It seemed a rather forceful way of expressing your displeasure.'

'I'm afraid I did it on the spur of the moment,' admitted Sarah defensively. 'You see, it was rather a private letter and I was afraid she might have had time to see a few words of it. But if she did I'll bet she forgot them the next second, because there is nothing like a really nasty shock for putting things out of your mind.'

'I'll remember that for future use,' said Charles gravely. He lit a cigarette and leant back in his chair watching her through the faint grey curl of smoke, while behind them in the ballroom the band played a slow foxtrot; a dreamy lilting tune that had been popular in the early years of the war.

Somewhere out in the darkness beyond the Club grounds a jackal howled eerily, and as other jackals took up the cry and blended it into a yelling, shrilling chorus as of souls in torment, Sarah shivered, and a sudden horror swept over her. A horror of the enormous, sunbaked land around her and the barren Khyber hills that lay just beyond Peshawar, menacing and mysterious in the starlight. Beyond those hills lay Afghanistan and the fierce and lawless tribes, while away and away to the northeast stretched the long line of the Himalayas, with somewhere among them the snow slopes of Khilanmarg.

A little breeze, rustling across the lawn, brought with it the smell of dust and flowering trees, and scattering the blackened fragments of Janet's letter, blew them away across the deserted terrace . . . It's no good, thought Sarah desperately: I know I promised, but I can't go back to Kashmir! I *won't* go. It's nothing whatever to do with me, and I never want to see those mountains again . . .

It was as though she were addressing the pale, accusing ghost of Janet. Telling her that as the letter had already been written and the envelope sealed down when she, Sarah, had come to Janet's room that night, it could not possibly have been intended for her, and that but for the chance that had brought her there, Janet would have given it to someone else. To Reggie Craddock, or Meril, or Ian Kelly . . . Anyway, it was burnt now so she could forget it. Surely she could forget it . . . ?

She saw in her mind's eye the long, winding hill road that climbed and twisted and dipped and turned for close on two hundred miles from the heat and dust of the cantonment town of Rawalpindi to Srinagar, the capital of the cool green valley of Kashmir. But the thought of returning to that valley, with its cold rim of watching mountains and black deodar forests, filled her with shuddering panic. She could not go back—she could not . . .

Charles Mallory's quiet voice broke into the tumult of her thoughts and brought her back to the present: 'What's the matter, Sarah? You're looking like a ghost.'

He had risen and was standing over her, and Sarah rose abruptly: 'I'm sorry. I'm a bit upset this evening. You go on in and dance with Helen. I'm better by myself.'

Her voice, even to her own ears, sounded thin and unsteady, and Charles said: 'Don't talk nonsense. You're shivering like a wet kitten. What's it all about, Sarah? You've been behaving for the last half hour as if you'd just been told where the body was buried. What's the matter? Bad news?'

'No,' said Sarah shakily, fighting a sudden desire to burst into tears. 'It's nothing really. I–I'm . . .'

'Feeling ill? Would you like me to take you home?'

'No. No. I'm all right. I mean, it's nothing.'

'Well in that case,' said Charles crisply, 'I suggest you take a pull on yourself and come in and dance. You can't sit here looking at ghosts all evening.'

'Oh, go away!' said Sarah, her voice trembling on the edge of hysteria. 'Can't you see I want to be left alone?'

'So that you can work yourself up into an even worse state of nerves, I suppose? But that won't help you, you know. Come on, Sarah. You don't look like the sort of girl who has hysterics. Show some guts.'

'You,' said Sarah furiously, 'would know about that of course.'

'About what?' Charles's voice was softly dangerous.

'Guts,' said Sarah distinctly. 'I understand your regiment's been ordered to Palestine?'

For one frozen second she thought Charles was going to hit her and, instinctively, she took a swift step backwards. But the chair was behind her and she stopped.

Charles looked down at her and laughed; though not pleasantly. And then, she did not quite know how, his arms were about her, sure and hard, and he bent back her head across his arm and kissed her competently.

'You have been asking for that,' said Charles, bored, 'for weeks.' He put her away from him and picked up his unfinished drink.

Sarah stood staring at him for a long moment. Then she snatched up her bag, whirled about and ran across the lawn to the lighted ballroom, leaving him standing alone in the starlight.

Part III

SRINAGAR

'Look for me by moonlight;
Watch for me by moonlight;'
Alfred Noyes, *'The Highwayman'*

8

It was the last week of May; ten days after the Charity Dance at the Peshawar Club; and the Creeds, accompanied by an unexpected passenger in the form of Miss Sarah Parrish, were on their way up to Kashmir for Hugo's leave.

Only a few hours ago on the long drive from Peshawar to Attock on the Indus, and on into Punjab to the great garrison town of Rawalpindi from where one of the main routes into Kashmir branches off from the Grand Trunk Road towards the foothills, they had been scorched by the heat and choked by the dust of the plains . . . and now they were picnicking by the roadside among pines and firs and deodars, and breathing cool mountain air.

'How did that dear old bolster, your Aunt Alice, take this sudden change of plan?' inquired Hugo through a mouthful of curry puff: 'I shouldn't have thought she would have approved at all.'

'Oddly enough,' said Sarah, 'she took it quite calmly. I think it has at last dawned on her that any girl who served in the forces during the late unpleasantness ought to be able to look after herself. Besides, the minute I said I was going up with you, all was well. Antonia is "a dear girl" and Hugo "such a *nice* man".'

'How right she is,' said Hugo complacently. 'About me, I mean. She has made a noticeable error of judgement in her estimation of my wife, but she can't really be blamed for that. She was probably mixing her up with two other women.'

A car swished past, covering them with dust, and drew up twenty yards ahead with a scream of brakes.

'I wonder what that's for?' said Fudge, waving the dust away from her nose with a chicken sandwich. 'Do you suppose they've run out of petrol, or want to ask the time?'

'As long as they do not wish to borrow beer,' said Hugo, 'all that I have is theirs, including my wife. Oh *blast!* It's Helen. I might have known it. Go and head her off, my sweet. She worries me worse than the hives.'

Fudge said: 'Vulgar brute!' and sliding off the low wall, went to meet the smartly clad figure that was advancing upon them from the car.

'*My dear!*'—Helen's voice had much in common with a peacock's—'I thought it was you! I made Johnnie pull up. We've been driving for hours, so I thought we might as well stop and have our lunch with you. I'd forgotten you were coming up today. What luck meeting you. God, how this journey bores me! If only there was somewhere else decent one could go. But of course there isn't. And anyway, none of us will ever go to the place again. At *least* this will be the last time, thank goodness.'

She checked suddenly at the sight of Sarah. 'Good heavens! It's Sarah. What on earth are you doing here, my dear? I thought you were supposed to be going to Ceylon or Singapore or somewhere? Don't tell me you're bound for Kashmir too?'

'Well, it looks that way, doesn't it?' said Sarah sweetly. She had a sudden and quite definite conviction that Mrs Warrender had stopped her car not because she had seen the Creeds, but because she had seen that there was a third person with them, and suspecting who it was, had wished to verify the suspicion. Her surprise was slightly overdone.

'But my dear! How nice. You'll simply adore Srinagar. Personally, I loathe it; but then of course Johnnie says I'm *far* too particular about the people I make friends with. Of course *I* always say one *can't* be too particular in that respect, but I know everyone else isn't quite so——Well anyway, I'm sure you'll have a lovely time. Not that there'll be anyone up here this year. In fact I hear it'll be *dead*—though I expect you'll find a sort of dying flicker here and there. Why, hello, Hugo!'

'Yes, this is me, Helen. In the flesh. Odd, isn't it? Even Fudge scarcely recognizes me in this pair of socks. What's happened to Johnnie? Is he busy with Mother Nature, or just sulking?'

'He's getting out the lunch basket. I'm afraid there are rather a pile of things on top of it. Here he is now. Oh, thank goodness you've got some beer, Hugo. I quite forgot to bring any with me, and we're both simply parched with thirst. I could drink six.'

Hugo closed his eyes and moved his lips in what may have been a silent prayer but was probably not, and Fudge said hurriedly: 'I'm so sorry, Helen, but I'm afraid that's the last bottle. However, if you can manage on half each, you're welcome to it.' She dropped her coat neatly over one of the two remaining bottles and turned to smile at Johnnie Warrender who came up carrying a large wicker lunch-basket under one arm and a car rug under the other.

'Hello, Johnnie. Here, don't put that down on top of the sandwiches! What time did you leave 'Pindi?'

'We didn't. I mean we spent the night at Murree,' said Johnnie depositing his burden on the wall. 'Hello, Sarah. I didn't know you were contemplating a Srinagar season.'

'Well, I always meant to do it sometime,' said Sarah vaguely, 'and as this seemed about the last chance I'd get, I decided to cadge a lift off Fudge and Hugo.'

'Good show. Pity you didn't see it in its heyday. It was a good spot once. We used to get some damned amusing polo there too . . . Oh well! Good God, Helen! Is this all you've brought in the way of lunch?' He regarded the sloshy mass of tomato sandwiches with unconcealed disgust, and having pitched them down the hillside, helped himself to one of Fudge's curry puffs.

Johnnie Warrender was an ugly little man who looked like a cross between a gentleman jockey and Groucho Marx, but possessed, despite this, a considerable portion of charm. Left to himself he would have been an attractive and cheerful nonentity; but he was not so left. From the time it had first been realized that Johnnie Warrender of the Lunjore Lancers could hit a bamboo ball farther and straighter, and with greater frequency from the back of a galloping polo pony than the majority of his fellow-men, the course of his life had been altered, and he became, in a small way, a celebrity.

Gone were the days of happy obscurity and unashamed and cheerful penury, for Johnnie's magic wrist and eye brought him into the circle of the rich, the leisured and the socially prominent. Government Houses and Residencies, together with the homes of every Brass Hat and Little Tin God in India, were open to him, and Maharajahs, Rajas, Nawabs and Princes were quick to follow suit: to lend him polo ponies and invite him to their Palaces as an honoured guest.

Unfortunately, there is something about Fame, even in such a comparatively narrow sphere, that is insiduous and corroding except to those of steady temperament and balanced judgement. And save in the matter of horseflesh and the polo field, Johnnie Warrender possessed neither steadiness nor judgement. He was still accounted a 'good fellow' and his capacity for gaiety and alcohol remained undiminished. But from being a happy-go-lucky and charming person, he became a spendthrift and a snob; in both of which his wife excelled him.

Helen, who had been a young and unaffected girl, became almost overnight a hard, selfish and scheming woman, and that worst of all Indian pests, an indefatigable social climber. Her goal was not a high one, and by dint of flattery and determination and her husband's prowess on horseback she achieved a fair measure of success—though at a cost. The children she had meant to have were the first casualty, because they 'could not afford the money'—or the time. Not now, anyway: though of course she would start a nursery one day. But somehow that day never came.

The friends of earlier years went next; ruthlessly discarded as she mounted to higher things, while money that Johnnie could ill afford went on the lavish entertaining of their newfound friends. The bills mounted and the Warrender overdraft achieved terrifying proportions. But Helen, if she possessed any fears for the future, refused to face them, while Johnnie's motto was 'sufficient unto the day'. And now their world had crumbled round them, never to be rebuilt.

The first blow had been the mechanization of the cavalry. 'It could never happen,' said Johnnie and his type. But it did; and with the departure of the horses and their replacement by tanks and armoured cars, the standard and opportunities for polo among the less wealthy regiments shrank perceptibly. Then Hitler marched his storm troops into Poland, and the tide of the Second World War, damned for twenty years behind slowly rotting barriers, roared hungrily across the world. And for Johnnie and Helen, as well as for thousands of their class and kind, it was not the beginning, but the end of an epoch. A *Götterdämmerung;* a Twilight of the Gods.

Something of all this was in Sarah's mind as she sat on the low stone wall at the side of the Kashmir Road, listening to Johnnie talking horses and Helen complaining about the impossibility of the British officers who had been sent out to India during the last years ('My dear, half of them simply don't know a racehorse from a tonga pony!'); and seeing, in the merciless midday sunshine, the marks of dissipation and weakness on the one face, and the bitter lines of discontented middle age on the other. Perhaps, with the ending of the war, they and many like them had subconsciously expected the clock to turn back again. But the old days were over for good. India was to be given her freedom and 150 years of British rule would end. There was nothing left for the Johnnies and Helens except memories and debts . . .

Suddenly Sarah felt acutely sorry for them both and for the inevitable tragedy of their kind. There is always something more pitiful in the destruction of petty but prized possessions than in the crash of dynasties, for the latter is at least spectacular and dramatic, while the former is of no more account in the eye of history than the breaking of a child's toy.

Hugo courteously handed the last of the chicken sandwiches to the ever hopeful Lager and slid off the wall: *'En avant, mes enfants!* "The sun is sinking fast, the daylight dies"—Hymns A. and M. In other words, it's almost five past two and we've been hogging it here for over an hour. If we're thinking of getting to Srinagar this evening we must put on no ordinary turn of speed. I refuse to navigate this tortuous road in the dark. Our headlights are rotten and my nerves are worse. Get off that rug, Helen, it goes in the back of the car.'

Helen rose languidly and, stooping to the lunch-basket at her feet, produced from it a battered-looking watermelon. 'Here, have this Hugo. Johnnie simply loathes watermelon and after all, we have eaten a good many of your curry puffs. But fair exchange is no robbery, is it?'

'Must I, Helen? Oh well–very thoughtful of you.' Hugo took the green globe with unconcealed reluctance and stowed it gingerly in the boot of the car.

'You can eat it for breakfast tomorrow. Where are you staying in Srinagar, Sarah? At Nedou's?'

'I expect so,' said Sarah. 'I may take a houseboat though. "When in Rome" you know.'

'Oh, then you aren't staying with Fudge and Hugo?'

'Of course she's staying with us,' said Hugo. 'We have hired four houseboats for the season. One for each of us and one for the dog. We are people of large ideas. You must come and look us up some day. Hi! Ayaz!'

Hugo's bearded Mohammedan bearer appeared round the bend of the road where he had been eating his own meal, and Helen said: 'Of course we will. And I must get Gwen to ask you to the Residency one day. We're staying with the Tollivers you know. Well, *au revoir*. Shall I give your love to Charles Mallory when I write, Sarah? But no!—you're sure to be writing to him yourself. All the girls do.'

'Sarah,' said Hugo cheerfully, 'is always too busy reading letters to have time to write any herself. You wouldn't believe the number of people who write to her. In fact, all the boys do. Well, so long. See you at Philippi.'

The car slid away, swung round the corner and was gone.

'Crude,' remarked Hugo, lighting himself a cigarette with one hand, 'but probably more effective than subtle methods. Sarcasm and subtlety are wasted on Helen. Well, it's nice to have you with us, Sarah, and I'm glad you decided to give Ceylon the miss-in-baulk at the eleventh hour.'

'Yes,' said Sarah slowly, 'I think I am too.'

She leant back and closed her eyes against the sunlight and the mountain scenery, and thought again of the events that had led up to her decision to return to Kashmir.

Sarah had returned home after the Charity Dance shaken with fury at Captain Mallory, and determined to leave for Ceylon as soon as possible. But she had been unable to sleep. She had accused Charles Mallory to his face of cowardice, yet she was no better than a coward herself.

It was no good hiding behind the excuse that Janet had never meant that message for her. Of course she had not! Nevertheless it was to Sarah that she had been forced to entrust it. And she, Sarah, who had promised to help—should 'anything happen' to Janet. Well, it had happened. So how could she back out of her promise now? For all she knew, the record that Janet wrote of might be of desperate importance, not only to a few individuals but to hundreds of thousands—perhaps to millions of people.

Yet supposing she did go up to Kashmir herself, and took over Janet's boat, and found it? What could she do with it? No, of course it was impossible! She must forget all about it and let sleeping dogs lie. If only there was someone she could give the letter to. Someone to whom she could hand over the whole responsibility . . . She considered going to the Governor, or the Chief of Police. But she could not forget that Janet had said: 'Of course I can't go to the police! What could I tell them? Give away the results of months of work and planning, and ruin everything at the eleventh hour?'

What could she, Sarah, tell them, when she had burned the only piece of evidence she had—Janet's letter? She wondered now what had possessed her to do it. Cowardice again, she thought wryly. The urge to be rid of this thing that threatened to disturb her peace of mind. Well at least it left the ball firmly in her own court, and sooner or later she would have to make up her mind what she proposed to do about it.

On this decision she fell asleep at last, and dreamt that Charles was kissing her: not scornfully, as he had kissed her upon the Club lawn, but tenderly and with passion. And had been quite unreasonably infuriated when her dream had merged into reality, and she had awakened in the morning sunlight to find Lager enthusiastically licking her face.

Later that day Sarah had gone out into the garden and fought a battle with herself among the flowering jasmine bushes and the beds of yellow and scarlet cannas. In the end it had been Janet's unconscious paraphrase of Edith Cavell's dictum that *Patriotism is not enough* rather than her own lightly given promise that had swung the balance. No, it was not enough just to be 'patriotic', to love your own country and your own people, if you were not prepared to take any risks, or make any sacrifices, on their behalf. And if that was 'jingoism', then Shakespeare had been a founder-member, and she was in good company!

She would go to Kashmir and take Janet's boat, and find the record Janet had left there. Though what she would do with it once she had found it, she had no idea. That situation, however, could be dealt with when it arose. In the meantime at least her conscience would cease to trouble her, or torment her with accusations of cowardice. She would send a wire to

Ceylon and then ask the Creeds if they would take her up to Srinagar with them. There would just be time to arrange it . . .

So here she was once again upon the winding Kashmir Road. Being borne swiftly towards the city of Srinagar, and the Dal Lake where Janet had lived on a houseboat named *Waterwitch*.

9

It was past five o'clock by the time the Creeds' car left the mountains and came out upon the level valley and the long, straight, poplar-lined road that leads from Baramulla to the city of Srinagar—that curious admixture of ancient and modern India that stands astride the Jhelum River, sheltered by a curving arm of the mountains and near a chain of beautiful lakes.

The sun was low in the sky, and its fading rays turned the white snowpeaks that ring the valley to rose-pink and amber; and here the river that had raged through the narrow mountain gorges behind them, spread out into a broad and placid stream that flowed serenely between green banks lined with willows and chenar trees.

On either side of the road lay long fields of yellow mustard, the emerald green of crops, patches of late iris, purple and white, and small, huddled villages ringed by willow and walnut. Flocks of slow-moving sheep strayed homeward in charge of brown-robed shepherd boys who played upon small reed flutes, and the twilight was sweet with birdsong and tinged with a sense of nostalgia and lost dreams and the scent of spring.

It was dark by the time they reached Srinagar, so Sarah spent the night on board the Creeds' houseboat; but soon after breakfast on the following morning she set off in a *shikara*—one of the slim, flat-bottomed, gaily canopied boats that are the gondolas and water taxis of this eastern Venice —in search of the *Waterwitch*.

It did not prove difficult to find, and the agency with which the boat was registered for hire accepted Sarah's explanations and the receipt without undue interest, and dispatched her in charge of a polite young Kashmiri to Chota Nagim, some few miles outside Srinagar City where the *Waterwitch* was moored. She had not looked forward to this return visit, but that first trip to Nagim enchanted her.

The *shikara*, once clear of the city, slid away down cool, sun-dappled waterways fringed with willows; past ancient wooden houses perched upon stilts above the stream and crazily reminiscent of Hansel and Gretel.

Through villages whose walls rose out of the water, and whose carved and fretted balconies overhung the passing boats. Villages whose main street was the waterway.

As the heart-shaped paddles rose and fell in unison, the boat glided under old, old bridges and by temples whose glittering roofs were discovered on closer inspection to be plated not with silver, but with pieces of kerosene tins. Brilliant blue kingfishers flashed and darted above the quiet reaches of the stream, and innumerable bulbuls twittered among the willows. And at last they came to a quiet backwater near an open stretch of lake where, moored against a green bank and sheltered by the boughs of a gigantic chenar tree, lay a small houseboat.

It was a trim little craft, and according to Sarah's guide contained a living-room, and a small dining-room with an adjoining pantry from which a narrow wooden stair led up to the roof. The forward part of the roof was flat, and supported an orange and white striped awning, and beyond the pantry lay two small bedrooms which led off each other, and were each provided with a minute bathroom.

Unlike the majority of houseboats upon the lake, the sides of the *Waterwitch* had been painted white, while the wooden shingles that covered the peaked roof above the after section of the boat were stained green, so that the whole effect was rather that of a child's Noah's Ark. It formed such a gay and attractive picture, backed by the green of the willows and mirrored in the clear lake water, that Sarah was aware of a sudden and overpowering sense of relief.

She could not have said what she had expected, but subconsciously she had supposed that an air of darkness, decay and mystery would linger about the boat in which Janet had lived and where she had written down and hidden her secret. But there was nothing dark or mysterious about this trim little boat with its freshly laundered curtains fluttering in the breeze.

As the *shikara* drew alongside, a sliding-door in the centre of the boat was drawn back and the red-bearded *mānji*, * the owner, popped out upon the duckboard wreathed in welcoming smiles, and after a brief conversation with the man from the agency, salaamed deeply and hastened to usher Sarah on board.

The *Waterwitch* was furnished in much the same style as any other houseboat upon the lake. The wooden panelling of the walls was unstained and unpainted; as were the low ceilings, which were formed of small sections of wood cut into squares, diamonds and hexagons, pieced together to make a complicated mosaic overhead. There were cheap cotton curtains at

* A boat-owner.

the windows and the living-room was crowded with furniture: a sofa, upholstered in faded and much worn plush, whose springs looked to be in urgent need of repair; three armchairs with clean but faded cretonne covers, a large writing-desk, two occasional tables of intricately carved walnut, and several others in brass or papier mâché, in addition to a standard lamp of horrifying design.

A narrow shelf with a fretwork rim ran round the entire room at the level of the top of the windows and was crammed to over-flowing with dusty, dog-eared books and out-dated periodicals, and Sarah regarded this tattered array of literature with blank dismay.

There if anywhere she thought, is where I shall have to look; and her heart sank at the prospect of leafing through all those thousands of musty pages. She had hoped to be able to complete her search of the little houseboat in a matter of hours, but she had not calculated on several hundred assorted books and magazines as possible hiding places. It was going to take days, not hours, to conduct a really thorough search through the contents of those close-packed shelves . . .

'Very nice room!' urged the *mānji*, extolling the beauties of his boat. 'Good chairs for sittings. All covers I wash new. Many beautiful books. Many sahibs are leaving books on my boat for long time now. Here is dining-room. Take a look, Miss-sahib, very fine dining-room.'

There was no door across the opening between living-room and dining-room, its place being taken by an old-fashioned bead curtain, and the *mānji* held a bunch of the coloured, clashing strings and ushered Sarah through into the next room.

This was better! The dining-room appeared to contain the minimum of furniture and hiding-places, which after the clutter of the living-room was a relief. The table was a work of art in polished walnut wood; oval in shape with a deeply cut and beautifully carved pattern of chenar leaves running round its rim, and Sarah ran her hand appreciatively across its shining surface as she passed on, urged by a lyrical running commentary from the *mānji*, to a small pantry, half of which was taken up by the short wooden staircase that led up through a species of trap-door to the roof.

A bedroom, a small bathroom, a second bedroom beyond it, and another bathroom. The little boat was clean and neat. Swept and garnished and empty of all feeling. An impersonal, placid little boat that gave no hint, no whisper of the secret lurking somewhere within it. Blobs of sunlight reflected off the water outside danced a silent saraband upon the ceilings, the uneven floorboards creaked loudly and cheerfully under Sarah's feet, and the little boat rocked gently to the movement, slapping the water in small gay splashing sounds against its sides.

There seemed to be nothing of Janet here. Janet belonged to the grey skies, the white snowfields and the black winter forests of Gulmarg; not to the gay green and gold and blue of maytime on the Dal Lake.

An hour-and-a-half later Sarah was on her way back to Gagribal Point and lunch with Fudge and Hugo, having completed all the necessary arrangements with the man from the agents, and given orders that the *Waterwitch* was to remain at its present moorings. She had also provisionally booked the next-door *ghat*, or mooring-space, on behalf of the Creeds: 'You won't mind mooring your houseboat there instead of at Nagim, will you Fudge? It's only just round the corner really, and it looked so peaceful and sheltered. Nagim seemed to be full of boats.'

'*Mind?* My dear child, for this I will leave you half of my overdraft in my will,' said Hugo cordially. 'Fudge has a single-track mind in these matters, and merely because some four score years and ten ago, when we first visited this salubrious health resort upon our honeymoon, we parked our barque upon Nagim, she cannot conceive of any other pitch. This regardless of the fact that what was once a blossoming Eden far from the madding crowd, has since had endless monstrosities of wood and stone built all round it, in the form of club-houses, cafés, boarding-houses and what-have-you, and is so thickly jammed with houseboats that one's left-hand neighbour is never ignorant of what one's right-hand neighbour doeth. No. Speaking for myself, I shall be delighted to park elsewhere. For one thing, I do not fancy floating upon sewage; and for another——'

'That will be quite enough!' interrupted Fudge hastily. 'It's a lovely idea, Sarah. We'll have our boat taken out there immediately after lunch.'

The afternoon had been spent sitting upon the roof of the Creeds' big houseboat, as it was poled by a team of husky Kashmiris down the same waterways that Sarah had passed through that morning. And with the evening they came to their mooring.

The *Waterwitch* had been connected, via several hundred feet of wire, to the main electric light cables that ran alongside the Nagim road, and as all her lights were lit, her windows glowed cheerfully in the twilight, and Fudge, who had been trying to persuade Sarah to remain on the *Sunflower*, was relieved at the sight of the gay little boat. 'It doesn't look so bad,' she admitted. 'How did you manage to find it, Sarah?'

'Oh, just looking around,' said Sarah vaguely. 'Don't worry darling. I shall be quite safe. I shall have Lager with me, and your boat is so close that I've only got to raise a yell if I feel nervous.'

The Creeds' houseboat had been moored about thirty yards below the little *Waterwitch* and facing it, so that the cookboat, which housed their *mānji* and his family and would also provide accommodation for Ayaz, lay behind it and out of sight. The *mānji* of each houseboat usually combined the office of cook, headwaiter and *valet de chambre* with that of owner; but tonight Sarah declined the culinary services of her own factotum and dined on board the *Sunflower* with the Creeds.

They were not more than halfway through the meal when a *shikara* bumped alongside in the darkness and a voice hailed the cookboat in Kashmiri. A few minutes later Ayaz, the Creeds' bearer, appeared in the doorway with an envelope on a small brass salver, which proved to contain an invitation to a cocktail party at the Residency on the following evening, addressed to Major and Mrs Creed and Miss Parrish.

'That's quick work,' commented Sarah, as Fudge scribbled an acceptance and handed it to Ayaz: 'How did they know we were here? Helen, I suppose.'

'I don't think so,' said Fudge. 'Hugo and I wrote our names in the book this morning, and put yours in too for good measure. We were having coffee at the Club and met the new P A—an erstwhile acquaintance of yours.'

'Forgive a poor ignorant newcomer,' said Sarah, 'but what exactly is a P A?'

'Personal Assistant,' translated Hugo, helping himself to cream: 'A poor wretch whose job it is to send out the invitations to Residency Tea-Tipples and Bun-Battles. I believe it also includes such onerous duties as translating the *khansamah's* menus into French, arranging the rhododendrons on the dining-room table, fetching and carrying for the Lady Resident, and prompting her in a hissing whisper when she mixes the names of her guests. This sinecure is at present held locally by a bootfaced damsel by the name of Forbes.'

'Forbes? You don't mean *Meril?*'

'The same. No Helen of Troy, as you will be the first to admit. But doubtless oozing with efficiency.'

'I shouldn't have thought she'd be in the least efficient. However, she was a pretty good skier.'

'Was she, indeed? I can't say I ever noticed her performance in particular. It's those spectacles I suppose. I must admit I am sorry for the wench.'

'Why? Because "girls who are spectacled never get their necks tickled"?'

'That, of course,' admitted Hugo. 'But the girl is also gravely handicapped by an aunt who holds the All-India Gold-Plated Cheese Biscuit, open to all comers, for sheer undiluted louse power.'

'*Hugo!*' expostulated Fudge indignantly.

'I apologize, m'dear. An ill-chosen simile, but doubtless Sarah gets the idea.'

'I have heard rumours,' admitted Sarah, recalling certain forcible remarks of Janet's on the subject of Meril's aunt. 'What's the matter with her?'

Hugo said: 'You will undoubtedly meet the lady at this binge tomorrow, and be able to judge for yourself. Speaking for myself, she fascinates me, and I cannot help regretting that upon her demise it will not be practicable to have her stuffed and placed in some public museum.'

'And they say that women are cats,' commented Fudge, selecting a banana from the fruit dish. 'For sheer concentrated cattiness, you can't beat the male!'

'Nonsense!' said Hugo. 'I speak but the limpid truth. Lady Candera is the Original Boll Weevil. She has an eye that can bore holes through six feet of armour-plating, and a tongue that could skin an elephant. Take it from me—a tough baby! Strong men blench before her and women take cover.'

'Is she quite as formidable as Hugo makes out?' inquired Sarah of Fudge.

'Well, almost,' admitted Fudge, dipping her banana thoughtfully in the coffee sugar and ignoring Hugo's outspoken criticism of the action. 'I'm scared of her myself; but then I take jolly good care to avoid her.'

'*Worm!*' observed Hugo, removing the coffee sugar.

'Worm yourself! You're terrified of her. She prides herself on always saying exactly what she likes as rudely as possible. And that's always pretty unnerving to the general public.'

'Tell me about her,' said Sarah, interested. 'She sounds full of entertainment value.'

'She is, in a way,' admitted Fudge with a laugh. 'I've often thought that life would be a lot duller if it were not for these highly coloured characters. If everyone were all a nice pink, like the Hoply girl or Mrs Ritchie, how bored we should all be! I appreciate the addition of a few nice splashy reds and purples myself. They add a dash of paprika to the mixture, if nothing else.'

'Lady Candera,' pronounced Hugo, 'is a type that is, or was, fairly common all over the world. But we grew a special brand of them in the Indian Empire. Next year there will be no Indian Empire, and so that brand will become extinct—along with the Johnnies and Helens and their ilk. They won't go to ground in England, because it will not be able to give them what they want; so the Lady Canderas will retire to infest places like Cyprus and Madeira, while the Johnnies and Helens will probably get themselves dug into Kenya. *Ehu fugaces!* And if you shove that slimy chunk of fruit into the coffee sugar once more Fudge, I shall arise and assault you.'

'You still haven't told me much about this Lady Whatsiz,' complained Sarah. 'What's she like?'

'Nothing on earth,' said Hugo promptly.

Fudge threw him a withering look. 'She is tall and thin and, as Hugo says, she's got an eye like a gimlet. I believe she's half French or Afghan, or something of that sort. They say she used to be a raving beauty when she was a girl. She must be about ninety by now—well anyway pushing eighty—and she looks like something that has been dug up from the ruins of Byzantium.'

'*Miaow!*' said Hugo, handing over the cream jug. Fudge ignored him.

'Her husband was something or other in the I C S—the Indian Civil Service. Or am I thinking of the F and P?'

'Foreign and Political Department,' translated Hugo kindly, 'the chaps who only had to keep breathing in order to end up with a four-figure pension and a handle to their names.'

'Well anyhow, he was something big in some Indian State,' said Fudge. 'But he's dead now, and she lives in a houseboat near Gagribal with Meril and a sort of dim companion-woman called Pond.'

'And a very suitable name too, if I may say so,' interpolated Hugo: 'I have seldom encountered anyone so damp as that female. If there is a breeze about, she ripples.'

Fudge ostentatiously returned the cream jug: 'Where was I? Oh yes. They live somewhere near Gagribal in a huge houseboat.'

'Chiefly noticeable,' said Hugo rapidly, 'for the outsize telescope erected on the roof, by which means they are enabled to keep an indefatigable eye upon the misdeeds of the unwary.'

Fudge giggled. 'They used to spend a lot of time peering through it, and years ago Lady Candera tried to start a "Purity League" in Srinagar. She said that the goings-on she observed in other houseboats and passing *shikaras* were flagrantly immoral and should be stopped. She even tackled the Resident about it, and he apparently replied that he would consider taking action provided he could have a good look at the "goings-on" through the telescope first. She never spoke to him again.'

'Poor Meril!' said Sarah. 'No wonder she looks so harried.'

'Let's go and sit up on the roof,' suggested Fudge, rising. 'There's a moon tonight.'

'Not me,' said Hugo firmly. 'I have no desire to waste my last leave in Kashmir scratching mosquito bites.'

'Is it really that? Our last leave in Kashmir?' sighed Fudge. 'Oh dear!

Somehow I can't believe it. We've spent so many leaves up here. Do you suppose we shall ever come here again?'

'No,' said Hugo. 'Unless, of course, the Amalgamated Brotherhood of Mangle Manufacturers, of whom you will by then be an unwilling member, come here for their Communal Workers-of-the-World Jamboree and Butlin Binge one day. Then, standing by the rows of cosy, communal, Comrades Dormitories, and gazing out at the Concrete Lido that will have blossomed by the lake, you will drop a tear into its medicated waters and murmur, "Ah me! How lovely it used to be when it was merely sewage!" '

'Disgusting brute!' said Fudge. 'There was a time when you used to spend hours holding my hand in the moonlight.'

'Undoubtedly. But that was in the days when I was merely betrothed to you, or endeavouring to become so, and that was all I could do about it. However, having successfully pressed my suit, should I now be overcome by the romantic yearnings that once drove me to moongaze, there are other things I can do about it.'

'Hugo!'

'Not before the child!' said Hugo. 'Shove off and shiver on the roof and leave me and the port in peace.'

'I think I shall go to bed, if you don't mind Fudge,' said Sarah. 'It's been a long day, and I feel sleepy.'

'Very sensible of you,' said Hugo, yawning. 'We will see you onto your yacht.'

They escorted Sarah down the gangplank and along the few yards of turf that separated the two boats, Lager frolicking and barking in the moonlight and chasing imaginary cats in the shadows.

'Are you sure you'll be all right?' asked Fudge anxiously. 'Shout if there's anything you want.'

'Quite sure. I will. Good-night Fudge. Good-night Hugo. Come in Lager, you little pest.'

Sarah turned and walked up her own gangway, and the little *Waterwitch* rocked and creaked to her footsteps. At least, she thought, it would be impossible for anyone to come on board without instantly advertising their presence, since even the lightest step on a houseboat could be both heard and felt. The floorboards creaked and the boat vibrated slightly to every movement of those on board.

She closed and latched the sliding-doors behind her and snapped off the lights in the living-room, dining-room and the small pantry as she passed through them on her way to her bedroom. After which she undressed and got into bed, suppressing, with an effort, a strong desire to look over her shoulder and jump at every slight sound aboard.

Lager leapt onto the foot of her bed and curled himself up into a small velvet ball, and Sarah turned out the light and lay for a while staring into the darkness, until, moved by a sudden impulse, she reached out a hand and pulled back the curtain from the window beside her bed.

The glassed frames had been pushed back into the thickness of the wall leaving a wide square, screened by wire gauze against flies, mosquitoes and night-flying insects, that looked out across the moonlit lake to the shadowy mountains beyond.

Gulmarg lay somewhere over there—an unseen hollow below the white levels of Khilanmarg and the long ridge of Apharwat.

The moonlight would be shining on the little ski-hut, as it had shone that night when she had talked to Janet in the snow. It would be lying cold and clear along the verandah of the silent hotel, as it had lain on the night that she had stood and stared down at a line of betraying footprints on a thin film of snowflakes; and it would peer into the garden of a deserted house near the Gap, where the wind swung a gate idly to and fro on a broken hinge . . .

Sarah shivered, and closing the curtains against the white night, fell into an uneasy sleep.

10

The late evening sunlight shone warmly upon the smooth lawns and towering chenar trees of the Residency garden where peonies, roses and canterbury bells bloomed in gorgeous profusion in the long flower-beds, and wafts of scent from the direction of the kitchen gardens spoke of sweetpeas already in bloom.

In an ordinary year the British Residency in Srinagar gave many parties during the course of the season, but this year was not as others. It marked the end of an epoch—of an era—and something of this feeling seemed to pervade the present party. A tinge of restlessness; of farewell to familiar things. Next year there would be no time for parties. Only for packing and goodbyes. So let us eat, drink and be merry, for tomorrow we shall be scattered as chaff before the wind and the familiar places will know us not . . .

Their hostess greeted Sarah and the Creeds in the dim hall of the Residency, and directed them into a spacious green and white drawing-room full of guests and flowers.

'Hello, Meril!' said Sarah, turning to accost a hurrying figure.

'Oh, it's you Sarah! I heard you were up here with the Creeds. I thought you said you weren't coming to Kashmir again.'

'I wasn't,' admitted Sarah, 'but it seemed a pity to miss what may be my last chance of seeing this place. It was rather a spur-of-the-moment idea.'

'Well, I hope you'll like it. It isn't going to be very gay this year, what with everyone trying to get home. Still, you'll like being out at Nagim. The bathing's quite decent.'

'What's quite decent?' inquired an all-too-familiar voice behind them. 'Personally, I've yet to find anything decent about this place.'

'Oh hello, Mrs Warrender. May I introduce Miss Parrish? Mrs—oh of course, how stupid of me! You've met before. You were both at the Ski Club Meeting, weren't you.'

'Yes. Sarah and I know each other well. *Do* tell me, how is Charles? And what do you think of Srinagar? *Quite* deadly of course. No life in it.

Gulmarg is the only place worth going to in Kashmir, but even that is simply finished this year. Anyway, it was becoming too shatteringly provincial. Isn't that George McKay? What on earth's he wearing that frightful blazer for? It looks exactly like a striped awning! Some ghastly Cricket Club or other I suppose . . . Hello, George. I thought you were busy doctoring people in Sialkot?'

'I was until yesterday. At present I am on embarkation leave.' Major McKay shook hands with Meril and bowed to Sarah. He was a solidly built man of medium height and in his early thirties, with a pleasant but rather humourless face and a certain primness of manner that made him seem older than his years.

'Yes, I'm really off,' he said in answer to inquiries. 'I thought I'd give Kashmir a last look before I left. There are more people up here than I thought there'd be. All doing the same thing I suppose. Saying goodbye.'

'Well I hope for your sake that Srinagar will leave a better taste in your mouth than Gulmarg,' said Helen with a laugh. 'All those post-mortems must have made it rather a busman's holiday, and I hear our hardworking Secretary, Reggie, didn't see eye to eye with you about one of them. Was that true?'

'I'm sure I don't know,' said Major McKay stiffly. 'It's a subject I cannot really discuss.'

'Oh dear! Have I said something I shouldn't? How awful of me! Where are you staying?'

'At the Nagim Bagh Club, for the moment; but I hope to get some fishing later on. Is your husband up here?'

'Yes, Johnnie's somewhere around. Heavens! Here's that Candera woman. Why on earth Gwen asks her I don't know. Oh sorry, Meril. I forgot she was your aunt.'

Meril smiled wanly and glanced over her shoulder with a somewhat hunted expression at the latest arrival: a tall, elderly woman clad in impeccable tweeds, who stood in the doorway surveying the assembled company through a pair of jewelled lorgnettes. No; not elderly, corrected Sarah mentally—old. But despite her age she was holding herself with that erect carriage so admired by the Victorians.

'If she's coming over here, I'm off,' said Helen Warrender, and removed herself swiftly.

Meril looked as if she were about to follow her example, but a harshly imperious voice arrested her.

'Ah, Meril,' said Lady Candera bearing down on the shrinking Miss Forbes: 'Gossiping, I see? I understood you had certain official responsibilities connected with these functions. Obviously, I was mistaken.'

Meril flushed an unbecoming shade of red and shuffled her feet like a small child: 'I'm sorry, Aunt Ena. Can I get you anything?'

'Yes. A brandy and soda please. You know I detest cocktails.'

'Yes, Aunt Ena. Of course, Aunt Ena.' Meril left at what was almost a run, and Lady Candera turned her lorgnettes upon Sarah, observing her from head to foot with the peculiar rudeness of the undisputed autocrat. Sarah remained unruffled and returned the old lady's scrutiny with equal interest.

Lady Candera showed little signs of the beauty that legend credited her with. Though perhaps a hint of it lingered in the modelling of jaw and temple and the line of the thin, beaked nose. Her face sagged in innumerable yellow wrinkles and was curiously blotched, as is the skin of some elderly Indian women, and her eyes were an odd, pale grey that appeared lighter than the tone of her somewhat swarthy complexion—and were certainly a paler shade than the iron-grey of her hair. She wore a magnificent rope of misshapen pearls, and her bony fingers were loaded with diamonds and emeralds in heavy, old-fashioned and not over-clean settings.

Sarah's appearance, or possibly her calm gaze, appeared to interest her, and raising her lorgnettes she addressed Major McKay in commanding tones: 'Major McKay, who is this gel? She's new. Not like the usual run of cheap stuff we get up here this time of year. Or is she?'

Major McKay, his ruddy countenance betraying a mixture of embarrassment and frigid disapproval, said stiffly: 'Lady Candera, may I introduce Miss Parrish. Miss Parrish——"

'—of London and Hampshire,' interpolated a gentle voice as Hugo drifted up, glass in hand. 'How are you Lady Candera? Hello Doc, nice to see you up here again.'

'One of these tourists, is she?' said Lady Candera, with a sound that in anyone less majestic would have been termed a sniff.

'Please! Please!' deprecated Hugo, waving his glass in a pained manner. 'Let us say "A bird of passage"—and what a bird! In my opinion, a golden oriel.'

'Ah,' said Lady Candera, bringing the lorgnettes to bear again. 'Very interesting.' She nodded briefly at Sarah, turned abruptly and walked away.

'Hugo, that was outrageous of you!' said Sarah, attempting severity and relapsing into a giggle.

'Why? I am a keen soldier and believe in keeping in practice.'

'What were you practising then?' inquired Major McKay.

'Counter-attack,' said Hugo solemnly. 'Have a sausage?' He collected a plate of small hot sausages speared on cocktail sticks, and a glass of sherry for Sarah. 'The sherry is a far, far better thing than that weird mixture they are dishing out,' said Hugo. 'I recommend it. Here's cheers! By the way McKay, perhaps you can——' He stopped. The Major was no longer with them. 'Odd,' commented Hugo. 'He was around a moment ago.'

'Why, hello Sarah!' a tweed-clad figure was pushing its way between the guests towards them: Reggie Craddock, whom Sarah had last seen in Tanmarg, superintending the departure of the Ski Club members: 'Oh . . . hello Hugo; I didn't see you' . . . Reggie sounded less than pleased. 'Up here again?'

'What do you mean "again"? I am practically a fixture. In fact they are considering according me the status of a Protected Monument. What brings you here, Reggie?'

'Last spot of leave in Kashmir,' said Reggie. 'I'm due home soon. We're selling up, you know. Nearly seventy-five years and three generations in this country, and now—oh well. You know the Nawabzada, don't you?'

He caught the arm of a slim, flannel-clad figure and dragged him out of the crowd.

'Yes, of course,' smiled Sarah. 'We met skiing.' She held out her hand to Mir Khan who bowed over it gracefully.

'It is nice to see you again, Miss Parrish. I do not ski now. The snow has gone. So I play tennis and golf instead. Do you play these games also?'

'A little,' said Sarah.

'Don't you believe her, old man! She plays both with distressing competence,' said Hugo.

Sarah laughed, and catching a glimpse of Johnnie Warrender through the crowd, asked Mir Khan if he included polo in his list of sports?

Mir Khan shrugged. 'When I can find it,' he said. 'But polo is dying in India; even among the Princes.'

Reggie said: 'Don't you ever do any work, you idle plutocrat?'

'Not if I can help it,' admitted Mir with a disarming grin. 'One of these days work may catch up with me, but just now I run very fast and so I keep just out of reach. For the moment I am what the Americans would call a playboy.'

'And very nice too,' sighed Hugo, accepting a fresh and brimming glass from a passing *khidmatgar*. 'I only wish I was in a position to follow your admirable example. But what with an expensive wife to keep in socks and headgear, not to mention keeping myself in pants and footwear, I am reluctantly compelled to apply my classic nose to the grindstone. It's all very sad. "Skin off your nose",' said Hugo.

'And what do you think of Srinagar?' asked Mir Khan turning back to Sarah.

'Well, we only arrived the day before yesterday,' said Sarah, 'but I like what I've seen of it so far.' The talk turned for a time to the valley and the various beauty spots Sarah must visit before she left, until Hugo said: 'By the way, Reggie, there's another member of your skiing flock here this evening. McKay.'

'Oh,' said Reggie Craddock briefly; his pleasant face all at once blank and uncommunicative. The oddly uncomfortable silence that followed was broken by their hostess, who bore down upon Mir Khan and whisked him away to meet a Frenchman who wrote travel books and knew his father, while Hugo was removed to entertain a Mrs Willoughby.

Sarah was left with Reggie Craddock, who began to talk skiing; but she was not really listening to him, being more interested in gazing around the crowded room to see how many faces were known to her. Surely that was one of the Coply twins talking to a pretty blond girl by the piano? The boy half turned his head; yes, it was Alec. Or was it Bonzo? She never could tell which was which unless they were standing together, when it was possible to pick out the small differences that distinguished them from each other. Apart, few people were aware which one they were addressing.

Reggie Craddock talked on and on. But now he was speaking of Janet Rushton, and the name served to jerk Sarah out of her inattention . . .

'Damned shame about Janet,' said Reggie. 'She was a really good sort: and one of the best women skiers I ever saw. Kandahar class. Why the hell women jib at obeying perfectly clear and rational orders, I'm hanged if I know. It wasn t as if I hadn't expressly ordered everyone to keep off Blue Run, and explained why. Good Lord, you'd have thought one fatal accident was enough to scare 'em off the run, apart from a direct order. Never been so upset in my life. Gives the Club a bad name too. Puzzles me though; she was no fool, Janet. Not the sort to do a damn' silly thing like that. To tell you the truth, Sarah'—Reggie dropped his voice to a confidential undertone—'I've never been quite satisfied about that business of Janet.'

He stopped and looked at Sarah intently, as though he had perhaps expected to surprise some flicker of agreement on her face. His eyes were very bright and as curious as a bird's in his brown, nutcracker face.

Sarah felt herself flushing under his gaze and was furious with herself; it was a trick she had never outgrown and which she mentally designated as Victorian and 'missish'. She spoke quickly to hide it, and with perhaps a shade too much emphasis: 'What rubbish, Reggie! I didn't suspect you of being imaginative.'

'Imaginative in what way?' asked Reggie Craddock. He lowered his gaze and examined the contents of his glass with exaggerated interest, but Sarah did not reply, and after a moment he said, apparently at a tangent: 'You knew Janet quite well, didn't you.'

It was not a question but a statement of fact, and the suspicion darted across Sarah's mind that he said it casually—too casually—in order to . . . what? Was she herself getting over-imaginative? Why should she suddenly imagine that Reggie Craddock, of all people, should be laying a trap for her? Fishing slyly for an unguarded statement?

Reggie's eyes were upon her again, bright and bird-like. No, not bird-like, thought Sarah. A bird's eyes were bright and soft and inquisitive. Reggie's eyes were bright and inquisitive, but they were hard too. As hard as flakes of steel; and somewhere deep down in them there glimmered something that was wary and alert.

His question seemed to float in the air between them and she realized that she must answer it as casually as it had been asked. 'No,' said Sarah, aware of an odd constriction of her throat. 'I can't say I knew her at all well. I'd spoken to her, of course. But then I spoke to most people at the Meeting.'

'She had the room next to you in Gulmarg, didn't she?' Reggie was once more intent upon his glass, twirling it slowly so that the lights moved on the olive at the bottom.

'Yes. But I didn't see much of her. She was in a different class from me as a skier.'

'I see,' said Reggie Craddock slowly. He poked at the olive in his drink with a small cocktail stick. 'I thought you must have known her well, since you've taken on her boat.'

His glance flicked upward to Sarah's face, and something jumped and fluttered in her throat, and her mouth was suddenly dry. She lifted her glass with a hand she was surprised to find steady, and sipped at her sherry before replying.

'Yes?' said Sarah with a composure she was far from feeling. Her tone was gently interrogative and her slightly lifted eyebrows managed to convey a faint suggestion of polite surprise at this inquiry into her personal affairs.

Reggie Craddock flushed an unbecoming red and looked away. He said hurriedly: 'I knew Janet pretty well. She was here last summer when I was up on leave. We were on one or two parties together; and of course we were both interested in skiing.'

He paused to eat the olive and tuck the discarded stick absently into a bowl of pansies that stood on the grand piano at his elbow: 'She had a rather jolly little houseboat,' continued Reggie more slowly. 'I remember her telling me last year that she'd taken it on a long lease for this year as well, because one of the best moorings on the lakes went with it, and decent moorings were often hard to get. When I came up here this year I thought I'd take it on, but the man from the agents was out when I called about it, and the next time I went along, which was this afternoon, they told me you'd taken it.'

Sarah said nothing and continued to sip her sherry.

Reggie cleared his throat and fidgeted with the stem of his glass. 'I suppose you wouldn't consider sub-letting it to me? I wouldn't ask except that—well I know it sounds damn silly, but I've rather a hankering to take on that little boat. Reasons of sentiment, and all that rot, and this looks like being my last chance. Of course I'd get you another one just as good, and you could keep the same *ghat*. I don't suppose it makes any difference to you what boat you're on, as long as it's a decent one and you're next to the Creeds. Tell you the truth, I was a bit cheesed off when I heard you'd got in ahead of me with Janet's boat. Well—er—how about it?'

Sarah regarded Reggie Craddock thoughtfully over the rim of her glass. An assortment of quite incredible theories were running through her mind, whirling and flaming like catherine wheels on Guy Fawkes night.

Reggie had known Janet well. Reggie had taken the trouble to find out, or remember, that Janet had occupied the room next to hers at the hotel in Gulmarg. Reggie had tried to rent the *Waterwitch*, and having failed to do so was trying to persuade her to give it up to him. He had, it was true, issued a strongly worded edict against the use of the Blue Run; but supposing that had been a blind?

Added to all that there were two other facts worthy of note: Reggie Craddock had been in the ski-hut at Khilanmarg, and was the only skier up that year who was entitled to wear on his lapel the little gold K on a blue enamel ground that was the badge of the Kandahar Ski-Club.

All these things and many others raced and jostled each other through Sarah's brain, intermingled with a feeling of blank incredulity. It was, of course, utterly fantastic, and she was letting her suspicions run away with her. It was ridiculous, absurd, impossible, to imagine for one moment that a man like Reggie Craddock . . . And yet Janet Rushton was just as absurdly and impossibly dead, and all at once words that Janet had spoken repeated themselves in Sarah's brain: 'If anyone had told you a few hours ago that I was a Secret Service agent, would you have believed them? . . . Of course you wouldn't! Because I don't look like your idea of a Secret Service agent.'

'Well?' said Reggie Craddock.

Sarah collected herself with an effort. 'I'm terribly sorry to disappoint you Reggie, but I'd rather not. I've taken a fancy to that boat, and once

I've got settled into a place I hate having to move.' Her tone was light and friendly, but perfectly definite.

A rather ugly look crept over Reggie's face, but he answered easily enough: 'Oh, that's all right. I merely thought it was worth asking. But of course, as you were a friend of Janet's . . .'

'I've already told you,' snapped Sarah with some asperity, 'that I barely knew the girl.'

Reggie finished his drink and put the glass down upon the piano with a brisk clink. 'I think I forgot to mention,' he said, 'that when the agents told me that you had taken on the *Waterwitch*, they also told me that you held Janet Rushton's receipt for the boat, without which you could not have moved in.'

There was a brief moment of silence. Then: 'What month were you up here on leave last year, Reggie?' asked Sarah.

'August. Why? What's that got to do with it?'

'Only that it interested me to hear that Janet had told you last August that she had paid for the *Waterwitch* in advance for this year.'

Reggie's brows drew together in a scowl. 'I don't see . . .' he began.

'That receipt,' said Sarah softly, 'was dated 3 December.'

Somebody in the press of guests stepped back and inadvertently jostled Sarah's elbow, jerking the remains of her sherry in an amber stream down her grey linen dress, and a breathless voice began to gasp incoherent apologies: 'Oh dear! Oh, dear me, I am *so* sorry! How *exceedingly* clumsy of me!'

Sarah turned with overwhelming relief to find a small, anxious woman struggling to extract a handkerchief from a large and overcrowded handbag, with which, when she had succeeded, she made futile little dabs at the stained dress. At any other time such an accident would have been annoying, to say the least of it. As it was, Sarah could have kissed the offender, since but for this timely interruption she would have become involved in some impossible explaining. For her retort to Reggie Craddock had been a double-edged weapon.

If, as she had insisted, she had barely spoken to Janet Rushton, how was it that Janet's receipt for a lease of the *Waterwitch* was in her possession?

Turning away to reassure her rescuer, Sarah was aware that a large, hearty woman wearing puce-coloured crêpe de Chine had borne down upon Reggie Craddock and swept him away on a spate of voluble chatter, and she breathed a deep sigh of relief. She really *must* learn to keep her temper and guard her tongue. It had been stupid and foolhardy to make damaging admissions merely to score off Reggie Craddock, and she was not at all sure that by doing so she had not allowed Reggie Craddock to score off her!

'I *cannot* apologize sufficiently,' the small woman was saying unhappily. '*Most* careless of me. Your pretty frock! But these parties—so crowded.' She groped agitatedly for a pair of rimless pince-nez that had fallen off her diminutive nose and were now swinging aimlessly from the end of a thin gold chain.

'Please don't bother,' urged Sarah with her most charming smile. 'As a matter of fact, I'm really terribly grateful to you.'

'To *me?*' said the small woman blankly. 'Now you are making fun of me!'

'No, really,' Sarah assured her earnestly, 'I mean it. I was involved in a most awkward conversation, and your bumping into me like that simply saved me. Sherry won't stain. I'll rub it down with a sponge when I get home, and it won't show a mark, I promise you.'

'It is so kind of you to say so,' fluttered the small woman. 'I am sure you cannot mean it, but it has made me feel a little better about my clumsiness. May I introduce myself? My name is Pond. Miss Pond.'

'Oh!' said Sarah with interest. 'I'm Sarah Parrish.'

'How do you do,' said Miss Pond primly.

'Fine, thank you,' said Sarah. 'Here, let's sit down, shall we? That sofa looks quite comfortable.' She steered her companion towards a chintz-covered sofa from which they could look out over the garden, and having seated herself, turned with frank interest to look at the companion of the formidable Lady Candera.

Pond, thought Sarah. Hugo was right. It really was a most suitable name. A small patch of somewhat weedy water; the haunt of homely, foolish things like ducks and tadpoles.

The little woman seated beside her might have been any age from thirty to sixty, and her features seemed to consist of a series of buttons: a small flat button of a nose, a primped button of a mouth and a pair of brown boot-button eyes. She wore, in addition to an anxious expression, a haphazard collection of garments that gave an impression of having been flung together in a hurry, and Sarah's fascinated eye observed that she was wearing short buttoned boots in addition to such miscellaneous items as a Batik silk scarf, mustard-yellow fabric gloves, and several strings of assorted beads.

Her voice was soft and breathless and she appeared to speak in a series of gasps. Was this Sarah's first visit to Kashmir, and what did she think of the dear valley? Where was she staying? And did she not think that the Lake was *too* beautiful?

Sarah, grateful for her escape from Reggie Craddock, replied suitably, while outside the windows the daylight faded and the garden filled with shadows and the scent of mignonette and night-scented stock.

They were still talking when, well over a quarter of an hour later, a stentorian voice cut through the cocktail party hubbub as a knife cuts through cheese: 'Elinor!' trumpeted Lady Candera.

Miss Pond sprang up as though she had been stung in a sensitive spot by a hornet. 'Oh dear! I'm afraid that is for me . . . Yes Ena, I am coming. So nice to have met you, Miss Parrish. I am so sorry. About the sherry, I mean. Yes, Ena, yes . . . I'm coming.' And gathering up a scattered collection of gloves, handbag, handkerchief and scarf, she scuttled out of the room.

'What are you giggling about?' demanded Hugo, plumping himself down on the window-seat near Sarah. 'Has the human doormat been amusing you? Incredible creature, our Pondy. How do you suppose she does it?'

'Does what?'

'Puts her clothes on. I have a theory that she first covers herself with glue and then crawls under the bed, gathering up fluff as she goes.'

Sarah burst out laughing. 'You *are* an idiot, Hugo. But possibly you're right, at that.'

Fudge came across the room and leant on the back of the sofa: 'What are you two laughing about? Do finish that drink, Hugo. It's quite time we left. They'll be sweeping us out with the crumbs soon. Sarah! What on earth have you spilt on your dress?'

'Sherry,' said Sarah. 'And believe me, I was never more grateful for anything in my life. Is Reggie still around?'

'Reggie Craddock? No, I think he left about twenty minutes ago with Mir.'

'Thank God for that,' said Sarah devoutly. 'Come on, Hugo.'

They said goodbye to their host and hostess and moved out into the hall to wait while a red-robed *chaprassi** went off to summon the car.

Twilight was merging into dusk, and the lights of the Srinagar Club twinkled through the trees beyond the Residency gates as Sarah went out on to the front steps—Fudge and Hugo having stopped to talk with some friend—and stood looking up to where the bright blob of light glittered from the summit of the Takht-i-Suliman temple, high above the chenar trees of the garden.

A lone figure, obviously one of the departing guests, appeared suddenly at the far end of the drive near the gateway, from the shelter of a clump of

* An office-servant.

bushes. There was a strong light above the gateway, and as the figure passed through, Sarah noted that it was wearing a striped blazer and wondered idly what Major McKay had been doing in the garden? A moment later someone came swiftly out of the shadows across the gravel drive from the direction of the tennis-courts, and ran lightly up the steps.

'Hello Meril,' said Sarah. 'You're just in time to see us off.'

Meril stopped, and putting up an uncertain hand to push back a lock of hair that was straggling untidily across her brow, said anxiously: 'Is it late? I felt I couldn't bear that stuffy room a minute longer, so I went out to walk round the garden. The flowers all seem to smell so much sweeter at night. I didn't realize it was so late. Are people leaving?'

'They've mostly left I think,' said Sarah, turning to look over her shoulder into the lighted hall: 'Your aunt is still there—telling Hugo where he gets off, judging from her expression! And at a guess there are still quite a few people left, so you don't have to worry: you're in time to speed at least a dozen departing guests.'

Meril looked alarmed. 'Oh dear, I suppose I shouldn't have gone out.' She pushed ineffectually at the errant lock of hair, and inquired abruptly: 'Why did you come up here again?'

Sarah raised her eyebrows, more at the tone than the question itself, and said with a laugh: 'It's a free country!' and Meril blushed suddenly and hotly in a wave of scarlet colour that temporarily eliminated her freckles. 'I–I didn't mean it like that,' she said. 'I only wondered——' Her voice trailed away as she turned to peer anxiously over Sarah's shoulder to where her aunt stood among a small group of departing guests in the hall, and Sarah suffered a pang of conscience: poor Meril! It was a shame to snub her. She must lead a dreary and frustrating life with that aged autocrat of an aunt. No wonder she was such a milk-and-water nonentity!

'As a fact,' she explained, 'the Creeds were coming up, and everyone told me that I really ought to see Kashmir without its snow before I left India. So here I am. We're parked in a sort of backwater just outside Nagim. You must come out and bathe and have lunch with me some day.'

'I'd like to do that,' said Meril absently, her eyes still intent on the group in the hall: 'We don't get much bathing here.'

'Then it's a date. We're just the other side of the Nagim Bridge. Chota Nagim, I think they call our backwater. My boat's the green and white one. It's called the *Waterwitch.*'

'The *what?*' Meril turned quickly.

'The *Waterwitch.*'

'But–but that is—that was Janet's boat!'

'Yes,' said Sarah pleasantly. 'Was she a friend of yours?'

'Janet? Well no—not really. I knew her of course. She was up here all last year. She lived in that boat out at Nagim, but she went about a lot. Tennis and parties and things. Everyone knew her. Aunt Ena doesn't like me going to parties. Not that I get asked to so many,' added Meril with an uncertain smile.

Sarah said: 'Would you say Reggie Craddock had been a special friend of hers?'

'Of Janet Rushton's? I don't know. Why do you ask?'

'Oh nothing. Idle curiosity, I suppose. Something he said this evening gave me the idea.'

'Reggie Craddock and Janet,' said Meril thoughtfully. 'Perhaps he did like her. I never thought about it before. He was up here on leave last year, of course, and Major McKay said——'

But what Major McKay had said was lost, for at that moment Fudge and Hugo came out of the hall and swept Sarah down the steps and along the wide gravelled drive towards the car park and home.

11

Sarah devoted the next few days to an exhaustive search of the *Water-witch*. But the task proved far from easy, since Fudge and Hugo were apt to appear on the boat at all hours of the day, demanding her presence at bathing parties, picnics or expeditions, and she found it hard to produce an adequate supply of plausible excuses for not accompanying them.

On more than one occasion she had been sorely tempted to tell them the whole story and ask for their assistance in her search, and the only thing that restrained her from doing so (apart from a conviction that this was a matter best kept to herself), was the fact that she possessed no shred of proof with which to support her incredible story, and did not relish the prospect of its being received with polite or derisive incredulity.

Examined in the cold light of day it frequently appeared, even to her, as both fantastic and impossible, and she still sometimes wondered if she had not dreamt or imagined the whole thing. But the evident anxiety of some person unknown—Sarah suspected Reggie Craddock—to obtain posses-sion of the *Waterwitch* did little to support that theory, for it was on the morning after the Residency party that a Kashmiri who said he came from the agents had endeavoured to persuade her to exchange the *Waterwitch* for another boat.

Sarah had refused to consider it, and suspecting bribery, had sent the man away with a flea in his ear. But though she remained on the boat and continued with her solitary search, she found it wearisome and disheartening work.

She had begun by looking in all the obvious places—enthusiastically assisted by Lager, who barked and scratched and evidently laboured under the impression that he was being encouraged to hunt rats. But her main difficulty lay in the fact that life on a houseboat could only be compared to living in a goldfish bowl, since apart from the sudden and frequent appear-ance of one or other of the staff, who were liable to walk in on her at any moment, the attention of water-borne hucksters requesting her to examine their wares, or attempting to sell her fruit or flowers, was as maddeningly recurrent as the clouds of mosquitoes and midges: and less easy to repel.

On one occasion she had been surprised by the *mānji*, while engaged in unpicking a section of her mattress in order to make sure that no folded paper had been concealed among its lumpy, raw cotton stuffing. (Lager had been particularly noisy, and she had been cross and preoccupied, and had not noticed the *mānji's* approach). Her explanation, that she was in search of some sharp object that had pricked her from the mattress, was not well received. The *mānji* informing her that never before had it been suggested that evil insects inhabited his boat, and not so much as the smallest flea would the Miss-sahib find—unless perchance one had entered the boat upon the person of the Miss-sahib's dog, and for this he accepted no responsiblity. Sarah's attempts to clear up the misunderstanding merely made matters worse, and the *mānji* had retired, offended dignity in every whisker.

But since it was impossible to move noiselessly on a houseboat—and nothing larger than a mouse could have stirred without advertising its presence—thereafter Sarah saw to it that Lager did not run excited races with himself while she was searching.

Unfortunately, there was nothing she could do about the numerous vendors of shawls, carpets, papier mâché and underwear, whose *shikaras*—drifting silently over the water—would appear suddenly outside the windows with the request that the Miss-sahib should 'Only look—do not buy!' The sudden and unheralded appearance of these gentlemen never failed to startle her, and she began to wonder how Janet had ever been able to make a record of anything without the entire population of Srinagar being aware of it! She must have written it and hidden it by night; when the lamps were lit and the curtains close-drawn, and every door and window bolted and barred . . .

Only when all the obvious hiding-places had been exhausted did Sarah turn resignedly to the bookshelf in the living-room, and taking down the volumes one after another, go methodically through them. It proved to be a weary, dusty and thankless task, for the books were for the most part old and tattered, and they smelt of dust, mildew and mice. The dust made Sarah sneeze and her head ache, but she plodded doggedly on: occasionally coming across one that had been Janet's and which bore her name on the flyleaf—written in that sprawling school-girl hand that Sarah remembered so well from her one sight of it in the letter she had burnt at the flame of Charles Mallory's cigarette lighter.

These particular books she had examined page by page, and in one of them she found several sheets of paper covered with Janet's handwriting and stuffed between the cover and the dust jacket—and for a marvellous five minutes was convinced that she had found what she was looking for, since it appeared to be a code. But its appearance was deceptive, for it proved to be a laundry list.

On the following day she had barely settled down to work when an unexpected caller arrived in the person of Helen Warrender.

Helen had evidently driven out to the Club at Nagim, which lay only about a quarter of a mile from where the *Waterwitch* was moored, on the far side of the narrow strip of land that separates the Nagim Bagh lake from the backwater of Chota Nagim. Leaving her car there, she had walked across the fields to call on Sarah.

A flurry of barks from Lager announced her approach and gave Sarah just time to push the day's quota of unsorted books under the frill of the sofa and hurriedly brush the dust from her hands, before going out to greet her. Helen, it appeared, had come to make her an offer for the boat.

Friends of hers, explained Mrs Warrender airily, had specially wanted this particular boat, and been most disappointed at hearing that it was already occupied. But on hearing that Helen knew the present occupant they had asked her to approach Sarah with a view to an exchange of boats: 'And of course dear,' concluded Helen, casting a disparaging eye about the cluttered living-room of the *Waterwitch,* 'I knew you couldn't possibly have any objection, so I told them they could consider it fixed. That's right, isn't it?'

'No,' said Sarah coldly. 'I'm afraid it isn't. I have absolutely no intention of giving up this boat, and when you next see Reggie you can tell him that from me!'

'*Reggie?*' exclaimed Helen Warrender blankly.

'You can add,' continued Sarah, with a dangerous sparkle in her green eyes, 'that I am a moderately easy-going person, but I don't like being pushed around.'

'I don't know what you're talking about,' said Helen Warrender. Her customary drawling voice had suddenly lost its veneer of affectation and was quick and harsh: 'Reggie? What Reggie? You mean Reggie Craddock? The man who—but *he* can't be . . .' Helen stopped abruptly and bit her lip. 'I'm sorry ' she said more slowly. 'There seems to have been some muddle. It wasn't Reggie Craddock who wanted the boat. It was—oh well. Someone you wouldn't know. A friend of mine.'

She turned and stood for a while staring out of the houseboat window in frowning concentration and tapping her teeth with the edge of her sunglasses. She seemed to have forgotten about Sarah.

Presently she swung round and said: 'Why did you think I was trying to get the boat for Reggie Craddock? Has he been after it too?'

'It looks that way, doesn't it?' said Sarah. 'I'm sorry I was rude, Mrs Warrender, but——'

'Oh, call me Helen,' said Mrs Warrender impatiently. 'There's no need for you to apologize. I didn't realize your boat was so much in demand. Why did Reggie Craddock want it?'

'Sentimental reasons,' said Sarah. 'Or so he said. I didn't really go into it. Srinagar is full of houseboats and most of them appear to be empty this year. But as I happen to have taken this one, I prefer to stay on it.'

'And that goes for me too, I suppose?' said Helen.

'Well, yes; I'm afraid so. I'm sure your friends will be able to find a dozen boats as good as this one, and probably at half the price. After all, prices should have fallen considerably this year.' She realized suddenly that she had made a tactical error and stopped.

'Oh,' said Helen Warrender in an interested voice. 'So you booked this boat last year? But you can't have done that. You weren't here. How did you come to take it? And why are you paying higher than you need for it?'

Sarah considered for a moment. She was strongly tempted to tell Mrs Warrender to mind her own business, but realized that this would only create an impression of secrecy; in addition to being rude. It was not that she had any particular objection to being rude to Helen Warrender (who in Sarah's opinion had asked for it), but she particularly wished to avoid a suggestion of any mystery being attached to her occupancy of the boat. She therefore decided that an edited version of the truth would serve her best: 'I took over this boat from a friend of mine,' she said carefully. 'Janet Rushton.'

'You mean the girl who killed herself skiing in Gulmarg? But I knew her!'

'Yes, that's the one. She had this boat last year, and she'd taken it on for six months of this year as well. Then she changed her mind about it, and happened to tell me one day that if I ever wanted to come up here later in the year before the lease ran out, I could take it on. I thought it might be a good idea, so I took over her lease, hoping that I could sub-let if I didn't come up after all. But I did, and I like the boat; and I like this *ghat*. But I don't expect I shall stay up here long, and as soon as I've gone your friends and Reggie Craddock and the agent's uncle's brother-in-law, and anyone else who wants it, can fight it out between them. Until then I intend to stay on it myself.'

Mrs Warrender said 'Oh' in an uncertain tone of voice, and sat down on the arm of the sofa. 'Well, that's that, isn't it? It's damned hot all of a sudden; I shouldn't be surprised if we were in for a thunderstorm. I could do with a drink if you've got one around.'

'I'm so sorry. I should have offered you one before,' apologized Sarah. 'What'll you have? Lemon squash?'

'As long as you put plenty of gin and a spot of bitters in it, yes.'

'Sorry, no gin on board. But if you'll wait a minute I'll run across to the Creeds' boat and hijack some of Hugo's.'

'That would be darling of you,' drawled Helen, dragging off her sun-hat and fanning herself with it. 'I confess I loathe soft drinks, and I could do with a stiff John Collins.'

Sarah ran down the gangplank and across the short strip of turf that separated the two boats, but it took her a minute or two to locate the gin which Hugo had left behind a flower vase on the writing-table, and when she returned it was to find Helen Warrender sitting on the floor with a pile of books strewn around her. She had one in her hand and looked up, unabashed, as Sarah entered: 'Funny place to keep your books,' she observed. 'Your sausage puppy started rooting them out from under the sofa, so I thought I'd better rescue them. Your *mānji* must be an untidy devil. There are lots more under there.'

'Are there?' said Sarah, in what she hoped was a disinterested voice; and mentally consigning Lager to perdition, she mixed a John Collins and handed it to her unwelcome guest. 'I'm afraid there's no ice. Do you mind?'

'Not at all, darling. Thanks. Well, here's cheers.'

Helen downed half the glass while continuing to gaze at the book in her hand, and Sarah saw that she was looking at a fly-leaf across which Janet had written her name.

'This Rushton girl,' said Mrs Warrender. 'Wasn't she supposed to be rather a spot skier?'

'Yes,' said Sarah briefly.

'Damn silly thing for her to do. She ought to have known better. I rather wonder at your wanting to take over her boat after that.'

'Why?' inquired Sarah coldly.

'Oh, I don't know. Rather gruesome, don't you think? Still, if you don't mind. It's been an unlucky year for Kashmir in the way of accidents, hasn't it? First the Matthews woman and then the Rushton girl. I keep on saying there's bound to be a third one. These things always go in threes, don't they? Well, I suppose I'd better be going.'

Sarah did not attempt to dissuade her and Helen stood up and brushed her skirts, and tossing Janet's book onto a chair, walked over to a looking-glass in an atrocious Victorian frame of plush and shells hung on one wall, and replacing her sun-hat, peered at herself and exclaimed: 'Heavens, what a mess I look! It's this heat. Let's hope we get a good storm to clear the air.'

She dabbed at her nose with a rather grubby powder puff, and having touched up her mouth with lipstick, said: 'Well, my visit seems to have been rather abortive, doesn't it? Sorry you don't feel like giving up the boat. Still—there it is. If you feel like changing your mind, let me know.'

Sarah continued to say nothing, and Mrs Warrender snapped shut her handbag, adjusted her dark glasses and trailed out of the boat into the sunlight. At the bottom of the gangplank she turned and said: 'Thanks for the drink. I do hope you won't regret it. The boat business I mean.' Upon which cryptic remark she waved a languid hand and walked off between the willows.

'Now what was that intended for?' mused Sarah, addressing herself to Lager: 'A threat or a promise? Either way, I'm not sure I like it. No. I do not like this set-up one little bit and I've half a mind to——No, I haven't! I won't be pushed around!'

There were two gangplanks on the *Waterwitch*. One that led from the bank to the pantry, and was used almost exclusively by the *mānji* and the other houseboat servants, and a second that led to a small open space on the square prow of the boat from which one entered into the living-room. Sarah stood on the prow in the hot sunshine and watched Helen Warrender take the field path that led between young corn and a blaze of yellow mustard towards the Nagim Bagh road, and presently she said again, and with more emphasis: 'No, Lager. I will *not* be pushed around!'

12

Having replaced the books so tactlessly exposed by Lager, Sarah postponed any further search through the houseboat's tattered library, and spent the remainder of the day with the Creeds.

I'm beginning to imagine things and to be suspicious of everything and everybody, she decided ruefully; and that's fatal. After all, why *shouldn't* Reggie Craddock's story be true? How do I know it isn't? He did know Janet, and for all I know he may have been fond of her. Suppose Mrs Warrender's friends really do want this boat, and for quite unsinister reasons? It *is* rather an attractive little boat, and quite a reasonable size compared with most of these outsize floating palaces I've seen. I must try and cultivate a sense of proportion . . .

With this laudable object in view she lunched with the Creeds, accompanied them in the afternoon on a picnic to the Shalimar Gardens, and returned to dine with them on the roof of their houseboat, though their original plan had been to dine and dance at Nedou's Hotel, and they had booked a table there. But since Major McKay, who was to have made the fourth member of the party, had sent an eleventh-hour message to say that he had pulled a muscle while playing tennis, they abandoned the dance with some relief and ate a scratch meal, hurriedly concocted by the houseboat staff, instead.

The day had been hot and breathless, but with nightfall a light wind began to blow from the mountains, ruffling the surface of the lake and driving little waves in crisp slaps against the side of the houseboat.

Normally, on moonlit nights the lakeside was noisy with frogs; but to-night for some reason the croaking chorus was silent, and though the sky overhead was still cloudless, away to the southwest summer lightning licked along the distant ranges of the Pir Panjal, and there was a mutter of faint, far-off thunder in the air.

Beyond the willow trees a line of tall lombardy poplars bent their heads before the freshening breeze, the *mānjis* came out upon the bank and began to tighten mooring-ropes and chains, and Hugo, who was dispensing coffee, got up from the table and went to the roof's edge to observe the operation.

'*Ohé, Mahdoo!*' called Hugo in the vernacular: 'What dost thou do?'

'Perchance there will come a storm in the night, Sahib. We make the boats secure so that should the wind be great, it cannot pull them away to drift and sink in the lake.'

'That's a jolly thought!' said Hugo, returning to his seat. 'Nice thing for yer uncle to wake up in the small hours and find himself drifting rapidly away from the home bank and about to turn turtle at any moment.'

Sarah yawned and got to her feet. 'Well I'm off to bed, I think. Good-night, and thanks for a lovely day.'

'Good-night Sarah. Sweet dreams.'

Sarah strolled along the bank in the moonlight and waited at the foot of her gangplank while Lager scampered off into the shadows to chase imaginary cats. He was away for an unconsciously long time and Sarah, growing impatient, whistled and called. She could hear him scuffling about somewhere in the shadows beyond the willow trees, but he would not come to her, and when at last he reappeared he was licking his whiskers and prancing in a self-satisfied manner.

'Lager, you little horror,' reproved Sarah sternly, 'you've been scavenging! What have you been eating? You know you aren't allowed to eat rubbish!'

Lager's ears, nose and tail drooped guiltily and he pattered docilely up the gangplank at Sarah's heels.

The *mānji* had left the lights burning and Sarah made a tour of her little boat, checking that the windows and doors were fastened before returning for a last look round the living-room. She had already commented caustically to Fudge upon the feeble lighting in Srinagar, for the Power Station being unable to supply the load demanded of it, even a 60-watt bulb produced only a feeble yellow glow. But tonight, for some reason, it seemed to her that the lights were suddenly over-bright and garish and that in their glare the small houseboat appeared larger and less overcrowded and strangely empty.

Outside, the night was full of noises. The slap of wind-driven water against the sides of the houseboat, and the jar and whine of the ropes and chains that moored it to the bank; the sough of the wind through leaves and branches, and the chorus of creaks and groans from the boat itself as it rocked and jerked and fidgeted at its moorings. But inside the small living-room it was comparatively quiet.

The harsh yellow light poured down on the faded covers of the chairs and sofas, the tortured carving of the overornate tables, the shabby Axminster carpet and the long row of dusty books and tattered magazines. And looking about her, Sarah was seized with the uncomfortable fancy that everything in the boat—each piece of furniture—was endowed with a peculiar life of its own, and was watching her with a curious, sly hostility. So must they have watched Janet. Janet scribbling her record with fear-stiffened fingers and repeated glances over her shoulder. Janet hiding it away somewhere on this small boat.

The room knew. The room was aware. The blank eyes of the window-panes blinked and brooded, reflecting a dozen Sarahs in lilac linen dresses. The cheap cotton curtains billowed faintly in the draught, and the bead curtain in the dining-room doorway swayed and clinked softly as though some unseen presence had just passed through it . . .

Outside the wind was rising, and as the boat began to rock to the gusts, Lager pattered restlessly about the room sniffing at the skirting-boards and the shadows of the chairs, and whining. Sarah spoke to him sharply, and having pulled the curtains to, snapped off the lights and marched deter-minedly to bed.

She turned off the dining-room lights as she passed through, but left the pantry light burning so that when she was settled in bed with Lager curled up at her feet, and switched off her bedroom light, she would still see its glow through her half-opened door. It gave her a vague feeling of reassur-ance, like a nightlight in a nursery, and she fell asleep lulled by the rocking of the boat and the wail of the wind through the branches of the big chenar tree. But some two hours later she awoke suddenly and sat bolt upright in bed. She had no idea what had awakened her: only that one moment she had been fathoms deep in dreamless slumber, and the next moment wide awake and with every sense tense and alert.

The threatened storm had skirted the lake and passed on down the valley towards the mountains of the Banihal Pass, but the boat still rocked and creaked at its moorings, and the water still slapped noisily against its sides. The wind was blowing in savage gusts, and in a brief lull between them Sarah could hear the scuffle of rats in the roof and the steady snoring of Lager, who had burrowed under the blankets. It was several minutes before she realized, with a sharp pang of alarm, that the pantry light was no longer burning and the entire boat was in darkness.

Stretching out a hand she groped for the curtains of the window near her bed and pulled them aside, but no moonlight crept in to lighten the little room, for the sky was covered with clouds and a light rain was falling on the uneven surface of the lake. Sarah felt for the switch of the bedside lamp and heard it click as it turned under her fingers, but the light did not come on and the room remained shrouded in darkness.

It's the storm, she thought. The wind must have torn down the wires or blown a branch of a tree across the line somewhere. There's nothing to be frightened of . . .

Then why was she frightened, and what had awakened her? Why was she sitting so rigidly upright in the darkness, listening intently for the repetition of a sound?

And then she heard it: and knew that this was the sound that had jerked her from sleep into tense wakefulness.

It came from the front part of the boat. From the dining-room, thought Sarah, trying to place it. She heard it quite clearly in a pause between the gusts of wind, despite the multitudinous noises of the night: a muffled scraping sound that was quite unmistakable. The sound made by one of the sliding houseboat windows being drawn stealthily back in its groove.

Sarah knew those windows. They were guarded by outer screens of wire flyproof mesh that also slid back into the thickness of the houseboat walls when opened. They had no bolts, but were fastened together on the inside by inadequate latches of the hook-and-eye persuasion. And as the frames, owing to warping and slapdash workmanship, hardly ever fitted quite accurately, it was a simple matter to slip a knife blade between them from the outside and lift the latch.

Somebody had just done that. Someone who was even now easing the stubborn ill-fitting frames apart, inch by inch.

Sarah sat rigid, her heart hammering; waiting for what she knew would be the next sound. Presently it came: a barely audible thud, followed by a slight extra vibration of the uneasy craft as someone stepped down through an opened window into the boat.

A scurry of wind drove the rain against the window-panes by her bed, and in the resulting rocking and creaks from the *Waterwitch* she could not pick out any further sound of footsteps.

If I just sit here, thought Sarah frantically, and don't move or make a sound, perhaps they won't come in here. Perhaps it's just someone after the spoons. If I keep still . . . But she could not do it. There was Janet—and Mrs Matthews. Why had she been so stupid and so stubborn as to sleep alone on this ill-omened boat? It was all very well to tell herself not to panic or do anything silly, because nothing really bad could happen to her. Look what had happened to them? No: she dared not sit still and wait. She must get away quickly. But she had forgotten Lager. If she got out of bed he would wake up and bark . . .

Of course! That was it—Lager. Lager would save her! He would race off into the darkness, barking defiance and create a diversion, for darkness would be no problem to him, and he could, when the occasion demanded it, make as much noise as a hurdy-gurdy. It might well be sufficient to frighten away the intruder—though on this wild night it would not wake the Creeds—and under cover of the noise Sarah herself would escape by the back of the boat and rouse the cookboat.

She leaned forward in the darkness and dug Lager out of his nest of blankets. He was warm and velvety and relaxed, and he continued to snore gently. But he did not wake. Sarah shook him and spoke urgently into his floppy ear in a tense whisper: *'Lager! Lager! Wake up. Rats, Lager!'*

But the dachsund puppy did not move. Sarah shook him violently. He's doped! she thought incredulously. He's eaten something. Where? When? And then she remembered how he had scuttled off into the shadows when she returned from the Creeds, and had reappeared licking his chops. He had eaten doped food. Food that had in all probability been put there for this special purpose . . .

A sudden fury of rage shook Sarah, temporarily submerging her panic, and clutching the unresisting Lager under one arm she slid to the floor and groped her way across the room.

For one wild moment she had considered opening the window and shouting. But she knew that the wind would tear the sound to tatters and it would only be a waste of breath. She would have to go through the empty second bedroom behind her and through the bathroom and out at the back of the boat, from where she could rouse the *mānji.* Or better still, feel her way along the narrow duckboards that ran along both sides of the boat, until she reached the gangplank by the pantry door, and go down it and along the bank to the Creeds.

The *Waterwitch* rocked to another sudden buffet of wind, and Sarah banged her head violently against the open door of her cupboard and dropped Lager. For a moment she clung to the edge of the cupboard door while a variety of coloured sparks shot through the darkness: she must have forgotten to latch it and the draught and the uneasy motion of the boat had combined to swing it open.

After a moment or two she stooped dizzily and groped about in the darkness. Lager still snored gently, and guided by the soft sound she gathered him up and made unsteadily for the spare bedroom door, moving this time with more caution.

It seemed a long way in the dark. The door was ajar—presumably the wind again—and Sarah passed through it. There was no gleam of light from the black night beyond the curtained window-panes, and the wind shrilled through the cracks in the houseboat and sent cold draughts along the floors. Once something touched her cheek and she started back, her heart in her mouth. But it was only a curtain billowing out on the draught.

She tried to remember how the room was furnished. A bed against the wall, and the door into the bathroom to the left of the bedstead; the dressing-table under one window. Was there a chest of drawers under the other? She could not remember, but once she touched the bed she would get her bearings.

Sarah moved forward an inch at a time, one hand held out before her. Where *had* the bed got to? And then suddenly her hand touched polished wood. But it was not the end of a bed. It must be the dressing table. No, it was too high for that and too smooth, and it had a carved edge. Surely there was no table in the spare bedroom that had a carved border to it?

She stood still, confused and uncertain, her head still aching and dizzy from its violent contact with the cupboard door. And as she stood there, she became aware of something else: a curious clicking sound somewhere near her. She could hear it between the blustering gusts of wind. *Click . . . clack . . . click . . .* Very softly, like someone telling beads. *Beads!* The garish bead curtain that hung in the open doorway between the dining-room and the living-room . . . That was it! . . . it was here, close beside her; swaying and clicking in the dark. And with a sudden, sickening shock of panic she realized what she was touching. It was the oval dining-table with deep, carved, chenar-leaf border.

She wasn't in the spare bedroom at all. She was in the dining-room! She must have lost her bearings when, confused by the blow on her head, she had stooped down to grope in the dark for Lager. And the curtain that had touched her cheek was blowing out from an open window; that was why this room was so much colder. There was a window standing open in it; which could only mean that the sound she had heard—the sound of a window being opened—had come from here.

She was in the wrong room. And in the same instant she realized that someone else was in the room with her.

Sarah stood frozen, not daring to move. Even her heart seemed to have stopped beating. She could hear no sound other than the noises of wind and water and the creaking of the boat as it rocked and strained at its moorings, but she did not need any sound to tell her that someone was there, close to her; almost within reach of her hand. Sheer animal instinct, that sixth sense which warns us of the near presence of one of our own kind, was sufficient . . .

I mustn't move, she thought frantically. I mustn't breathe . . . She felt the floorboards under the feet vibrate, and the air about her stirred as though something solid had passed her in the black dark.

There was a sudden lull between gusts of wind and in the brief silence Lager gave a loud snuffling snore.

She heard someone draw a hard breath in the darkness, and something —a hand—brushed against her bare arm.

Sarah dropped Lager, backed wildly away, and screamed at the top of her voice. And as she did so a light flashed on; the white glare of an electric torch, full in her face, and an incredulous voice said: 'For God's sake! Sarah!'

The next moment arms were about her holding her closely, and she was struggling frantically, still in the grip of terror. Her captor held her with one arm and with his free hand turned the torch onto his own face.

'Charles!'

13

Sarah burst into overwrought tears, and Charles, holding her, said: 'I'm sorry, Sarah. I didn't know there was anyone on board. Don't cry, dear. It's all right now. There's nothing to be frightened of now.'

No, there was nothing to be frightened of now. All at once Sarah knew that. The terrors and confusions and doubts that had haunted her since that white night in Gulmarg when she had awakened in the moonlight were over: Charles was here and she was safe. For a long moment she let herself relax against his shoulder, and then jerked away; aware of a sudden and entirely unfamiliar feeling of shyness.

'Here,' said Charles. 'Handkerchief.'

Sarah accepted it thankfully, blew her nose and sniffed childishly.

'Could we turn on the lights do you think?' said Charles. 'I'm not sure how much more life there is left in this battery.'

'There aren't any,' said Sarah unsteadily. 'I think the line must be down somewhere. But there are candles in the next room, if you've got any matches.'

'I've got a lighter. That'll do instead. Good Lord! What on earth's that?'

Charles retreated a swift step and flashed the beam of his torch onto the floor.

'It's Lager,' said Sarah, dropping onto her knees beside the limp velvet bundle: 'I'd forgotten him, poor lamb. I dropped him when you touched me. I was so scared.'

'What's the matter with him? Is he ill?'

'No. He's doped.' Sarah lifted wide startled eyes to Charles's face above her. 'Did you do it?' she asked sharply.

Charles went down on one knee and turned the puppy over. 'Do what? Dope him?'

'Yes,' said Sarah in a whisper.

'No. Why the hell should I want to?' said Charles impatiently. He turned back one of Lager's eyelids and studied the eye for a moment. 'Opium, I should say. He'll be all right.'

Sarah said in a shaky whisper: 'Someone did. If it wasn't you, then there's someone else who meant to get on this boat tonight.'

'What's that?' said Charles sharply. 'Look—it sounds to me as though something pretty tricky has been going on around here. This is no place to talk. Let's find these candles.'

Sarah got up holding Lager in her arms and they went into the living-room and lit two dusty, yellowed candle-ends that still remained in a pair of tarnished candlesticks of Benares brass. The flames flickered wanly for a moment or two in the draught and then steadied and burnt brighter, and the small room was once again just a room: overcrowded with furniture of a vanished era, shabby, over-ornate, uninteresting and uninterested; and remembering the vivid impression of tense and watchful awareness that it had given her earlier that night, Sarah wondered at herself.

She looked up to find Charles watching her with an unreadable expression in his eyes and the shadow of a smile about his mouth, and became abruptly conscious of the fact that she was wearing nothing but an exceedingly flimsy chiffon and lace nightdress: and in the next instant, with fury, that she was blushing.

'You look very nice,' said Charles pensively. 'All the same, I think you'd better put on something else or you'll catch cold. Besides,' he added thoughtfully, 'there are a lot of things I want to talk about, and I'd like to be able to keep my mind on the job.'

'Oh!' said Sarah breathlessly. 'Oh! You . . . you . . . Give me that torch!'

She thrust Lager into his arms, snatched the torch from his hand and fled. To return a few minutes later wearing a severely tailored dressing-gown of dark green silk that clothed her from throat to ankles, and with her bare feet thrust into small green morocco slippers. An observant spectator might have noticed that she had also found time to apply a discreet amount of lipstick and powder and to run a comb through her red-gold curls.

She found Captain Mallory lying on the sofa nursing Lager in his arms and blowing smoke rings at the ceiling. 'Please don't get up,' said Sarah frigidly, seating herself in the armchair opposite him. 'And now, if it's not too much to ask, you will please tell me what you were doing on my boat?'

'I didn't know it was yours,' said Charles, 'and I didn't know anyone was on board. So few of the houseboats have been taken this year that it seemed a safe bet that it was unoccupied.'

'Look,' said Sarah leaning forward, 'do you see any green in my eye?'

'Yes,' said Charles with disconcerting promptness: 'emeralds and peridots and jade, sprinkled with gold dust and steeped in dew. Perfectly lovely.'

Sarah flushed rosily and drew back with a jerk. 'Thank you. But what I wanted to point out was that though I may have green eyes, I'm not all *that* green. If you thought the boat was empty you'd never have come creeping into it in the small hours of the morning.'

Charles blew another smoke ring and regarded her meditatively over the tip of his cigarette before replying. He appeared to be turning something over in his mind. After a moment or two he apparently came to some decision, for he swung his heels off the sofa and sitting up spoke in a voice that was wholly free from flippancy: 'All right. I didn't think it was empty. I had been told that it was occupied by a "maiden lady". The description is my informant's, not mine. Her name was given as Harris. It rang no bell. I was further informed that she would be attending the dance at Nedou's Hotel tonight and would not be back until well after midnight. By the way, do you mind my smoking? I should have asked.'

'No,' said Sarah. 'Go on. Why were you on this boat?'

'I wanted to have a look at it, and at the same time I did not want to appear in any way interested in it. I decided that the task of scraping an acquaintance with a maiden lady called Miss Harris in order to take a look at her boat, might take more time than I had at my disposal. So I came along to give it the once-over unofficially. I was therefore surprised, to put it mildly, to find Miss Parrish not only in residence but remarkably vocal.'

Sarah said: 'That's not true either. Is it?'

'What makes you think so?'

'Because I don't believe that you're the kind of person who makes mistakes. Not when it really matters.'

'I appear to have made one this time,' said Charles dryly.

'No you didn't. You thought I'd be at the dance. So I should have been if Major McKay hadn't strained a muscle. And as the dance goes on until one o'clock tonight, and it takes nearly an hour to get back here by *shikara*, you knew you had plenty of time. You didn't expect to find anyone on this boat, but you knew I had taken it, didn't you?'

'Maybe,' said Charles non-committally, watching Sarah with half-closed eyes. 'Why do you think this is an occasion that really matters?'

'Because——' Sarah checked suddenly. 'No. Tell me first why you came here.'

Charles hesitated a moment, staring down at the glowing tip of his cigarette and frowning, and then he said slowly: 'I knew the girl who had this boat last year. Her name was Janet Rushton.'

Sarah drew a sharp breath and Charles looked up swiftly: 'You knew her too, didn't you. That letter you burnt on the lawn of the Peshawar Club was in Janet's writing. I was fairly sure of it. We checked back on you. You were in Gulmarg for the Spring Meeting. You had the room next to Janet's. You came up here and took over her boat, using the receipt signed by her. How about it, Sarah?'

Sarah did not answer. She sat quite still, her eyes meeting Charles's level, penetrating gaze while a minute ticked slowly by.

The wind blew another flurry of rain against the windowpanes and the candle flames swayed and flickered to the draughts, throwing leaping shadows onto the panelled walls and the intricately inlaid woodwork of the ceiling, and the houseboat jerked and rocked, creaking and groaning at its moorings.

Sarah spoke at last, and uncertainly: 'I don't understand. If you are— one of them—if you were keeping tabs on me . . . What *is* it all about, Charles?'

Charles transferred Lager to a sofa cushion, and coming to his feet took a restless turn about the small room, and came back to stand over Sarah, frowning down on her and fidgeting with his cigarette.

After a moment he said abruptly: 'I've no idea how much you know, but it's obviously a good deal more than is healthy for you. I think you'd better tell me. Everything please, right from the beginning and without leaving anything out.'

Sarah told him: sitting in the shabby armchair that Janet must have sat in, in the boat that had been Janet's boat, with the guttering light of the candles that Janet must have used throwing leaping shadows across her white face. And as she talked, it was as though she was reliving the incidents that she described: as though she saw again the lamplight glint along the barrel of Janet's automatic, and stared unbelievingly at a line of footprints in the blown snow on a moonlit verandah. Once again she seemed to hear Janet's voice in the shadow of the ski-hut on Khilanmarg, and to watch the flying shadow swoop across the snowfields and vanish into the darkness of the forest: once again to stare down across the shadowy bowl of Gulmarg at a far-off pinpoint of red light . . .

She told, her voice a dry whisper with the returning terror of that moment, of the thing that had followed upon Janet's departure—the sound of a door stealthily closing among the shadows under the snow-hung eaves of the ski-hut. Of the finding of Janet's body in the Blue Run, and her own visit to the house by the Gap. Every incident seemed etched so clearly in her mind that she could tell it all as though it had only happened yesterday. The tracks on that snow-covered pathway. The darkness and silence of the empty house. The faint odours that lingered in the cold rooms—

cigarette smoke, damp, cordite, and that other cloying, elusive scent that she could not place. She told him of the bullet hole and the stain upon the floor. Of the man in the snowstorm, and, finally, of the arrival of Janet's letter months later in Peshawar.

She told it all in meticulous detail up to the burning of Janet's letter, while Charles sat on the arm of the sofa and listened; his face expressionless and his eyes intent. And when she had finished she shivered convulsively, and gripping her hands tightly together in her lap to hide the fact that they were trembling, said: 'What's it all about, Charles? I don't understand, and I'm scared. Yes I am! I'm scared stiff. I wouldn't mind if I thought it was just some of the usual anti-British stuff . . . Indian terrorists. But it isn't. There was someone listening in the ski-hut. And then Reggie Craddock trying to get me off the boat, and someone who said he was from the agents, too. And this morning Mrs Warrender turned up with a story about a friend who wants to swop boats with me. What's it all about—? or am I going crazy?'

'Say that again?' said Charles sharply.

Sarah laughed on a high note. 'I said "Am I going crazy"?'

'No, I mean about Reggie Craddock and Helen Warrender. Let's hear about that: word for word, please.'

So once again Sarah took up the tale and repeated all she could remember . . .

The cigarette burnt out between Charles's fingers and he swore and flicked the smouldering fragment into the ashtray. 'Hell!' said Charles. 'This needs a lot of thinking out. Go to bed, Sarah. You've had enough alarms for one day. We'll defer any further explanation until the morning.'

Sarah's mouth set itself in a stubborn line and her green eyes sparkled in the wavering light of the candles.

'I am not budging,' said Sarah firmly, 'until you tell me what it's all about. I shouldn't sleep a wink, and you know it. It's no good trying to be discreet and hush-hush and Top Secret, because like it or not, I'm in this too. Up to my neck, as far as I can see! What's it all about, Charles?'

'If you mean Reggie Craddock and Co., I don't know. As for the rest, I can't tell you much more than Janet told you . . .' Charles stood up and began to pace the small expanse of faded Axminster carpet once more; his hands in his pockets and his frowning gaze upon the floor.

'A year ago,' began Charles slowly, 'one of our agents sent word that he was onto a big thing. He didn't even give a hint as to what it was, but he sent a–a signal. One that we only use very rarely, and which means that we are onto something white-hot and must be contacted with all possible speed.'

Sarah said: 'Janet told me that Mrs Matthews had sent for help last November. Before they even moved into Nedou's Hotel.'

'She had. And a Major Brett was sent off as soon as it was received. But——'

'Wasn't he the man who fell out of the train?' asked Sarah on a gasp.

Charles nodded, and turning away, resumed his pacing: 'But the first warning arrived last May. It came from Srinagar and had been sent by my best friend. We sent someone to contact him at Murree, but Pendrell never got there. The car he was travelling down in was involved in an accident on the way, and he was killed. It was a very well-staged accident.'

'Like–like that Indian who came up in December to meet Mrs Matthews,' whispered Sarah.

Charles glanced at her and nodded again. 'Ajit; yes. Mrs Matthews was sent up to take over after Pendrell died. There were a few lines to go on, but nothing very much; for though there were several of our people up here, they weren't in the same class as Mrs Matthews. Janet came up as a sort of Number Two to her, and we heard nothing more from either of them until we got that signal from Mrs Matthews towards the end of November. It meant that she had got the goods and to send someone at once.'

'I still don't see why she didn't go herself,' said Sarah frowning: 'Janet said they weren't allowed to, but——'

'They weren't. If Pendrell had sat tight he might be alive today; who knows? But he decided to leave Kashmir, and the move was fatal. He must have been suspect already, and when they heard he was leaving for 'Pindi they obviously decided to take no chances. They played safe and rubbed him out.'

'But Janet——? And you said there were others . . .'

'It's far easier to send a new agent who has nothing against him or her, to contact one "on the ground." Any move on the part of Mrs Matthews or Janet Rushton to leave Kashmir would perhaps have been construed as suspicious; supposing the other side were in any doubt about them. It was safer, in theory, to stay where they were—though unfortunately it didn't prove to be so in practice. And after Ajit and his car and his driver were swept over the edge of the road by a convenient avalanche, we realized that the chances were that Mrs Matthews and Janet had been spotted, and that there was a far more efficient team operating against us up here, and in northern India, than we had hoped.

'With Ajit dead, it was decided to use the Ski Club Meeting as protective colouring and send up a skier, ostensibly just another winter-sports addict, to contact one or other of those two women. The agent was to arrive after dark and the meeting would take place in great secrecy. After which he would stage a second, and public arrival, on the following day, and for the rest of the time avoid being seen speaking to either of the women except in the middle of a crowd.

'The meeting-place and the signal—that red light you saw—was worked out and sent to Mrs Matthews by catalogue. It was a risk of course, but after what had happened to Pendrell and Major Brett and Ajit, less of a risk than trying to send any plan by word of mouth. One or other of them, Janet or Mrs Matthews, were to have watched for that light every night after they arrived in Gulmarg: if it had been noticed by anyone else it would only have been taken to mean that the *chowkidar*—a watchman— was cooking a meal or sleeping the night in an empty hut. Having seen it, either Mrs Matthews or Janet would have visited the hut. They were both excellent skiers and it would have been a great deal easier than it sounds for one of them to have slipped out of the hotel in the small hours and skied over, and back again half an hour later, without being observed.'

'But suppose there was a storm or something, and they couldn't see it?' asked Sarah.

'If they didn't come the first night, the messenger was to remain two more nights. No longer.' Charles stopped in front of one of the candles and said irrelevantly: 'These things will burn out soon.' He stood staring down at the unsteady flame for so long that Sarah moved restlessly in her chair and said: 'Go on.'

Charles lifted his head with a jerk as though he had temporarily forgotten about her.

'That's about all,' he said curtly. 'You know the rest.'

'No I don't,' said Sarah, her voice barely above a whisper. 'What happened to the man? The messenger. They killed him too, didn't they?'

'There wasn't a messenger,' said Charles slowly. 'He was held up on the road and arrived too late.'

'But how . . . ?' Sarah found she could not complete the question.

'We don't know how they found out,' said Charles bleakly. 'About the hut and the signal I mean. But there's obviously been a bad leak somewhere, because the light was a trap, and Janet walked into it.'

'But somebody else *was* there. I've told you! I saw the bullet hole and— and there was blood on the floor.'

'I know,' said Charles. 'I saw it.'

'*You!*' Sarah's voice was a whisper.

'Yes,' Charles's eyes, watching her over the guttering candle flame, reflected small dancing glints of yellow light. 'You see I was the messenger. I was the man you bumped into in the snowstorm on the *marg.*'

'*Oh!*' said Sarah on an indrawn breath. 'I didn't know. I only knew that —' she stopped abruptly.

'Only knew what?' asked Charles curiously.

Sarah flushed and bit her lip. 'Nothing,' she said curtly. She did not intend to explain to Charles that the intense interest she had taken in him in Peshawar had sprung partly from a strange and persistent conviction that she had met him before.

Charles regarded her curiously for a moment but did not press the question. He sat down again on the sofa and pulling a thin gold cigarette-case from his pocket offered it to Sarah, and when she shook her head took another cigarette himself and lit it at one of the candles.

Sarah, studying his face as it bent above the wavering flame, was astonished at herself that she should not have instantly recognized him as the man of the snowstorm. How could she have forgotten the line of cheek and chin, even blurred as it had been by darkness and falling snow? The grey eyes, or the voice with its faint suggestion of a drawl and its unintentional but instinctive note of command, which could only belong to Charles?

Charles looked up suddenly and caught her intent gaze. His mouth curved in a shadow of a grin and he said: 'It was easier for me. You had red hair.'

Sarah blushed rosily and for no apparent reason, and to distract attention from the fact, said hastily: 'Tell me what happened. What did you do?'

'There wasn't much I could do,' said Charles soberly. 'It had been arranged that I should be among the later arrivals at the Meeting—there were several people who could only manage the last few days—so that I could leave with the rest of the crowd not too long after collecting the information. Just long enough to be seen to have no contact with Mrs Matthews and her supposed niece! But though the reasoning behind that decision was sound it turned out to be a mistake, because the weather was obviously batting for the opposition——

'A flash flood on the Kabul River meant that I took a full day to reach Rawalpindi, then just beyond Uri I found that the road was blocked by an avalanche that had brought any amount of rock and trees with it, and no motor traffic was likely to get through for three or four days. So I came on foot and skis, which was slow going and delayed me badly. I was met near Babamarishi by one of our men, a Kashmiri, who acted as a guide as far as the outskirts of Gulmarg and happened to mention, casually, that an elderly memsahib had been killed in a skiing accident. His version of her name was near enough for me to realize who it was. So I had that much warning, at least. But there was still Janet.

'I went on, keeping to a woodcutter's track through the forest that

Kadera had shown me, in order to keep out of sight as much as possible. I had a key to the hut, and I meant to lie up there until it was dark enough to light the signal lamp that was in my pack. I wasn't far short of the hut when I met a coolie who was employed by the hotel to collect and carry wood—he had a great load of it on his back and had stopped to rest, and he asked me for a cigarette. He too told me about the old memsahib who had died, and he said that the young Miss-sahib who had come up with her had been killed that very morning in a similar accident; which he attributed to evil spirits. That was how I learned about Janet . . .'

Charles was silent for a time, twisting the cigarette between his fingers and looking tired and grim. And at length he said: 'Since it seemed that they had both died on one of the ski runs there was no reason to suppose that anyone knew about the hut near the Gap, so I went there anyway. Because I badly needed somewhere to rest before tackling the long slog back to Babamarishi, and there was obviously no point in staying on in Gulmarg any longer, or in turning up officially as a latecomer to the Meeting. I meant to turn back and say I hadn't been able to make it because of the hold-up on the road, and that it hadn't been worth waiting for the way to be cleared. Which is what several other people did——

'It wasn't until I got to the hut and saw those tracks on the path and found that I didn't need my key because the door was open, that I realized that a fuse had blown somewhere—and at a very high level. *You* know what I found inside. It didn't take long to work out what had happened, or realize that whoever stage-managed those two "skiing accidents" also knew all about the hut and the signal. In fact there was only one thing I couldn't understand.'

He paused for a moment, frowning, and Sarah said: 'Why they didn't lay for you too?'

Charles nodded. 'Yes. If they knew so much, why didn't they wait for me? They obviously knew that another contact was coming and what he was going to do; though it's doubtful if they knew his identity, because any one of a dozen people might have been detailed for the job. Well, why not wait until I arrived and gave the signal, knock me off, and then wait until Janet arrived and do the same by her?'

'Perhaps they had meant to do that,' said Sarah, 'and then something happened to hurry them up?'

'The storm,' said Charles. 'I came to the conclusion it must have been that. They probably waited in the hut for me for a night or two, and then realized that there was a storm brewing.'

'Bulaki said so,' interrupted Sarah in a half whisper.

'What's that?'

'My bearer. He told me on the morning we left for the Khilanmarg ski-hut that there was bad weather coming.'

'That would be it,' said Charles. 'If they waited any longer for the contact to show up they might hit bad weather and be unable to use the signal: so they decided to get Janet. After all, she was the main objective. Once she was dead it didn't really matter how many messengers came up to the hut. It's some consolation to realize that she must have got one of them. She carried a gun, and I'm prepared to bet a good deal that the bullet that made that hole came from it.'

Sarah said: 'Were you in that house when I came into it?'

'I don't think so. I must have missed you by a pretty narrow margin. I don't mind telling you that I didn't stay long! I saw everything I needed to see, and then I went up through the trees at the back and did a recce to see if I could find the body of the man who was shot in the sitting-room. There were tracks running slantways up the hill, and I followed them for a while; but I didn't like the look of the weather, so I came back, and I only noticed then that there was a broken latch on a side door. I went in by it to see if I'd missed anything, but there was nothing there but a pile of dusty furniture, and as I saw that it had started to snow I chucked my hand in and came away. I cut across the back garden and came down parallel to the path and onto the *marg*, and I hadn't gone far when I hit into you. Gave me a considerable jar, I assure you.'

Sarah laughed a little shakily. 'Not half as bad a shock as it gave me! So it was you I heard in the hut.' She sat silent for a moment and then said, 'Then—there is nobody who knows.'

'Knows what?'

'The—the "Big Thing" you talked about. The thing your friend found out—and Janet and Mrs Matthews too. Now that they are dead, does no one else know?'

'No one human,' said Charles slowly.

'What do you mean,' asked Sarah sharply.

'There is still something that knows. This boat knows.'

In the little silence that followed upon his words a candle flame flared and went out, sending up a thread of evil-smelling smoke into the deepening shadows of the room.

The draught whined along the floor and lifted the worn carpet in uneasy ripples as the boat lurched to a wilder gust of wind, and once again, as earlier on that same night, Sarah became aware of the inanimate objects that furnished the small room. Once again they seemed to her imagination to become endowed with a sentient personality, a mysterious entity of their own, so that even with her eyes held by Charles's steady gaze, she could still see them. The carved tables, the shabby chintz-covered chairs, the cheap brass trays and the rows of dusty books upon the shelf. All those things that had watched Mrs Matthews: that had watched Janet, and were now watching her, Sarah Parrish . . .

'Yes,' said Sarah in a dry whisper. 'Yes, the boat knows.'

A savage gust of wind raged across the lake, accompanied by driving rain, and shook the little houseboat as a terrier shakes a rat. The tables and chairs jerked and shifted and the candlestick that bore the last remaining candle toppled onto the floor, plunging the room into darkness.

Then, as suddenly as it had come, the wind died away. One moment the night was riotous with sound, and the next it was quiet save for the slap and splash of water against the sides of the boat, the whisper of light rain falling on leaves and lake water, and a faint mutter of far-off thunder.

Silence seemed to flow into the valley, smoothing out the turmoil of the storm as oil smooths out rough water. And in that silence, though there was no sound of footsteps, the boat jerked suddenly to a different rhythm as someone trod quietly up the gangplank and scratched very softly on the pantry door . . .

14

Sarah's terrified gasp was loud in the silence, and Charles switched on his torch, and throwing an arm about her shoulders felt the tension of her accumulated fear as vividly as though he had touched something charged with static electricity.

He said quickly: 'Don't, dear! It's only Habib. I'm sorry—I ought to have warned you. But what with one thing and another, I forgot. I put him off on the bank and told him to keep an eye on the approaches, and to come aboard if anything worried him. I left the boat outside the dining-room window.'

'Who—who's Habib?' quavered Sarah, struggling to collect herself.

Charles released her, and stooping to pick up the fallen candlestick, replaced it on the desk before replying.

'Officially, my bearer-cum-driver,' said Charles, relighting the candle with the flame of his cigarette-lighter: 'Actually, an invaluable assistant. I'd better go and see what's up.' He walked to the doorway, and then turned and came back again.

'Can you use a gun, Sarah?'

'I . . . I think so. But——'

Charles drew out a small black Colt automatic barely larger than a cigarette-case and tossed it into her lap. 'Be careful of it. It's loaded. I'm going out to talk to Habib and do a bit of reconnoitring, and if anyone you don't know comes onto this boat before I get back, don't wait to ask questions. Shoot first and argue afterwards! I won't be long——'

Without giving Sarah a chance to protest, he turned and vanished into the darkness of the dining-room, and a moment later she heard the sound of the pantry door being eased open in its groove, and then the boat vibrated again to noiseless footsteps descending the gangplank.

Sarah sat tense and still, straining her ears to listen in the stillness, and fighting a frantic desire to follow him and run screaming down the bank to take refuge with the Creeds. But between the prow of her own boat and theirs lay almost thirty yards of wet darkness, bounded by reeds and scrub willow: and Charles had taken the torch. Her fingers tightened round the tiny gun, and the feel of the cold metal steadied her; but she was still sitting tensely on the extreme edge of the sofa, listening, when Charles returned some fifteen minutes later. The candle had guttered out, and the entire houseboat was in darkness.

This time Charles came from the shore and up the gangplank, and Sarah collapsed onto the sofa cushions with a sob of relief at the sound of his voice. He spent some time moving about in the pantry, from where she could see the reflected gleam of his torch, and presently he came into the room carrying a lighted hurricane lamp that he had found in one of the cupboards. It flared abominably and the oil smelt, but Sarah was grateful for any form of illumination.

'Well?' she inquired, trying to make her voice sound cool and casual: 'What was worrying him?'

'Habib? Nothing much,' said Charles shaking the wet out of his hair. His clothes were patched with damp and leaf mould and his shoes were caked with wet earth. 'Your electric line is down: he tripped over the end of it on the bank, and was afraid that it might have been cut on purpose. Which would have proved that someone other than myself had designs on this boat tonight. However, we managed to trace the other end without drawing attention to ourselves by showing a light, and it was obviously brought down by the wind.'

He broke off to fiddle with the wick of the hurricane lamp that was flaring lopsidedly and darkening the glass with smoke, and poking at the wick with a matchstick, observed in an abstracted voice that judging from the ease with which he had been able to break into her boat earlier in the evening, he suggested that she fit the door and windows with some strong bolts tomorrow. If, of course, she intended to stay on it.

There was the faintest suggestion of a query in those last words, and Sarah replied shortly that she had every intention of doing so. But though the words were brave enough, the effect was somewhat marred by the fact that she had been unable to bring them out without her teeth chattering. Because even as she spoke she wondered what would have happened to her, and if she would still have been alive, if it had been someone other than Charles who had forced the latch of the dining-room window that night?

Staring at him with dilated eyes, she said in a harsh whisper, and as though the words were forced out of her: 'I'm afraid. Charles, I'm afraid.'

Charles knelt swiftly, and catching her cold hands held them tightly against him. His own were warm and steady and very reassuring, and he smiled at Sarah; a smile that did not quite reach his eyes.

'No, you're not. Brace up, Sarah darling!'

'It's easy for you—' began Sarah on a sob.

'That's where you're wrong,' interrupted Charles roughly: 'It's damnably difficult for me!'

He dropped her hands, and standing up abruptly returned to the dining-room where Sarah, following him, found him hunting in the cupboard under the sideboard with the aid of the torch. 'Don't you keep anything to drink on this boat except orange squash and soda water?' demanded Charles irritably.

'There's brandy in the corner cupboard.'

'Thank God for that! We could both do with some.' He splashed a generous amount into a glass and held it out. 'Drink that up and you'll feel better.'

'No thanks.' said Sarah distantly.

'Don't be so missish,' advised Charles with a suggestion of a snap.

'I'm not. I just don't like brandy!'

'Who asked you if you liked it? Just drink it up, there's a good girl. We still have a lot of the night before us!'

He pushed the glass across the table and grinned unexpectedly. 'You needn't worry,' he assured her. 'I fully realize that I am alone on this boat with you, and that it is long past midnight. In fact not one of the charms of yourself or the situation has escaped me. But I'm not trying to make you drunk.'

Sarah glared at him furiously and instantly drained the glass, and Charles reached out and patting her shoulder approvingly said: 'Good girl.'

'I believe you said that on purpose,' accused Sarah, thinking it over, 'just to make me mad enough to drink the stuff. Did you?'

'Well, it worked anyway,' said Charles equably. He poured a strong peg for himself and taking Sarah by the elbow returned to the living-room.

'And now let's get back to business,' said Charles, ensconcing her on the sofa with Lager on her lap. 'First of all, what was in that letter of Janet's that you burnt? The sooner we get that clear the better. Try and remember it word for word.'

Sarah told him, knitting her brows in an endeavour to remember the exact wording, and Charles said 'Hmm,' now I wonder why on earth she didn't——Oh well, she didn't, and that's that. At least we know that she hid something on this boat. The trouble is that several other people appear to know it too. Or so it would seem. But how?—and why? Did you tell anyone else about that letter?'

'No.'

'Could anyone else have seen it at any time? Did the envelope look as if it had been tampered with when you opened it?'

'N–o,' said Sarah doubtfully. 'I don't think so. You see, I didn't think of looking for anything like that. I came back to the house that day—it was the evening of Aunt Alice's party for the Blue Cross Ball—and I was late back and there was a big mail in. I read all the home letters first, and I hadn't time to read this one. It looked dull, so I put it into my bag to read later.'

'How long had it been on the hall table?' asked Charles.

'I don't know. Two or three hours, maybe? I had been out since about three o'clock and I didn't get back until past seven.'

'Then anyone could have seen it there and steamed it open and read it and put it back again?'

'Of course not!' said Sarah indignantly. 'Only someone in the house; and as we were all out watching polo that afternoon, there would only have been the servants, and none of them would read or write English. Anyway, what would have been the point? If anyone had wanted to see it, it would surely have been simpler just to steal it and be done with it? Then I should never have known about it.'

'Oh well,' said Charles. 'Let it go. What then? Did you leave your bag about anywhere?'

'No. You see it was one of those bags that are meant to go with a certain dress. It had grey roses on it and hung on a band round my wrist. The only time it was out of my hands was during dinner, and then it was hung on the back of my chair. You were there. You could have touched it. No one else.'

'Yes,' said Charles slowly. 'That's true. To think I had the damned thing not six inches from my hand for nearly an hour on end! If I'd only known ——Well, go on.'

'I didn't open the letter until halfway through the dance, and as I didn't know what was in it I didn't think of looking to see if the envelope had been tampered with. Anyway, there wasn't very much light. Only those paper lanterns. And then Helen Warrender interrupted and—well you know what happened after that. You were there. You——'

Sarah was struck by a sudden thought, and sitting upright with a jerk that almost dislodged the comatose Lager from her lap, she stared accusingly at Charles: 'Was that why?' she demanded.

'Was what why?'

'You know! Did you come to the party because of me? Was that why you seemed to be around so much and yet never——' She stopped and bit her lip.

Charles's lips twitched, but his voice was perfectly grave: 'But of course,' he said. 'How could I keep away?'

Sarah flushed pinkly. 'I didn't mean that,' she said with some heat. 'You know quite well what I meant! I mean was it because I had known Janet? Were you only keeping tabs on me?'

'Yes,' admitted Charles frankly. 'I was—interested.'

Sarah laughed. It was, despite herself, a somewhat bitter little laugh. 'And I thought—' she said, and stopped again.

'Did you?' asked Charles softly. He watched the smoke from his cigarette spiral slowly upwards for a moment or two; then: 'But you see Sarah, you might have been the one.'

'What one? What do you mean?'

'The one who killed Janet.'

Sarah's gasp of rage made a soft explosive sound in the quiet room and she struggled for words: 'You–you–you think that I—you thought that I——'

'All right,' said Charles calmly. 'I'll take it as read.'

'Do you really think—' began Sarah.

'No,' said Charles, as one giving the matter his consideration: 'I don't. Not now. But it was perfectly possible. It has also been said—and proved with regrettable frequency—that most female criminals are also good actresses. You knew Janet and Mrs Matthews. Your fingerprints were on the brass poker in Janet's room, and I met you in that snowstorm not a hundred yards from the hut by the Gap. You had to be watched.'

'And you watched me,' said Sarah tartly.

'Among others, yes,' admitted Charles with a grin. 'And as luck would have it, I happened to be present when you opened Janet's letter. I even had to watch you burn it—and with my own lighter!—when every instinct was urging me to reach out and grab it.'

'Then why didn't you?' demanded Sarah. 'Oh! . . . Oh, I think I see. If I *had* been the one, then . . . yes, I see. Very difficult for you.'

'Damnably,' admitted Charles cheerfully. 'Still, even if I didn't know what was in that note, I knew where it had come from, and could check up on it to a certain extent.'

'How did you know that?' asked Sarah sharply. 'Did you know her so very well?'

'Who? Janet? No. Hardly at all.'

'Then you are asking me to believe that you could recognize her handwriting from just that glimpse? The letter wasn't signed and I held it so that it couldn't be read.'

For answer Charles drew out a leather pocket-book from his breast-pocket, and after hunting through it, extracted a small sheet of folded paper that he tossed onto Sarah's lap.

Sarah jerked it open and stared at it incredulously. It was the covering note from the firm of lawyers in Rawalpindi that had accompanied Janet's sealed envelope.

She looked up at Charles and discovered that he was watching her with the same curious intentness that she had observed before, and she said a little unsteadily: 'I–I don't understand. How–how did you——?'

'How did I get that letter? I picked it up off the lawn. You'd forgotten it.'

'But I couldn't . . . I would have noticed . . .'

'No you wouldn't. You see you gave me an excellent piece of advice— have you forgotten? When you knocked that whisky and soda all over poor Helen Warrender you said that there was nothing like a good shock for putting things out of people's minds. You then very obligingly presented me with an opening, and I provided the shock. Remember?'

A slow wave of colour, starting at the base of her throat, mounted to the roots of Sarah's hair, and she stood up, dropping Lager in a velvet heap onto the floor. *'Oh!'* breathed Sarah stormily. 'You–you——'

'Go on,' urged Charles. 'Let's have it. What about "You cad, sir!"?'

Sarah sat down again abruptly, and Charles laughed.

'It's no use, Sarah darling. All's fair in love and war, you know. And it worked. It worked like a charm! You swept off like an insulted Archduchess, entirely forgetting that letter, which had fallen onto the grass and which I had carefully edged under your chair. What's more, the shock was apparently sufficient to keep you from realizing you'd lost it right up to this very minute. And—if it's any consolation to you—I enjoyed it very much, thank you.'

'I think,' said Sarah with dignity, 'you are the most insufferable man I ever met.'

'And you,' said Charles, 'are without any doubt at all, the most attractive and infuriating woman I have yet encountered in the course of a long and varied experience of crime.'

A dimple appeared unexpectedly in Sarah's cheek and she collapsed into a sudden fit of slightly hysterical mirth.

'Oh dear! I am sorry. But I suddenly thought of "Olga-Poloffski-the-Beautiful-Spy" and all those. Is it really true, do you suppose? I mean, do you meet dozens of ravishing female spies?'

'You'd be surprised,' said Charles. 'And now let us abandon these fascinating personalities and get back to business. How long have you been on this boat?'

'Five days,' said Sarah promptly.

'Found anything yet?'

'No. I've made a start though. I looked in all the obvious places first of course, and then I thought it was probably in one of those wretched books up there. I've been through about half of them, but it's a tough assignment; specially when you don't know what you're looking for.'

'Well now you'll have me to help you. A "record" she said?'

'That's it. There were some old gramophone records in the bottom drawer of that desk. I thought at first she'd used the word literally, so I had them out and played them over on the Club radiogram. But they were just tunes; and cracked at that.'

'A *record*,' said Charles thoughtfully. 'Might be anything. Scratched on a window-pane, written on the underside of a floorboard. Hidden behind one of those fiddling little bits of wood on the ceiling. Hell! It isn't going to be easy. But we've got to get it even if it means taking this boat apart plank by plank. And the sooner we find it the better, for it seems to me that too many people are interested in this boat.'

'That reminds me,' said Sarah slowly. 'You never answered a question of mine. If you were keeping tabs on me, how was it that you didn't know I was on this boat?'

'I did,' said Charles. 'But as you surmised, I was assured that you would be at the Nedou's dance. A nasty accident of the usual sort overtook one of our local agents, and the understudy wasn't as efficient as he might have been.'

'Accident? You mean—*murder?*' Her voice cracked oddly on the word.

'It isn't so unusual, you know,' said Charles gently.

'Yes, I know,' said Sarah with a little catch of her breath. 'I saw it happen to Janet. I didn't believe it, but I saw it happen.' Her fingers twisted together in her lap and she said jerkily: 'Charles, why is it only now that I've taken the boat that so many people want it? After all it's been empty for months. Why do they want it now?'

'Ah, that's the question,' said Charles. 'I'd like to know the answer to that one myself. The way I see it is that our lot aren't the only people who linked you up with Janet Rushton. The chances are that someone else, or possibly several people, have been keeping a watchful eye on you as well— just in case. You can also bet your bottom dollar that this boat was searched pretty thoroughly after Janet died, if not before.'

'Then if you think that, what's the use of our searching it? The record was probably found weeks ago!'

'Use your head, Sarah,' urged Charles. 'If it had been found, no one would have taken any further interest in the boat. Whereas quite a surprising amount of people are taking an active interest in it. So it stands to reason it wasn't found.'

'But I don't see——'

'Listen,' said Charles patiently: 'Janet lived in this boat, and paid a cash deposit on it, reserving it up to the end of June this year with the proviso that should she be unable to make use of the boat herself, whoever held the receipt for the money could do so instead. That clear?'

'Quite, but——'

'*Ssh!* Janet dies, and you can be sure that this boat was searched from top to bottom. Not because they had any idea that she had hidden anything in it, but just to be on the safe side. Nothing is found and the boat ceases to be of any interest. Then, suddenly, a Miss Parrish, who had been present at the January Meeting of the Ski Club, occupied the room next to Janet Rushton's and been seen talking to her in the moonlight outside the ski-hut (you say there was someone watching), and is therefore, in all probability, an object of suspicion, receives a mysterious letter.'

'But no one could *possibly* have known about that!' objected Sarah.

'Don't interrupt. On receipt of this letter she suddenly changes her plans, and instead of going to Ceylon, decides to return to Kashmir. Now I don't suppose that anyone else got onto that letter of Janet's. We did—through you! But I admit I think it's unlikely that anyone else did. *But*—Miss Parrish, still almost certainly under surveillance, arrives in Kashmir *and produces the receipt for Janet Rushton's boat.* Now do you see?'

'I suppose so,' said Sarah slowly.

'There's no "suppose" about it. Why has Miss Parrish decided to come to Kashmir? And where did she get the receipt for the *Waterwitch?* Obviously, from Janet Rushton. The *Waterwitch* immediately becomes worth watching again—and so does Miss Parrish!'

'But if, as you think, they have already searched the boat—' began Sarah.

'Of course they've searched it. But that doesn't mean they feel any easier about letting someone whom they have every reason to be suspicious of do a bit of independent searching. Because you *have* been searching; and I bet you any money you like, your *mānji* has reported to that effect. In fact the whole set-up is probably causing a lot of uneasy speculation. Why are you here? How did you get hold of Janet's receipt for the *Waterwitch,* and what are you looking for? The sooner they get you off the boat the better.'

'Of course,' said Sarah slowly, 'there's another thing. I might even find it for them.'

Charles gave her a curious slanting look and said softly: 'That, I should imagine, is pretty well at the top of their list. For all they know you may have been told where to look. If so, and supposing they can't shift you off the boat, and next best thing is to keep tabs on you and let you do the finding. Should you turn up anything——' Charles broke off and frowned.

'Go on,' said Sarah. 'And should I turn up anything?'

'Oh well,' said Charles lightly. 'I imagine they'd find it fairly simple to steal if off you. They'd have saved themselves a hell of a lot of brainwork, and pinching the solution off you would be child's play.'

'That isn't what you were going to say,' pointed out Sarah.

Charles stood up suddenly and walked restlessly across the small room, his hands in his pockets. Then he turned and came back to Sarah and stood in front of her, frowning down at her.

'I've changed my mind,' said Charles shortly. 'The sooner you get off this boat and out of this country the better. You can pack up and move into Nedou's Hotel tomorrow morning, and we can get a car to take you down the hill the next day.'

Sarah smiled disarmingly at him. 'Suppose I don't want to go?'

'You'll do as you're told,' said Charles curtly. 'As long as you are here you are a nuisance and a liability.'

'Oh no, I'm not,' corrected Sarah firmly. 'That's where you're wrong. As long as I'm here there is just a chance that I may be merely a simple-minded tourist after all, who has got mixed up in this entirely by mistake and doesn't know a thing. And who quite possibly *bought* the receipt off this Miss Rushton, at that! For all they know, Janet may have decided she didn't want the boat, and seen a chance of getting her money back by selling it to someone who wasn't likely to know that houseboat rents would fall considerably this season. Don't you see? They can't be sure.'

'That's not the point,' said Charles roughly.

'Yes it is. And there's another thing. If I go, this boat goes to the next applicant on what seems to be a nice long list.'

'No it wouldn't. I should take it on.'

'And become a marked man at once? You've said yourself that once anyone in your job becomes suspect his usefulness is reduced to a minimum. That's right, isn't it?'

'Yes, but——'

'No, it's my turn to hold the floor. I'm not going! It isn't because I don't know exactly what you were going to say just now when you pulled yourself up. You were going to say that if and when I find anything, I should go the same way as Janet.'

'Exactly!' agreed Charles grimly. 'In fact the chances of your being allowed to survive any discovery on this boat are nil. That's why I'm packing you off to Ceylon tomorrow.'

'Charles—wait a minute. All this that you're working on, it's very important, isn't it?'

'Very.'

'How important? Is it only going to affect one or two people or hundreds of people—or what?'

'I don't know,' said Charles slowly. 'That's the hell of it. We simply do not know yet. But it could be millions.'

'Well then, do you think you've got any right to take chances with something like that? Suppose they *are* suspicious of me? It doesn't really matter, because they can't be quite sure. As long as I'm on the boat you stand a better chance of keeping other people off it, and unless it can be proved that I'm up to my neck in this, I doubt their doing anything very drastic just now. Can't you see that?'

'Maybe you're right,' said Charles thoughtfully. He stood still, his hands deep in his pockets, staring down at the faded carpet, and presently he jerked his shoulders uncomfortably and said: 'All right, you win. But with conditions.'

Sarah said: 'It depends on the conditions.'

Charles ignored the remark. 'First of all,' he said, 'you will carry a gun with you always, and use it without hesitation in a crisis. If you shoot some innocent citizen by mistake, I'll get you out of it. But as I've said once already this evening, the golden rule in the present situation is shoot first and argue afterwards. I'll give you a heavier gun. That one hasn't much stopping power. Next, you will get a set of bolts and fix them to every available door and window. You can do that, can't you?'

Sarah nodded.

'Finally,' said Charles, 'you will go nowhere by yourself. Always keep in company when you leave the boat. Is that clear?'

'As pea soup,' said Sarah flippantly. 'All right. I'll do it. But where do we go from there?'

'We take this boat to bits if necessary,' said Charles. 'And as we haven't any time to lose, we may as well get on with it now. Sleepy?'

'At the moment,' confessed Sarah, 'I don't feel as if I shall ever be able to sleep again.'

'Good,' approved Charles callously. 'In that case let's get on with it. How far did you get with the books and what were you looking for?'

'A loose sheet of paper or else pages marked so that you could read off a code. That was all I could think of!'

'And not a bad idea either. Oh well, let's get to work.'

They settled themselves on the floor, surrounded by stacks of novels, and proceeded to go through each one methodically; looking down the spine of each book and investigating the thickness of each cover with a penknife. The night was at last both quiet and still, and although they could occasionally hear a far-off growl of thunder no breath of wind returned to disturb the lake, and the houseboat lay motionless at her moorings in a silence broken only by an occasional soft arpeggio of plops as a frog skittered across the water from one lily-pad to the next, the splash of a leaping fish or the cheep of a sleepy bird from the branch of the big chenar tree.

They worked methodically, stacking each book to one side as they finished with it, and reaching for the next. Hour after hour seemed to slip by, and Sarah's back began to ache and one of her feet had gone to sleep. She began to listen for sounds on the bank outside and to start nervously at each tiny night noise.

Charles, who had apparently never once glanced in her direction, appeared to be aware of the state of her nerves, for now he looked up from his work and smiled at her.

'It's all right,' he said, 'I told you no one would come back tonight. I think we've done enough for the moment. Let's put this lot back. Sorted on the right-hand shelves, unsorted on the left. OK?'

He stood up, and reaching down a hand pulled Sarah to her feet.

'Ouch!' said Sarah, collapsing on the sofa and massaging her left foot to restore the circulation while Charles replaced and stacked the long line of books. 'As a matter of fact,' she said defensively to Charles's back, 'I wasn't thinking of anyone trying to come on board—not with that man of yours on the bank. But suppose someone was watching from much further off? After all, they'd be able to see that a light was burning in this room, even though the curtains are drawn.'

'You forget,' said Charles with a grin, 'that you are a nervous spinster living alone. You would be more than likely to have a lamp lit in reserve on a night like this. In fact I bet you left one on when you went to bed, didn't you?'

'Well, yes. The pantry one,' confessed Sarah a little shamefacedly.

'I thought as much. You'd have to be an exceptionally strong-minded woman not to. No, I don't think you need worry about a light in this room being suspicious. And if your boat should happen to attract any more visitors tonight, Habib will deal with that.'

'How much does he know?' asked Sarah curiously. 'About all this, I mean?'

'Enough to be going on with,' said Charles noncommittally. 'No one knows much more than that—except for one, or possibly two men at the top.'

'Janet said something like that,' mused Sarah. 'She said that she and Mrs Matthews were only links in a chain . . .'

'Mrs Matthews was a little more than a link,' said Charles. 'But Janet was right. Too much knowledge too widely spread can be very dangerous. That's been proved over and over again: this particular business being a case in point! Somewhere along the line someone has either been bribed, blackmailed or tortured into telling what they know. We've got a reasonable number of people, like the man who met me in Babamarishi, up here in Kashmir: all of them working on their own particular line, and by no means all of them knowing each other. They are the real nuts and bolts of the whole system; but not the spark or the petrol. And, unfortunately, not at a level to be handed the kind of information that Mrs Matthews and Janet Rushton seem to have stumbled upon—which was their bad luck.'

He was silent for a time, staring unseeingly at the flame of the oil lamp that etched harsh lines and hollows in his face, and presently Sarah said: 'Charles——'

'Yes?'

'Who are *"they"*—the ones you call the "opposition"? The people who killed Janet and Mrs Matthews and–and all the others? I asked Janet that, but she wouldn't tell. So I supposed that they were the usual Freedom Fighters—the "Quit India!" lot. But now that we're quitting anyway, and they know they've won, I can't see that there would be any point in that.'

'There isn't.'

'Then who?'

'Work it out for yourself,' said Charles unhelpfully.

'That's no answer and you know it. You can't fob me off like that now— not after scaring me nearly out of my mind tonight; let alone in Gulmarg! Is it politics, revolution, mutiny, drug-smuggling, or what? You say "nobody knows". But you must have *some* idea.'

Charles sat down on the arm of the sofa, and said slowly: 'Yes. We have an idea. You see Sarah, every country in the world has an Intelligence Service—a Secret Service, if you prefer to call it that. Here in India it's often kept busy with what Kipling called "The Great Game". That game runs from beyond the Khyber to the frontier of Assam, and further. We have to keep an ear to the ground all over India, because a whisper heard in a bazaar in Sikkim may touch off a riot in Bengal. We have to keep eyes and ears in every town and village——

'Well, something very queer has been happening in India during the last year or so. Something beyond the usual underground stuff. There have been, for instance, a phenomenal number of burglaries. Not just the usual line in theft, but really big money. Carefully planned robberies of State

Jewels worth millions. Things like the Charkrale rubies and the Rajgore emeralds, that are almost beyond price. Some of these jewels have turned up in surprising places, but we have discovered that for some reason most if not all of them have passed into or through Kashmir. This State has been a sort of collecting house—a pool.'

Sarah said: 'I remember about the emeralds. I mean, that was why you were playing polo the day that—' she stopped suddenly, and Charles looked at her curiously. 'Those emeralds,' he said after a pause, 'are here in Kashmir.'

'How do you know?' asked Sarah, startled. 'Have you got them?'

'No. But we know they are here. We thought we had taken every possible precaution against them getting over this border, but someone's been too clever for us. They are here.'

'But what for?' asked Sarah.

'Well, in the first place, for re-cutting. A great many of the stones have been re-cut here, in grubby little jeweller's shops poked away among the back streets of the city. But the best of the stuff has gone out across the passes by Gilgit and over the Pamirs.'

'Where to?'

Charles looked at her slantingly under his lashes. 'Your guess is as good as mine,' he said dryly: 'I told you to work it out for yourself.'

'But—but they're our *allies!*' protested Sarah, horrified.

'They are no one's allies. They never have been . . . Except just for as long as it happens to suit their own book, and not one second longer! They will even ally themselves—and will continue to ally themselves—with the most blatantly fascist, reactionary and brutal regimes, solely to serve their own interests—and no one else's! There are a lot of things that the people of other nations will stick at doing because of that outmoded idea, "moral principles"; but they will stick at nothing, and their goal is always the same. Themselves on top; and everyone else either kneeling, or if they won't kneel, flat on their backs or their faces and very dead!'

'But the money—those jewels . . . I don't understand why . . . Do you mean it could be needed for starting something against us—another mutiny?'

Charles laughed; and then sobered suddenly. 'No. It's not that. As you've just told me yourself, there wouldn't be any point in starting one now that the British are quitting India.'

'Then why should you worry about it? Surely it's no longer your affair when you're clearing out?'

'Because the world has shrunk, Sarah. It's shrinking every day. It is no longer a matter of indifference to people in South America when a Balkan

State blows up. Whatever is going on here is something that may affect us all, and we've got to find out what it is. We've *got* to!'

Sarah said: 'Is that why Mrs Matthews came up here? Because of the money, and the jewels and all that?'

'Yes. Because every single lead we followed seemed to end up in Kashmir. We thought at first it was merely theft on a big scale and nothing more; but it had to be stopped. We put a lot of people onto it, but they were mostly small fry. Pendrell was a fairly big fish, and he got onto it. And he died. So we sent along another of the same—equally good—Mrs Matthews; and they got her as well. Two people have sent us the Top Secret signal, the one we only use for something white hot. Something's brewing all right, Sarah. Something black and damnable. And we've got to get onto it and scotch it before we quit this country, because after that——'

'The deluge,' finished Sarah.

'Perhaps. In the meantime, as I've already said, your guess is as good as mine. How many more of these beastly books have we got left to go through?'

'About forty,' said Sarah with a sigh. 'I'll do them tomorrow. *Ouch!*'

'What's the matter?'

'Pins and needles again. I've rubbed them out of one foot, but I've been sitting on the other and now that's died on me too.'

Charles went down on his knees, and pulling off the small green slippers, rubbed the circulation back into Sarah's numbed feet.

'Isn't it lucky that I have such nice ones?' mused Sarah complacently.

Charles looked up and laughed. 'Frankly, no,' he said. 'At the moment I should prefer it if they were the usual twentieth-century bunch of radishes that one sees so often on the bathing boats.'

'Why?' inquired Sarah curiously.

'Because they are distracting my attention. And also because I should feel distinctly better if I could find something about you that I didn't like.'

'Oh,' said Sarah in a small voice. Charles replaced her slippers and stood up, brushing his knees.

'Would it be any help,' suggested Sarah meekly, 'if I told you that I snored?'

'Do you?'

'I don't know.'

'I'll think about it,' said Charles gravely, '—and take the first opportunity of finding out. Thanks for the suggestion.'

'Don't mention it,' said Sarah primly. 'I am always happy to oblige any gentleman with whom I pass the night.'

'Good Lord!' said Charles, 'it's morning!'

'I was wondering when you were going to notice it.'

Sarah went to the window and drew back the curtain. Outside, the lake and the mountains were no longer black but grey, and to the east the sky was faintly tinged with silver and saffron. Birds were beginning to cheep and rustle in the trees, and faint but clear, from the direction of Nasim, came the melodious cry of the muezzin of the mosque of Hazratbal, calling the Faithful to prayer . . .

'Damn!' said Charles softly. 'I shall have to move quickly! Good-night, Sarah—I mean, Good-morning. Go and get some sleep. You'll be all right now. I'll be seeing you——'

There was a soft whistle from the bank.

'That's Habib,' said Charles; and was gone.

Sarah heard the muffled rasp of the pantry door being shut and then the boat trembled to swift footsteps upon the gangplank. There was a rustle among the willows and then silence.

Lager yawned and stretched and thumped his tail sleepily. 'Well thank goodness *you're* all right!' said Sarah.

15

It was past ten o'clock when Sarah awoke to find Fudge Creed standing by her bedside, shaking her.

'Wake up, you idle creature!' said Fudge. 'Do you usually oversleep to this extent? Anyone would think you'd been on the tiles all night!'

'You'd be surprised,' said Sarah yawning. She sat up, ruffling her hands through her red curls. 'Morning Fudge. Is it a nice day?'

'Heavenly!' pronounced Fudge pulling back the window curtains and letting in a ballet of sunblobs that danced across the ceiling. 'Your *mānji* reports that your breakfast has been ready for the last hour and a half, so I imagine it's uneatable by now.'

'Tell him I'll be ready for it in fifteen minutes,' said Sarah, sliding out of bed and stretching to get the sleepiness out of herself.

'Will do. And when you've finished, you're coming out shopping with us. We want to get some papier-mâché bowls to send off as a wedding present; and as Hugo thinks you'd like to see the city and the river, we thought we'd go to the Fourth Bridge shops. They make lovely stuff there. What about it?'

'It sounds just what the doctor ordered,' replied Sarah buoyantly, relieved at the prospect of getting away from the boat for an hour or two. Charles had said 'Don't go anywhere alone,' but he had not told her to stay on the boat, and she felt she had had quite enough of the *Waterwitch* for the time being. Having dressed she asked the *mānji* to buy a dozen bolts complete with screws and sockets in the bazaar, before sitting down to a belated breakfast which, as Fudge had predicted, was considerably the worse for wear and bore signs of having been kept hot over a charcoal brazier.

Sarah presented the kidneys to a grateful Lager and distributed most of the scrambled egg to a pair of friendly little bulbuls who hopped and twittered and flirted their pert black crests on the duckboard outside the open dining-room window, and drinking the lukewarm coffee she wondered why, after the alarms of the past night and her recent order concerning bolts for repelling intruders, she should feel so exceptionally gay and lighthearted?

'*Oh what a beautiful morning!*' sang Sarah. '*Oh, what a beautiful day!*'

'*Hell and damnation!*' yelled a voice outside the window. There was a crash and a thump, and Hugo erupted through the window clutching a dripping paddle: 'Why is it,' he demanded heatedly, 'that although I was presented with a Rowing Blue by my misguided University, I remain incapable of paddling these flat-bottomed, over-canopied punts for five yards without turning at least three complete circles and soaking myself from the waist up? Morning, Sarah. You're looking almost as good as you sound. Do you feel as good as you look?'

'I feel terrific!' said Sarah. 'It must be the air or something. I feel like rushing out and doing pastoral dances in a cornfield.'

'Well how about rushing out to the Fourth Bridge and holding my hand while Fudge reduces me to bankruptcy among the papier mâché merchants?'

'Are you thinking of rowing us there?' inquired Sarah cautiously.

'Have no fear! I am, alas, too corpulent for prolonged exercise and too incompetent a performer with one of these beastly fancy paddles to attempt it. I propose to drive. We might have lunch at Nedou's on the return journey: how does that strike you?'

'*Wizard!*' said Sarah. 'Just wait while I get a hat. "*I've got a beautiful feeling, everything's going my way . . .*" ' She vanished, singing, in the direction of her bedroom, while Hugo abstractedly finished off the toast and marmalade.

It was midday by the time they reached Ghulam Kadir's papier mâché shop at the Fourth Bridge, for Hugo had insisted on stopping at the Club for a beer *en route*, where they had found Reggie Craddock and Mir Khan, who had decided to accompany them.

Ghulam Kadir's showrooms overlooked the river and were stacked and piled with articles in papier mâché. Bowls and boxes in every conceivable size and shape, vases, candlesticks, dressing-table sets, lamps, platters, tables and dishes. On all of which birds and butterflies, leaves, flowers or intricate oriental designs had been painted in miniature and embellished with gold leaf.

Several brown-robed assistants wearing spotless white turbans of impressive size hurried forward to display the wares, uttering polite murmurs of greeting, and to the evident satisfaction of the aged proprietor—and the unconcealed amusement of Mir Khan—the pile of Sarah's purchases soon grew to alarming proportions.

Hugo, losing interest, eventually wandered off through a curtain-hung doorway, and they heard his voice raised in greeting in the next room.

'*Blast!* It's that old Candera pest,' grumbled Reggie Craddock, who was holding an assortment of finger-bowls while Fudge debated the respective merits of chenar leaves, kingfishers, lotuses and paisley patterns. 'Can't stand the woman. How Meril can stick it, beats me. Gossiping old bully!'

Lady Candera's astringent tones could be heard uplifted in comment and criticism from the next room: 'Well Hugo? Wasting your time and money as usual I see? Where's your wife? Why people buy this rubbishy trash I cannot imagine. No taste. No discrimination. I've just been telling Ghulam Kadir he's lucky that there are still so many tasteless tourists left in Srinagar. What are you doing here?'

'Imitation being the sincerest form of flattery,' said Hugo, 'I am following your example and acquiring—reluctantly and by proxy, so to speak—a collection of this rubbishy trash.'

Lady Candera gave vent to a high, cackling laugh. 'I like you, Hugo Creed. You are about the only person who has the gumption to stand up to me. But you malign me if you think I am buying this stuff. Heaven forbid! I am merely seeing that Meril's deplorable taste does not lose her her job. The Resident wants about two dozen pieces of papier mâché work and similar local rubbish to send to some charity bazaar, and he has asked Meril to get it. The man must be entering his second childhood to entrust the selection to Meril who, if left to herself, is certain to be grossly cheated over the price and return laden with all the unsaleable hideosities in Srinagar. Major McKay has very kindly come to support me.'

'Oh, God!' muttered Reggie Craddock.

Meril Forbes' voice was heard to say in trembling protest: 'But Aunt Ena, you know it was your . . .' 'Hold your tongue, child!' snapped Lady Candera sharply. 'I will not stand being argued with. Now run along and look out some nice powder-bowls. I don't like the last two that you have shown me. Major McKay can advise you.'

The dusty, heavily embroidered curtain swung back and Lady Candera entered, her lorgnette at the ready: 'Ah Antonia,' she observed to Fudge, 'increasing your husband's overdraft, I presume?' She turned the lorgnettes upon Reggie Craddock, inspected him silently and added: 'I see you have brought your faithful cavalier. Ah me, what it is to be young——! Though to be sure, in my youth, we missed a great many opportunities by observing a stricter regard for the conventions. You are about to drop one of those bowls, Major Craddock.'

Reggie Craddock scowled, and in an effort to retrieve the sliding bowl, dropped three more.

'Why don't you put them on the divan?' asked Lady Candera. 'So much more sensible. There you see, you have cracked that one and will have to buy it. However, I have no doubt you can use it as an ashtray. You are looking a little flushed, Antonia—or else you should use less rouge. If you modern women must use make-up, I do wish you would learn to apply it with a more sparing hand.'

Fudge said placidly: 'Dear Lady Candera, how you do love to torment us. But this morning I am determined to disappoint you. I refuse to rise.'

'You and Meril are two of a kind,' observed Lady Candera, seating herself regally upon the divan: 'No guts.'

Fudge smiled and said: 'But we are all scared of Lady Candera. She knows everyone's secrets and nothing is hid from her. Isn't that so?'

'I know yours, if that's what you mean,' snapped Lady Candera.

'Aha!' said Hugo. 'I see that you belong to the "All is discovered!" school.'

'And what is that, pray?'

'Kipling put it very neatly once: "Write to any man that all is betrayed, and even the Pope himself would sleep uneasily." In other words, if you whisper *"All is discovered!"* in a chap's ear, nine citizens out of ten will immediately take the next boat for South America, on the off-chance of its being true.'

'You mean, because there is no one who has nothing to hide?' asked Mir Khan.

'That's about it,' agreed Hugo. 'In fact if someone hissed *"All is discovered!"* in my ear, you would be unable to see me for dust.'

'That I can *well* believe!' said Lady Candera tartly. She turned her back on Hugo, and raising her lorgnette surveyed Sarah at some length. 'Ah, the rich Miss Parrish,' she observed.

'I'm afraid not,' said Sarah.

'What? Oh—But I thought all trippers who could afford to come out to India were rich.'

'Not this one, I'm afraid,' confessed Sarah with a laugh.

'Well, it's a good story, girl. Spread it,' advised Lady Candera. 'To be thought rich is the next best thing to being it. You will find it a great aid to popularity. You too are buying this rubbishy trash, I see.'

'Yes,' said Sarah, 'I think it's charming.'

'Before the war it had certain merits,' admitted Lady Candera. 'But like everything else, its price has quadrupled and its quality deteriorated—thanks to our various allies, who paid fantastic prices without any discrimination whatsoever so that it soon ceased to be worthwhile to maintain a decent standard of workmanship. Any trash would sell.'

It was perhaps fortunate that at this point they should have been interrupted by the arrival of Helen Warrender, accompanied by Captain Mallory.

Charles, who had included Sarah casually in a general greeting, did not look in the least as if he had spent a sleepless and strenuous night. Or that the proprietary hand that Helen kept on his arm was in any way unwelcome. And Sarah, noting these things, felt unaccountably depressed and irritated. Mir Khan had left her side to discuss the rival merits of candlesticks and table-lamps with Meril Forbes and Major McKay in the next room, and as the others had fallen into a group about the divan where Lady Candera held court, she found herself temporarily alone.

There was a small archway on her left, half covered by a heavy fringed and embroidered curtain, and driven by that feeling of irritation she pushed the curtain aside and slipped through, to find herself in yet another showroom; dim, dusty and crowded with tables.

The walls here were hung with folds of brick-red cloth embroidered in geometrical designs in reds and browns and lavishly strewn with small pieces of looking-glass no bigger than a man's thumbnail, while underfoot the floor was thick with Persian rugs. In the centre of the room and against the walls stood innumerable tables of carved and inlaid wood, piled high with articles in papier mâché, and yet more bowls and vases and boxes were stacked upon the floor in dusty pyramids upon the rugs. There appeared to be no exit from the room, other than through the archway Sarah had entered by, but on one side of it intricately carved shutters of painted wood guarded a window and a balcony that overlooked the river.

The shutters were closed, so that the only light in the small, dim room filtered through the interstices of the carving, and the atmosphere was both cold and stuffy. It smelt of dust and sandalwood and slow centuries . . . And of something else. Something that Sarah could not for the moment place.

She wandered about the room restlessly, picking up and examining various pieces of papier mâché and putting them down again without really seeing them, and listening with half an ear to the voices in the next room: Charles's voice, Hugo's, Helen's and Lady Candera's, which presently blurred together and grew fainter and faded to a mere murmur of sound. They have all gone somewhere else, thought Sarah.

The small, dusty, cluttered room was very quiet: quiet and cold and—and what? Sarah could give no reason for it, but all at once she found herself gripped by a feeling of panic that made her want to turn and run out of the room and after her companions. It was as if on entering this place she had somehow stepped out of the ordinary everyday world, for there was something here that frightened her. Something . . .

Quite suddenly she realized what it was. The smell that had been in the dark deserted hall of the hut by the Gap. It was here too! Faint but distinct, in Ghulam Kadir's showroom by the Fourth Bridge.

Sarah stood motionless: holding her breath and unable to move. There was no sound now from beyond the curtain, and even the noises from the river and the city beyond the carved wooden shutters seemed to sink into silence. Something rustled behind the drapery upon the walls, and the little mirrors winked and twinkled to the faint movement—a hundred sly, glinting eyes that watched Sarah and reflected her endlessly upon the dark, dusty hangings.

She did not hear footsteps upon the thick rugs, but the curtain that hung over the archway was jerked back and Charles stood on the threshold.

'I've been sent to round you up—' he began, and then the fear in her white face checked him, and he dropped the curtain quickly. Sarah's voice was a croaking whisper: *'The smell! The smell in the hut. It's in this room . . . !'*

'Hush!' said Charles. He took a swift stride forward and gripped her wrist in a clasp that hurt. 'Pull yourself together, Sarah!' he ordered in an urgent whisper. 'Quickly . . . That's the girl.'

'That smell . . .' repeated Sarah.

'Yes, I know. What the hell were you doing in here?'

'I just came in to see——'

'No. I mean here in this house?'

'Fudge wanted to do some shopping.'

'Are you——' There was a very faint sound from beyond the curtained doorway and in almost the same moment, as swiftly and surprisingly as he had done once before, Charles caught her into his arms and kissed her, holding her hard and close so that she could neither move nor speak.

The curtain behind them swung aside and Major McKay stood in the archway, looking pink and startled. His already ruddy face gradually assumed the hue of a beetroot, and he gave a small dry cough of embarrassment and stood back as Sarah, released, brushed past him with flaming cheeks.

She ran across the big showroom and through a doorway into another room beyond. A twisting wooden staircase led up from it, and from somewhere overhead she could hear Reggie Craddock arguing with Fudge, and Helen Warrender's high, affected laugh. Sarah stopped abruptly; daunted by the thought of Helen's mocking eyes, Mir Khan's clear, perceptive gaze, and Lady Candera's deadly lorgnette all levelled at her flushed face and ruffled hair.

She wished she could remember what she had done with her bag. There was a small square of looking-glass in it, in addition to a powder-puff and a comb. Had she given it to Mir Khan to hold or was it on some table in the room behind her? As she hesitated, Charles walked quickly through the door. His face was perfectly blank and he looked at Sarah with a faint frown as though he had for the moment forgotten who she was.

'I suppose,' said Sarah in a low, furious voice, 'that that was some more shock treatment? What am I supposed to forget this time?'

Charles's frown deepened. He caught her elbow, and jerking her round began to propel her up the narrow stairway.

'Don't be a fool, Sarah,' he advised brusquely. He paused for a moment at the turn of the stair to look swiftly upwards and behind him, and spoke in an undertone: 'Someone was coming in, and as I had no way of telling who it was I had to establish an alibi damned quickly. I've probably put years on McKay's life in the process; the poor chap was incoherent with apology. But that's his look-out; and for all I knew it might have been ——Well the fact of the matter is that I can't afford to be discovered deep in private conversation with you just now, Sarah. Not unless I can provide a very obvious and innocent reason for it. So there was nothing for it but to provide the reason.'

'I see,' said Sarah.

'I doubt it,' said Charles with an edge to his voice. 'This is an unhealthy house to visit just now, Sarah, and the sooner you're out of it the better.' He smiled down suddenly at her sober face. 'All right, I apologize. It was abominable of me, and that's the second time I've offended. If there is a third you'll know I really mean it! And now if you think you could try and look less like a girl who has discovered a body in the basement and more like one who has recently been kissed in the conservatory, we'll join the others. Think you can manage it?'

'I'll try,' said Sarah meekly.

'That's the spirit,' approved Charles, and followed her up the stairs to a large upper room where the remainder of Ghulam Kadir's customers were admiring furniture and carved ornaments of polished walnut wood.

'Oh, there you are,' said Fudge from the window recess. 'Where did you get to, Sarah? I told Charles to collect you in case you got lost among all these rooms and staircases. What do you think of these little walnut-wood tables? Aren't they sweet? I really think I must get a set of them.'

Hugo groaned audibly as one of the assistants, a fat little brown-robed man with a face deeply pitted by the marks of smallpox, hurried to stack the nest of small, polished tables one within the other, and surround them by vast sheets of paper and copious loops of string. Another assistant, a stately gentleman whose grey beard had been dyed an impressive shade of scarlet, was engaged in performing a similar office for Meril Forbes' purchases under the critical eye of Lady Candera, while a third assistant made out the bills.

Ghulam Kadir appeared in the doorway and gave a low-voiced order and the red-bearded assistant vanished through a curtained archway and reappeared with a large brass tray loaded with tiny cups of black coffee which Ghulam Kadir handed round with flowery compliments.

Charles proffered his cigarette-case to Helen Warrender who looked at it and laughed. 'Thank you, but I won't deprive you of your last one.' 'Sorry,' apologized Charles: 'I didn't realize I had only one left, but for you, Helen, I will even sacrifice my last cigarette!'

'Dear Charles, I wish I could take you seriously! You know I never smoke anything but Sobranies, but after that I shall honour you by accepting your last gasper.' She bent her head over Charles's proffered lighter as the pockmarked assistant hurried up with a box of cigarettes, and Charles accepted one with a word of thanks and glanced at his watch: 'I hate to hurry you, Helen, but it's past one o'clock, and since we are supposed to be joining Johnnie and the Coply twins for lunch at Nedou's Hotel at 1.15 we shall be a good half hour late even if we start now.'

Helen gave an affected little shriek of dismay and began to hunt through her bag. 'What is it I owe you for, Ghulam Kadir? Oh yes—the powder-bowl and the tray and the eight table-mats. That's seven rupees eight annas, and twelve rupees, and let me see—the mats were four each, weren't they? I'm sure not to have brought enough money. Charles darling, your arithmetic's better than mine, how much do I owe?'

'Fifty-one rupees eight annas,' said Charles promptly. 'Here, I've got it, you can pay me back at lunch.' He handed over a collection of crumpled notes while Helen said: 'You *are* an angel, Charles! Don't forget to remind me, will you?' and Lady Candera remarked, 'A nice morning's work, Helen,' in acidulated tones.

'Shift ho, for all of us,' said Hugo. 'My stomach has been commenting on the lateness of the hour for some time past. What is the ghastly total, Fudge? . . . Heaven save me! Here you are, Ghulam Kadir, you old robber. Pity we didn't arrive in a pantechnicon. Good God, Sarah! You don't mean to say you've acquired all that? On second thoughts, I regret that we did not come in two pantechnicons.'

They went down the twisting staircase in single file, and when they reached the main papier mâché showroom, Ghulam Kadir, who had preceded them, produced a handful of small objects—little papier mâché containers made to hold a box of matches—and formally presented one to each of his customers.

'Oh, thank you! they're charming,' exclaimed Sarah, examining her gift which bore a design of gold chenar leaves and brown, furry chenar buds on a cream ground.

'And now we really *must* go,' said Fudge. 'What are you looking for Sarah?'

'My bag,' said Sarah. 'I left it somewhere down here and I haven't paid my bill yet.'

'Ah, Captain Mallory; your cue again, I think,' observed Lady Candera with malice.

Sarah flushed angrily. 'I must have put it down somewhere here.'

'Anyone seen Sarah's bag?' demanded Hugo. 'Anyone ever seen any woman who did not end up a shopping expedition by mislaying something? Is there a doctor—I mean a detective—in the house?'

Parcels were abandoned while the party hunted through the rooms. 'Oh dear—I am sorry,' apologized Sarah contritely. 'It's a white one. Not very big. I can't think where——'

'Is this it?' inquired Hugo patiently, fishing up a white suede bag from between a carved sandalwood table and the end of the divan.

'Bless you, Hugo!' Sarah reached gratefully for her property and paid her bill, and the party once more collected its respective parcels and pieces and went down into the street where they were joined by Major McKay, who had been soothing his ruffled feelings with a quiet cigarette on the river steps.

Lady Candera, Meril and the Major, who were also apparently lunching at Nedou's Hotel, were going as far as the First Bridge by *shikara,* and Charles, who had left his car on the other side of the river, accepted a lift for himself and Helen as far as the opposite bank. Sarah, Reggie Craddock and Mir Khan piled into the Creeds' car, and were driven away through the maze of narrow and tortuous streets that twist and turn through Srinagar City.

16

It was almost two o'clock by the time Hugo's car drew up outside Nedou's Hotel and decanted its passengers.

'You and Reggie will lunch with us, won't you, Mir?' asked Hugo, disentangling himself from a pile of paper parcels.

'I should be delighted.'

'What about you, Reggie?'

'Well,' said Reggie doubtfully, 'I didn't warn out for lunch at my pub, so——'

'Oh give 'em a ring, if that's all that's worrying you. They'll have given you up by now, anyhow.'

'You're probably right,' admitted Reggie. 'In that case, thanks very much: I'd like to.'

Nedou's Hotel, in contrast to its recent crowded years, seemed very quiet and sleepy, and there were only a few people in the entrance hall as Fudge and Sarah passed through. From the bar came a subdued murmur of voices and the clink of glasses, and Sarah, glancing in through the open door as she passed by, caught a glimpse of Johnnie Warrender and the Coply twins throwing dice.

Hugo led the way to a table by the window and presently Helen, followed by Johnnie, Charles and the Coply twins, took their seats at one nearby. But there was something curiously depressing about the vast, echoing room with its sea of empty tables, and even Hugo seemed oppressed by it and to have temporarily mislaid his customary good humour.

Lunch was for the most part a silent meal, and when it was over they took their coffee out into the entrance hall where they sat facing the empty spaces of the big ballroom. There was a stage at the far end of it—the scene of many amateur performances and cabarets in past years—and the heavy, dark curtains of crimson plush that hid it from view seemed to add to the gloom of the deserted ballroom.

Hugo, Reggie and Mir drifted away to the bar in search of liqueurs, while Fudge and Sarah sat on, sipping their coffee and making desultory conversation to Major McKay, who appeared to have lost his party, and presently Charles came across the hall and sat down on the arm of Fudge's chair.

'Cigarette, Fudge? You don't, do you Sarah? Well St George, what have you done with the dragon?'

Major McKay was betrayed into a smile. 'If you are referring to Lady Candera, she went to sleep over the coffee. We had luncheon in the private dining-room upstairs to avoid having to mix with the *hoi polloi*—that's you, Charles.'

'*Touché,*' said Charles with a laugh. 'Well good luck to you. I hope you pull it off. If you do, you'll deserve the Albert Medal with bars.'

Major McKay turned a rich shade of beetroot and Sarah said: 'Pull what off?'

'George knows,' said Charles with a grin.

'On the contrary, I have not the least idea what you are referring to,' said Major McKay frigidly. He consulted his watch, and rose. 'Well—er—time's getting on. I suppose I'd better go and see if Lady Candera's car is back. I shall be seeing you all at the Nagim Club this evening, I expect.'

He made his escape, and Fudge turned reproachfully to Charles: 'You really shouldn't pull his leg like that, Charles! It's too bad of you. It upsets him. Besides, it may only put him off.'

'I find it irresistible,' said Charles. 'George is a good old stick, if only he'd stop taking himself so seriously. And if that sort of thing is going to put him off, he's not worth any woman's time.'

'What *are* you two talking about?' demanded Sarah, bewildered. 'Put him off what?'

'Meril, of course,' said Fudge impatiently. 'You don't suppose George McKay is dancing attendance on that old dragon for fun, do you? We're all madly hoping that he'll run off with Meril.'

Sarah laughed. 'What an old matchmaker you are, Fudge! But why run off with her? I'm quite sure that Major McKay would never do anything so unconventional.'

'Well he'll never get her if he doesn't,' predicted Fudge. 'The minute Lady Candera realizes that it is not her witty and stimulating conversation that the gallant Major is interested in, but her despised niece, she will show him the door in no uncertain manner. And Meril, poor child, will never have the courage to do anything about it.'

'I don't believe it!' said Sarah flatly. 'Not in this day and age. That sort of thing went out with Victorian novels and the vapours. Meril isn't a minor. She doesn't need anyone's consent. Besides, you're wrong when you say she hasn't any courage. I've seen her take a slope, skiing, that *I* wouldn't dare face.'

'Ah, but that's quite a different sort of courage,' said Fudge wisely. 'Lots of people with plenty of physical courage haven't an ounce of moral courage to go with it. Meril's one of that kind, and where her aunt is concerned she behaves like a hypnotized rabbit.'

'Sounds as if she'll make the Major a perfect wife!' commented Sarah caustically. 'But what makes you think he's interested in her, anyway? Lady Candera seems to hypnotize a lot of people. Maybe he's one of them too?'

'Well, he was up here last year and he went around quite a bit with them. But it certainly wasn't Lady Candera who drew him up to Gulmarg. Meril used to give him skiing lessons every day. Now here he is again, in spite of the fact that he could have taken his leave in England instead. Of *course* it's Meril! Besides, didn't you see the beautiful shade of puce he went when Charles pulled his leg about it?'

'Personally,' said Charles, 'I can imagine nothing duller than having to go through life tied to such a model of rectitude and propriety as George McKay. No woman of spirit could bear up under the strain.'

'Nonsense,' said Fudge firmly. 'He's a good man. He's kind and he's reliable. Besides Meril isn't a woman of spirit. She'll make him a perfect wife, and they will stodge along together and be as happy as . . . as . . . well, I can't quite visualize George as a lark, I must admit. Anyway, it's too late in the afternoon to think up suitable similes. Where on earth has Hugo got to? It's time we were making tracks for home.'

Fudge got up, and accompanied by Charles, crossed the hall and disappeared in the direction of the bar, and Sarah, left alone, turned to look across the gloomy spaces of the deserted ballroom.

The sun was shining brightly outside the line of tall windows that ran down one side of the room, but between the windows and the dance floor stood a row of pillars that supported a long gallery overhead, and formed an open corridor between the windows and the ballroom below: a corridor that was furnished with sofas, chairs, tables and writing-desks, but which owing to that line of pillars, kept much of the daylight from the ballroom floor.

It was a gaunt and not very attractive room, and in the afternoon light, gloomy and bare and unfriendly. But Sarah was peopling it with the gay dancers of other years and picturing it ablaze with lights and full of noise and music and laughter; and presently she moved out onto the polished floor, humming softly to herself and took a few dancing steps across the shining surface.

Except for her own tuneful humming, it was very quiet in the big ballroom. And indeed the whole hotel seemed to be taking a siesta, for she could hear no sound from the hall or the passages beyond the ballroom. Even the subdued murmur of voices from the bar had ceased, and beyond the tall windows the garden drowsed in the afternoon sunlight, empty and silent.

The sprung floor vibrated under Sarah's feet as she swayed and turned to the strains of an imaginary band: *'The moonlight, and the moon, and every lovely lilting tune . . .'* hummed Sarah, and stopped. That tune again! Janet's tune. Perhaps this ballroom *was* haunted. Perhaps Janet had danced to that tune here last year—and other years . . .

Sarah stood still in the middle of the dim, deserted floor, trying to visualize Janet in a ball dress, and thinking of all the young men up on leave who had danced here during the war years, and gone away to die in Burma and Malaya, North Africa and Italy; in Japanese prisoner-of-war camps and on the infamous Death Railway . . .

As she stood there, her eye was caught by a faint movement. The curtains that hung in front of the stage rippled very slightly as though someone had drawn them an inch or two apart in order to peer out between them, and then dropped them softly back into place.

Sarah stayed very still, listening. Yes. There was someone on the stage behind the curtains, for in the stillness she could hear, very faintly, the pad of quiet feet moving across bare boards. A dog or a cat? But the curtains had moved at the height of a man's head. A hotel servant, then?—snatching a brief siesta in the shelter of the curtains.

A hundred to one it's only a servant! Sarah told herself firmly. It was silly to start imagining things even in innocent places like this, and she would go and see for herself.

She ran lightly across the floor and up the short flight of steps that led to the stage, and taking a deep breath, pulled aside the folds of the curtains and went through onto the stage behind them.

It was much larger than she had expected, but nothing moved upon it save the lazily drifting dust motes in a shaft of sunlight. The wide stretch of uncarpeted boards sloped slightly upwards towards the back wall in which there was a single tall window, and after the gloom of the ballroom the stage, on this side of the curtains, seemed full of light.

The sunbeams streaming in through the high window made symmetrical patterns on the bare boards and slanted across the piles of chairs and tables that stood against the walls of the stage, one upon the other. On one side a small flight of concrete steps led down to what were probably dressing-rooms, while on the opposite side, where the sunbeams did not penetrate, a steep, enclosed staircase wound up into the shadows of a gallery above. A gallery that was the continuation of the one that ran overhead along one side of the ballroom.

There was someone or something on that staircase; though Sarah did not know why she should be sure of this. Perhaps a board had creaked, or something had flickered among the dusty shadows . . . The empty stage stretched silent and still in the drowsy afternoon light and the heavy folds of the curtains hung dark and unmoving; and no sound came from the ballroom behind her. The furniture against the walls, the neatly stacked tables, the wicker chairs turned one upon the other, the smug outlines of cretonne-covered sofas and armchairs and the red plush curtains seemed to hem Sarah in, and she straightened her shoulders and walked steadily across the stage to the foot of the spiral staircase and looked up into the dusty dimness overhead.

Something moved sharply above her on the stairway and for the flash of a second she glimpsed a face that peered down at her from the shadows overhead. Then its owner turned and she heard a scurry of bare feet on the staircase, followed by the swift pad of retreating footsteps in the gallery overhead.

Sarah whirled about and running across the stage, slipped back between the curtains. From the front of the stage she could see up into the ballroom gallery and she was just in time to see a figure whisk out through its far door: a figure wearing the brown voluminous robes and white turban of a Kashmiri, and that she might have taken to be a member of the hotel staff if it had not been for the brief glimpse of its owner's face that she had received from the dark stairway.

She had a good memory for faces, but even if she had not, there would have been little excuse for forgetting this one, since she had seen it only an hour or so ago. It was the pockmarked face of the fat little assistant in Ghulam Kadir's papier mâché shop at the Fourth Bridge in Srinagar City.

As she stood there, staring up across the ballroom to the half-seen door of the gallery, the curtains at her back moved again and Sarah whirled round, her heart in her mouth.

'Charles!'

'Hello, Sarah.'

'Gosh!' said Sarah in a gasp. 'You gave me one hell of a fright. What were you doing back there?'

'Watching you,' said Charles. He lit a cigarette and his eyes regarded her thoughtfully over the small yellow flame of his lighter. 'You know Sarah,' said Charles softly, blowing out the flame, 'you are too curious by half. Too curious and too courageous. And in the present circumstances, that is an unfortunate combination. I would feel a lot happier about you if you'd allow discretion to be the better part of valour for a change.'

'Do you know who was behind that curtain?' demanded Sarah. 'Well I'll tell you——'

But she was unable to, because Charles had taken a swift stride forward and the palm of his left hand was over her mouth.

'*Ssh!*' said Charles softly. 'There are too many eyes in this place, Sarah, and too many ears.' He raised his voice, and said as though continuing a conversation, '—it was a pretty good band too. Run by a man in the Police called Chapman, who played a darned good game of golf and——'

But it was only Meril Forbes who came hurriedly through the doorway below the stage that led out of the ballroom into the long, whitewashed cloakroom passage.

She was wearing her usual air of distressed uncertainty and she checked at the sight of Charles and Sarah: 'Oh! . . . Have–have either of you seen Aunt Ena? She sent me to get some cigarettes, and I've got them. But goodness knows where she's gone to: I've looked everywhere. She does so hate to be kept waiting. Oh dear, anyone would almost think she did this sort of thing on purpose!'

'Of course she does,' observed Hugo, strolling in through the doorway, hat in hand: 'Didn't you know? *"She only does it to annoy because she knows it teases."* You should refuse to rise, Meril dear. As a matter of fact your elderly relative is outside in her car, sizzling slightly.'

'*Oh dear!*' repeated Meril helplessly, and hurried away across the ballroom.

'Poor kid,' observed Hugo kindly, watching the retreating figure. 'Pity someone can't make her a present of some backbone. Ah, there you are, Sarah. I've been sent to hunt you up. My spouse has been demanding your immediate apprehension. She is thinking of making a beeline for home. Coming?'

'Yes,' said Sarah gratefully. She turned and ran down the steps from the stage and joined Hugo on the ballroom floor.

'Charles been taking you on a Cook's Tour?'

'Yes,' said Charles, coming down from the stage: 'I've been telling Sarah all about the Gay Days.'

'Believe it or not,' mused Hugo, 'there was even a historic occasion when I myself performed upon that bally stage. If memory serves, I sang a duet with a girl called Mollie someone. A tasteful ditty about a bench in a park—or was it something about tiptoeing through tulips? I can't remember. I do recall, however, that my braces lifted the occasion to the heights of immortality. They gave under the strain of a high C and my trousers descended. It went well with the audience. In fact, I think I may say without vanity that I was a riot. The customers rolled in the aisles, and had anyone been able to supply a piece of string, or a safety-pin of suitable dimensions, I could have taken a dozen encores. As it was, our prudent stage-manager blacked us out and hurried on with the show. Ah me! Those were the days!'

From somewhere in front of the hotel came the sound of a car horn blown in a series of impatient toots.

'That is undoubtedly my better half beginning to simmer at the edges,' said Hugo. 'Come on, Sarah. Let us leg it with all speed.'

17

Sarah had tea that day on the flat roof of the Creeds' houseboat, looking out across the lake to the mountains behind Shalimar. Willow boughs
made a swaying curtain of green lace above the tea table, and a trio of
perky little bulbuls flirted their crests among the leaves and twittered for
crumbs.

The lake seemed to drowse in the late afternoon sunlight, the reflections
mirrored in its placid surface broken only intermittently by the passing of
an occasional country boat or *shikara*, or the splash of a brilliant hued
kingfisher. And Sarah, toying abstractedly with a cucumber sandwich as
she tried to make up her mind whether or not to return to the *Waterwitch*
and continue her search, decided against it. The thought of leaving the
sunlit peace of the comfortable deck-chair at Fudge's side to rummage
through the dark, dusty corners of the *Waterwitch* was repellent, and
though conscience fought with inclination, inclination won, and Miss Parrish stayed on: watching the shadows lengthen across the water and the
mountains turn saffron and pink and rose in the rays of the setting sun,
while Subhana, the Creeds' *mānji,* cleared away the tea things.

Lager, entirely recovered from his last night's adventure, snuffled and
skirmished among the reeds and willows on the bank, and Fudge and
Sarah sat idle, their hands in their laps, looking out across the lake
through the soft blue shadows while below them homeward-bound
shikaras and country boats from Nasim passed down the water lane towards the Nagim Bagh Bridge, their paddles splashing in musical rhythm.

A scent of woodsmoke drifted across the quiet air, and presently, like
the first star in a pale sky, the light on the top of the little stone temple that
crowns the hill of the Takht-i-Suliman shone out, wan in the warm evening
light, and from somewhere in the Creeds' cookboat a voice began to sing a
plaintive Kashmiri song full of odd trills and quavers.

'Where's Hugo?' asked Sarah suddenly.

'What?' Fudge woke from her reverie with a start.

'Hugo? He went along to the Nagim Club to meet some chap who's putting up there, and who's advertising a trout rod for sale on the Club's noticeboard. Hugo wanted to have a look at it. I think this must be him now——'

There was a sound of voices from beyond the willows that screened the field path leading from the houseboat to the Nagim road, and Fudge sighed and said: 'Damn! he's brought somebody back with him; and I did so want a peaceful evening doing nothing. Now we shall have to sit about drinking short drinks and making polite conversation for hours on end. I suppose it's this rod man.'

'No, it isn't,' said Sarah, who had risen and was peering down through the willow boughs. 'It's Charles.'

'Oh,' said Fudge on an odd note. She looked sideways at Sarah and laughed. 'Still interested in him, Sarah?'

'No of course not,' said Sarah hastily.

'Which means you are. Well—now's your chance.' She stood up and waved to Hugo who had arrived on the bank below.

'I've brought a guest,' called up Hugo. 'Rustle us up a drink, darling. We're coming up.'

Fudge crossed the deck and called down to Subhana, as Hugo and Charles, enthusiastically greeted by Lager, came up onto the roof of the houseboat.

'I found him at the Club,' said Hugo, waving an explanatory hand at Charles. 'I hadn't realized he was staying there. He wishes to take you poodlefaking in the moonlight, Sarah.'

'*Hugo!*' said Fudge. 'I do wish you wouldn't use that disgusting expression.'

Charles laughed. 'As a matter of fact,' he said mildly, 'I wondered if you would all dine with me tonight? There is apparently a gramophone dance on at the Club, and though I don't imagine the attendance will be large, it might be quite fun. The Secretary has put out a plaintive appeal for support.'

Fudge smiled and shook her head. 'That's sweet of you, Charles. But I don't think I could face a gramophone dance tonight. I've got a bit of a headache and I feel like a peaceful home evening and early bed. You take Sarah. I'm sure her Kashmir education will not be complete without a dance at Nagim on a moonlight night.' Fudge turned her head and looked out across the lake to where the setting sun was transforming the Gulmarg range into a flat lilac silhouette against a saffron sky: 'It's going to be a lovely night,' she said.

Charles turned to Sarah. 'What about it, Sarah? Would you like to come? I'm afraid I can't promise you a very amusing evening: we shall be lucky if half a dozen couples show up at the Club.'

Sarah hesitated a moment, looking from Fudge to Charles and back again, and Charles, turning a little so that his back was to the Creeds, lowered one eyelid for a fraction of a second. 'Yes, I'd love to,' said Sarah promptly. 'Are you sure you and Hugo won't come, Fudge?'

'*Quite* sure!' said Fudge firmly. 'Thanks all the same, Charles.' She smiled across at him, and Hugo said sadly: 'I, you notice, get no say in the matter.'

'Oh, darling!' said Fudge remorsefully, 'do you really want to go? All right then, I'll go if you'd like. I can easily take an aspirin.'

'Nonsense,' said Hugo. 'I was only pulling your leg. I could do with early bed myself after the ghastly schemozzle of that storm last night. I hardly got a wink of sleep. Besides, I am reaching the sere and yellow leaf. My dancing days are done. It is now up to young and sprightly creatures like Charles and Sarah here to carry on the good work of making the nights hideous with revelry. All that I shall now contribute to the racket will be a snore.'

Subhana and Ayaz Mohammed appeared upon the roof with an assortment of drinks and glasses, and Hugo having dispensed sherry and whisky with a liberal hand, the four of them sat on into the green twilight, talking and laughing, while a huge, apricot-coloured moon lifted above the mountains beyond Shalimar and laid a shimmering silver pathway across the lake.

Eventually, glancing at her watch, Fudge inquired of Charles what time he was thinking of dining?

'Round about eight, I suppose. The dance won't begin until after nine.'

'Well it's nearly eight now,' said Fudge. 'I don't want to hurry you, Sarah, but if you intend to change you'd better think about moving.'

Sarah jumped up, and Charles said: 'I'll wait for you. Then we can go along to the Club together. That is, if you won't mind looking at the papers while I change? Or would you rather I came back and fetched you in about half an hour's time?'

'No. Wait for me here. I won't be more than ten minutes,' said Sarah; and vanished down the hatchway staircase, calling to Lager to follow.

Abdul Gaffoor, her *mānji*, was switching on the lights in the *Waterwitch* when she reached the boat, and pausing only to tell him that she would not be in for dinner, she made for her bedroom—conscious of a little shiver of distaste as she passed through the silent rooms, and grateful for the scuttering patter of Lager's feet and the sound of his small excited snufflings and whimperings as he sniffed at the floorboards, beneath which lurked an entrancing smell of rats.

Strewn all over her bed was the untidy heap of paper-wrapped parcels that she had bought that morning and which Abdul Gaffoor and the Creeds' bearer had carried in from the car; and Sarah was annoyed to see that every parcel had been opened, the string round each one cut and the paper roughly replaced. Abdul had evidently been curious as to her purchases and had peered at them all with the inquisitiveness of a squirrel. 'He might at least have had the decency to do them up again tidily!' said Sarah aloud and crossly.

She bundled the entire collection hastily into an empty suitcase, and had removed her shoes and dress when a sudden and unpleasant thought slid into her mind and she stood still, staring down at the bed where the parcels had lain. A moment later she whirled round to open the cupboard and have her suspicion instantly confirmed; for it needed no second look to see that someone had been going through her belongings.

Neat piles of underclothing were not quite as neat as she had left them. A nest of carefully rolled stockings had been disarranged, and the order of the line of shoes on the bottom of the hanging cupboard had been changed —Sarah invariably put walking shoes at one end of the line, followed by house shoes and then evening slippers; but now a pair of gold evening sandals stood between blue suede house shoes and brown brogues . . .

There were other indications too; small in themselves, but enough to show that someone had been taking an exceedingly thorough look at all her possessions. Was it only curiosity on the part of Abdul Gaffoor, or was there some other less pleasant explanation? Sarah was suddenly intensely thankful that she had taken the precaution of carrying Charles's gun with her in her bag which had not been out of her sight, except——

She snatched up her bag in a panic and opened it, but the gun was still there, wrapped about with a chiffon scarf, and she drew a deep breath of relief and regarded it thoughtfully. She really could not carry a gun to a dance! Besides, she would be with Charles, and since her room had already been searched it was highly unlikely that anyone would search it again for some time. On that decision, she took out the gun and stuffed it under her pillow, and straightening up, saw with dismay that according to the little travelling clock that stood on her bedside table she had already overstepped the ten minutes she had promised to be away.

Heavens! thought Sarah, I'm going to be appallingly late, and Charles will think I'm one of those deadly women who say ten minutes and mean thirty! She turned hurriedly back to the cupboard, selected a deceptively simple evening dress of white linen boldly patterned in black leaves, and slipped her feet into a pair of white sandals. That should do for a gramophone dance, thought Sarah—and for Charles.

A few minutes later she was dressed and ready. She gave a final glance at herself in the inadequate mirror and looked in the cupboard for an evening-bag. But the assortment that presented itself to her proved unsatisfactory, and with another look at the clock and an exclamation of annoyance, she snatched up the white suede one from which she had removed the little automatic, and having reached for a brief fur cape, switched off the lights, and with Lager frisking at her heels, returned to the Creeds' boat.

Charles must have been watching for her, for he came down the gangplank as she arrived opposite the boat. 'Are you intending to bring that pup?' he inquired, 'because he won't be allowed inside the Club rooms you know.'

'Don't worry, I'm going to ask Hugo to keep an eye on him: Lager dotes on him, and he'll stay quiet as long as Hugo is around. It's only when I leave him alone that he behaves abominably and yelps non-stop like a lost soul. We left him behind this morning in the charge of the *mānji*, but I'm afraid he's a snob. He doesn't consider that *mānjis* are "company", and I gather he hardly paused for breath. He started yelping when we left and we could hear him still at it from the Nagim road when we got back at half past three. But he behaves like an angel with Hugo, don't you Lager, you little horror?'

'Who is taking my name in vain?' inquired Hugo appearing in the open doorway at the top of the gangplank.

'Me,' said Sarah ungrammatically. 'Hugo, be a darling and look after Lager for me. He's had his supper, and if I leave him alone on my boat he'll only howl until I come back.'

'OK,' sighed Hugo. 'Sling him along. Here, Lager boy—no, there is no need to chew holes in me to show your appreciation of my person. Goodnight, Charles. Have a good time, Sarah.'

'I intend to,' promised Sarah. 'Good-night, Hugo.' She raised her voice and called up through the willow boughs: 'Good-night Fudge,' but there was no reply from the roof of the boat and Hugo said: 'She's gone to bed—it's that headache, I'm afraid. I'll say good-night for you.' He waved a cheerful hand, and they turned away along the bank to pass round the shadowy trunk of the big chenar tree and come out onto the moonlit path that ran across the fields towards the Nagim road.

'Nice work,' said Charles, taking Sarah's arm and hurrying her down the path between the young corn. 'I need an alibi tonight Sarah, and you're it. Damn that thing!' . . . he had trodden on a piece of rusty tin, laid down by one of the *mānjis* to cover a depression in the path that the last night's rain had filled with muddy water, and it had creaked loudly and protestingly under his feet as though a nightjar had screamed in the fields.

'I had to ask the Creeds to come along for the look of the thing,' said Charles, 'but that providential headache of Fudge's has saved me a lot of trouble.'

'What do you mean? "want me for an alibi"?' asked Sarah.

Charles glanced over his shoulder before replying, but the moonlit expanse of field offered little or no cover, and they were out of earshot of the boats and the trees. Nevertheless he dropped his voice to an undertone: 'I have an assignation for tonight,' said Charles, 'on an island in the lake. Not the sort of place I should have chosen for it myself, but I suppose it has its points. However, under the circumstances I do not want to go floating about the lake by myself. It's not the sort of thing I'd be likely to go in for, and might well give rise to comment and curiosity. On the other hand, if there is one thing that chaps go in for more than another in Kashmir, it is floating round the lake in a *shikara* with a girl. So no one is likely to consider it in the least odd if I take the beautiful Miss Parrish for a moonlight ride. Even if Fudge and Hugo had decided to join the party, it would still have raised no more than a tolerant eyebrow and an indulgent laugh if I had gone off with you in a boat for an hour or two.'

'What is this assignation?' asked Sarah, her eyes sparkling with excitement. 'Who is it with?'

'One of our men. You saw him today—twice, if I am not mistaken. In fact you scared him considerably the second time!'

Sarah checked to stare up at him, her brows wrinkling: 'I don't understand,' she said. 'I haven't seen anyone I don't know today except——' She drew her breath in on a sudden gasp and stood still. 'Not–not the man from that shop?'

'That's it,' said Charles. 'The assistant with the pockmarked face. You saw him again at the hotel I think.'

'But–but I don't understand,' said Sarah again. 'What was he doing at the hotel?'

'Trying to see me,' said Charles, hurrying her onwards. 'He's one of our best men. We planted him there two years back. A pretty neat bit of work it was too. He had hoped to get an opportunity to speak to me this morning during the time that we were all at the shop, but due to the mob of customers who turned up he was kept too busy and didn't dare risk it. The most he could manage was to make me a sign to that effect, which he did when he handed me the cigarettes.'

'What was it?' asked Sarah in a whisper.

'Nothing in the least exciting, I'm afraid,' said Charles with a grin. 'He merely scratched his chin with the little finger of his left hand, in a gesture that is shorthand for N B G, or "sorry, no can do—over to you." So I immediately mentioned Nedou's Hotel and that I was lunching there, and talked of the stage.'

'Yes,' said Sarah slowly. 'I remember.'

'Ahamdoo is pretty quick, and that was quite enough for him. But the meeting at Nedou's was a frost—largely due to you, I may say! You walked in on us before he had time to say a word. We heard you coming, and he whisked round and was halfway up those stairs to the gallery when you appeared on the scene positively radiating suspicion. By the time I was able to catch up with him he'd got the wind up good and proper—either he thought he'd been followed or he'd spotted someone he was scared to death of, because he was in a blind panic and couldn't wait to get away. He merely hissed at me that he'd be on the Char-Chenar island at eleven tonight, and was off like a scalded cat: I wasn't given time to draw breath, let alone argue the toss; and I have to admit that when you bust up that initial meeting I could cheerfully have strangled you!'

'You ought to have warned me,' retorted Sarah, employing the popular tactic of attack being the best form of defence. 'And anyway, where were you?'

'Sitting in one of the armchairs that had its back to you. The back was a high one, but I don't mind telling you, Sarah, that you gave me a few very nasty moments. You couldn't see me unless you started peering round among the furniture; but I couldn't see you either, and I didn't know who the hell it was. I didn't dare move until I heard you walk away towards the staircase, and believe me it was a weight off my mind when I realized it was you.'

'Why didn't you tell me at once?' demanded Sarah indignantly. 'I was scared stiff. You might have explained!'

'With the place simply teeming with people? Not much!' said Charles firmly.

'What people in particular?' asked Sarah curiously.

Charles looked down at her and shook his head, for by now they were near a small village, and a few yards further on the path left the field to wind between a handful of tall, ramshackle Kashmiri houses before joining the main road that stretched away on either hand, white and deserted in the moonlight.

The acacia trees that bordered it patched the dusty road with shadows and filled the air with fragrance, and the few shops—rickety buildings hurriedly constructed of unseasoned deodar-planks during the brief boom years of Nagim Bagh—were for the most part shuttered and silent. Once safely past these and walking in the direction of the Club, Sarah repeated her question.

'Well,' said Charles meditatively, 'there's Reggie Craddock for one.'

'But he couldn't be mixed up in a thing like this?' gasped Sarah, horrified. 'Yes I know he tried to get me off the boat, but——Oh no! He couldn't. Not really. Besides, he's an Englishman!'

Charles said dryly: 'My dear Sarah, money talks in all languages. And there has been big money spent here.'

'Then you think that Reggie . . . ?' began Sarah.

'I don't know,' said Charles curtly. 'He might be in debt. When chaps get into the hands of Indian money-lenders they can end up in some ghastly tangles. I don't say he is; but I'm curious about Reginald Craddock. He knew Janet Rushton, and for all I know he may have been genuinely fond of her; though somehow that doesn't strike me as sufficient reason for wanting to get you off Janet's boat. Craddock was a member of the party at the ski-hut, and he was at Ghulam Kadir's shop this morning at a time when a very important message was due to be passed to someone there.'

'*What's that?*' Sarah stopped for a moment on the moonlit road. 'Oh, you mean the one that pockmarked man meant to give you?'

'No, I don't. That shop is used as a cover for a lot of things. Not active things: strictly passive ones. I think you would find that its aged and respectable proprietor is careful to know nothing of plots or plans. He merely allows his premises to be used, in return for a nice fat sum, as a sort of post office and receiving centre that collects and passes on information for the opposition. Something was due to be passed today: Ahamdoo was onto that much. I have my own ideas as to how it was done, but I can't be sure. We've had a check on everyone who entered or left that shop today, and Reggie, of course, was one of them.'

'So was I, for that matter. And so were lots of other people—including you,' retorted Sarah.

'I know. But all the same I am distinctly interested in Major Reggie Craddock . . . Left turn here—this is the Club.'

They turned in through an open gate, to walk down a long, tree-shaded drive that wound through an orchard and ended in lawns, neat flowerbeds, and a low Club building on the extreme edge of the Nagim Bagh lake. As they neared it Sarah, who had been silent for a few minutes, said thoughtfully: 'I wonder if you could work up a case against everyone who was in that shop this morning?'

'Of course,' said Charles cheerfully. 'I can produce a different theory to fit each one of you; and yours is still the best of the bunch.'

'In that case, I'm surprised that you trust me with all this information,' said Sarah with a laugh.

'How do you know I do?' asked Charles softly. Sarah stared at him blankly, but before she had time to frame an indignant reply Charles had steered her inside the Club and seated her in a chair on the edge of the ballroom floor, and having ordered tomato juice and promised not to keep her waiting long, vanished in the direction of the Club's residential block, leaving her alone with a pile of illustrated papers and two bored Club *khidmatgars* who were whispering together by the bar at the end of the room.

On the far side of the ballroom floor a row of french windows faced the lake and gave onto a long, roofless verandah, supported by wooden piles and set with chairs and tables. Sarah left her chair and went out onto it, to find herself looking across a sheet of moonlit water bounded on the far bank by a row of dimly seen houseboats, from which an occasional square of light threw a thin quivering line of yellow across the lake. The majority of them, unlike the many boats that were moored to the near bank, appeared to be unoccupied, and behind them, above the dark, distant tree-tops, rose the crouching bulk of fort-crowned Hari Parbat; silhouetted blackly against the moonwashed plain and the long line of glittering snow peaks that fringed the far wall of the valley.

Sarah leaned her arms on the verandah rail and gazed out across the water to where, shimmering in the moonlight, the snowy slopes of Apharwat lifted above the dark tree-line that marked Khilanmarg. Somewhere over there, a dot in the waste of whiteness, was the little ski-hut, and somewhere below it, among the miles of trees, lay the rambling hotel buildings and the small hotel room where, for her, this fantastic adventure had begun. And once again, as she looked at those far mountain ranges she wondered why she stayed on in Kashmir, where so many frightening things had happened to her since the night that she had been awakened by the moonlight on her face.

She had quitted the place with such deep relief, feeling thankful that she need never see it again. But a mixture of curiosity, bravado, and a promise given to the dead girl had brought her back, and ever since her return she had been living in a constant state of fear and tension. So why did she stay, when it would be so easy to send a cable to the Pierces in Ceylon, to hire a car and be in Rawalpindi in less than a dozen hours, and on the Frontier Mail speeding south the same day? If she were in her right mind she would be thinking of packing and leaving immediately, if this was any concern of hers. Yet she knew that she had no intention of going, and was, on the contrary, conscious of a feeling of intense exhilaration, even though last night on the *Waterwitch* she had experienced pure, undiluted terror, and again that morning, both in Ghulam Kadir's shop and as she stared up the dark staircase at the side of the stage in Nedou's Hotel. But it did not seem to matter. All that mattered was that she was young and alive, and life was glorious and exciting—because she was going to dine with Charles.

Sarah smiled to herself a little ruefully in the moonlight, and thought: You may as well admit it, you're not staying on here and allowing yourself to be scared out of your wits just for the fun of it or from any altruistic motives. You are staying because you've fallen in love with a man who is engaged to a beautiful blond called Cynthia! You've had a lovely time playing at being in love and enjoying having men fall for you, but now you've burnt your fingers. And Cynthia or no Cynthia, you don't really give a damn *how* many people get themselves bumped off, or if the whole British Empire and the sub-continent of India goes up with a bang, as long as you can stay around near Charles.

Women, decided Sarah cynically, are wonderful! At which point her musings were interrupted by Captain Mallory, correctly dinner-jacketed, who joined her at the verandah rail carrying two glasses of sherry.

'Here's to you, Sarah.'

'Thanks,' Sarah sipped her sherry and looked at Charles over the rim of her glass. 'Who is Cynthia?' she demanded abruptly.

'Cynthia? Sounds like a song: *"Who is Cynthia, what is she, that all her swains commend her?"* What Cynthia—or should I say which Cynthia? Or do you mean my sister?'

'Your sister! Have you got a sister called Cynthia?'

'I have indeed. You'll like her.'

'Oh,' Sarah smiled widely and dizzily. Yes, she was young and alive, and life was glorious and exciting because she was going to dine with Charles . . .

Except for a depressed gentleman wearing tweeds and a pince-nez, and a youthful couple who were holding hands under the table-cloth and conducting an intense conversation in whispers, the dining-room in the residential block of the Club was empty, and Charles and Sarah dined in the comparative privacy of a table set by a bow window, from where they could look out over the lawns and the lake to the mountains. The depressed gentleman finally departed, to be followed shortly afterwards by the intense couple. But Charles and Sarah sat on deep in conversation . . .

Sarah was enjoying herself. Her green eyes sparkled and her copper curls glinted in the wan light of the drably shaded ceiling bulbs, and the conversation, by mutual consent, did not touch on the business that had brought Charles to the valley. It was not until almost the end of the meal that she remembered to tell him of the search that had been made of her room and the opening of her parcels. 'You hadn't anything there, had you?' asked Charles frowning. 'Anything incriminating, I mean?'

'No, thank goodness. The only incriminating thing I've had was that little automatic, and I'd carried that about with me in my bag. Lucky I did!'

'Very,' agreed Charles soberly. 'But I can't understand why anyone would have been interested in the stuff you bought this morning. That makes it look as if it could be only a bit of curiosity on the part of your *mānji*. Let's hope so, anyway.'

A white-coated *khidmatgar* appeared with coffee and inquired if they would prefer it served over in the ballroom or out on the lawns, but Sarah did not want to move: 'It would be cold by the time it got over there anyway, and the kind of coffee they make in this country is bad enough when it's hot.'

She poured out the pale, unappetizing brew and handed a cup to Charles, inadvertently spilling some on her dress in the process. *'Bother!'* exclaimed Sarah cheerfully: and reaching for her bag, opened it to pull out a handkerchief. Something else came out with it and fell onto the table-cloth—the little papier mâché matchbox container that Ghulam Kadir had presented to her that morning.

'Complete with box of matches, I see,' said Charles, idly turning it over with one finger. "You've been favoured. Mine was only the case without the box of matches.'

'So is this one,' said Sarah. She put away her handkerchief and picked up the little box. 'No it isn't! But I'm almost sure . . . Why, it's not mine at all. Look! Mine had almost the same design, gold chenar leaves on cream. But it had those little furry chenar seeds in the pattern where this has got bulbuls. I know what must have happened! We all put our things down when we were hunting for my bag just after we'd been given these boxes, and I suppose I must have picked up someone else's by mistake. They're very alike.'

'You did *what?*' said Charles sharply. 'Here! Give me that box! It's a thousand to one chance, but——' He drew out the box of matches that the little case contained, but there were no matches inside it. Only a small slip of folded paper.

'A thousand to one chance,' repeated Charles in an awed whisper, 'and,

by God, we've pulled it off! This is what they were searching for of course, when they went through your room with a small-tooth comb.'

He smoothed out the scrap of paper on the palm of his hand. It bore a single line of graceful curving eastern writing, and Charles studied it, frowning.

'What is it?' asked Sarah urgently. 'Can you read it?'

'I can read it all right, but I haven't an idea what it means. It's a line from a poem in Persian.'

'What does it say?'

'Well, rather freely translated, it says "the author"—literally, the teller of tales—"threads his bright words as beads upon a string".'

' "The teller of tales threads his bright words as beads upon a string",' repeated Sarah slowly. 'What on earth does it mean? Is it a code?'

'God knows,' said Charles. 'It may mean anything. Perhaps it's a password. Anyway, we've got something at last. And what is better, the very fact that it hasn't reached the person it was intended for will almost certainly have thrown a largish-sized spanner into the works. I should imagine that no ordinary hair-tearing is in progress somewhere.'

Charles rolled up the small scrap of paper and tucked it into his breast-pocket. 'Now for heaven's sake Sarah, try to remember where that match case was when you picked it up. Can you get any picture in your mind of where it was lying or whose things it was with? If we could only get a line on who had it originally, the battle would be practically in the bag. Think, Sarah!'

Sarah put her head between her hands and frowned down at the table-cloth for a long minute.

'It's no good,' she said. 'I'm terribly sorry, but I just haven't got an idea whose it could have been. Someone found my bag for me—Hugo—and I saw this box and thought it was mine. It was so like, and I hadn't had time to look at any of the other people's boxes. I suppose I just picked it up and stuffed it into my bag. I think I picked it up off the big carved table. Or it could have been on the divan? I can't be sure. But—oh *no*——!'

'What is it?'

'Don't you see, if this really is the message that was due to be passed to someone, then that someone must be one of *us!* One of the party in the shop. A European. English . . . !'

'Not necessarily,' said Charles slowly, turning the little box between his fingers. 'We've got to think of everything. Every possibility. There were several other people who visited that shop this morning besides the ones we met there, and it is just within the bounds of possibility that someone who had left before we arrived made the same mistake that you made. Put a box down and picked up the wrong one. There were quite a few of these matchbox cases scattered around the showroom tables.'

'But you don't think it's likely?' said Sarah shrewdly.

'No,' said Charles slowly. 'I don't think it's likely.'

'Then you think it could——'

'I think that the sooner we dispose of this ornamental trifle the better,' said Charles grimly. 'Under the circumstances, I imagine you'd be safer walking about with a time-bomb in your pocket than with this box.'

'I don't believe it!'

'No? Then the sooner you do the better.'

'I don't mean what you've just said, I mean I don't believe that's the message. Why would anyone bother to wrap it up like that?—be so devious? It sounds silly and complicated and—and far-fetched to me!'

'What you don't realize is that the East *is* devious. It will always prefer to walk bye-ends to an objective rather than march up to it from the front; and it's the failure of the West to understand this that trips us up so often. Besides, as I've already told you, that shop was no more than a post office —for collecting and being collected from only. Whoever sent that message would not have delivered it there personally, or gone anywhere near the place. It probably passed through several hands *en route,* just to muddy the trail and make sure that it could not be traced back to its source.'

' "Bye-ends", in fact,' said Sarah.

'That's right. Everyone who touched it would certainly have taken a good look at it, and made nothing of it. But you can bet your bottom dollar that it would have made sense to the one it was intended for—and to no one else! Come on, Sarah, let's go and dance . . .'

He stood up, and taking her arm led her swiftly out of the house and along the moonlit path to where strains of music from a large radio-gramophone in the ballroom showed that the dance had officially begun.

By this time, the Club was looking considerably gayer. Several of the high bar-stools were occupied by partnerless males, while between eight to ten couples were dancing to music provided by the Club's radio-gramophone: among them, several people whom Sarah knew . . .

Meril Forbes, wearing pale blue taffeta, was dancing with Major McKay, and one of the Coply twins was partnering an unknown blond. Reggie Craddock was there, and so was Helen Warrender: the latter, wearing a décolleté creation glittering with green sequins and more suited to a Vice-regal Ball than a Club gramophone hop, was dancing with a tall bowlegged man with a vast straw-coloured moustache whom Charles said was a Colonel Grainger; adding that he was a four.

'What on earth does that mean?' inquired Sarah blankly.

'Polo handicap. He was considered to be worth four goals to any side he played for. Johnnie was a seven.'

'What is he now?'

'A has-been,' said Charles briefly.

'Isn't that Johnnie at the bar?' asked Sarah.

'I expect so, that's his usual pitch and that is what it did for him, poor devil.'

The record ran to a close and the dancers stood about the floor and applauded in a desultory manner while the Club Secretary put on another one. 'Hello Meril,' said Charles, pausing beside Major McKay and his partner. 'Your Aunt Ena here tonight?'

Meril started nervously and turned. 'Oh! . . . Oh hello Charles. Er . . . No. Aunt Ena wasn't feeling very well. She was coming. I mean . . .' Meril fumbled nervously with a small evening-bag embroidered with multi-coloured beads and sequins, dropped it and made a clumsy dive to retrieve it.

She was forestalled by Charles who handed it back and said with mock severity: 'Do you mean to tell me that your aunt thinks you two are sitting soberly at the Institute?'

'Well—well, yes,' said Meril on a half gasp.

Charles looked at Major McKay's blushing countenance and whistled expressively. 'George, I'm surprised at you! I had no idea you concealed so much duplicity and rash courage behind that innocent façade. Have you considered what Aunt Ena is going to say when she discovers that far from escorting her niece to a lecture on "Three Years in Borneo"—with hand-coloured slides—you have taken her out on a round of mad revelry?'

'Well—er—as a matter of fact,' began Major McKay uncertainly, 'I—er —that is——'

'I asked him to bring me!' interrupted Meril defiantly. Two bright patches of colour burned in her usually pale cheeks and Sarah noted with surprise that she looked positively pretty. 'I hate lantern lectures and I hate the Institute, and I didn't see why I shouldn't dance instead. After all, it can't really matter a bit to Aunt Ena. She went to bed.'

'And I wouldn't put it past George to have slipped something in her coffee,' said Charles cheerfully. 'You want to watch these doctors, Meril. Darned dangerous chaps.'

'My dear Charles,' said Major McKay huffily, 'a joke's a joke, but you really should not——' he caught Charles's eye, grinned, and said unexpectedly: 'Thanks for the suggestion, all the same. I will bear it in mind.'

Charles laughed and pulled Sarah back onto the dance floor.

'I have misjudged George,' he said. 'I believe he may even be capable of rousing Meril to stand up for herself, when Lady Candera finds out what he's up to and orders him never to darken her doorstep again.'

'If you ask me,' said Sarah with some asperity, 'Meril won't need any rousing. If she is to be believed, it was her idea that they duck this lantern-slide lecture and take in the nightspots instead. So it's my bet that you and Fudge, and anyone else who is interested, can go ahead and buy the fish-slices and plated toast-racks in perfect safety.'

'You sound a little crisp, Sarah darling. But then to you, Meril is only a sort of Boneless Wonder. You haven't seen as much of her aunt as we have. If you had, you would realize why we get such a kick out of seeing old George advancing cautiously to the rescue. It gives us the same feeling we'd get watching some solid London Bobby, backed by the full resources of the local fire brigade, crawling up a forty-foot ladder to rescue a kitten that has got itself stranded on a factory roof.'

Sarah laughed. 'I know. And I'm not really being crisp. It's only that it goes against the grain to see one of my own sex—specially one who can ski like Meril and has a nice figure and could even be pretty if she made the least effort—behaving with such—such *hysterical* flabbiness!'

'That's what comes of serving in the W R A F and wearing uniform,' said Charles with a grin. 'The sight of a really womanly woman, complete with fluttering nerves, timidity and the vapours, not to mention migraine and a horror of mice, inspires you with acute irritation.'

'It does indeed! This is the Atom Age—more's the pity—and anyone as spineless as Meril Forbes should be dumped straight back into a Brontë novel where she belongs. However, if she can sneak off dancing the minute her aunt's eye is off her, I feel there's hope for her yet. If she has any sense she'll get roaring drunk and go home and recite——'

Sarah checked, frowning, and missed a step.

'What's the matter?' asked Charles.

'Nothing—it's just that I suddenly had a funny feeling that I was quoting something that someone else had once said . . .' And even as she spoke, she remembered.

Of course. It had been Janet, speaking impatiently in the Khilanmarg ski-hut: 'What you need, Meril, is to get roaring drunk and recite the Declaration of Independence to your aged aunt . . .' But she refused to think of Janet tonight, and she thrust the memory resolutely away from her and was grateful that the ending of a record at that moment gave her an excuse to change the subject. The Secretary dutifully played a few more records, and then closed the gramophone for a break, and the dancers scattered to various tables on the edge of the ballroom or to the bar or the verandah.

Charles led Sarah to a chair on the lawn outside and hailed a loitering *khidmatgar* to order drinks. Twice a car purred past them, bringing late arrivals; dances came and went, and they had been there for some little time when they heard the crunch of gravel on the path beyond the lawn as someone walked down it in the direction of the car park.

'Who was that?' asked Charles, turning in his chair.

'Reggie, I think,' said Sarah, peering through the mixture of moonlight and shadow. 'But I couldn't really see. Why?'

Charles did not answer, and presently they heard a car start up. It drove off and, by the sound, turned to the left in the direction of Nasim, and when they could hear it no longer, Charles stood up and said: 'Let's go back and dance. We've got about another quarter of an hour to fill in before we need start.' They walked back together across the lawn, and as they re-entered the ballroom, he glanced down at her and said: 'Do you think you could look as if you were romantically interested in me? In about a quarter of an hour's time we are due to leave this Club, ostensibly to go moon-gazing together. Try and look the part, will you?'

' "*Merely corroborative detail intended to give verisimilitude to an otherwise bald and unconvincing narrative*"?' murmured Sarah wickedly.

Charles laughed and pulled her into his arms. 'Perhaps. Anyway they've put on a suitably inspiring tune for us to dance to.'

They moved out into the floor as a rich and fruity tenor voice from the gramophone announced that *'People will say we're in love!'*

'Let us hope so,' said Charles. He was an excellent dancer and Sarah dropped her long lashes and relaxed to the sweet swing and sway of the music:

> *'Don't sigh and gaze at me—*
> *Your sighs are so like mine,*
> *Your eyes mustn't glow like mine,*
> *People will say we're in love . . .'*

'You're doing it beautifully,' approved Charles, his mouth at her ear. The music stopped and Sarah opened her eyes and applauded automatically.

Although the dance had still over an hour and a half to run, several people had apparently already left, and looking about the room, Sarah could see neither Reggie Craddock nor Helen Warrender. A Coply twin was sitting out in the verandah talking to some girl whom Sarah couldn't see, but whom she imagined, judging by the fold of blue material just visible beyond the open doorway, to be Meril Forbes. However, there were several new arrivals: among them Mir Khan in a party of six, all of whom were strangers to Sarah. He bowed and smiled, but did not speak.

Johnnie Warrender was still at the bar and appeared to be rapidly approaching a state of extreme truculence. His voice was clearly audible through the babble of voices and the latest record whirling on the gramophone.

'Helen?' said Johnnie thickly, 'how sh'd I know? P–probably off p–poodlefakin' shomewhere. She dish–dis–pises me. Thash what. Like that Sh–Shakespeare woman. *"Infirm of purposh, g–gi' me the dagger!"* Thash Helen!'

'Hmm,' said Charles, swinging Sarah past the bar. 'Very illuminating. I wonder——' He did not finish the sentence, for at that point Johnnie Warrender slid off his stool with a crash of breaking glass, picked himself up with the assistance of his neighbour and left the building, walking unsteadily.

The music changed again, and a moment later Sarah shivered.

'What is it?' asked Charles quietly. 'Cold?'

'No. It's that tune. It seems to haunt me.'

> *'The moonlight and the moon,*
> *And every gay and lovely tune*
> *That's played for you . . .'*

'Why?' asked Charles gently.

'Janet sang it outside the ski-hut on Khilanmarg; while she was strapping on her skis. And–and it seems to have kept cropping up ever since. They played it that night in Peshawar. The night I read her letter——'

'Yes,' said Charles, 'I remember.'

'And now here it is again!'

'Perhaps it's an omen. A good one this time, let's hope.'

The big clock on the wall struck the quarter hour. 'Come on,' said Charles. 'This is where we make a move.' He glanced down at his watch and gave a sudden exclamation of dismay. *'Damn and blast!'* said Charles furiously, under his breath. He seized Sarah by the arm and hurried her off the floor.

'Why? What's the matter?'

'It's my own bloody fault,' said Charles savagely. 'I shouldn't have taken my time by that clock. It's almost fifteen minutes slow. Come on, Sarah. Step on it!'

'I'm sorry,' said Sarah firmly, 'but as I gather this is going to be a longish trip, I'm going to dive into the Ladies Room first.'

'Must you? Oh all right, only make it snappy! I'll go and get my *shikara*. Meet you at the top of the water steps. Turn right at the end of this building. *Hurry!*'

He disappeared into the night and Sarah whisked into the Ladies cloak-room.

The Ladies Room at the Nagim Club was entered through a small vesti-bule leading off the entrance hall, and Sarah closed the door behind her, and putting her bag down upon a dressing-table took a swift look at her face in the mirror. Light, running footsteps sounded on the path outside the window, followed a moment later by a slight sound from the end of the passage that led out of the dressing-room to the left, where the lavatories were, as though someone had either quietly opened or closed a door.

Sarah flicked her nose with a powder-puff and ran across to the passage. She tried the door of the first lavatory and found it locked, but the next in the line was open, and as she closed the door behind her there was a faint scuffling sound from the passage outside followed by a smothered laugh. Sarah paid no attention, but when she turned the handle again to leave, the door would not open. Oh bother the thing! thought Sarah frantically. It *would* take this opportunity to stick! She tugged at the handle, but the door remained obdurate.

A system of oriental sanitation prevailed at the Club, as in most of Kashmir, and therefore each lavatory had two doors: the back one opening into a narrow passage reserved for the use of lavatory attendants. Sarah hastily unbolted it, only to find that this door too was fastened from out-side. Fastened . . . That was it of course! The doors had not jammed. Someone had locked her in. Some silly fool of a practical joker, thought Sarah, remembering that smothered laugh. But Charles had said 'Hurry!' and he was waiting for her at the foot of the water stairs: she *must* get out.

She hammered at the door with her fists and shouted at the top of her voice until the noise echoing loudly round the little whitewashed cell al-most deafened her. But when she stopped to listen she could hear no sound from outside except, very faintly, the strains of the radio-gramophone in the ballroom, and she realized with a stab of dismay that until some other woman entered the Ladies Room, she could shout herself hoarse without a chance of anyone hearing her above the noise of voices and music in the ballroom. There was nothing for it but wait until someone else entered the cloakroom.

Locked in a lavatory, of all places! thought Sarah furiously. Of all undig-nified, silly, stupid situations!

The words of a ribald song of her earlier schooldays rose unbidden to her mind:

'Oh dear, what can the matter be?
Three old ladies locked in the lavatory!
They were there from Monday to Saturday.
Nobody knew they were there . . .'

Sarah giggled hysterically and immediately afterwards was seized by another stab of panic. *'Nobody knew they were there.'* That was the trouble. Charles knew where she was, but he could hardly come charging into the sanctity of the Ladies Cloakroom in search of her. However urgent his desire for speed, she was sure that a proper Anglo-Saxon respect for decorum would forbid such an impossible breach of etiquette.

But it appeared that she had over-estimated Charles's respect for the conventions.

She heard the door into the dressing-room open violently, and shouted again, and Charles's voice called: 'Where the hell are you?'

'In here!' called Sarah. 'I've been locked in!'

There was a sound of quick footsteps and of a bolt being jerked back, and the door swung open suddenly and precipitated her into Charles's arms.

'Are you all right?' demanded Charles sharply. 'What happened?'

But Sarah was unable to answer, for she was suddenly overcome by a gale of unseemly mirth.

'For God's sake stop giggling!' snapped Charles.

"I c–c–can't help it,' choked Sarah. 'It's so s–s–silly! Three old ladies I– locked in a lavatory. Oh gosh——!'

Charles gripped her shoulders and shook her until her hair resembled a red-gold Japanese chrysanthemum. 'Pull yourself together, Sarah!' he said urgently. 'How did it happen?'

'I don't know,' said Sarah, dabbing her eyes. 'When I went in there I heard a slight sound and someone laughed, and when I wanted to come out again I found that some idiotic humorist had locked me in, so I banged and yelled for a bit and then you came. That's all.'

'Who was it?'

'I tell you, I don't know! I only heard someone laugh. I suppose they thought it was frightfully funny. It must have been a practical joke.'

'Let's hope so,' said Charles grimly. 'Come on, we've got to get out of here. Where's the back door?'

He caught her by the elbow and hurried her down the passage past the bathing cubicles and out at the far door, but once in the open he was forced to slow his steps, and they walked decorously down the path.

Something glinted and sparkled with a flash of green fire on the moonlit gravel near the dressing-room window, and almost without thinking, Sarah stooped and picked it up. It was a small green sequin.

18

Charles led the way along the path and round the end of the Club building to a flight of wide stone steps that descended to the water's edge where a number of *shikaras*, their crews sleeping soundly and small oil riding-lights blinking smokily in each prow, lay moored in the shadow of a big chenar tree.

A single *shikara* was drawn up at the bottom step, and a shadowy figure in Kashmiri robes stood with one foot on the prow and one on the stairs, steadying the boat. Charles handed Sarah in, murmured a few words to the man and followed, and the man pushed the boat off from the shore, and leaping aboard, passed them and swung himself into the stern where the rowers sat.

They drew away from the shadows of the bank and out into the brilliant moonlight on the lake, and Sarah, leaning out to peer around the high padded partition that served as a backrest for the passengers and screened them from the crew, saw that there were four men paddling the boat. She turned to Charles who was sitting beside her, his shoulder touching hers, and said in an undertone: 'Is is safe?'

'Is what safe?'

'Going off on this sort of trip in a public *shikara*.'

'It isn't a public *shikara*. It's a private one—and they're all picked men.'

'You mean they're British? In disguise?'

Charles gave a short laugh. 'Don't be such a little owl! Of course not. There are all creeds and classes in our job. Hindus, Mussulmans, Sikhs, Dogras, Pathans, Parsees, Punjabis, Bengalis—any amount of 'em. One of our best men is a quiet little *bunnia** who keeps a shop in a Delhi bazaar. Another drives a *tonga†* in Peshawar City.'

'*Um,*' said Sarah, and was silent for a space.

'What's worrying you?' inquired Charles in an undervoice; aware that she was troubled.

* A shopkeeper.
† A two-wheeled horse-drawn vehicle.

'All these people,' whispered Sarah, 'and the man who was watching out for you last night—Habib. And there was the one you met at some place near Gulmarg, and the pockmarked man in the shop, who we're going to meet . . .'

'What about them?'

'Well, weren't they here when Janet and Mrs Matthews were alive?'

'They certainly were—except for Habib, of course.'

'Then—then why weren't they able to help them? Why didn't one of them leave Kashmir and carry a message to someone in British India?'

'I thought I'd already told you why,' said Charles with a trace of asperity. 'The fact that we have a certain number of people, such as these men tonight, whom we can call upon to help us, doesn't mean that they know more than a fraction of what is going on. Any more than a junior employee in some big Multi-National Corporation knows what is going on in the mind of the Chairman of the Board of Directors! Unfortunately, whatever those two women stumbled upon was too hot to be handled by any of the resident helpers in this State. And even more unfortunately, neither of them realized—according to what you told me about your conversation with Janet—that they themselves had been spotted, until it was too late to call up a squad of watchers to keep an eye on them. Or perhaps Mrs Matthews considered it wiser at that juncture to refrain from hedging her bets? That's something else we shall never know.'

'I suppose so,' said Sarah, and relapsed into silence.

The paddles fell softly, rhythmically, with a soothing monotony of sound as the boat slipped smoothly through the water. There was no wind on the lake that night, and the breeze of their passage was barely enough to do more than stir the faded cotton curtains that hung from the decorated canopy overhead.

Charles shifted restlessly and though he was lying back against the cushions in apparent relaxation, Sarah was aware that his body was tense and strained.

'What's the matter? Why don't you tell them to hurry?'

'I daren't,' said Charles briefly, shifting his shoulders again in a small jerky gesture of anxiety. 'There may be people watching and we mustn't look as if we're in a hurry until we're well out of range of the Club. We're supposed to be out for a sentimental moonlight row, not a boat-race. The trouble is that we're badly behind time.'

'But surely he'd wait?' asked Sarah anxiously.

'Ahamdoo? Of course. But it could be dangerous for him to hang around for too long. I suppose he chose the island because it would be a comparatively easy place for me to reach. And a much safer spot to get to because I'd have to come by water, instead of by land through all those bazaars and mean streets. But it still seems a pretty dicey choice to me.'

'Then why did you agree?' whispered Sarah.

'I told you. I hadn't any choice!'

'I'm sorry. I–I forgot.' Sarah fell silent again, and Charles turned and looked back to where the lights of the Club were mirrored in the lake behind them. A minute or so later he said: 'OK I think we can safely step on it now.'

He gave a low-spoken order to the rowers, and immediately the tempo of the paddles quickened. Sarah would not have believed that the shallow wooden boat could move at such speed. The four heart-shaped paddles dipped and rose as one, driving the pointed prow through the water with a sound of tearing silk, while the curtains fluttered and flapped in the draught of their passage.

As they neared the end of Lake Nagim, where the wide expanse of water breaks up into the narrower channels that lead towards Srinagar or to the main stretch of the Dal Lake at Nasim, Charles gave another order. And once more the pace slowed, and swinging left, they passed under the shadowy arch of the Nagim Bridge in a leisurely manner.

There was a figure upon Nagim Bridge. Some night idler who leant against the wooden rail at that end of the bridge where a tree threw a patch of shadow, and whose cigarette-end made a spark of orange light against the darkness.

Beyond the bridge and away to the left stretched the backwater of Chota Nagim, and Sarah could see the outlines of the Creeds' boat and, behind it, the solitary riding-light that marked the *Waterwitch.* Then they were paddling past reed beds and dark patches of lotus leaves, and presently the *shikara* entered a willow-bordered channel between banks that were not more than a dozen yards apart, so that the thin boughs arched over the water, interlacing above it and breaking the moonlight into a thousand silver fragments that powdered the black water below. But even here the paddles still did not change their rhythm.

Charles jerked back his cuff and peered at his watch, and the greenish, luminous circle of the watch face, glowing faintly in the shadows, reminded Sarah that she was still clutching the small green sequin she had picked up on the gravel path outside the window of the Ladies Room at the Nagim Club.

As the *shikara* left the gloom of the short willow-shadowed channel and came out again into open water, she examined her find. The small green sequin lay on the palm of her hand winking and glittering in the clear moonlight, and she was just about to drop it overboard when something seemed to click like a shutter in her brain.

A green sequin. Helen Warrender had worn a dress embroidered with green sequins. Then sometime that evening Helen Warrender must have passed along the path that led to the back door of the Ladies Cloakroom at the Club. Why? Only someone wearing a bathing costume would be likely to make use of the back door. Anyone else would naturally enter it by the main entrance in the hall.

Sarah's mouth tightened and her green eyes sparkled dangerously. Practical joke nothing! thought Sarah angrily, she wanted to make me look silly to Charles, and anything sillier than getting oneself locked in a lavatory I can't imagine. She'd like Charles for herself. Well, she can't have him, that's all——!

'Cat!' said Sarah, unaware that she had spoken the word aloud.

'What's that?' asked Charles, startled.

'Nothing,' said Sarah, flushing guiltily. 'I was just thinking of something.'

She flicked the little sequin overboard, where it flashed briefly in the moonlight like a wicked little green eye, and was whirled away in the wake of the paddles—for now they were moving swiftly once more.

The *shikara* passed through a narrow neck of water where a grassy island bearing a row of tall poplars reached out an arm towards the shores of Nasim, and entered the wide, glimmering expanse of the Dāl Lake. On their left, among the dark masses of trees along the curving shore, lay the village of Nasim and the mosque of Hazratbal; and away in the distance, at the far side of the lake, lay the Shalimar Gardens and the mountains, misty with moonlight.

The lake stretched before them like a vast mirror, smooth and shining, and the night was so still that the dip and thrust of the paddles seemed intolerably loud in that silver silence. Yet theirs was not the only boat on the Dāl that night. There were a few little low-lying native boats, barely more than dark streaks on the gleaming water: fishermen out spearing fish, or houseboat *mānjis* returning from visits to friends in the villages. And further out on the lake, their white canopies ghost-like in the moonlight and the oil-lamps on their prows pricking warm pinpoints through the silver, were two more *shikaras.*

By now their own *shikara* was heading away from the Nasim shore towards the centre of the lake, and Charles had ceased to lounge back against the cushions. He was sitting upright, leaning a little forward with his hands clenched on his knees, staring intently ahead; and Sarah, following the direction of his gaze, saw a ghostly shape afloat on the water ahead of them, and realized that it was an island. A tiny island with tall trees upon it, lonely and lovely in the middle of the moonlit Dāl.

At first it was only a shadow, a silhouette in silver point; but as they drew nearer to it the outlines sharpened and darkened, and she could see that there was a small building on the high ground in the centre of it, while at each corner a huge chenar tree leaned its boughs out over the water.

As she looked, Sarah's eye was caught by a movement away to the right of the island. There was yet another *shikara* out there on the lake, a white moth in the moonlight. But since this one carried no light at its prow, it was impossible to tell if it was moving towards the island or away from it.

Charles had seen it too, for he gave a curt order to the rowers and they checked their paddles. For a moment or two their boat moved ahead on its own momentum, the water whispering along its sides; then it slowed and drifted quietly to a stop.

Sarah moved, her dress rustling on the cushions, and Charles made a brief imperative gesture of the hand, demanding silence. He was staring out into the moonlight, his head a little on one side, and Sarah too sat still, listening. In the silence she could hear the quick breathing of the rowers behind her and the *drip, drip,* of water from a paddle. A fish jumped and a frog croaked from a patch of floating weed. Then, very faintly, she heard the sound of paddles and realized what it was that Charles was listening for.

The sound of those other paddles was not growing louder, but softer; which meant that the boat beyond the island was moving away: and there was yet another sound from somewhere far away out on the lake. So faint that it was little more than a vibration in the stillness. The *pht–pht–pht* of a motorboat . . .

Charles turned his head and gave a brief order, and the *shikara* moved forward again; softly now, as though the need for haste were gone; and almost before the prow grated against the bank he had gone forward and leapt ashore. Sarah followed more gingerly, her boldly patterned frock nearly invisible against the chequered black and silver of moonlight and chenar shadows.

The little island could not have been more than thirty yards square. The four great chenar trees were rooted on the level turf, while in the centre the ground rose in a series of artificial terraces banked with Persian lilac, to a small summer-house. It did not take more than a couple of minutes to walk round the entire island. But there was no one there.

Charles looked at his watch again and stared out across the water to where a faint white dot showed against the reflections of the mountains. It was the *shikara* that they had seen beyond the island and it was moving in the direction of Srinagar.

A bird rustled among the lilac bushes, but no other sound broke the stillness, for the faint beat of paddles and the throb of the motorboat had both died away: and watching Charles's tense profile, white against the inky shadows of the chenar trees, Sarah was seized with a sudden shiver of fear and unease that made her glance quickly over her shoulder, as though she half expected to see someone standing behind her among the shadows.

'Why isn't he here?' she asked, forming the words with an effort. She had meant to speak them aloud, but somehow they had been spoken in a whisper. And it was in a whisper that Charles answered: 'I don't know. Either he never came, or else . . .'

He did not finish the sentence and after a moment Sarah said uneasily: 'Or else what?'

Charles turned slowly, and his face in the clear moonlight showed drawn and rigid, the face of a stranger. It was as though he had aged ten years in as many minutes. He said under his breath and as though he had forgotten Sarah and was thinking aloud: '. . . or else—he's still here.'

Sarah took a swift step backwards, her hands at her throat. 'Still here? You mean—on the island?' Her voice cracked oddly: 'Don't be ridiculous, Charles! There's no one here but ourselves and the boatmen.'

'Perhaps,' said Charles curtly. 'Anyway, we can make sure.'

He turned away abruptly and began to search among the lilac bushes, and it was a moment or two before the full significance of that dawned upon Sarah. Her brain felt cold and numb and stupid and she did not seem able to move. She stood as though frozen, staring unseeingly ahead of her into the dense shadows, while the bushes about the little summer-house rustled as Charles searched among them.

Directly in front of her, outlined blackly against the expanse of moonlit lake, stood one of the four huge chenar trees that gave the island its name. Its massive trunk was hollow with age, and as Sarah's eyes became accustomed to its darkness, detail after detail emerged from the shadows as though it were a photograph in a developing tray.

Charles had made the circuit of the lilac bushes. 'He's not there,' he said.

'No,' said Sarah. Her voice sounded husky and strange and as if it did not belong to her—as though it belonged to some other girl who stood there in a black and white patterned frock among the black and white patterns of shadow and moonlight. She lifted one arm and pointed stiffly, like a jointed doll: 'He's over there. In the tree . . .'

And suddenly, as though her legs would no longer bear her, she sat down abruptly on the dew-damp grass and began to laugh.

Charles leant down and quite deliberately struck her across the cheek with the back of his hand.

Sarah gasped, choked, and caught her lower lip between her teeth, and for a long moment she stared up into Charles's quiet, unwavering eyes, and seemed to draw strength from them.

'I'm sorry,' she said in a subdued voice. 'I'm—I'm behaving very badly.'

Charles said: 'I shouldn't have let you come. Go and sit in the boat, darling.'

'No,' said Sarah. 'I'm all right now. Let me stay, please.'

'It won't be pleasant.'

'I know,' said Sarah: 'Janet wasn't pleasant . . . or—or Mrs Matthews, either.' Charles did not argue further, but turned and walked over to the tree.

Sarah had been right. The sprawled fingers of a plump, clutching hand that showed so still among the dead leaves and grasses at the foot of the old chenar tree were Ahamdoo's. The rest of him lay huddled inside the hollow tree-trunk with the haft of a Khyber knife protruding from his breast.

Charles and the tall rower who had stood at the bottom of the water steps by the Club lifted him out and laid him on the grass in the bright moonlight. The round, pockmarked face that had been ugly in life was uglier in death: the dark eyes wide and staring, ringed with white, the lips drawn back from uneven teeth in a grimace of agony or fear.

Charles knelt and searched through the voluminous brown robe, and pulling off the curled-toed leather slippers, felt inside them and examined the soles. But if Ahamdoo had carried any tangible message, it was not there. Only . . . only . . . about the folds of those robes there lingered, faint in the fresh night air but quite distinct, that same curious odour that both Sarah and Charles had met with twice already: first in the deserted hut by the Gap, and then again, that very morning, in the dusty showroom of Ghulam Kadir's shop at the Fourth Bridge.

Now it was here too; on a little island in the middle of the moonlit Dāl, clinging about the robes of a murdered man.

Charles lifted a fold of the robe and sniffed at it, frowning. Letting it drop again, he rose to his feet and spoke to the tall rower, who fetched a torch from the boat, and together the two men searched the island inch by inch: the grass verge, the terraces and the steps up to the little summer-house, the bushes of Persian lilac and the hollow trunks and twisted roots of the old chenar trees. But they found nothing there but dead leaves and the debris of old picnics. And though there were footmarks in plenty, it was impossible to tell who had made them or when, because too many country boats stopped at the island on their way across the lake.

Charles returned to the *shikara*, and lying prone along the shallow prow, peered into the water around the shore with the aid of the torch while one of the rowers paddled the boat in a slow circuit of the island. He had obviously forgotten Sarah, who stood backed against the lilac bushes in a patch of bright moonlight, her hands gripped tightly together. Now and again she shivered, but she did not move.

The *shikara* completed its circuit of the island and Charles returned to the body of Ahamdoo. There was no other boat, and nothing to show how Ahamdoo had come to the island. Charles stood for a while in silence, staring down at the huddled figure with an intense, frowning concentration, as though he could wrench the secrets from that dead brain by an effort of will. Then abruptly he went down on his knees again.

Ahamdoo's right hand, which Sarah had seen protruding from the hollow trunk of the chenar tree, was lying with clawing, outspread fingers on the grass. But the other one was clenched, and Charles knelt again and lifting the closed fist, forced it open. Rigor had not yet set in and the body was still warm, but the fingers had been so tightly clenched that it was only with difficulty he opened them.

There was something in the palm of Ahamdoo's hand on which, at the moment of death, he had clenched those podgy, brown fingers; something that gleamed dully in the moonlight. A single blue china bead.

Charles picked it up and turned it over between his fingers, smelt it, shook it, looked through it and touched it gingerly with his tongue. Finally, with a faint shrug of the shoulders, he produced a handkerchief in which he wrapped the bead carefully, and having replaced it in his pocket, rose to his feet, dusted his knees and spoke to the tall rower in the vernacular.

Together they lifted the small, plump body of Ahamdoo and placed it in the shadow of the chenar tree, and a second man came over from the boat carrying a coarse blanket with which he covered the body. Charles spoke to them in a low voice and they nodded without speaking. The tall man thrust his hand into the bosom of his robe and for a moment Sarah thought she saw the glint of a revolver. Then Charles touched him on the shoulder, and turned towards her: 'I'll take you home,' he said curtly. 'There's nothing more we can do here.'

He took Sarah's cold arm and led her back to the boat, while the tall man and the man who had brought the blanket squatted down, India-fashion, in the shadows near the shapeless dark heap that had been

Ahamdoo. And presently the *shikara*, now with only two rowers, drew away from the island.

Sarah found that her teeth were chattering, though whether from cold or shock she could not be sure, and Charles picked up her fur cape from where it lay on the floor of the boat and fastened it round her unresisting shoulders. There was a folded travelling rug on the forward cushion, and he shook it out and drew it up over her knees.

Sarah said, trying to keep her voice steady: 'What are those two going to do?'

'Wait here until I send the boat back for them.'

'Aren't you going to send for the police?'

'No,' said Charles curtly. 'The less the local police, or anyone else for that matter, knows about this, the better.'

'But—the body. You can't just leave it there. What are they going to do with it?'

'Dispose of it,' said Charles bluntly.

'How?'

Charles shrugged his shoulders. 'Oh there are ways. It's better for everyone concerned that Ahamdoo should just disappear. I assure you it isn't an unusual occurrence in this country.'

He relapsed into silence; frowning down at the tasselled shadow of the canopy fringe that jerked in time to every thrust of the paddles; his hands clasped about his knees.

Sarah drew the fur cape closer about her throat and shivered again, and Charles evidently felt the slight movement, for he glanced round at her.

'Cold?'

'No,' said Sarah. 'I–I was thinking. Did they—was it because we were late? If we hadn't been late——'

Charles shook his head. 'We were bound to be late. If one thing hadn't delayed us, another would. I've been too sure that they weren't onto me.'

Sarah drew a sharp breath and jerked round to face him: 'You mean, you think they know about you?'

Charles laughed; but without amusement. 'Of course. But I'd like to know how they spotted me. I've walked on eggshells for years, waiting for this to happen.'

'What difference will it make?'

'Don't be silly, Sarah,' said Charles impatiently. 'It's the chap who isn't suspect who is useful. The others are about as much use as a sick headache.' He struck his knees with his clenched fists: 'I should have been on the island before moonrise if necessary, and stuck there until Ahamdoo arrived. Instead of which I go putting up a lot of unnecessary smoke-screens and providing myself with completely redundant alibis at the Club, and allow myself to be neatly delayed there while someone else keeps my appointment and rubs out Ahamdoo under my nose.'

'But you couldn't know—' began Sarah.

'Couldn't know what?' demanded Charles bitterly. 'I knew Ahamdoo would arrive at the island at the exact time he said he would. Our people don't arrive late or early on a job I assure you: it isn't considered healthy. I had taken the trouble to find out exactly how long it would take me to get to the island from the Nagim Club, and I should have taken my time by my own watch. But I didn't. Instinct made me keep an eye on the Club clock, because I happen to know that it is checked daily by the wireless; and it was easier to keep an eye on it rather than be continually looking at my own watch. And because I was too sure of myself I fell into a trap that shouldn't have caught a baby!'

'What do you mean?' asked Sarah. 'What trap?'

'The clock, of course. Tonight, for some unaccountable reason, that clock which was right by mine and the wireless at five this afternoon, was nearly twelve minutes slow. To have made it any slower would have been to run too great a risk of having it spotted—but a lot can happen in twelve minutes It probably didn't take more than twelve seconds to kill Ahamdoo! All the same, twelve minutes is cutting it a bit fine, so they take another chance . . . Nearer a dead certainty than a chance, when you come to think of it!'

'How do you mean?'

'I mean that as soon as you and I arrive together at the Club, obviously intending to dine and dance, they realize what I mean to do. And they bet on your paying a fleeting visit to the Ladies Room before setting off for an hour or so on the lake! All things considered, it was a dead cert that you would, and someone was probably alerted hours ago to keep an eye on you and the moment we looked like making a move to leave to delay you— using that particular ploy for starters! There would have been other ones in reserve, in case that one failed. But it didn't. It worked like a charm, and as a result another eight or ten minutes are wasted, so that even by making up what time we could by paddling flat out whenever possible, we arrive at the island a good twenty minutes beyond time.'

Sarah said desperately, remembering the green sequin: 'But how can you be sure that it wasn't a coincidence? The clock I mean? And locking me in *might* have been only a joke? You *can't* be sure!'

'I'm not much of a believer in coincidences of that type,' said Charles. 'Especially when I arrive at a rendezvous to find that someone has beaten me to it. It's all too convenient.'

'But—but surely it was far too risky? You could have looked at your watch and not at the clock—there could have been other women in the cloakroom who would have heard me and let me out, and stopped them from trying anything else.'

'In that case,' said Charles grimly, 'you can be quite certain that something equally innocent to the eye would have delayed us. And even if all the innocent-seeming devices had failed, I still do not believe that we should have been allowed to reach the island in time. Some nasty accident would have occurred.'

'What sort of accident?' asked Sarah in a small voice.

'God knows. But . . . Well just think how easy it would have been for instance, for someone who had seen us leave on time, to get into a car or onto a bicycle—or even to leave pretty briskly on foot!—and reach the Nagim Bridge, or better still that neck of land just beyond it, ahead of our *shikara?* We'd have been a sitting haystack in the moonlight at that range. They couldn't miss!'

'You mean you think—you can't really think that someone would have tried to *shoot* us?'

'Not us; one of us. It wouldn't really have mattered which one, if the object was either our late arrival or non-arrival at the island.'

'I don't believe it!' said Sarah breathlessly. 'I won't believe that anyone would——'

'Oh, possibly not,' interrupted Charles impatiently. 'I'm merely telling you that some way would have been found to stop us getting to the island in time, and that if the simpler ways of preventing it had failed, something damned unpleasant would have been substituted!'

He paused to stare out across the moonlit lake, and after a moment spoke as though he were thinking aloud.

'Whoever did it must have been waiting on the island. The motorboat of course. That would cover the time problem. A motorboat could drop a man on the island and be away again in a matter of minutes, and Ahamdoo would never have landed if there had been another boat there already. He would have made certain there wasn't one before he went on shore. And the murderer, of course, would have used Ahamdoo's boat to get away in. The only thing that doesn't make sense is why didn't they remove the body?'

'Why should they?'

'Oh, just to confuse the issue a bit. If there had been no sign of him I couldn't have been a hundred-per-cent certain that he hadn't developed cold feet at the eleventh hour. And they can't really have supposed that they'd scare me off by demonstrating what they were capable of. Sarah, somehow I've got a hunch that leaving him there was a mistake on the part of the murderer, and I trust it's going to prove a pretty costly one.'

'What doesn't make sense to me,' said Sarah, 'is why they didn't wait a bit longer.'

'You mean until I turned up, and then dispose of me too? Well for one thing, they would have known that I wouldn't have arrived there alone, and that I and anyone with me would certainly be armed. And for another, that a gun battle at this hour, on a night as quiet as this one, would create a hell of a racket—not to mention the resulting blaze of publicity! You notice that to date nothing noisy has been used. A blow on the head for Mrs Matthews and Miss Rushton, and a knife for Ahamdoo——'

'But you've just said that someone on the bridge or that neck of land, could have shot us!'

'If they had, they'd have used something like an air-gun—it would have been enough, at that range! Or a silencer. But they couldn't bank on us doing the same. They had to stop Ahamdoo's mouth, and the moment they'd done so they knew they had to leave pretty smartly—and did!'

Charles relapsed into silence, occupied by his own thoughts, while Sarah stared ahead of her seeing not the beauty of the moonlit lake, but a small glittering green sequin, winking up at her like a little evil eye from the gravel of the path outside the Club.

If Charles was right and locking her in had all been part of a plan, then Helen . . . No! it wasn't possible! It couldn't have been Helen. It must have been someone else. Then what had Helen Warrender been doing on that path this evening? How long had the sequin lain there? Or was there anyone else who had worn a dress with green sequins on it? People one knew did not do these things—plot and spy and lend themselves to murder. It could not possibly have been Mrs Warrender. And yet . . .

Sarah's mind went back to the story that Johnnie Warrender was badly in debt. It was no secret, for Helen was eternally referring to the extent of his overdraft, and she also made no attempt to disguise her preference for the society of those who were socially and financially better off than herself. All the same would any amount of money tempt her to involve herself in murder? It did not seem credible . . .

Sarah's thoughts ran round and round in a helpless circle of suspicion and denial, like a squirrel in a cage, as the *shikara* turned out of the Dāl and crossed a small open stretch of water, heading for the dark, willow-bordered channel that led into Chota Nagim where the *Waterwitch* and the Creeds' houseboat were anchored.

The moon was sinking towards the mountains beyond the bulk of Hari Parbat Fort, and the *shikara*'s canopy no longer threw a shadow down upon its passengers. The cold clear moonlight illuminated every corner of the boat, and Sarah turned her head and looked at Charles. He was frowning thoughtfully down on something that he turned over and over between his fingers, and she saw that it was the cheap, blue china bead that he had taken from Ahamdoo's clenched hand.

For some reason the sight of it filled Sarah with shuddering repulsion: a renewal of the horror she had experienced as she made out the outlines of those plump, rigid fingers among the dead leaves at the bottom of the hollow chenar trunk. She said suddenly and violently: 'Throw it away Charles! How can you touch it?'

Charles tossed it lightly into the air and caught it again. 'Throw it away? Not much! This means a great deal Sarah, if only we can work it out.'

'Why should it mean anything? It's only a china bead.'

'You're forgetting something,' said Charles, rolling the bead in the palm of his hand.

'What?'

'The writing on that bit of paper in the matchbox.'

Sarah caught her breath. 'Of course! I'd forgotten. It was something about beads——'

' *"The teller of tales threads his bright words as beads upon a string",* ' quoted Charles. 'Quite a coincidence, isn't it?' He tossed the bead in the palm of his hand, throwing it and catching it again.

'I thought you didn't believe in coincidences,' said Sarah.

'I don't. That's why I'm interested in this bead. Very interested. That line out of a poem would obviously have meant quite a lot to the person for whom it was intended. And I don't believe Ahamdoo was carrying this for fun. There's a link between the two, and I mean to find it. This may not be much to go on, but it's something.'

Sarah looked at the small blue oblong as it glinted in the moonlight. It was about half an inch in length, made of coarsely glazed china, and the hole through it was large enough to take a fairly thick piece of twine. One saw strings of these beads in shops in the native bazaars and round the necks of *tonga* ponies: they were said to bring good luck and avert the evil eye, and even the wiry little pack-ponies who had ploughed through the snow on the Gulmarg road had worn ropes of them slung round their necks.

'Could there be anything inside it?' she asked.

'No,' said Charles, squinting through it at the moon. 'Not a thing. However I will crack it up when I get back, just to be on the safe side. Hello, here we are in the home stretch. I hope Fudge and Hugo haven't been waiting up for you. I promised Fudge I wouldn't keep you out too late. Do they take their chaperoning duties at all seriously?'

'Lager's the only one who is likely to be awake,' said Sarah. 'I only hope he doesn't bark and wake everyone up.'

The *shikara* had turned out of the main stream and was now being paddled softly up the backwater of Chota Nagim, and Sarah peered ahead to where the *Waterwitch* lay moored in the shadows of the willow trees beyond the Creeds' boat. She had turned out all the lights in the boat before she left, with the exception of one over the front door that lit the prow and the top of the forward gangplank. But the *mānji* had evidently considered this insufficient, for now a welcoming orange glow lit up the drawing-room windows, adding a warm note of colour to the waning moonlight and the black shadows as the *shikara* nosed its way gently through a patch of lily-pads and bumped alongside.

There was no one on board except Lager, warm from sleep and whimpering an enthusiastic welcome, and Charles looked about the narrow crowded drawing-room, and having tried the lock on the door, said: 'Did you get those bolts I told you to put on your doors and windows?'

'Not yet,' confessed Sarah. 'But the *mānji* said he'd have them fixed by tomorrow. I'll be all right. Lager will protect me, and this time I'm going to lock myself into my bedroom as well, and anyone who likes can come on board and burgle the boat—I shall put my head under the bedclothes and refuse to move.'

Charles frowned and jerked his shoulders uneasily. 'Can I count on that?' he asked, unsmiling.

'I promise,' said Sarah. 'I've had enough of rushing in where angels fear to tread. And quite enough "alarums and excursions" for one night. Don't worry. Look at Lager. He's simply bursting with beans and bounce, and if anyone puts a foot in the boat tonight he'll bark his head off and wake up everyone for miles. There's no storm tonight, and you could hear a mouse move in this quiet. Listen.'

She held up a finger and the silence seemed like a wall about them.

'You see? It was different last night. The storm was making such a racket that a troop of elephants could have boarded the boat without my hearing them; and Lager had been drugged. But you could hear a pin drop tonight, and if I yelled, Hugo and Fudge and the *mānjis* and Hugo's bearer would all be buzzing round like bees. Besides, I shall turn all the lights on and no snooper is likely to come sneaking up on a brilliantly illuminated boat in the small hours of a night like this.'

'No, there is that,' said Charles slowly. He went over to the nearest window and stared out into the moonlight: 'It will be dawn in less than four hours.' He swung round on Sarah. 'Have you got that gun?'

'Yes,' said Sarah. 'It's under my pillow, if you want to know.'

'Good. Well you do just as you said. Lock yourself into your bedroom, and if you hear anyone move on the boat before morning, yell the roof off and don't hesitate to shoot.'

'I know,' said Sarah: 'I hear someone trying the bedroom door, and *"Bang!"*—I've shot the *mānji*, who was trying to bring me my morning tea. I hope you'll bail me out?'

Charles laughed. 'I'll do that. We'll move you off this boat tomorrow, anyway. It's not worth the risk. I wouldn't leave you on it tonight if I hadn't got it under pretty close observation.'

'You've *what?*' said Sarah. 'You mean——?'

'Oh, I've had some of our people watching this boat in shifts since this morning—I mean yesterday morning,' corrected Charles, glancing at his watch.

'Where are they now?' asked Sarah, interested. 'I didn't see anyone.'

'You weren't meant to. One of them is keeping an eye on the approach from upstream and another from the bridge end, to keep a check on anyone who comes past here by water; and a couple of chaps are posted on the landward side. Anyone who looks as if they are coming towards this boat will be followed. I want to know the names of any intending visitors.'

'Where are you going now?' asked Sarah. 'Back to—back to the island?'

'No. I've sent the boat back there. That's a job they can do better without me. I'll walk back to the Club from here.' He turned away, and Sarah accompanied him out onto the prow.

The night air was cool and fragrant after the stuffy atmosphere of the little houseboat drawing-room, and Charles walked down to the foot of the gangplank and stood there, peering into the shadows beyond the big chenar tree. He drew the torch out of his pocket and flashed the light briefly, twice, and a figure detached itself from the shadows fifty yards or so from the boat, where the willows grew thickest, and moved into the moonlight.

Sarah heard a faint rustle of footsteps on grass and presently a tall Indian stood at the foot of the gangplank. He wore a dark blanket wound about his shoulders and drawn over his head so that it threw a deep shadow over his features, and Sarah could only catch a gleam of eyes and teeth.

Charles spoke in a low voice in the vernacular and the other answered as softly.

'Has anyone been near the boat?'

'No one Sahib; save the *mānji* who has returned to the cookboat and is now asleep, and the big sahib who brought back the Miss-sahib's dog. There have been no others as yet, either from the water or the land.'

'Remain then and watch. Now that the Miss-sahib has returned, allow no one to enter the boat before morning.'

The man saluted and withdrew noiselessly into the shadows and Charles turned and came back up the gangplank, and said: 'Wait here, Sarah. I'm just going to take a look round the boat to see that the *mānji* hasn't left anything unlocked.'

He went away down the narrow duckboard that ran all round the outside of the boat on the level with the window-sills, trying each window and door as he passed, and disappeared round the far end. Presently he reappeared again from the opposite side having completed the circuit of the boat.

'OK. Everything appears to be locked up safely. You'd better bolt this door too, just to be on the safe side.'

'All right,' said Sarah slowly. She felt a sudden aversion to entering the stuffy atmosphere of the cramped and shuttered little boat in which Janet had lived and worked, and hidden her secret.

A bittern called from a reedbed on the far side of the backwater: a lonely, mournful cry. Sarah shivered, and seeing it Charles said: 'You're quite sure you're all right? You don't think you'd better go over and ask Fudge and Hugo for a bed?'

'No I don't,' said Sarah with asperity. 'Good-night, Charles. I won't say "thank you for a lovely evening" because it's been the most gruesome evening I've ever spent, and I hope I never have another one like it. But thanks all the same.'

Charles smiled down at her, his face drawn and tired in the moonlight. He laid the back of his hand lightly against her cheek in a brief caressing gesture and said: 'Go on in and let me hear you bolt the door,' and she turned away obediently and went in.

19

The bolt shot home and Sarah leant tiredly against the closed doors and listened to the sound of Charles's footsteps descending the gangplank.

The little boat rocked and creaked for a moment, and then steadied again and the silence flowed back once more.

Lager came pattering back into the room from some expedition into the darkened rooms at the other end of the boat and frisked about Sarah's feet, and she gathered him up into her arms and sat down in one corner of the shabby sofa, feeling very tired. Too tired for the effort of getting to bed, and yet not in the least sleepy.

Sitting huddled and relaxed, her chin resting on Lager's silky head, she remembered that she had told Charles that the night was so still that you could hear a pin drop. It had been true while he was beside her, but now that he was gone and she was alone the night seemed full of little sounds; the soft lap of water against the side of the boat, the scutter of a rat somewhere beneath the floorboards, the creak of a board contracting in the night air and the croak of frogs from among the lily-pads; Lager's gentle breathing, and the soft *click, clack* as the bead curtain in the doorway between the drawing-room and the dining-room swayed in a draught.

Slowly, very slowly, a queer sense of uneasiness stole into the cramped little room: a feeling of urgency and disquiet that was almost a tangible thing. It seemed to tiptoe nearer to Sarah and to stand at her elbow, whispering—prompting—prodding her tired brain into wakefulness and attention. As though, perhaps, Janet herself had entered the room and was trying to speak . . .

For a moment the feeling that someone—was it Janet?—was watching her was so vivid that Sarah jerked round and looked behind her. But the room was empty and there was no gap between the motionless folds of the cheap cotton curtains that shielded the dark squares of the window-panes and shut out the moonlit night.

But there was still something there that clamoured with a wordless persistence for attention, and Sarah's tired brain shrugged off its lethargy and was all at once alert and clear. She sat quite still; tense now, and very wide awake, staring about her.

The room was just the same, and nothing appeared to have been moved since she had left it. There were the chairs with their shabby cretonne covers and the sofa on which she sat. The over-ornamented tables with the dust of long years lingering in the endless crevices of their intricate carving, and the lines of tattered books and aged periodicals that leant limply against each other on the long wooden shelf that ran round the narrow room. A yellowing calendar dating from the restless, long-ago twenties still hung from a nail on the wall beside the carved walnut-wood desk, and the time-worn Axminster carpet that had been made in some murky factory of Edwardian England, and travelled ten thousand miles from the loom of its birth to end its days on the floor of a houseboat on the Dāl Lake among the mountains of Kashmir, still spread its faded reds and blues under her feet . . . That carpet could tell a tale, thought Sarah, gazing down at its worn surface. *'The teller of tales threads his bright words as beads upon a string . . .'*

A frog skittered across the water outside and a soft breath of wind from off the mountains ruffled the leaves of the chenar trees. The draught lifted the threadbare Axminster in a soundless ripple and stirred the quiet cotton folds at the windows, and the curtain in the doorway that led into the dining-room swayed and clicked. Beads—red and green and white and yellow glass beads, winking and glinting; china beads, opaque and smooth. Blue china beads . . .

Click . . . clack . . . click. A small voice in the silence saying over and over again, *'Look! . . . look! . . . look!'*

Something clicked, too, in Sarah's brain, like the shutter of a camera, and she was unaware that she spoke aloud: 'Of course!' said Sarah. ' "As beads upon string!" Of course. Why didn't I think of it before?—it's there —in the curtain. Janet's record!'

She dropped Lager onto the floor and stood up.

Why hadn't she noticed before that there was no design about the curtain? That the beads fell into no pattern? Small beads interspersed at brief irregular intervals by large blue china beads. That was it—irregular intervals. Dots and dashes, short beads and long beads, with blue china beads to mark the divisions. So simple. As simple as a page of Morse code . . . and so very quick and easy to make——

Sarah found herself trembling with excitement as she ran to the desk and snatched up her writing-block and a pencil, and pulling forward a carved chair, sat down facing the curtain and began to write down the order of the beads from the top to the bottom of each string in turn.

The letters made no sense but they read off smoothly in dots and dashes. Long beads and short beads and blue china beads. It'll be in code of course, thought Sarah, but Charles will know it. She scribbled on in the silence.

A night bird called again from among the reeds, and another breath of wind from across the lake ruffled the lily-pads and sent the water lapping softly once more against the side of the boat. Lager snored peacefully on the sofa, but all at once Sarah's pencil slowed and stopped, and her eyes became fixed and still . . .

Someone was watching her. She was quite sure of it. A queer, unmistakable, prickling shiver of awareness crept up her spine and tightened the skin of her scalp, and she had to force herself to look over her shoulder. There was nobody there, and with the curtains closely drawn no one from the shore or the lake could possibly see into the room, while if anyone had come up onto the duckboards or paddled close in a *shikara* she would have heard them in this stillness. Her nerves must be playing tricks on her.

Yet the feeling of being watched, and the awareness of another presence close at hand, persisted and grew stronger and stronger until it was not a feeling any more, but a deadly certainty, and Sarah sat rigid, straining her ears to listen.

Somewhere in the darkness on the other side of the bead curtain a board creaked sharply, and a faint tremor of movement shook the floor beneath her feet. So she had been right! There *was* someone on the boat. A creaking board by itself was nothing—they creaked all night and for a dozen trivial reasons—but that quiver of movement that had run through the *Waterwitch* was unmistakable. Someone, somewhere on the boat, had taken a step in the darkness.

Sarah listened, tense and trembling: thinking that no one could come on board, either from the lake or from the land, without making far more noise and a great deal more vibration than that which had been produced by a single stealthy footstep . . .

It was only then that she remembered, with a wild rush of relief, that Charles had left a watcher on the bank. Several watchers! The one out there now must have put a foot on the gangplank and caused that slight tremor, for no stranger would have been able to come onto the boat without being seen by one of Charles's men. It was stupid of her to panic. She was perfectly safe.

She picked up her pencil again. And once more a board creaked in the darkness and the little boat vibrated to soft footsteps. Once—and again—and again . . .

Lager stopped snoring and lifted his head, his eyes bright and alert and his head cocked a little on one side.

Someone was moving on the boat. No. Not *on* the boat. *In* the boat——

The doors and the windows were locked and barred and there were watchers on the bank; but none of that was any use. No one was trying to board the boat, for someone was there already. Someone who had been there all the time, waiting in the darkness beyond the sly, winking lines of the bead curtain.

Sarah sat quite still, not daring to move, her body rigid with fear and her mind darting about like a terrified animal in a trap.

Charles had said she was safe—she had a gun and there was a watcher on the bank not twenty yards away. She had only to cry out. But the gun was under her pillow in the bedroom, away in the blackness beyond the bead curtain, and she seemed to have lost the power to move or breathe. She opened her mouth to call out, but her throat seemed to have dried up. It was as if she were trapped in a waking nightmare.

She heard Lager jump off the sofa behind her and land with a little *flump* on the floor, and he pattered over and stood beside her, peering into the darkness beyond the glinting beads. The boat vibrated gently to soft footsteps as someone moved across the dining-room, and now it seemed to her that she could hear breathing—or was it only the wild thudding of her own heart that sounded so loud in the silence?

Something flickered and moved in the darkness beyond the bead curtain: eyes were looking at her and a hand came forward to draw aside the curtain—a horrible hand . . .

Sarah tried to scream, but no sound came from her fear-constricted throat, and Lager, beside her, thumped the floor with his tail as the curtain swung aside. And it was only Hugo who stood there in the doorway looking down at her.

'*Hugo!* Oh Hugo—oh God! you gave me such a fright! Hugo you *beast* —I nearly died of heart failure. I suppose you've just been snoring away on my bed ever since you brought Lager back—and I thought——*Oh Hugo!*'

Sarah collapsed in a limp heap, gasping, choking, sobbing in hysterical relief, and after a moment or two she dashed the tears from her eyes with the back of her hand and laughed up at Hugo.

But there was something wrong. Something out of true. Why wasn't Hugo laughing? Why didn't he say something? Why did he look so–so——

The cold hand that had for a moment released its clutch upon Sarah's heart, began to close again—very slowly—and she struggled to her feet and stood staring at Hugo, her hands clutching the back of the spiky, carved chair. There was an odd smell in the room—so faint that had the windows been open she would not have noticed it. A smell that conjured up terrifying memories . . .

Hugo said: 'What were you doing, Sarah?'

His voice was the voice of a stranger; soft and without any expression—almost a whisper.

Sarah said: 'Hugo! Don't look at me like that! What's the matter?' Her voice cracked oddly.

Hugo did not take his eyes off her face. He said again: 'What were you doing, Sarah? You were taking it down, weren't you?'

Sarah did not answer. She could only stare numbly, her eyes held by that curious fixed look on Hugo's face.

Hugo said: 'I saw you. I was watching from the pantry doorway. You were writing it down, weren't you? I never thought of it being here. How did you find out?'

Sarah's brain seemed to be full of wavering, ludicrous thoughts that swooped and darted like swallows. Incredible, impossible, fantastic ideas that chased themselves across her brain, whirling and absurd; gone before she could see them clearly or put them into words.

Hugo leant down and picked up the writing-block and Sarah's eyes, released, flickered and closed and opened again.

Hugo—Hugo's hands holding the writing-block. Bright red hands: shiny, slippery, horrible . . . Why, he was wearing gloves! Rubber gloves . . . *Red rubber gloves,* drawn up over his wrists, smooth and taut except where a jagged tear at the edge of the left-hand glove showed a small triangular patch of sun-tanned flesh . . .

He was holding the writing-block in his left hand, and in the right a curious object that looked like, and yet unlike, a gun. And he was speaking again, though his words did not seem to make sense to Sarah. She could only stare at those smooth, slippery, red hands and try to remember something——

Red . . . like blood . . . and shiny; and that smell . . . the smell in the dark, musty hall of the house by the Gap. That was it!—the tiny triangular patch of wet blood at the edge of the chair, that hadn't been blood at all but a fragment of red rubber——

Hugh was saying: 'I'm sorry, Sarah, but there it is. You know too much. You shouldn't have meddled. Why the hell couldn't you leave well alone?' His voice was all at once absurdly querulous and aggrieved, like that of a spoilt child.

Sarah forced her gaze away from those scarlet hands and up to Hugo's face. She said, her voice a frozen whisper: 'Then it was you in the hut, waiting for Janet. Oh no! No, I don't believe it. It's crazy—you couldn't, Hugo!'

'I had to,' said Hugo, still in the same queer, querulous voice. 'You don't suppose I liked doing it did you? The damned girl was too clever for her own good. Besides, the end justifies the means—you believe that, don't you? The individual doesn't matter—can't matter. Janet was just grit in the machine. She had to be removed.'

He's mad, thought Sarah wildly, he's quite mad! he *must* be. She said: 'Hugo—don't! You don't know what you're saying.'

Hugo laughed suddenly and when he spoke again his voice was quite normal. He came forward into the little cramped drawing-room, and as the bead curtain clashed behind him he glanced at it, frowning, and said: 'I shall have to cut that damned thing down, or our dear friend Charles might drive up to it in the same way you have. Odd to think I've been through this bloody boat with a small-tooth comb and missed what was right under my nose. Damned smart of you to spot it, Sarah: I always knew you were a smart girl. How did you do it?'

Sarah said wildly: '*Hugo*—Hugo I don't understand. Why did you . . . ? Oh, I think I must be going mad!'

Hugo sat down astride a chair facing her, his arms along the back of it and his chin on his sleeve, but he kept the odd-looking object in his right hand pointed at Sarah. His hand was quite steady, and suddenly Sarah was afraid as she had never been before, even when she had first heard the footsteps in the dark behind the bead curtain. And curiously enough, her fear steadied her.

She looked at Hugo, and it was as if she were seeing him for the first time.

The Hugo she had known, the gay, babbling, easy-going Hugo, was no more a real person than a piece of painted canvas scenery is real. That Hugo was merely a façade; a smokescreen; and behind it lived the real Hugo. Looking at him now, Sarah could not understand why she had ever thought those hard, implacable eyes were gay, or had failed to notice the cruelty of the small tight mouth. I suppose, she thought dazedly, it was because he was always laughing—or talking. His mouth was always open and his eyes crinkled up. One listened to him and laughed at what he said, and didn't really look at him at all . . .

She said desperately: 'But why?—What did you do it for?'

'The Party,' said Hugo; as one who says 'for God.'

'What party? I don't understand—you're English!—you can't mean——'

'As a matter of fact,' said Hugo, 'I'm half Irish, but——'

'Oh God!' interrupted Sarah. *'Cromwell,* I suppose!'

Hugo threw back his head and laughed; but the unaffected gaiety of that sound did not deceive Sarah any longer. It was a habit and no more. Part of his stock in trade. It went no deeper than the surface.

'I'll spare you that,' said Hugo, 'but if you think that any waving of the Union Jack is going to affect me, you waste your breath. No, it was always the Cause. One life, Sarah, that's all we get, and we're a long time dead. Have you ever thought of that? No, I don't suppose you have. You're young yet. But there are millions of people who spend it in misery and sickness and grinding poverty, slaving their guts out to earn power and money and leisure for a pampered handful of profiteers or effete layabouts who still think of themselves as "the Aristocracy" and regard all those who work with their hands, or are less well born or well connected than themselves, as "the Common Herd" . . .

'Now that this war is over the scum will be coming up to the top once more and imagining that they can carry on in exactly the same way as they did before. Well they are due for a series of nasty shocks! Much nastier ones than the election results that put a cat among the pigeons last year! The People are moving, and nothing can stop them now.'

'You mean—you're one of *them?'* gasped Sarah. 'A *red?'*

'If you like to call it that. Though it's not a word we use much.'

'But you're a serving officer . . . you can't . . . Doesn't your country mean anything to——No, I can see it doesn't. But Janet—and Mrs Matthews—and, and—Ahamdoo——Oh God! was that you? How many were there? How *could* you——'

'Don't be a fool, Sarah!' said Hugo roughly. 'They were on the other side, and they knew the risks of the game. They took a gamble and lost. That's all there is to it. Do you suppose that any of them would have hesitated to shoot me if they'd been able to get off the mark quicker? Of course not! Your precious Charles wouldn't hesitate to shoot me in the back if he had half a chance. And quite rightly. I'd do the same to him if I thought I could get away with it. I'd only just tumbled to Charles. Clever chap. Makes me boil to think I never dreamt . . . Oh well——!'

Sarah said uncertainly: 'Does—does Fudge know?'

Hugo's face changed. His brows twitched together in a black frown, and his voice was suddenly harsh and rasping: 'No, she doesn't! Fudge has nothing whatever to do with this. She knows where my sympathies lie of course, which was why she insis . . . persuaded me to give up my job in Intelligence—because she was afraid I might be "too biased". She hadn't the remotest idea that it was much too late in the day for that, or that the damage, from her point of view, was already done. She still doesn't know. Not yet, anyway.'

Sarah said: 'Then how did you manage about Janet? You were at Khilanmarg with her when . . . No you weren't! That was why Janet stayed: you said you'd strained a tendon. You hadn't, I suppose.'

'No. I merely didn't want to go to Khilan because I was still hoping to catch whoever came to that hut near the Gap: Charles, I imagine? Oh yes, we'd cottoned on to the hut all right. It wasn't too difficult, because one of the great advantages of having worked for Intelligence is that you get to know a reasonable number of your fellow-workers, and to learn how some of them tick. For example, that a select few of the more erudite, who are not all that certain that their Indian servants don't understand English and may not be averse to accepting bribes and listening at doors, elect to conduct their top-secret discussions in Latin, in the belief that not a word of it will be understood by any inquisitive ear. And how right they would have been if I hadn't got wind of it and contrived to plant a few exceedingly innocent-looking Indian ears here and there, whose owners, convincingly disguised as humble servitors, were all in possession of Classical degrees acquired at English universities.

'That hut scheme was only one of several interesting bits of news we managed to collect in this way: and very useful it proved——Though I admit it never occurred to me that Janet would take my place up at Khilan just when it had become a case of "Now or Never", with the possibility of the weather turning nasty and still no sign of any ruddy lamplighter. Fortunately it made no odds, since she came anyway. I nipped across from the hotel and lit my own signal lamp, on the off-chance that it might fetch her down, and it did. All I had to do was wait. The only casualty on our side was that idiot Mohan Lal, who apparently hadn't realized that she'd be bound to have a gun. She plugged him very neatly.'

'Who—who was Mohan Lal?' asked Sarah shakily.

'Oh, just one of the boys. Rather a nasty bit of work and no loss. But it annoyed the third member of the party, who we'd managed to plant as a waiter in the hotel, quite considerably. I had the greatest difficulty in preventing him from shooting the girl out of hand, which would have caused no ordinary mess. Nothing like a purely accidental death for closing a tiresome episode without trouble. Missing bodies, or corpses with bullet holes in 'em, are a hell of a nuisance and stir up streams of awkward questions.'

Sarah said: 'How did you do it? Why didn't they——' Her voice failed her and she could not go on.

'Why didn't they make a fight for it? Ah! See this little gadget?' He gestured with the curious weapon he held. 'Gas. A very clever invention of an exceedingly clever man. It can either stupefy, anaesthetize, or kill instantly. Depends on your trigger finger and how much you wish to use. It leaves no trace and it makes no noise. A whiff of this, and then it's a simple job to knock someone on the head in the sort of place that they might be likely to hit themselves if they'd had a bad fall. Or stick a knife into them with no fuss at all: not a cheep . . . !

'I've got an excellent staff, but the brains are here,' Hugo tapped his forehead, and suddenly flung back his head and laughed loudly and uproariously: 'God, how I've laughed up my sleeve sometimes at all our pompous brass-hats and gilded Foreign and Political snobs—the lordly "heaven-born"! If only they'd known that all the time I held 'em here—here, in the palm of my hand!' The hard blue eyes held for a moment a fanatical glow and his voice dropped to a whisper: 'But nobody knows. I've been too clever for them. Nobody knows. Good old Hugo—the station silly ass.'

Sarah said, trying to keep her voice steady, trying to keep the wild panic from showing in her face: 'Why are you telling me all this?'

Hugo looked at her for a moment as if he had forgotten she was in the room. He said petulantly: 'Now don't be silly, Sarah. You know quite well why. You know too much. Far too much. I'm sorry, but there it is.'

'But–but——' the words seemed to dry in her mouth, 'you can't kill me, Hugo! You can't. If–if I promised . . .'

'You wouldn't keep it, and I'm too near the end of the job to take any chances. The stakes are too big. No, my dear. A little whiff of this and the question will be settled. I'm not sure what they will decide that you died from. However the local MO is not likely to amount to much, and the chances are that he'll put it down to some heart trouble and leave it at that. In your fall, suffering from this inexplicable attack, I think you will have stumbled against the bead curtain and pulled it down with you. Yes, that will be the best idea. Two birds eliminated with one stone. And if you are considering screaming, I shouldn't. This stuff can work like chain lightning.'

Sarah fought with blind panic and managed to steady her voice. She said: 'It's no use, Hugo. You can't get away with it this time. There are men watching this boat and they must have seen you come on board.'

'You mean the bird in the bushes along there?' said Hugo with a laugh. 'That's all right. He's the only one within sight of the boat. The others are merely watching the various approaches.'

'You mean, you *knew?*' Sarah's grip tightened on the back of the chair.

'Of course I knew. I'm no fool. The chap over there saw me come on board. In fact he couldn't have missed me: I made as much noise as possible. And why should he worry? He sees you hand over Lager to me when you leave, in the presence and with the approval of his boss—Charles was a party to that transaction, remember? Then not long before you return I come along the bank complete with dog, and go onto your boat turning on the drawing-room light in the process—always a disarming act. No criminal turns on a light. As you could see, he's not posted near enough to overhear much, and he undoubtedly supposed that you and Charles were greeted affectionately by me when you came on board.

'I hope you've noticed that I haven't kept my voice down? Your amateur watchdog will have heard loud voices and laughter proceeding from this boat for the last ten minutes or so. The Miss-sahib having a jolly chat with the stout sahib who is her friend. No sounds of alarm. Not a bark from the dog. When I've dealt with you and set the scene here, I shall go out, chatting merrily, call back a gay "good-night" to you, and leave with the same amount of ostentation as I arrived. The watcher will think nothing of it. I shall then—which is a bore but necessary—have to deal with him. A very simple business.'

'You couldn't!' breathed Sarah. 'You couldn't! He'll have a gun . . .'

'Oh, almost certain to. But what more natural than that you or Charles have told me—the old familiar friend—that he is there, lurking in the bushes? I shall hail the bird in a conspiratorial whisper and say you have a message for him. Naturally he will bite. Here is a sahib who is obviously in on the whole thing. And at close range he can get a whiff of this, and since we don't want to overdo the heart-failure idea, he can be found in the morning—drowned, I think. All very murderous and harrowing, but absolutely nothing to do with that nice Major Creed, who will be simply prostrated with manly grief and emotion. See?'

'Yes,' said Sarah slowly. 'I see.'

Her brain seemed suddenly to have cleared. Hugo was not mad: it was worse than that. He was a dedicated, dyed-in-the-wool fanatic in his loyalty to his own ruthless dogma and his equally ruthless masters, and he meant just exactly what he said. He would kill her without a qualm; as he had killed Janet and Mrs Matthews and Ahamdoo—and how many others? He would deem himself justified, because to those of his kidney the end would always justify the means—any means! however brutal and degrading. And what he had said was true—no one would ever suspect him. Even Charles would never suspect. Those who were employing Hugo had chosen a good tool, for like Caesar's wife, he was above suspicion.

There must be some way out. This could not be happening to her—Sarah Parrish.

The light. Could she make a jump for it and smash it? In the dark she could have a chance, for the weapon Hugo held had one disadvantage. Except at point-blank range he could not use it without grave risk to himself. And if he tried to use it in the dark he might himself fall a victim to it.

The switch was near the far door and out of Sarah's reach; but the single bulb that lit the room was nearer, and though it was still too far away, the wire that led from the switch sagged across the ceiling, held in place by a few rusty nails, and if she could jump for it and wrench it down the lights would go out. But would it break or hold? And even if it did break, would the shock from the current knock her out? If so, she would be in as bad a position as before . . .

Hugo followed her gaze with complete understanding, and grinned.

'You can't do it, Sarah. Well, I must be getting along. Any last messages or anything?'

And then Sarah heard it. Coming from that distance it was a very faint sound, and if all her perceptions had not been screwed to their peak by panic her ears would never have caught it.

Someone was coming down the field path, and whoever it was had trodden on the sheet of tin that lay over the wet patch.

Lager had heard it too. He lifted his nose from his paws and his eyes turned to the window behind Hugo's head.

'Lager—!' pleaded Sarah desperately.

Lager dropped his head back on his paws obediently, and Hugo said: 'I'll look after him. Don't worry.'

I must talk, thought Sarah, I must keep him talking. There's a chance . . .

Hugo sat up and lifted his right hand. His eyes had widened curiously so that the whites showed all round the irises. Odd, pale eyeballs, hard and glittering like wet pebbles. That small, cruel mouth. Henry VIII—who had said that? It had seemed funny once, but it wasn't funny now. How could they all have been so blind? 'Bluff King Hal,' who in spite of his bluffness and his bulk and his joviality had been a killer. This was a killer too.

Sarah said frantically: 'Listen Hugo—if I tell you—all that I know—what they know . . .' her voice was coming in gasps, and Hugo's eyes narrowed a little, but his right hand did not move and Sarah realized that he too was listening. She began to talk loudly, wildly: 'Look, Hugo—I can tell you things. I can tell you everything you want to know—anything you like, I——'

Lager lifted his nose again and said 'Wuff!' and Hugo turned his head.

Sarah could never remember very clearly what had happened then. It had all been a churned-up horror of panic and noise.

She only knew that Hugo's eyes had moved aside from hers at last, and terror lending her strength, she jerked up the chair she had been clutching. It caught Hugo under the chin and he fell over backwards.

She had a confused recollection of Lager barking, Charles's voice calling her name and someone else shouting: a crash of breaking glass, and then blackness.

Sarah recovered consciousness to find herself lying in the open on the prow of the *Waterwitch*, with Charles bathing her head with cold water. The drawing-room seemed to be full of people and there was a queer sickly sweet smell in the air—a smell that she knew.

She stared up at Charles and said: *'Hugo!'*

'I know,' said Charles. 'He's dead.'

'Dead?' Sarah sat up with a jerk, clutching at the wooden edge of the prow with frantic hands. 'Did you—did you——'

'No,' said Charles quietly. 'He killed himself. He knew the game was up, and so he turned that devilish weapon on himself.'

Sarah stared wildly into the small brightly lit room where every window and door had been thrown open, the curtains drawn back and the night air was swiftly dissipating the sickly odour. There were three Indians in the room and Reggie Craddock: two of the former wore Kashmiri dress and the third was Mir Khan. Reggie Craddock was kneeling on the floor beside Hugo's body, stripping off the rubber gloves from the limp hands.

Charles stood up and went back into the room, and Sarah dragged herself to her feet, and following him, subsided onto the sofa and began mechanically to brush the water from her face with the backs of her hands, while staring down incredulously at Hugo . . .

Hugo lay on his back. His eyes were closed, and the small, cruel mouth had fallen into the lines he had trained it to take in life. He was smiling, an amiable and vacuous smile, as Mir Khan went through his pockets, removing papers and replacing cash, a cigarette-case, a box of matches and other objects of no interest.

Reggie got up from his knees and handed the gloves to Charles, who wrapped them gingerly round the weapon that Hugo had held, and picking up a carved wooden box from a table beside him, emptied out the oddments it contained and placed the small bundle inside it. Mir spoke to the two Kashmiris in their own tongue, and they went out, one of them carrying the box, and Sarah heard the sounds of their footsteps on the gang-plank, and then silence.

Mir rose and offered her a cigarette, and when she shook her head, lit one himself, and Charles left the room—to return almost immediately with a small glass of brandy which he handed to Sarah without speaking.

She swallowed it down with a grimace, and Charles said gently: 'Do you think you could tell us what happened?'

Sarah nodded dumbly, and as the brandy began to take effect she pulled herself together with an effort, and told him all that had happened since he left her, in a voice that she did not recognize as her own as it repeated, tonelessly, everything Hugo had said and what she herself had done.

At the mention of the curtain, Mir Khan turned sharply away from the window and going over to it stood fingering the beads while she spoke. But no one interrupted her.

There was silence for a while when she had finished, and Reggie Craddock said, looking down at Hugo: 'Can you square the doctor?'

'Yes,' said Charles curtly.

'You'll have to explain things to him a bit.'

'Of course.'

Mir swung the beaded strings, and listening to them click and clash together, said: 'It is better this way. We cannot afford a public scandal. But can you be sure he spoke the truth when he said she did not know?'

'I think so,' said Charles.

Sarah looked helplessly from one to the other. 'I don't understand,' she said wearily.

Charles turned and walked over to the open door, and stood looking out into the night towards the Creeds' boat, his hands in his pockets. 'We were talking about Mrs Creed,' he said.

Sarah caught her breath in a little gasp: she had forgotten about Fudge, and suddenly she found her eyes full of tears. 'But I told you that Hugo said she didn't know anything about this!'

'I can believe it,' said Charles quietly, 'and I see no reason why she should be told.'

'But you'll have to, now.'

'No we won't,' Charles turned back from the doorway. 'I think this is what had better be the official version. Mir, Reggie and I escorted you home after the dance, and found Hugo here on the boat having brought Lager back. We were all sitting round having a drink, when Hugo had a heart attack and died before any of us could do anything. We're all witnesses to it, and as that foul stuff appears to be everything that Creed claimed, I think you'll find that we won't even have to square the M O. The medical verdict will be heart failure. I'd better go and collect the M O now.'

'Take my car,' said Mir. 'It's standing in the road.'

'Thanks, I will.'

Reggie said: 'What about Fudge? Hadn't you—hadn't one of us better go over and tell her?'

'No,' said Charles curtly. 'We'll have to get the doctor first.'

'But surely she'll miss him and come over?'

'I doubt it. It's my guess that you'll find Hugo slipped his wife a sleeping-draught on every occasion that he wanted to do any night work. He was too clever a chap to take chances. Come on, Sarah. Time for you to go to bed.'

'I can't,' said Sarah. 'I couldn't sleep. And—and—I'd better be here when the doctor comes and when Fudge comes. It would look all wrong if I'd gone to bed.'

'She's right,' said Reggie briefly. 'Cut along and get your medico. The sooner we get this beastly business settled the better.'

'And I,' said Mir, 'shall take down the rest of this bead code.' He stooped and picked up the fallen writing-block.

Sarah heard the sound of Charles's footsteps die away and the night was quiet again.

Mir's pen made a small, monotonous, scratching sound in the silence as it marked down line after line of dots and dashes, and Reggie leant against an open window, staring out into the night while the sky paled to the first, far-off, whisper of morning. And on the floor, Hugo lay and smiled.

Sarah found that tears were pouring down her cheeks, but she was too tired to lift her hand and brush them away.

20

It was three days before Sarah saw Charles Mallory again: by which time Hugo had been buried and the stir caused by his sudden death was already subsiding, for his had not been the only death in Srinagar that week.

Within a few hours of the news of Major Creed's death from heart failure, there had been another tragedy; equally sudden and unforeseen. Johnnie Warrender had broken his neck while exercising some of His Highness's polo ponies.

There had been other happenings too; arrests and disappearances. But since these had been among the crowded mazes of the city, they had not come to the ears of the European visitors, and it is doubtful whether they had aroused much attention even in the city itself, owing to the surge of rumour, counter-rumour, speculation and uncertainty aroused by the imminent passing of the British Raj.

Sarah was sitting on the grass under the willows, looking out across the lake and the open strip of water where the *Waterwitch*—now paid off and retired to some mooring on the Jhelum River—had recently lain. It was almost six o'clock, and the sun was moving down the western sky towards the mountains of the Pir Panjal. Lager was snuffling and digging among the roots of the great chenar tree, and overhead a pair of bulbuls were conducting a vociferous domestic argument.

Someone was walking down the field path, for the battered sheet of tin was still in place, and though the hot suns of the last few days had baked the ground beneath it to a bricklike hardness, it still creaked protestingly when trodden on. Sarah heard that familiar sound and turned swiftly; and all at once there was a tinge of colour in her cheeks and something strained and stiff in her attitude relaxed. A few moments later, Charles came towards her across the grass.

He looked very tired, and there were lines in his face that she did not remember having seen before. But his eyes were quiet, and the watchfulness that had been in them had gone.

'Don't get up,' said Charles and subsided cross-legged on the turf beside her. 'Where's Mrs Creed?'

'She's gone for a walk.'

'Alone?'

'Yes. I wanted to go with her, but she preferred to go alone. She's all right; I mean——'

'I know,' said Charles. 'She has a lot of courage, and I'm very sorry for her. But not nearly so sorry as I would have been had her husband lived, and she had found him out.'

'Do you think she would have done?'

'Of course. In the end it would have been unavoidable. For one thing there were the children, who are both in England at the moment. Like a lot of British kids, they were here in Srinagar at the Sheik Bagh School during the war, and their parents took them home as soon as it ended and put them into boarding-schools in England. But Hugo had planned a family holiday in the Lebanon at the end of the summer term, and it's beginning to look as though from there they would all have vanished—to end up in some comfortable dacha outside Moscow, where the kids could have been educated and brainwashed and transformed into rabid little Stalin-worshippers.'

'Oh no!' said Sarah unhappily. 'He couldn't have been so cruel! Fudge would have *hated* it so!'

'Maybe. But she couldn't have done anything about it, because once you walk into the particular spider's parlour, your chances of getting out are nil. And even if she did get the chance, she'd never have been allowed to take the children with her, and she wouldn't have abandoned them—not in a million years. At least she's been saved that.'

'Didn't she . . . do you think she ever suspected anything?'

'Not the real truth. That's something she can't have conceived of. But she's told us that she was afraid her husband was involved in something that he didn't want her to know about, and that was why he was under stress. I think she suspects some kind of black-market deals. No more than that. They had been poor, and suddenly they seemed to be rich. Money was coming from somewhere and she didn't know from where. There were other things too that she couldn't account for. Mir says she has been lucky, and that there is a verse in "one of your Christian books" (it's in the Psalms, as a matter of fact) that says: "Keep innocency and take heed unto the thing that is right: for that shall bring a man peace at the last," and that Mrs Creed has kept innocency and so will gain, perhaps, peace at the last. I hope so.'

Sarah said: 'She loved him . . .'

'Yes, she loved him. Very much, I think. But there are worse things than losing someone you love. There is finding out that they are not *what* you love. Mrs Creed is a truly "good" woman, and she admired his political views because they seemed to her compassionate and kind and caring. He never let her know more than that, and she could not have borne to discover the truth, and find that her beloved husband was not only a traitor but a murderer. And a thoroughly bad hat into the bargain!'

Sarah said restlessly: 'Nobody can be *all* bad.'

'That's true, and there was one good thing in him: though he himself would probably have considered it a weak spot. His love for his wife and children. All the rest was bad. Not even grandly bad: only mean and vain and cruel and egotistical.'

'Why? *Why* Charles?'

'I'm not sure. But from what we've learned, and from what his wife has unconsciously given away, he was a man who was eaten up with envy of those who had more than he had. More money, more brains, more personality, a better education, a better social background. It is an only too common failing in these days,' said Charles bitterly.

'But he *was* clever. And popular—people liked him. Everyone liked him.'

'Oh yes. He was clever. But not clever in the right way. He was cunning. His childhood had bred in him an envy of those who had more than he, while his vanity made him wish to lead in everything. He went to a university where he fell in with a very radical and distinctly precious set, most of whom had enough pull to get them into cushy jobs when they left. Hugo hadn't, so he plumped for the Army where he found, as so many find in so many walks of life, that an average man with money and a good social background could get ahead of a better man with neither.'

'But a brilliant man—' began Sarah.

'A brilliant man will rise to the top anywhere. You can't stop him. But Major Creed was not brilliant. Only cunning: and in his own view, "penniless", because he had very little in the way of a private income. He was passed over once or twice in favour of men he considered were inferior to him except in pocket and background, and he could not rise above it. He allowed it instead to sour him and destroy him. He had already acquired strong Communist sympathies at his university, but now he went over to the Party heart and soul, and for the meanest of motives: "Envy, hatred, malice and all uncharitableness!" He transferred into the Indian Army in 1937, and shortly after the war broke out managed to get himself attached to the Intelligence Corps of all things.'

'Yes, he said something about that. About knowing people in it and being able to find out about that hut in Gulmarg because they . . . But I didn't believe he could ever really have been in it. I thought he was—was just inventing. Lying again, I suppose . . .'

'He wasn't, worse luck. No; Hugo of all people was involved in intelligence work, and what's more he was carefully vetted for the job; which proves that he must either have covered his tracks very well, or else the "vetting" was pretty slack in those days! That's one reason, of course, why he was above suspicion. And why the opposition always knew so much about what was going on. It seems that he organized and ran a very effective under-the-counter Intelligence Service of his own at one and the same time as the official one; and without anyone ever suspecting it! Oh, he was clever all right. I suppose all traitors have to be—those who get away with it! And all the time he remained, on the surface, "Hugo the Good Fellow", "Hugo the Joker", the "Life and Soul of the Party"——Pity no one every dreamed *which* Party . . . !'

Charles paused and began to tear up the grass stems, shredding them between his thin, tanned fingers, and presently Sarah said: 'Tell me about it, Charles. What was in Janet's curtain?'

'Everything,' said Charles. 'Everything except a name: Hugo's! That was something they hadn't yet discovered. You know, of course, that there is to be a transfer of power from Britain to India.'

'Of course,' said Sarah with the ghost of a laugh. 'Nobody around here talks of anything else these days.'

'Quite,' agreed Charles dryly. 'But what you don't know is that the transfer will not take place next year, as was originally announced, but in August of this year.'

'*What!*' Sarah sat bolt upright. 'But—but——'

'Unfortunately, it's true: you'll hear the announcement very soon. As far as that part of it is concerned, we have found Janet's curtain too late.'

'Why? What difference could that have made? And why do you say it's "unfortunate"? Don't you want them to run their own country? How would *we* like it if——' She saw that Charles was laughing at her, and stopped and bit her lip. 'I'm sorry. I should have known. What were you going to say?'

'I was going to say that it's a great pity that so many people fail to realize that the war that has just ended is only a taste of what is to come. That this "Peace" we are enjoying is only the lemon, the very sour lemon, that both teams suck at half-time. The big struggle is to come, and it is going to be far more bitter: because it will be between ideologies and not nations.'

'But what has this got to do with the transfer of power?' demanded Sarah. 'Everyone knew it must come one day.'

'Of course. But there are those who profit enormously from chaos and disaster, and who will therefore ensure that both occur when that day comes. To this end, money has been spent. It has been poured out!'

Sarah said: 'But, Hugo? What was he doing in all this?'

'Hugo handled the money. And from here. What better place was there? This is not "British India". It's a protectorate: an Independent Native State ruled over by a Maharajah, who is "advised" by a British Resident and can only be disposed—and that only as a last resort—if he behaves *really* badly. Even then, he must be replaced by his heir. Kashmir is, in a way, national—almost international—ground; and moreover, it has a largely Mohammedan population and a Hindu ruling class. That was an asset to begin with! But it had a better one. It was a famous holiday resort for both Indians and British. People from all over India came here, and needed to give no explanation for doing so beyond that they were on holiday.

'Huge sums of money came in here: American dollars, brought by American Communists wearing American Army uniforms. Oh yes, some of them were in it too! English pounds and Indian jewels, bar gold, and silver rupees. All kinds of money was collected here: much of it the proceeds of large-scale robberies. Here it was changed into whatever currency was needed, and here the leading plotters and agitators came for orders and pay, and for funds. There were a great many helpers—among them British men and women.'

'I know,' said Sarah soberly. 'Johnnie Warrender was one, wasn't he?'

'No, not Johnnie. Helen.'

'*Helen!* Then it was——But why—I mean Johnnie is dead. I thought . . .' said Sarah incoherently.

'Oh yes, Johnnie killed himself. It was no accident, but he faked it very well. You see he had learned about his wife. And besides, I think he was a dead man already.'

'What do you mean?'

'He was finished. What Americans would call "washed up". There was nothing any more for him. He had been living on an overdraft for years, and now there was no hope of paying it off, or of paying his other debts. Or playing polo again. With the transfer of power the world of people like Johnnie Warrender will come to an end. It was Helen who worked for Hugo. I don't think she really knew what she was doing: she probably didn't want to! She is a stupid woman of limited outlook, who thought only of the money and nothing else at all. A perfect tool for Hugo. Do you remember the theft of the Rajgore emeralds?'

'Yes,' said Sarah. 'There was a lot about it in the papers; and you mentioned them too—you said they were here.'

'So they are. We suspected that those emeralds would come to Kashmir, as a good many other stolen jewels had done, and we set a watch for them. But they slipped through. Mrs Warrender brought them and passed them to Hugo on the road.'

'But she couldn't have done that!' protested Sarah. 'I was there: and Fudge too. She didn't give him anything!'

'She's told us herself. She gave him the emeralds. They were inside some fruit—a grapefruit or a papaya or something.'

'No,' said Sarah slowly. 'It was a watermelon. I remember now . . .'

'Helen Warrender would have done almost anything for money. There are too many people like that.' Charles pulled up a long grass stem and sat chewing the end of it thoughtfully, looking out over the lake, and after an appreciable interval, Sarah said: 'You can't stop there. Tell me about the rest of it. There are so many things I want to know. That message in the matchbox—how did they find out? About the curtain, I mean? And how did that pockmarked man, Ahamdoo, know?'

Charles said thoughtfully: 'Now that he's dead, I don't suppose we'll ever know the answer to that. We can only guess.'

'Then how did *they* know?'

'That question,' said Charles with a faint smile, 'should be "Why didn't they find out sooner?"—considering how little privacy there is on a houseboat!'

'You're telling me!' sighed Sarah with deep feeling: 'That's why I can't imagine how Janet managed to make that curtain without every Kashmiri within a radius of ten miles knowing all about it.'

'But they *did* know. That's the whole point. It is also a beautiful illustration of why the thought-processes of the East so often succeed in baffling the West. There is an old saying, which originated in this part of the world, that "It is always darkest under the lamp". Janet Rushton knew that to be true, and being a smart girl, she put it to good use. She knew very well that if she attempted to make that record in secret—say, after dark when the curtains were drawn—she would undoubtedly have been found out, and however carefully she had hidden it, it would have been discovered. So she did it openly and in full view, and when it was finished, she hung it up where everyone could see it. Therefore, because it was common knowledge, no one even thought to mention it . . .

'From what the *mānji* now tells us, she must have planned it all very carefully. And since she had the advantage of being born in India and spending a good slice of her childhood here, she knew a lot about the mind of India. She knew, for instance, that because it was inclined to be devious, it could be deceived by openness: and she traded on that knowledge.'

'But the bead curtain?' prompted Sarah.

'The *mānji* says that there had always been one on the *Waterwitch;* apparently many boats had them in the old days. But one day in late November, Rushton Miss-sahib destroyed it. She seems to have tripped and fallen, and grasping at the curtain as she fell, brought it down with her. It was old, so the strings broke easily, and he says that the Miss-sahib was very upset and insisted on replacing it. When she found that such things were no longer made locally, she sent him to the bazaar to buy string, and also extra beads, since many of the original beads had fallen between the floorboards and been lost.

'This, of course, ensured that the maximum number of people would hear the tale. She even went to the bazaar herself and bought more beads, and as there was a last sunny spell towards the end of the month, she sat out on the roof of her boat and threaded them in full view of every passing *shikara,* while Mrs Matthews sketched on the bank. She worked on it for the best part of ten days, and by the end of that time it had become such a familiar sight that it was taken for granted, and ceased to be of the slightest interest. In other words, she deliberately sat under the light and flaunted the thing that must be hid.'

'Yes . . . yes, I see,' said Sarah. 'It was a sort of double bluff.'

'Exactly. And it succeeded in fooling everyone. It might have continued to do so if a certain dealer in carpets (now behind bars and telling us a lot of interesting things in the hope of escaping death!) had not been a lover of Persian poetry. He was one of the many who had actually seen Janet Rushton working on her curtain when he came alongside in his *shikara,* hoping to sell her a carpet, and he had also been one of the people who searched the *Waterwitch* after her death, just in case she had left behind anything either useful or incriminating; and found nothing. But only recently, happening to read that poem, the connection between words and beads suddenly struck him, and he began to wonder . . .

'Since he does not live in Srinagar—his main shop is in Baramulla—he sent this line of verse by a sure hand (whose owner is also now in jail!) to Ghulam Kadir's shop, concealed in a matchbox inside a papier mâché cover, with instructions that it must be passed to Creed-sahib whom he knew would be visiting the shop on a certain day. The man who took delivery of it had the bright idea of presenting similar boxes to any customer who happened to be in the shop at the time, to cover this simple transaction. And as a result of trying to be too clever fell a victim to chance, because your box happened to be too like Hugo's.'

'And I suppose Ahamdoo saw the message?' said Sarah slowly.

'That is the assumption. It wouldn't have been too difficult, since he was one of the assistants in the shop, which—as you saw—has plenty of hiding-places. And he had sharp ears and excellent eyesight! He'd already overheard enough to let us know that a message was to be passed to a *feringhi,* a foreigner, who would come to the shop on that particular day, ostensibly to buy papier mâché, and he suspected either Lady Candera, or her niece Meril, whom he thought might be working for her as a spy. Presumably he managed to take a look at the message—a glance would have been enough!—and when you interrupted us at the hotel, and he saw both Lady Candera and Meril Forbes there, he fell into a pond of panic, and decided to meet me on that island instead, because he thought it would be safer.

'He'd worked with Mrs Matthews, and he too had seen the bead curtain that Janet was making. He had also, on our behalf, searched both their boats after they were dead. So when he read that line of *Farsi* (Persian)—which it seems he must have done—he too would have begun to puzzle over it. And when he set out for the island he took a blue bead with him, presumably to illustrate a theory that the blue china beads could have been stops at the end of words. Though that, of course, is something else we shall never know . . .'

'Is that all?' asked Sarah. 'I mean all that was in Janet's curtain? Just—just about the money and jewels . . . to pay the agitators and saboteurs?'

'No,' said Charles slowly. 'No, there was something else.'

'I thought there must be. You needn't tell me if you don't want to, you know.'

'If I didn't, it would be because I still can't quite make myself believe it. You see it was a plan, a very well worked-out plan, to take over Kashmir as soon as the British moved out, and turn it into a Communist State.'

'But what ever for? What would be the point of that?'

'The point would be that with a Communist Government in power the President or the Dictator, or whatever he liked to call himself, would, in the name of the new Government, call upon Russia for help if either India or the Muslim tribes of the Border country tried to move against them.'

'But what *for?*' repeated Sarah.

'Come on, Sarah, use your head! For a bridgehead, of course! For a base from which, in due time, Russian troops could move against Afghanistan or the North-West Frontier, or India herself, eventually. Just take a look at the map. Any of the nearby territories could be knocked off one by one by anyone who was strongly entrenched in Kashmir, if Kashmir itself was a fully paid-up member of the USSR.'

'I don't believe it. It couldn't be done!'

'No? Think again. On the day of the transfer of power—and probably for some weeks before—the communal hatreds that have been so carefully fostered by the paid agitators will be given their head. And if the country is *really* partitioned, there will be riots and killing and terrible disturbances. Under cover of that, and while everyone's eyes are elsewhere, Kashmir was to have been cut off from the world. Believe me, it would have been quite easy! Far easier than anyone thinks possible. There are not many ways into this country, and those ways are through high mountains and easy to block: and there is only one aerodrome—not a very good one, either! With riot and bloodshed breaking out all over India, it would not be considered so very extraordinary if no news came out of Kashmir for several days. And by the time anything was done about it, it would have been too late . . .'

Sarah said: 'Do you really believe it would have been possible?'

'Yes. I think so. The ownership of the State is already in dispute, so there would be a well-built façade for agitators to shelter behind. The battle cry would be: "We are neither Indians nor Pakistanis! We are Kashmiris!—*Kashmir for the Kashmiris!*" And with the troubles that the new Government will have upon its hands, a *fait accompli* in Kashmir might have proved very difficult to deal with.

'Oh believe me, it may sound wild and improbable, but it was perfectly possible! A handful of men could close the airfield and cut every road into this country—and defend it against an Army. Besides, possession is still nine points of the law! Then later on, when India was ready to turn her serious attention to re-taking Kashmir, the new junta and its boss would yell for help to the Kremlin, who would hurry to assist a defector from the tyranny of capitalist countries, and rush in troops and bombers and fighters and Uncle Tom Cobley and all. Yes, I think they could do it all right.'

Sarah moved restlessly, her fingers pulling off the heads of the daisies that starred the grass. 'But you were in time?'

'Yes, we were in time. We've rounded up a good many people, and some of them have talked, so that we have been able to fill in the gaps in the knowledge Janet Rushton recorded. We've been able to make raids and we have found scores of documents and blueprints. It has been like a net pulled in from the sea. At first you do not even know where the net is, for the marking corks are small and the sea rough. Then you find the first mark and begin to pull the net in, foot by foot. To begin with you pull in only net and water and bits of weeds. But when the last bit of the net comes up it is heavy with fish who can't escape. That's how it's been with us.'

Sarah shivered suddenly, as though the evening air had become cold. 'Were they going to use that–that gas?'

'What gas? Oh, you mean that gun of Hugo's? No, that was just one of the many nasty little inventions that scientists of every nation like to come up with. Hugo thought this one would be useful, and got his friends to make that little gun for him. He used it to stupefy his victims, thereby making it easier for him to polish them off in a way that could be made to look like an accident, and probably the only person to be actually killed by it was himself! It had one bad drawback: that smell. That's why he couldn't store refills on his own boat, and kept a few stashed away in that shop.

'I'm inclined to think that Ahamdoo must have found one and brought it along to show me, because the amount that was used on him to prevent him yelling and running ought to have been dispersed by the night air, as it was used in the open. But his clothes smelt strongly of it; as if he'd carried some hidden under the folds of that smock. They'd have found it when they took his gun, of course. That was missing; and so was his own knife. He wouldn't have come out unarmed.'

Charles flipped the stub of his cigarette into the lake where it broke the reflections with a little hiss and sent a tiny ripple out across the quiet water.

'What about Mir Khan?' asked Sarah. 'Did he know, all the time?'

'Know what?'

'That Janet was an agent; and Mrs Matthews. And you.'

'That I was, yes. The others, no. We don't all know each other: as I told you once, it isn't considered necessary, and often it only adds to the risks. Mir had been on a job in Gilgit and was in Gulmarg only by chance, and because he likes to ski.'

'And Reggie Craddock?'

'He's not one of us. But it seems that he was more than halfway in love with Janet Rushton, and he didn't believe her death was an accident. Also, because he was interested in her, he noticed what no one else did and what you yourself only discovered by accident. That she was very much afraid of something. People in love often do not need words to tell them things . . . You ought to know that!'

Sarah flushed faintly and turned her attention to the daisies once more, and Charles said slowly: 'Reggie watched Janet Rushton, and he knew. It was he who stood in the shadows of the ski-hut and watched her go away across the snow. It was he whom you heard close the door.'

'Was it Reggie who made those footsteps on the verandah?' interrupted Sarah. 'I suppose he——No, of course it wasn't . . . They were too small.'

'Helen,' said Charles. 'She told us about that. The Warrenders had the end room on that block, and the reason for that surreptitious bit of snooping was nothing more than curiosity. She happened to be suffering from an attack of insomnia, and remembering that George McKay was a doctor, decided, Helen-like, to wake him up and demand a sleeping-draught. By chance she opened her door at the exact moment that you started scratching at Janet's; and retreating hastily, she watched you through a crack and saw you let in and the light go on. It stayed on for a long time, and then suddenly went off again—that was when Janet looked out!—and when it came on once more she couldn't resist sneaking along to see if she could find out what on earth was going on. However, by the time she got there Janet had put the radio on, so she couldn't hear a thing and retreated, baffled. Thereby letting George enjoy uninterrupted slumbers, as I gather she'd forgotten all about the insomnia by then!'

Sarah laughed, and felt the better for it: she had been wondering if she would ever laugh again after the shock of that appalling night. Remembering that she had interrupted Charles when he had been telling her about Reggie, she said hastily: 'Go on with what you were saying about Major Craddock. How much did he hear when he was listening to Janet and I talking outside the ski-hut?'

'Very little; he says you were both whispering. But that wasn't what worried him. You see, he is a skier: possibly one of the best who have ever come to Kashmir. So he did not accept the explanation of Janet Rushton's death, because she too was a good skier; and a good skier would not have fallen in that particular way. He suggested as much to Major McKay, but George was no skier and paid little attention. They had a difference of opinion about it, and McKay was angry.

'Reggie is not very clever, but he's stubborn. And it is surprising how much information a stubborn and dogged man can ferret out if he really sets his mind to it. Reggie set his mind to it and decided to carry out some investigations of his own. At one time he suspected you.'

'*Me!* Good heavens!' Sarah sat bolt upright.

'Only because he had seen you talking to Janet outside the ski-hut that night, and you had never mentioned it. Later he became convinced that there was something on the boat—Janet's boat—that you were after. When he found he couldn't get you off it, he watched it.'

'Oh he did, did he!' said Sarah, stormily.

Charles noted the fact, and smiled. 'You owe your life to him, all the same! To him, and to your dog.'

'To *Reggie?* How? It was you——'

'Not entirely me, I'm afraid. I didn't suspect Hugo. But Reggie had been secretly watching the boat, and he had seen Hugo searching it. He had also seen Hugo put down, very carefully, a piece of meat among the roots of the chenar tree on the night that Lager was drugged.'

'*Hugo* did that?'

'Of course. Who else?'

'The beast!' said Sarah wrathfully. 'The *beast!* And he always pretended to be so fond of Lager! I have had moments of feeling I could almost be sorry for Hugo, but I shan't have them again!'

Charles leant back and laughed delightedly. 'Oh the inconsistency of the British! How is it that we will always be able to feel "almost sorry" for a murderer, but have no mercy for anyone who ill-treats an animal? I'm sorry, Sarah. It was rude of me to laugh.'

Sarah was compelled to laugh with him. 'You're quite right of course. Oh dear, it's disconcerting to find out how childish and unreliable one's reactions can be! I suppose Hugo meant to come on board that night, and didn't because of the storm. Or else he saw that there was a light on and thought it meant that I was awake. Poor Lager! Go on about Reggie, please.'

'Reggie didn't fully understand what he'd seen. But then he had never liked Hugo——You knew that?' for Sarah had nodded. Now she said: 'Well . . . Hugo was always very friendly to him, but I did sometimes think that Reggie seemed to find him irritating. That's all.'

'Reggie began to wonder if it were not possible that Hugo had an affair with Janet Rushton. If perhaps she had become too demanding, and a threat to his marriage and reputation: even that he might have killed her to rid himself of that threat. It's curious that his romantic imaginings should have led him so near to the turth! He thought that there could be letters hidden on the boat—love letters from Hugo to Janet—and he went away and brooded on this. Do you remember that when I left you that night I spoke first to one of the watchers?'

'Yes. Why?'

'I asked him if anyone had been near the boat, and the man replied that no one had, except the *mānji,* who had returned to the cookboat and was now asleep, and the big sahib who had brought back your dog. He didn't add *"and who is still on the boat",* because it didn't occur to him to do so; any more than it occurred to me to notice that although the man had mentioned that the *mānji* had gone back to his cookboat, he had not said that Hugo had returned to his boat. You see Hugo was above suspicion. The watcher, seeing Hugo go on board, supposed later that you and I had been talking to him. But what more natural, if there was danger to the Miss-sahib, that Creed-sahib should remain when Mallory-sahib left?'

'That's what Hugo said. So he was right.'

'Yes, he was right. All the same, I was worried. It seemed to me that there was something not quite right; something that didn't fit. A false note. But I couldn't pin it down. It nagged at me in the way that a name or a face that one can't quite remember does, and then just as I reached the gate of the Club, I suddenly realized what it was—Lager! You had told me that when you left him alone he would whine and bark without ceasing.'

'Yes,' said Sarah. 'It was true. He's a little beast that way. He'll yelp and howl for hours on end.'

'But he was not yelping or whining when you came back to the boat that night.'

'No, but that was because—' Sarah stopped suddenly.

'—because Hugo was on the boat,' finished Charles. 'Exactly. That's what suddenly occurred to me. The pup had been making no noise. Why? Because someone was with him. Someone he knew. It was then that I remembered what the watcher had said—or rather, what he had *not* said. He hadn't said that Hugo had left the boat: only that he had gone on board. Then Hugo was still on the boat. Where? Why hadn't he shown himself? Had he taken a nap on one of the beds and fallen fast asleep?'

'Yes, that's what I thought when I first saw him,' confessed Sarah, and shivered suddenly and uncontrollably. 'So what made you come back?'

'Because I met Reggie, and because Reggie had been talking to Mir Khan. The dance was over and Reggie and Mir had stayed on talking in the Club garden. Reggie had probably had too much to drink, and he was worried and lonely and off his guard. And when Hugo's name happened to come up in the course of conversation, Reggie confided to Mir that he didn't trust him—he was "up to no good", was the way he phrased it—and he went on to say that he himself had been watching your boat, and what he had seen . . .'

Charles drew out another cigarette and lit it, and said through the smoke: 'Fortunately, Mir is an Indian. Had he been British the chances are that he would automatically have been on the side of a fellow-countryman, and so Reggie's information would have meant very little. As it was, he had no reason to be biased for or against Hugo; but since he knew we were suspicious of anyone who was interested in the *Waterwitch*—and clearly, Hugo was interested—he told Reggie to come with him at once and they'd wake me up. Mir seems to have thought I'd be in bed and asleep by then but that the matter was too urgent to be left. They were actually crossing the drive on their way to my room when they met me coming up it, and Mir told me what Reggie had seen.

'A few minutes earlier and it might not have meant very much. But now, when I'd just realized that Hugo must already be on your boat, it meant the end of the world—or that's what it felt like!' Charles laughed suddenly, and said: 'It's a long time since I won the quarter mile at my school. But I must have lowered my own record that night! There wasn't time for explanations. I just said "He's on her boat now!" and turned and ran, with Mir and Reggie pelting behind me——

'We had to slow down a bit when we reached the field path, because it was vital to move quietly and there was that damned piece of tin some-where on the path. Even then, Mir put a foot on it, but otherwise we made no noise. We could hear voices; and then the dog barked, so I called out——

'Hugo couldn't expect to explain away a dead body, or those gloves and that smell. Had it been anyone else who called, I think he would probably have killed you at once, and then gone out with some story that you were asleep, and tried to bluff it through. But he knew I would come on board.'

Sarah said: 'He had that awful stuff. He could have killed us all. Why didn't he?'

'Because he couldn't have got away with it. He must have realized within seconds that I wasn't alone, and he can't have known how many people I had out there with me: though he would have known that some if not all of us would be armed. And then he'd be coming out from the light into the dark—the moon was down by then—so we'd see him before he could see us. Worst of all, from his point of view, that filthy weapon of his was only useful at short range and against a single target. It would have been useless against an unknown number of men whose positions he couldn't pinpoint. The odds against him were too great, and he must have realized it and turned that foul gun on himself.'

A silence fell between them. The smoke of Charles's cigarette spiralled up slowly in the quiet air, and behind it the lake lay like a sheet of topaz in the twilight. The sun had dipped behind the Gulmarg range, and the mountains behind Shalimar were no longer rose and cyclamen, but slate-grey and cold blue against a pale jade sky flecked with tiny apricot clouds as soft as a fall of feathers from the breast of a wounded bird. A veil of wood smoke from the evening fires drifted across the darkness of the trees at the far side of the lake and a lone frog began to croak among the reeds.

Charles said: 'That's Mir coming across the fields. I suppose someone told him I'd be here.' He came to his feet and stood waiting.

'I have only come to say goodbye,' said Mir walking towards them. 'No, do not get up, Miss Parrish. I cannot wait.' He shook hands with Charles and smiled down at Sarah: 'I shall see you again, I hope. But tomorrow I leave Kashmir.'

'More . . . work?' asked Sarah, standing up to shake hands and brushing daisy heads off her lap.

'I am afraid so.'

'Why do you do this kind of work?' she asked curiously. 'You don't have to.'

Mir laughed. 'There you are wrong, Miss Parrish. We all have to do the work we were sent into this world to do. This is my work: I do not know why it should be so, but I know that it is. And I help my country, also. There is some satisfaction in that. Goodbye—and . . . I wish you much happiness. *Khuda hafiz!*'

He sketched the graceful Oriental gesture of farewell and turning away among the willows, walked quickly back along the field path.

There were so many more things that Sarah had wanted to know. So many questions that she had meant to ask. But suddenly they ceased to matter. It was only Charles who mattered, standing before her in the dusk under the willow trees.

The moon had risen while they waited, and now it floated silver and serene in a sky that still held the last faint flow of sunset. It laid a shining pathway across the quiet water and lost itself among the lily-pads at the lake's edge.

Charles's tall figure seemed etched against it in black on silver, while Sarah's white face and pale frock gleamed from the shadowy background of the willow boughs, silver on black.

Charles reached out and took her hands in his, and Sarah said softly: 'You said that if there was a third time, you'd really mean it.'

'This is the third time and I really mean it,' said Charles gravely.

'Good,' said Sarah contentedly.

The two figures, the black and the silver, drew together and became part of the moonlight and the shadows: so still that a heron, alighting in the shallow water at the lake's edge, remained within a yard of them, pricking between the lily leaves, until Lager, returning from a foraging expedition beyond the chenar tree, sent it flapping out across the moonlit Dāl.

Postscript

For those who are interested in facts, the first ski-hut on Khilanmarg was destroyed, together with its occupants, by an avalanche that roared down from the ridge of Apharwat, leaving a track that is still there—a long, wide, silver-grey smear on the mountainside. The ski-hut in this story, which was built to replace it, has by now, I am told, been demolished and re-placed in turn by a hotel with a ski-lift that connects it with Gulmarg.

The original H.B. *Sunflower* (there could be a new one of that name by now), which I have allotted to the Creeds in this book, was our houseboat —rented by my father for several years, together with its mooring in Chota Nagim ('small' Nagim), the *ghat* with the huge chenar tree, massed willows and the field path that one followed to reach the Nagim Bagh Road and the bridge of that name, or the Club. I should not be surprised to learn that the piece of rusty tin on that path, laid down by our *mānji* to cover a depression where rain would collect in wet weather, was still there.

The Club certainly is. And so too is the bridge and the little island known as the Char-Chenar—four chenars—though the central pavilion and the tiers of rising ground on which it stood have been bulldozed to the level of the surrounding turf, and the thickets of Persian lilac have gone. Sadly, so has the ancient wooden mosque of Hazratal, the sacred hair; so named because it enshrines a precious relic in the form of a hair from the Prophet's beard. It has been demolished in favour of a showy white marble mosque from which the once melodious and haunting voice of the muezzin, calling the Faithful to prayer, has given place to a metallic and vociferous one that emerges, at full blast, from a cluster of outsize loudspeakers, wired for maximum sound at the top of the new minaret.

Importunate salesmen in *shikaras* loaded with every kind of local produce from Kashmir carpets to cabbages and cut flowers still tout their wares alongside every occupied houseboat, and the old, picturesque, wooden houses where the makers of papier mâché, carved wood and embroidered *pashmina** live, still crowd together on either side of the Jhelum

* Handwoven cloth of goat's wool.

River where it flows through Srinagar City. The one-time British Residency, standing among its green lawns and gardens in the shadow of the
Takht-i-Suliman, looks much the same as it did in the old days, though
nowadays it houses a series of showrooms for the display and sale of the
many arts and crafts for which Kashmir is famous.

I suspect that by now both of the Nedou's Hotels—the stonebuilt one in
Srinagar and the rambling, ramshackle, much-loved wooden one in
Gulmarg—have been modernized and 'improved' out of all recognition.
But as far as I am concerned, they will always be there, unchanged and
unchanging. Enshrined, like flies in amber, in my memory; complete with
the stage upon which I appeared more than once in charity cabarets. For I
was the girl to whom my fictional Hugo Creed refers briefly near the end
of Chapter 15; the 'girl called Mollie someone' with whom he once sang a
duet: 'A tasteful ditty about a bench in a park—or was it something about
tiptoeing through tulips?' Hugo could not remember. But in fact it was
both, though on two separate occasions; and my partner on that bench was
not in the least like Henry VIII being a lissom young officer in an Indian
Cavalry regiment, one 'Bingle' Ingall of the 6th Lancers.

Oddly enough, there is a postscript to that particular duet. Years later—
over forty of them I fear, during which I had completely lost track of him
—we suddenly met again in, of all places, the Book section of a famous
department store in San Francisco where I was signing copies of *The Far
Pavilions* and *Shadow of the Moon*. He had, it seemed, become a profes-
sional actor, married an American girl and settled in a suburb of that city;
and having seen in some local paper that I was in town signing books, had
dropped in to say, "Fancy meeting you here!" It is a far cry from Kashmir
to San Francisco, but as Hugo would probably have said: 'If I may coin a
phrase, "It's a small world." '

It is indeed! And getting smaller every day.